From Culbone Wood – in Xanadu

FROM CULBONE WOOD – IN XANADU
notebooks and fantasias

Tom Lowenstein

Shearsman Books
BRISTOL

Contents

Culbone Wood Journal 1   1

Journal 2   32

Journal 3   57

On Kubilai Khan: an essay   80

Journal 4   129

The Great Khan's apartments   159

Notes taken from an Alpine landscape   174

Topographical descriptions   192

Note to the reader   217

From Samuel Purchas   222

The Travels of Marco Polo   224

Acknowledgements   229

Bibliography   230

Notes   232

Illustrations   235

I note merely the discord between Somersetshire now and the timelessness of Xanadu's appearance before me. And while I might wish to travel in person to such far flung places, I must be content to versify them into an existence which makes them my own and in which I may dream without too great a repining at not having arrived there.

To reach, even in imagination – Purchas's *Xaindu* – one must travel through a great deal of mud and much hot, stormy desert. Then on arrival one finds that it is a Paradise presided over by a tyrant. Was this, in Eden, our First Parents' experience?

Between what is here and the place which, in a vision, we have visited, exists a tension. It is through such a stretch, in a stiff-bridged sort of dreaming, that we achieve the difficult, intoxicating juncture we were seeking in our labyrinthine aberration.

In Culbone Wood
A poor Fool stood.
He pitched his mind
In spiced Serinde:
At the court of the Khan
And his pastures of Yuan.

Flowers at his feet
Spread a soft seat.
Above in the oaks
A gay bird spoke:

'O come home, young man
From the court of the Khan.
Your fair Muse waits here
In green Somersetshire.'

The fool heeded this call
In his heart and his soul.
But his mind it ran on
To the East with the sun.

He replied to the bird
'I have heeded your word.
For I live with this scission,
This sore self-division.
I am here and I'm there:
To where I've been lured
And in which I'm immured.

But some better day
I'll forsake far Cathay.
But until that time come
I must live with the sum
Of what I've begun.
Soon enough this will end.
And self-severance – mend.

Culbone Wood Journal 1

An apple tree. The full, charged, fructified, complete effusion from itself, perfect in self-generating abundance – a variegated expression of what it stands through the summer to carry into October.

And so it raises its progeny to the air, and these hang in beauty, passive to allowance of the wasp, the ant and small red mite that crawl its mossy ridges. An apple tree in fruit is nature's noblest expression. The weight and colour of this harvest, *big with rich increese*, hung from a living and a supple wood. I've studied the bramble and the blackthorn bending with their pruinescent burden. But the apple is the richest of our legacies. One bite of it, moreover, from our First Parents, is engraved in every human brain. But much as I glory at this fruit, just two, if I consumed them, would throw me in a colic.

This was mankind's primal ill. Ingesting not one apple but the entire fruit tree. Indeed, the world's an orchard: rind, seed and core that germinated in the hearts of our *Grand Parents* and took root there. It's these seeds in the head I feel ripening and then corrupting me. The roots grapple in my physiology. I feed this tree. It fortifies itself in me.

A fool marching along the way marked his passage of return by the disposition of sheep on the hillside. He turned home in the evening and the sheep had been frozen into the pattern in which he had earlier found them. 'This cannot be,' said the traveller in his folly, and plunged into the woods where he lost himself for ever.

I proposed this, fresh-minted, as I missed my way thro' Culbone Wood and became lost, so I thought, to extinction, in the dark, steep chasm that leads, at last, up to the farm house where I've sheltered. It is a mazy and romantick wilderness: thunderous with stream water and threateningly enclosed with trees whose canopies thrust high to transcend the abyss whose shadow they have created. The ascent is precipitous and strewn with boulders, and there being no clear track, I was driven to stumble, in a zig-zag, now across stream, now through creeper-shrouded heaps of fallen old tree-trunks, and having, more than once, to tear from my face a curtain of wild clematis and ivy.

As viewed through semi-darkness, the sea below blinked dim through underwood and foliage: the water level, grey and dead or dying, as though October, which up here ministered to leaf and flower, had worked also on the ocean, which was pitted like a hammered metal, now pewter-tinted and now, as if soured, like a flat-iron, tarnished.

Weighed down also with the burden of my *Purchas*, clothes heavy and my linen faecal, I was, indeed, a sad sop in this soused condition. I thought this, as I climbed, however: that there slipped through my fingers that thread of Ariadne, whose paid-out glint might spin off lines of a recuperative poetry. And that these, like the silk with which the little spider builds, rise from deep in the self which was lost to itself in thickets and in mazings. Solipsistic peregrination!

Done in with the flux, I arrived at this farm and needs must, in my sorry frame, beg water and a lodging. And then here, that afternoon, the dose that stopped my bowel was *aperiative* to imagination: this latter, strongly coloured, alien and vivid, albeit fugitive to recollection.

I have borrowed what turned out to be a pruning knife from the farmer my host and cut a hole at the back of my britches in the place where I spoiled them with this afternoon's incontinence.

Mindful that the knife edge might contaminate some future cut in the branch of an apple, I cleaned the blade well, and so hope to have avoided contributing to our fallen world's infection.

I have, these few days, in consequence of my indisposition, been dressed in a shepherd's smock – a character-reversing loan for one who had been reduced to nakedness.

And thus strive now to sing without circumlocution.

It is morning and on the table lie the two sheets on which the last afternoon's composition is indited. How deep that vision! How distant and unwontedly complete. But how arcane its wild topography. The golden sun-glozed dome still glows – as though gold leaf beaten to an ultimate and airy thinness mantles the intelligence – and there, cooled by a breeze from the northwestern steppe, ample spaces gather to the palace and stretch thence through Asia.

Below the dome the Great Khan with his concubines perambulates. A dark spotted pard on a gold chain walks behind them. An Abyssinian servant follows. (Could I fashion gold from phrases such as these? Forced gold! Fool's gold! And for this reason: Howsoever distantly the Khan's power stretched west from Cathay and then south toward Corea, the shores of Africa lay far beyond the reach of Kubilai even. The association is evocative but derives from ignorance. The word *Abyssinian* comes to me, I think, for its combination of both like and unlike consonants and vowels. While these compound suggestions of *abyss/abysm*, whose sibilant percussion gently hammers.)[1]

Now as I write, I have not yet revisited the pages which are the product of my *prophetic fury*. For the circumstances of the phantasmagoria still live in my waking. And on this quotidian October morning, I am there now in Xanadu and would, were I able, immortalise the enchantment. Yet when I stretch my hand to position my ink horn, the quill dies in my fingers. My forearm is forestalled. I raise my left hand, bring it onto my brow, touch the fingers to a temple. This is English morning bristle. For am I not simply that hapless self that laboured yesterday through mud and briars to collapse among these hospitable premises? And am not I also that Tom O'Bedlam who entreated mercy

From the hag and hungry goblin
That into rags would rend ye ...

How close this touches! Xanadu and Bedlam lie adjacent in me. And I lie here in each, with a most nervous approximation.

I have breakfasted on a ham, and now in bustles the farmhouse maid to clear my dishes and to mend the grate. Up reaches a flame. And now a second. The tongues parry and embrace, fall, joust each other, withdraw into the timber, crawl on the bark as though clutching for a hold. The girl kneels at the hearth and builds in logs of ash and apple. Who invented this blaze? Who re-ignites it?

'Pardon, Sir?' as though she overhears my enquiry.

'Go, child,' I reply. 'It is nothing.' The girl thanks me. I know not for what. But as she passes through the door, I call her.

'Pray,' I ask, without knowing what I intend and without premeditation, 'Can you sing, lady?'

---

1 Entire possession eludes any Empire. Enquiry shows, as noted of the T'ang below, that Peking in the time of Kubilai was peopled diversely from beyond his *khaganate*. *Stet* therefore Abyssinia, wedded albeit with old Prospero's *abysm*.

3

'Why yes, sir. All about here have songs of the neighbourhood. And the hymns we do in chapel.' (A curious locution, 'do', and not unhappy.)

'Then as you go about your household duties – not here, mind, by me – will you, time to time, give voice to any song you might, in the ordinary way, sing at your own hearth or with your acquaintance?'

Supposing me to be mad, as well I may be, the girl retreated, something disconcerted. A whispered consultation followed, I surmise with her mistress. And then ensued a silence all that morning so much deeper than any I have experienced, so that (besides this renewal of *flamboyance* in the grate) all I could hear was the singing in my ears and the sound of still air on me in the parlour as, in my indolence, I moved between chairs and tarried, with some expectation of a compositional renewal, by the table.

And all this while, at a tree by a river, with a thin bridge to traverse it, a solitary damsel stands. She cries through the dusk and a slow wind stirs the instrument she carries.

At each short flurry, a dulcet and enticing tone arises: as if in the night air, sound became a prism and was lifted through the twilit glimmer.

Deranged? Beyond my latitude! And what right, I ask further, do I possess to idle here as though I'm privileged, by general acknowledgement, to have something to add to the universe that I share with this young woman? A girl, her mistress's instrument, who knows nothing. She eats. She cleans the farm and feeds the hens. She will marry, bear children and quickly grow old. Then Death will abruptly snatch at her mantle: remembered by a few and regretted for a moment when labour allows the luxury of mourning.

And yet, this morning she has accomplished what is an elemental, Promethean eventuality. In this, at her fire, she over-reaches me entirely. What better task is there than to create such a flame, this combustible heart for sustenance and comfort of another being? What more than this could I achieve? Indeed, from what coercion – except for that I am some species of ambitious gentleman with a smattering of languages, some books on his table and a headful of conceits, humours, images, associations and pretentions? What dignity, by contrast, this girl possesses, who contributes her labour and her pleasant manners to this unpretending household! All this so her master's sheep can feed, their wool grow thick, their meat become fat and each in this neighbourhood sit down sometimes to a dish of mutton. Have I something better to contribute?

Shakespeare suggests some elements of this society in his lovely *Winter*, where Joan, Tom, Marion and Dick maintain the hall: each labourer devoted to his rustic function. A frost encroaches. But once milk and firewood are carried from outside, then life – for the few – becomes supportable. The song connects in no intelligible way with the comedy of jests that goes before it. But just as the actors from *Love's Labours'* court evaporate for ever, so these humble figures make their brief appearances. None speaks: but each silently fills his line or stanza, and as they vanish, each pursues his necessary labour. Around them, fields, beasts and sheepfolds melt to nothing. And within the celebrated closing burden, fat Joan's ladle sings and clatters.

It is a rude-hewn vision in which work is either over-heated or else freezing. As for master and mistress, they exist at the edges of what they command and we do not see them. But they are, effectively, the hall itself: and this building, which will pass to their descendants, is their immortality. The servants meanwhile, who provision the manor, themselves are consumed in *slow-chap't* time's invariable progress. A mortality they suffer with patience.

I have looked through my poem. And very well, I acknowledge it to be a masterpiece. I will go further. This fragment is a masterwork of the English language. Nothing comparable precedes it. Little that comes later will emulate its scope and music, immediacy of coloration or that dramatic intensity that belongs less to the lyric than to epic and to Shakespeare's theatre (I mean the late romances). At the centre of the piece there lies an enigma: that *mysterium tremendum* lent, in part, by an historical grandeur and geographic majesty, but also by that mystical suggestiveness which radiates from its concealments.

The landscape, so quintessentially romantick, hearkens to an amalgam – in its evocations of two paradisal conditions – of the biblical and pagan: and this is just one stimulus to an imagination that would be transported to the antique clime which was brought to me in my realisation of Purchas. (The critics, should they one day read my poem, might well be disconcerted were I to disclose that the wilderness bounding the Great Khan's gardens derives from a view of the Bristol Channel as seen through the declivity, with its rocky contours and roaring freshet, of Culbone Wood – *pars densa ferarum tecta rapit silvis.*)

5

But no reader, beyond a circle of my intimates, will see this work for one or two decades hence. Of such I'm determined. This poetry shall stay near me as my talisman and not go out to be vilified by those who would have in their company only such things to which they are already habituated. This is a poetry of hazard and aesthetic peril. This to myself and likewise perhaps to those who would themselves be led to penetrate such a world as I have conjured in these remote broodings.

Already for myself it's over strong. And like some elixir, albeit benign, it is not for the unguarded or the non-initiate. People in a later age will variously approach it with their hermeneutic tackle. Others, all-too-knowing adults, will, as they do nursery rhymes, insensately chant it. The romantick who inclines to solitude will intone lines according to his predeliction with the borrowed menace of a dark, self-hypnotised inebriation, and school children memorize it alongside their tables of multiplication – and with as little relish. For myself, I shall maintain these lines in a privacy correspondent to the circumstances of their composition. Unchallengable though its presence, this demands asylum.

Not to be closeted too long with this solitary burden and clutching my papers, I walked to the yard in the early afternoon and having ascertained that this compound was deserted (the reconstruction of a hayrick having taken off the farmhouse), I stationed myself in the midst of the paving and emptying my throat of the used air from the parlour, gave voice to my fragment. This was the debut occasion that I heard the piece sounded. And in its movement from the paper to the eye and from eye to the voice, Xanadu imprinted itself strangely on this yeoman courtyard.

To our right stood the kitchen and its cobble-enclosed potager of lettuces and spinach, a stand of daisies and geraniums on the window ledge, straw scattered on the pavings, the sweet freshness of this and not unwholesome excrements enhancing the autumnal scents enclosed within this shelter.

As I chanted my poem (with an eye that cautioned as to possible embarrassment) I glanced up and observed that my voice had excited the attention of some eight or ten ewes that were fattening in the sheep pen against the prospect of this Friday's market. The woolly company was pressed together, but none too close, and consider my surprise and amusement to witness the manner in which some inclined their heads, and stretching their necks in my direction, gave the certain impression (some twitching up an ear, and others pensively inclining their long, mild faces, as though judiciously considering some compositional originality) of attending the recital.

I had reached the second page and was mid-way through this when the silence with which my companions had been patiently standing was now interrupted with a rhythmic grating, whose counterpoint transected the solemnity of my numbers. A party of sparrows had just then flown to the meadow. A chaffinch followed and two wagtails replaced it.

I aborted my recital, and for this reason. Rolling their eyes and with their slotted pupils angled, the sheep were grinding their teeth, and in reasonable unison! Nor was this pretty, for as each bared its long incisors and these scraped on their fellows, they gave out a screeching and dry dissonance. Putting up my pages, I retired to the meadow where the wind blew with a better music to the high tops of Culbone and allayed my disquiet. In mixed distraction, I walked there till evening with a few late butterflies. A large blue dragonfly with a black and green striped thorax hunted among the gnats. And the little white plume moth stumbled through the seeding grasses.

Disburdened of my lines, am I left here feeling yet more foolish? *Hier steh ich nun, ein armer Tor ...* The creaking of sheep's teeth continues to perturb me.

Among the butterflies still alive in the sunlight: Red Admirals and Peacocks. The former species flaunts a scarlet whose intensity is framed by black and white patterns: reminiscent of the fire that I'd left among its grey fragmenting embers.

If the Red Admiral is splendid, the Peacock expresses an aristocracy which I admire without sympathizing with it, as I do its sister: the *Vanessa atalanta* (Matchless appellation! In the balance of its consonantal/assonantal values, a short whole poem.) For the Peacock is beautiful in that it is too rich and there is an arrogance in the reserve onto which its blue climactic eye is painted. The Peacock's nobility is heraldic, whereas the *Vanessa* radiates the brightness, as its admirable English name expresses, of those jovial parades that cheer good people.

Back in the parlour, I opened the window and a Peacock flew in and vanished behind the dresser. A butterfly once hibernated in our own little kitchen and perhaps this individual, having supped on the last of its autumn nectar, had come to sleep here. Will it doze, I wonder, in that dream of Xanadu?

Less fancifully, I noted as the Peacock fluttered in, the ribbed, granular texture of its underwing which was utterly black, and thus blind, as it were, to the wide-awake blue eye that stares from its upper surface. This down-facing darkness is like shrivelled up lace which has been pulverised and reconstituted into dried out veins, which though they've long since ceased to work, retain their pattern.

Walking. Illness. Aberration.
　　Harbour with a book of histories.
　　A *drugged posset*. Sleep and reverie. Thence my poem.

Reverting to the Wood and birds I listened to, which then fell silent. It was as if they lived in Virgil, had fluttered from his lines and then flown back to roost in their proper hexameters. These are the numbers, most perfect in all literature, those creatures enacted:

> Nox erat et placidum carpebant fessa soporem
> corpora per terras, silvaeque et saeva
> aequora, cum medio volvuntur sidera lapsu,
> cum tacet omnis ager, pecudes pictaeque volucres,
> quaeque lacus late liquidos quaeque aspera dumis
> rura tenent, somno positae sub nocte silenti. *Aeneid* IV

Night. Fatigue. The forest. Ocean. Stars are setting. Quiet meadows empty. Animals and birds in wide, rough country sleep in silence.

The contained energy of moorland and its defensive architecture of rock that thrusts, as though wanting more of itself, toward the ocean. Where sea meets the sky there exists a perfection of silence that we, who are surrounded by land over which we beat our business, have yet to learn from. Still, we need that percussion. For the absolute would be as nothing without some differentiating relativity.

This house is full of noises – a very deep silence, notwithstanding. How this can be, is answered simply. For with coombs behind us rising steeply and meadows and woodland reaching to the Channel, the farm stands enclosed in quiet, natural limits.
　　Oh there are winds and bird song – rooks and magpies, chaffinches and sparrows – and a stag now and then that boveys in the twilight. At midnight, too, the owls chuckle and halloo each other, while far across the meadow, vixens – strangulating in the *act of darkness* – scream their lacerating hymeneals.

But there dwells in the house a serene suspension, through which softer, more domesticated music rises: the master and mistress – genial voices – children's laughter (which is both of the household and of heaven), rambling in and out the byre of cattle, dogs leaping to follow their shepherd up the pasture, horse-shoes scraping, the slow weight of cart's wheels and the rub of harness, clattering of ladles, women's pattens – there are two at the pump now: one fills a bucket – the ring and scratch of scythes, spades, hinges, pitch-forks, latches, and articulating silence, the cat's reticent and introspective *sotto voce*.

And then, as I breakfast, song, for which I've waited, reaches me from where the servant girl is working. Absorbed in her labour, she laments to herself, without inhibition.

Lacrimae rerum. Men and women
Disappointing one another –

Here is a region of which I know something!

Singing, as she sweeps, her voice comes through a twist of corridors above my ceiling, close now, then withdrawing through a casement and now stifled by old beams and plaster, as if her verses travelled along passages, winding thorough thresholds and down stairways, half audible from where I am secluded, as she moves from one task to another, her stanzas in fragments, now in an unwonted combination, separating and dispersing – *quo lati ducunt ... ostia centum*! – before invisibly she draws near again, her singing recovers its self-possession, and she voices it with harmonies, in synchrony and discord, where old occasions and the present hazard come together:

As though – In a wood there grew a tree.
And the green leaves grew around, around.
And I sowed the seeds of love, *she's singing. And now*
You have caused my dear heart's wound.

Where the pretty little birds do change their voice,
She calls. That I (*says he*) may give you a fair kiss.
And a girdle of red gold around thy waist.
I'd rather, *she replies*, rest on a true-love's breast.

And she has become a leaping hare.
Gently, my Johnny my Jingalo.
For poor, gentle John Barleycorn he's dead.
The dog goes before him everywhere.

Now as for those sheep they're delightful to see.
With my rue dum day, fol the diddle dol.
O Master John, do you beware!
And don't kiss the girls at Bridgwater fair.

And O pretty maid how far are you going?
With my whack fal lor, the diddle and the dido.
I will take thee down to some lonesome dale.
A pretty, pretty place for girls and boys to play.

When we have sheared our jolly, jolly sheep.
The green leaves grow around, around.
I'll place my love on a primrose bank.
For I'm sick to my heart and I fain would lie down.

She slept, she dreamed, she saw him by her.
Just in her bloom she was snatched away.
Young women they run like hares on the plain.
Hold up your cheeks my fair pretty maid.

And he went to the woods cutting broom, green broom.
Young women they sing like the birds in the trees.
And in the greenwood she lies slain.
Her clothing is made of the cold earthen clay.

Alas – here was hapless, inconclusive dreaming!

And did I lie thus with so mortal troubled mind?
In the jolly, jolly greenwood – or on *Elfin* ground?

There exists, in certain voices, a timbre belongs generally to the children. It is high-registered in a young woman and plaintive: but untouched, too young yet, by the melancholy and disenchantment of which she is innocent in her own ballads.

Such simplicity, with its musical attenuation and artless colour, may last through youth, and while sung from the stool or the apple-picking ladder, bespeaks a faery information: as if, through prompting of a similar effusion, the nether world folk – or the *gallybeggars* of this district, as they call them – communicate their yearning for the company of warm, quick, pretty and unknowing mortals – could they snatch 'em! (As with *Thomas the Rhymer* and Goethe's *Erlkönig* – of which more later.)

To be *not* thus detained, but live in the uncomplicated upper air, is one of my secure determinations. For I will not be ruled by fancy entirely. And in this I am confirmed by apprehension that this young woman's singing was a parcel of the homely *intermezzi* I have detailed. With the one goes the other. I'm reassured by that material equivalence. For songs are of the air, and without earth to sustain them, they'ld lead imagination wholly to the *elfin* – from which danger there's no certain egress.

And yet as I sat in reverie this evening, Great Kubilai's dome arose in my vision, and these rustic numbers soared up through it. Beware an ascension or a *katabasis* with that music!

The silence of the woods broken by the flux of sea from below. My system works in harmony with that and I am at pains to hold myself in a posture that resembles the human. Twice I squatted by the path and let fly with my bare arse. I heaped a tumulus of ivy and bracken on top of the stinking effluvium I had deposited and laid stones over these. Through the underwood, while I groaned out my innerds, I watched from above, the waves winnowing across the beach stones. Thus my vision oscillated. But in nature always.

Reverting to my Purchas. Here are countless divagations shut up in one volume. And yet I carry this along the narrow country track of my own small aberration. Narrative is voyaging through error. As Virgil expressed this: *Hic labor, ille domus et inextricabilis error.* There is no better vision, than in those last eight syllables, of man's errancy: that most complex ravel and unravelling followed by the thunderous finality of *error*, with its continuing suggestion of an uninterrupted blunder.[2]

A pear tree, outside Culbone Wood, overhangs the churchyard with a crop of late fruit encased in hard, russet-coloured skin. In the grass between graves, are rinds of two or three which have been eaten almost entirely away by birds and insects. One skin resembles some ancient long-boat, eviscerated and on its side. Another is a tattered web of indentations

---

2 Say the word 'journey' and I reply *vicissitude*. Worn soles, sharp wind and a poignant intestinal grinding. This volume of Purchas weighs ten pounds on my shoulder. The burden of its information drags down intellect and body. On every path we meet Misfortune. Anticipate that always when experience falls short of expectation. Commiserate with Purchas' lamentation! All men take disappointed journeys. Call it, as did Purchas, *pilgrimage*, and lend dignity – a nice delusion! – to its mishaps and hallucinations.

surrounding a pattern of holes, giving it the appearance, with the grass darkly showing through, of a mask, multiply fissured, that gazes back into the tree that bore it.

Metal and wood ring out, first in sequence and then together as the wicket closes. This is an expression of something that I could not at once identify. Then I was overtaken by a recollection: the clangour of ordnance: gun carriages, cannon, muskets and wagons. Milton in his *Book I* curses iron: its discovery and excavation. And a tree, which was at once dangerous and sacred, stands at the centre of his poem. Musket and wicket express the convergence. As I came through that gate, I imagined this fable:

Once Paradise was ended, a poor woodsman was passing through the forest and came to rest at the Tree of Knowledge which had, since in its primal state, grown into a giant.

Having rested in its shelter and hearkened to the song birds that innocently expressed themselves in its branches, the man took his axe and belaboured the tree trunk. As the hatchet bit the final inch of heart-wood, the tree fell down with a thunderous crashing. Crushed by his victim and still innocent of its nature, the woodsman died there in an agony of regret for all the great war engines that might have been fashioned from its timber.

Now, at the farm, there is a silence so complete that the sole sounds I detect are clucks and hisses emanating from my midriff, while deep in my brain, from fatigue and confusion, a symphonic roaring comes – as though Haydn here stood pounding with his *Paukenwirbel* – or van Beethoven belaboured his infernal anvil – and the joyous palaver of Signor Rossini broke forth in nightingale roulades and lark song – all these interwoven with an instrumental complication!

Encompassing this tumult, a primordial quiet leads me to an apprehension of the moments that preceded the world's first minutes – for as God proceeded through the creation, its augmentative expression made certainly a large commotion.

Before this, in Chaos (that miasma of elemental interfusions), no entity existed to strike on another. But with light and order, animation and then *separation* (which was Elohim's means of definition) came a wonderful clamour.

'Let there be Noise!' I conjecture the Creator crying as he sank back to his sabbath: and so things and creatures rushed out from him, and like children released from the asphyxiation of a school room and who race off to play by a cold stream in the meadow, there was spontaneous uproar. We who come later have inherited that pasture. While some run laughing through the grasses, others trample down the stream's edge and make puddles of its margin. And the poet? His task: to acknowledge and to build from mud, and enhance the creation with unbroken singing. So Ovid at the outset of his *Metamorphoses*:

> adspirate meis primaque ab origine mundi
> ad mea *perpetuum* deducite tempora *carmen*!

And if Ovid's *carmen* be a neuter, let us, with our own songs, nonetheless inseminate it with our consequent, perpetuating genealogies!

I, too, am a fruit of that tree onto which mankind was grafted. Once when I was a yunker, I held my ear to some apple bark and heard the coursing of the sap which later in the season would inform a hundred ruddy and delicious fruit that sang all summer as they swelled on the branches.

All things are endowed, in variable degrees, with singing voices. Not every person can attend to these; nor do all phenomena reveal acoustic properties. I can not, for example, hear this table over which I scratch – as chanticleer does, to pick grubs from the dung pile. But all bodies have a tune which is borrowed from the world whose stuff we are part of, and these, whate'er their provenance, I listen in to. Howsoever far-away and low in register, these *sotto voce* melodies are expressions of a character whose presence informs the part-song of fraternal, all-creating nature.

How gorgeous that initiating vision! And yet how insubstantial was its outcome. Here in muddy Somerset I squat with this trickle of the river I envisioned dried up in the twilight – while by some fastness of an Asian palace, fresh gold in its ardency pursues its rushing. I approach the table. But those pages do not draw me. They are paper merely: thin, poor, nothings. The good solid things in this parlour have more substance. Old workings of oak, turned in Devon last century. A dark tankard, coppers, and the tongs and shovels that lie haphazard at the hearth with its coals still aglow in a mountain range of ashes. See too the ravines inside this, pocked with faery dells and casements, shaggy humps and tumuli which let fall now, and then ensevelate, their strata.

I sense the ceiling beam inch down of a sudden, as though to forge from tensions in its old stability an oppression in me. My pen totters and then droops. It's filled with lead – not mercury! Here is a feather won't ascend again.

The Great Khan's portrait

No doubt this was a man, though not perhaps in any sense a gentleman, who knew pleasure, and that judging from the satiated but still greedy eyes and omnivorously sensual mouth, these pleasures were many and not all of them refined.

To contemplate this portrait is to encounter a cunning of enormous, if not total and secure power. The eyes that smile with confident self-containment are those of a ruler who has feasted on life and who intends, as though for a privately ordained *for ever*, to eternalise that privilege. There is policy and weight in these middle-aged cheeks, the full jaws and the long, fleshy nose which is somewhat European as to length and inclination. This is a nose that upholsters the skull comfortably, and it rests like the culminating feature of a great range of mountains on snowy wastes of chest and shoulders: while the folds of the simple and undecorated garment that encloses his torso appear like mountain passes: roads ascending and descending a monument whose presence is imperative and whose non-existence is unthinkable.

Onto this great expanse, or rather down into it, a manly beard flows. This is neither very thick nor sparse, but nonetheless has been developing since young manhood and expresses what can only be the project of longevity and an early matured masculinity. At once free growing and meticulously barbered, there is power in the hair too: the long striations combed with a view to revealing a pattern of individually cultivated strands, standing in by synecdoche for all the body's hair: and while the long moustache has elegantly inflected flow, and the eyebrows comely in their under-emphasis, no hair of the head is to be seen under the military hat except for the suggestion of a shadow that rises above the one visible ear.

But what an ear that is! Of a piece with the empty spaces of the forehead, it is a very paradigmatic and ceremonial ear. A single and perfectly fashioned organ of hearing: receptor of diverse advice and one that listens, as proprietor, to noises from the world that interest it. It hears the wind on the steppe – those great free places this one man controls; the wheeling round of horses, snorts and neighing, his lieutenants' orders, death cries, coarse shouting and the feeble movements, after battle, of the vanquished. And in every place to which it hearkens, bird song, music, the silence of his chamber which is broken only by the crepitation of his women's garments and cajoling whispers as his concubines compete for his attention.

If this be an object of poetic ratiocination – radiate as he does the pattern of an elevated and enigmatic human completeness – he is also,

14

while language merely circumambulates its object, in himself, the *epitome of the poem*. Words are loquacious, vain attendants. And the poem, that mere rectangle of scratches, is a short-lived exhalation, whose derivatives have been encoded by a feather which long since has come down from flight and *tottered* (Shakespeare's spelling).

Unseen in this portrait are the Great Khan's active and prehensile loins, his bent, belly-bearing legs and gouty ankles. But what does the Great Khan carry in his hand? Invisible albeit, I conjecture these, at different sittings, severally, include:

> A water pot which has been turned on a wheel from *loess* deposits in Shansi.
> Mangoes brought by camel from Khotan and ripened as they came through Central Asia to the summer capital.
> A relic to be placed in the Miaoying stupa or White Dagoba.
> A medicinal *mayabalam* seed.
> A handful of rock salt procured in Yunnan by Trade Administrator, Marco.
> Engraved in ivory and traced with gold, the year 1272, when he gave the name *Yuan* to his dynasty.
> A bundle of dried rhubarb root from the Suzhou mountains.
> A Blue-eared Pheasant feather, used to titillate his skin with.
> The thigh bone of a roasted Sandgrouse (*bagherlac* in the Tartar).
> A glove on which perches a Barbary falcon.
> A glove for hunting at the river with his goshawks.
> The skin of the sable. *King of Furs*, according to the Mongols.
> A dried Ferret-badger snout preserved as an amulet.
> A crocodile skin from the Irrwaddy River.
> A bunch of Mad Grass.
> A lacquered box containing ginger, pepper, cloves and *jujubes*.
> A Chinese pear – ten pounds in weight (to balance Purchas!)
> A yellow-fleshed peach from Hangzhou, which is two pounds roughly.
> The fragrant heart-wood of the lignum-aloes.
> Tong oil.

Am I preoccupied with the Khan for this reason mainly: that here was a person to be envied for having more access to pulchritude than any man perhaps in history? A fact that provokes me to recall how brief in a day's activity the matrimonial act is and, most germane for *man* here, how melancholy and bereft, as summarised by Aristotle, the after-experience.[3]

There are texts in the Hindu, so privately I have been told, which adumbrate in what must be sweet and lubricious detail the means by which erotic pleasure not only may be intensified but indefinitely prolonged. Such, no doubt is within the scope of persons of a leisured class, which like that of the Khan, enjoy the command of a complaisant *gynaeceum* and time to consummate what may be complicated theoretical and gymnastic recommendations.

All this is very well, if such information may be credited, but it begs the question of death. For is not such a prolongation of erotic expedition in effect based on a terror of the finish? (The plunge from a suspension and engorged horripilation through the vale of detumescence towards insipidity and indifference?)

And still during the act, we move restlessly and in a desperation of impatience for the end we overpoweringly desire and yet which, of all things, we most fear. The performance is accomplished in hurry and confusion, as though, as in a hunt, the quarry (our sensation) will escape us before we can intercept it.

We know, but half forget, in the ferocity of our engorgement that we are approaching an extinction: and in that state we will fall back very quickly into the humdrum of our ordinary character: all passion evacuated and our infatuated bewilderment devolved to the routine sequence of our appointments. But during that half ecstasy whose fulfilment is both a completion and an annulment, we wish that an entire lifetime might be spent in this posture of luxurious animality and that it should never end.

Of course what I am contemplating is the male experience. From Tiresias we learn that female pleasure is inordinately the greater and so, by complement, more difficult to attain (as also from experience we know that a woman falls not into a melancholy lassitude but rather into a healthy call for the repeat!). Herein lies one of man's greatest duties and it is one, no doubt, that a majority of our young husbands experience as an vacillation between primitive satisfaction and an impotent shame.

Any record of the Great Khan's own experience is of course lost. But the notion that a potentate in command of immeasurable armies should, in private, have conjugal encounters reductive to a high stomach, renders

---

3 Post coitum omne animal triste est – 'sive gallus et mulier' as completed by Galen!

me, even at this distance, melancholy. I will banish these imaginings and re-instate him as a stallion:

Rampant let the Great Khan stay
Among the beauties of Cathay:
Husband and lover, whose sweet pleasure
The spirits have ordained *sans* measure.
May every latest and entire delight
Resurrect him – every night.

From a dream by the fireside, as though in reflex from my oriental expedition, this minor, secondary vision. It was an old illuminated page, whose margin was broken by a scattering of moons and planets, and whose centre, which I gazed on from the congregation of surrounding spaces, was a rectangle or *targe*, of verses whose character I gaped at, in a rapture, as though I'd turned a page of the continuing creation and uncovered some passage – still I could not read it – Shakespeare, so I thought, had written at his terminating moment and which no-one but myself, before he'd drawn the curtain, witnessed – but which, like the *Phoenix*, burned on undiminished.

Such visions fluctuate. Their very character is instability. Indeed, at its heart was Shakespeare's absence. And yet, as one thing flows into another, that first illumination grew to be a sport of what it had itself created.

There was a dirty side room to this vision which lay closer than its primary medallion. This was a kitchen of a printer's in the late years of the Jacobean, in which a page stood straitened by its framework (the walls of a theatre likewise cram the apron), each character, as though by a reflexion, in reverse and topsy *tervy*: while from the Ptolomeian margin where a quarter moon consorted with some leading planets, I leaned forward and I saw it *was to be* a sheet of Shakespeare, whose iron glittered in the ink the printer's devil had applied that moment: and here, before the first time those metallic iambs touched paper, was Duke Prospero, in *Folio*, and I descried, before it could be printed, glimpses of his *baselesse fabricke* and *The Clowd-capt Towres* and *this insubstantiall Pageant faded*.

Were I Joseph, I might tell his King the meaning of my vision. Could it be perhaps that poetry, once got on paper, is a negligible facet of its origin and fabrication?

Could I in years ahead recall this parlour, its furnishings would be sufficient to o'ercrowd the memory – the chambers of my mind, indeed, would scarce contain them. And yet these multiplicities recalled, would warm a desolated evening (the very word to *de-solate*, withdraws the sun: uncanny reflex!) For here stands the perfection of a rustic parlour of this county. But such images recovered – I close my eyes to assay the experiment – would want one feature. Oh, it is a darkling journey! What lacks are those pages which had otherwise been weighted with the ore of yester evening's vision.

My quill, as said, hath been *informed* with lead.
And the goose from which it came? It laid.
Soon plucked and drawn. Then roast and ate.

I go to the table, stir round those pages. I pick two on the surface. Epitome, entombing all that's empty! I might as simply cut my poem with a pen-knife into granite as proceed into that desert paper: chilly and repellent as the frost embracing Greenland – whose ice sea lies here: and no axe to cut it. A carpenter's saw, a forester's indeed, I've read, has been deployed by the fellows of some whaling company to free their vessel, and at last let it breathe, as howling pressure threatened to asphyxiate it. But the mind, once drained of inspiration, is a dead thing – bloodless muscle. I am that null: inert and frozen.

On Samuel Purchas and his book I carried

Was it a mere chance I was reading about Kubilai when I fell asleep and dreamed my poem? There is no satisfactory answer to that question. A superstitious self might insist that I was *drawn* to Purchas, and some correspondence with the Great Khan joined me to him, and a bridge extending from myself to Xanadu had reached already into Kubilai's palace, and having touched there, arched back and enjoined my passage.

Thus my credulous self would have it that my poem was fated, and that it must have arrived from a relationship between myself and some particularity of the Asiatic, and that only a precipitating catalyst was needed to engender the connection. It was these elements, however, from which, I think, that stimulation was compounded:

I had carried Purchas through a lonely country which filled my eye with images of rocks, gorges and dark views of ocean. Indisposition, in this farmhouse quiet, heightened my susceptibility. I had swallowed laudanum and having descended the sublime abyss of an intoxication, returned, my unpremeditated numbers incarnated in the retrieval. This latter comprised a two-fold experience.

On the one hand it was as though I had travelled from a depth and that as I ascended – through the strait, steep chimney of the gulf into which I'd fallen – I found myself wrapped in my poem's self-transmission and that its lines were formulated, as though within the mantle of a parchment which had been scrolled around my waking.

At the same time, in a contrary manner, I was carrying my Fragment, in its original entirety, as though it were a great object inside me. And while that same envelope cocooned my person, poetry – that was made physical in the manner of a shaft of soft and vibrational radiance, in which light and sound had become one substance – infused my interior.

And just as in its extrinsic materialization, the poem had spooled an integument around me in such a way that I was, as it were, pupating within it and only awaited a return of consciousness to achieve the status of *imago*, so in parallel, I carried a whorling of this same matter in my body, through which it had dropped in the form of a granular-and-gold or honey-textured column from behind my eyes, as though suspended in a curtain that suffused the throat and hung behind the thorax and thus was contained within my very breathing which it partially interrupted in the approximation of a paroxysm. I mention this now, having just recalled it.

This said, the notion that I might have harboured mystic sympathy with Kubilai lacks sense altogether. The very notion is preposterous. I would hazard, indeed, that several other passages in Purchas might have taken me through parallel enchantment.

This proviso in mind, I have scouted Purchas' *Contents* and note here selections from his chapter listings:

Of Man, Considered in his First State Of Paradise – Of Babylonia – Of the
Sepulcres and Funerall Rites among the Turks – Of the Parthians and
Hyrcanians – A Generall Discourse of the Sea – Of Samatra and Zeilan – Of
Aegypt and her Famous River Nilus – Of Biledulgerid and Sarra, otherwise
called Numidia and Libya – Of Aethiopia Superior – Of Benomotapa and
the Parts adionying – Of the Kingdom of Congo – Of Groenland, Estotiland,
Meta Incognita – Of Iucatan and Nicaragua – Of Man-eating and other
Rites – Of Hispaniola and a touch Homeward at Bermuda.

Now based on these I might have chanced on, a question occurs which disturbs me not a little. What species of work might I have composed if, in lieu of *Xaindu*, I'd been reading *Biledulgerid* or *Bisnagar* or *Aethiopia*

Superior? But most especially, of *Great Tamerlane*:descendent, unrelated, of Great Kubilai? Of whom more, later.

Those are great wastes and spaces Purchas navigates. A fact that author notes, in several prefaces, with both pride and self-dubiety. And given my esteem for that indefatigable traveller who, on his own evidence, had 'written so much of travellers and travells, but never travelled 200 miles from Thaxted in Essex,' I would here indite a testimonial.

First, it is to Purchas that I owe my poem with its own narrow and yet far-flung geography. (Rest in well-earned peace, thou universalising labourer!) Second, I feel kinship with that sedentary traveller. For indeed, it is the discord between where Purchas sat (a marshland parsonage) and the incalculable countries towards which he cried God Speed to his imagination that has disturbed my waking and so *envolved* me in these aberrations.

True, I may love my native Somerset better than did Purchas Essex. Still, with one shoe here in farmhouse mud and the other foot sandalled among incense-bearing trees and flower-strewn grasslands with their rivulets and hunting courses, I feel, as Purchas may have, a division of my interests keenly. And King Kubilai, I wager, at once Mongol chieftain and Chinese Emperor, owned his share of self-division.

One can fall into a book, as one may tumble in a chasm. Both such adventures I have just experienced: first, as I've described, in my upland struggle. And second, at the farm itself where I dropped into Purchas, as though into a gulf of paper.

In my walk up through those woods from the Church, I am carrying the book in question, some ten pounds I conjecture, and a recent downpour having made the surface slimy, my endeavour is to keep my balance: for the drop is filled with bramble, undermined by fox and badger, pocked by rabbit – while trees, which struggle through the wreckage of the fallen, make a shade that lends the place a damp, unholy character.

Panting and sweating at one extremity and incontinently squirting at the other, I was hard put to it not to fall down sideways to my right and to possible great injury: anxiety on this account being compounded by a fear that the book itself would drag me down, or swing out in its wallet and so pull me into the abysm.

We were, myself and Purchas' book, as one in our exposure and joined in mutuality wherein I sensed my care for it was answered: as though by some inherent amuletic power within its sturdy neat-skin binding:

containing as this does a *whole round world*, condensed, complete and – as John Donne or Marvell might have noted when they held it – flattened *planispherically*: a soul-sustaining emblem of unbounded histories whose record has survived through countless periods of turbulence, compared to which my little insecurity's of paltry moment – and yet whose good that same book might benignly succour.

I did not fall over. Nor was a letter damaged. *Not so much as one hair.* But having sustained myself through Culbone's chasm, it was middle afternoon before I was secure in this farmhouse parlour: dried finally and, following hot water, less unwholesome. It was thus in the serenity of a chair by the fireplace and with mutton in my body, that I put my hand out finally and opened these old pages.

The letter *a* that gave rise to an *iamb*

Reverting to my poem, I should mention that my dream unfolded from a mere half-inch of Purchas' volume. For that alphabetic space enclosed between my own words 'In' and 'did' contains the crammed ambiguity, as to enunciation, of Purchas' *Xaindu*. And this in miniscule italic face embedded in a furrow such as we associate with what – romance! – lies only where imagination ventures.

'In *Xaindu*', begins Purchas. As though within these two last syllables lay energies from whose compression would emerge an expatiation which it lay within my sleeping mind to unleash through the interposition of the vowel 'a': Purchas's *Xaindu* exfoliating to become *Xanadu* – a tri-syllable which was easy enough to tessellate into an iambic sequence.

How, naturally, could I accomplish this transposition without some conscious organisational struggle? The solution, I think, lay within an inborn predisposition. I mean that rhythmic formulation that lies even within the sleeping intelligence. For all we English carry the iambic foot, like an hereditary tattoo, inculcated from the jigging thighs and even from the nipples of our mothers and nurses and from the games our brothers teach us.

The tavern songs that we subsequently learn embed this same measure. And thus while 'In Xanadu,' opens within no recognisable topography, the reticent, indeed, scarcely audible *anacrusis* of the monosyllable 'in' leads the mind, that has been historically disoriented, into an octosyllabic melody which, through the ear, becomes at once familiar and domesticated.

Further, while the trochee 'In *Xaindu*' would have struck the ear as though by assault back upon itself from a hammer, my own phrase lies within our native idiom. *In Xanadu did ...* 'In Scarlet Town there was ...' 'In Xanadu there was a maid ...'

How I unravelled or released the syllables, from *Xaindu* in its tight compression, to Xanadu, I do not recall. At all events, the latter seems to be my coinage, albeit suggested by Marco's *Cembaluc*, or by *Camdu* as inscribed on the *Atlas* of Ortelius three centuries later and which I have scanned to orient myself within my visionary latitude. Thus, as follows, are the two names, both in quantity and musical association:

Xaindu: constraint	*Xanadu*: alleviation
Xaindu: the germen	*Xanadu*: a branching flower
With *Xaindu* breath reined in	*Xanadu*: breezes
With *Xaindu* inflorescence	*Xanadu*: exfoliation
Xaindu: a containing cistern	*Xanadu*: a stream in movement
Xaindu: an unyielding in-growth	*Xanadu* flows forth, forward
In *Xaindu* a promise	With *Xanadu* reward

Further, the addition of the vowel *a* creates a consonance and euphony that is also found in *Samarcand*, which was Tamburlaine's city. For each of these names contains two *a*-s within its first two syllables: *Xana // Sama*.

This coincidence is by the way. All I have fixed on here lies within the play of vowels and thus the breadth of utterance which both allow. And this represents to me an ambience of air and a sense of the freedom which thereby flows. And while sunlit spaces spread from these letters, their contiguity with, and enclosure in, a stout surrounding architecture of consonants evokes also a milieu which is cultivated and urbane. And thus from each alphabetic agglomeration is suggested an exotic life in court and city which has prospered through the civilising exertion of its artisans and architects, through busy and successful trade, and not least on account of what has been accumulated through the exercise of war.

Reverting to euphony and to the music of those *a*-s with their supporting consonantal matrices, let me enlarge briefly on what properties are conjured for me by their combination. To wit: the opening vowels of *Xanadu* suggest – I speak here from the experience of my own idiosyncratic palate – a delectable liquor which is contained within crystalline rock that is itself constructed from some sediment of a sugar which is all too precious to violate or dislodge. This is the effect of the *X*, *n* and *d* on those glowing intermediate vowel sounds. While, perhaps equally in evocation, the *u* that concludes *Xanadu* suggests a drop into a cooler, twilit exiguity. In this I am perhaps influenced unduly by the environment of my poem in its final passage.

Within the name *Samarcand* there is, likewise, an occlusion of that bright, warm *a* vowel. But in this name there are *three*, and each is supported by, or set within, an ennobling consonantal architecture that is texturally harder and denser than those informing the word *Xanadu*.

And whereas *Xanadu* expresses a candied sweetness, spacious and expansive music and the cultivated subtleties of court, the name *Samarcand* suggests the polychromatism of the market place with its profusion of weavings, silken stuff and astrakhan, bold and geometrically pigmented ceramics, curiously worked metals, perfumed fruits from far oases, vegetables which have been pickled in the succulence of their early sprouting, and not least spices – those poignantly concentrated seeds, stems, barks and buds that yield a perfume in proportion to the sharpness, albeit imagined, of their colour.

Properties such as these are of course what we strive to achieve in our poetry through the juxtaposition of syllables and the process of extraction, substitution and elimination *via* the management of vowels and consonants. These being reduced, in so far as is possible, to a concentration of their most extreme associative sensuality.

We take language and its constituent elements as does the oriental who prepares a dish for the supreme monarch or one who is a connoisseur of the language of taste. For just as the flavour of a cardamon seed, when it has been broken in the teeth, spreads along the membrane and fills the mouth with both taste and aroma, radiating even into the illusion of a colour, so the syllables of a line give forth sensations that may be wrung from it as they are from a spice which has burst into life on the cognoscente's palate.[4]

---

4 Two lines of Shakespeare will be enough to render this obvious. At random for example:

Full many a glorious morning have I seen
Flatter the mountain tops with sovereign eye

Need I amplify at any length on the regal conjugation of 'glory' and 'sovereign'; the implication in 'full many', of gold in richness, thickness, multiplicity; lofty heights implied throughout which irradiate, from the empyrean, an entire universe in which the human eye ('have I seen') is homologised with Hyperion who lords it across, up and down, a brilliantly illuminated and gilded cosmos?

The patterning of vowels, as with most lines of Shakespeare, is exemplary of natural ease which does nothing to belie the art, albeit partially concealed, which controls the design. Viz. therefore, the sheer spread in line 1 of a kaleidoscopic deployment in which just one vowel sound is repeated, while 'flatter' in line 2 echoes

But here is a question. I fall asleep, amaz'd, on Purchas and I dream, my forehead on that saffron-shaded paper, which wrought on my unknowing of an after-dinner slumber.

But what if my brow had fallen on some other page (what, after all, was Xanadu to me and *vice versa*?) and I had slept, as had Marlowe perhaps, his brain on the Atlas of Ortelius, his eyelid advanced, on wastes of Asia, in the Samarcand of Tamburlaine – whose history Purchas outlines also? Here, then, was an exercise I set myself: to browse, in Purchas, that Tamburlaine's history, and attempt some new, inspirited effusion, thereby constructing a double set of poems that might evoke both ancient generals and from there embark on a *divan*, or series, such as poets of those regions, the great Hafez among them, have indited.

This was, I confess, a tedious employment. And yet as I persisted, I came, at last, to the history of *Aly*, Counsellor to Tamburlaine, on whose demise the Shepherd General raised a grand memorial of which Purchas writes this sentence:

Hee built a stately Tombe for him at Samarcand

Now here is an unassuming and yet burnished measure! Could but I emulate the slow stateliness and balance of this alexandrine! Perhaps Marlowe, only, in his honey numbers could rival that convergence of outlandish matter with an expression of reserve, suggestive, nonetheless, of majesty! (And therein the enigma of what syllables achieve. For Purchas, to whom poetry was frippery, wrote prose.)

But as to my own poetic voyage: perforce I must have read this line in reverie and translated the same into my *Fragment*. For the two are akin. There is affinity in rhythm and twinning as to the caesura. Synonymous in proclamation, the temperament of natural, geographic colour encloses monumental architecture.

Tamburlaine's *Tombe* and the Great Khan's *dome* present, furthermore,

---

its obliquely positioned 'a' in line 1, leaving the remainder of the line to run musically on, extemporising on yet a further expatiation of vowel sounds that have not, in their precise articulation, so far appeared. That is, until the telling end-word 'eye', which picks up clangorously the bombast of the initial 'I' in line 1, thus lending each word, in part by virtue of rhyme and repetition, the candour (in both senses) of the two principles: I mean the subject who experiences the sun and the sun in the self-substance of its radiance. Herein lies both a truth and amplitude which are inextricable from each other and which inter-reflect in a musically and experientially harmonising self-containment.

half rhymes with their 'o's and final 'm' sounds. And if 'tombe' suggests an earthy hollow and nobility in death, the convexity of 'dome' at once affirms both aspiration and the air, in whose convergence, vault the pleasures of the living.

In the light of such factors, these verses' consanguinity grows, by the moment, clearer and I'm struck how minds can borrow (copy!) what they seek in the arcana of their working without having recall of a source or occasion.

To continue with my struggle to eke poetry from Purchas. 'Twas empty employment. For Clio, alone, inspireth not true poesy. And thus following Tom Coryat, that *pedestical* fantastick (unlikely friend of the domesticated Purchas), who had 'pilgrimed', as he put it, into Persia with the hare-brained view to visiting the tomb of Tamburlaine, I too attempted to approach that sepulchre – resulting in these trifling and timid numbers, which, on the strength of crusts and tea, I wrote, just now, experimentally:

In Samarcand did Tamburlaine
A tomb of jade for his *reliques* ordain,
In whose green shrine his pride for ever might be sealed
And those high stories of his prowess and his fame
Be sung in strophes of speaking stone
Which cold and silence in the darkness yields.

Here would be told how long the round world bled
Till it was pale as every mortal's doom,
Which Death, with equal pallor,
Till he'd drained it, white from red,
Could neither counterfeit nor call his own.

Now would be blazoned in that obscure cell
The blood which erstwhile trimmed the crest of every fane
That Scythian Tamburlaine had razed in his advance
From scorching Inde to perfumed Isfahan.

But O those towers that climbed in glittering stone
Where Samarcand was watered by the blissful
Xanthine stream: such were the guardians of a harvest plain
Whose meadows, granaries and orchards held
The foison of each autumn's yield:
And all who dwelled therein rejoiced with tributary song

That their triumphant Shepherd King
Enclosed their lives with bounty and renown.

Thus without the frontier of his rumoured tents
The name lives on where geste and threat and conquest
Are interred. For all, that thrived there once, is laid to rest:
The flaunted colours faint, then fade and now are spent.

Once, in a vision, ranting Tamburlaine I saw,
As he the milk-fed steeds spurred west to east,
Turning the sun back from its shining road,
All challenges reversed: kings, cities, nature even, in retreat:
How man, like the sun (I saw) may rise and scorch his track
And lay waste everything that stands to intercept his path:
Bending the world's objects to his will
And binding whole empires to his royal hearth.
So, as in the fable of a dream, all earthly beings pass into decay.
All aspiration, hope, imperial design, the laws of destiny obey.
And even that great rock that seals with jade
The reliques of exultant conquest in their tomb will pass,
And in the dissolution of its green accumulated dust
Will drift from this great globe as will the globe, too, roll
Toward its last, enduring and predestined waste.

Alack, this dependence on a single *sic transit* world-worn notion! I shall,
nonetheless, retain it as a curiosity. And warning!

The last digression – *finis*

In Purchas' small details – shrunk as the wax in a dried old hive – lie
golden cells of honey. A nectar that a dreamer may, like hymenoptera in
their quaint devotions, husband.

Note thus how inspiration's passed along in series. Viz. after Genghis,
Kubilai rides to China. Then how Marco, from Cathay, in Genoa, retails
his narrative to Rustichello and how Purchas strips from this what glean-
ings he needed.

Note too in the *Pilgrimage* I carry, some previous eighteenth-century
reader's memoranda: scribbles in Latin and Greek characters, in broken
marks, whose ink once glittered. Now this joins my destiny. And half-
nescient, I've leaned an opiated brow against its pages and, in sleep, have
made my supper of it. (What started as an impulse or a thought, becomes

a book. And where that book stops and the self connected to this starts are questions neither I nor book can answer.)

Of Purchas's friend, the *fantastick* Thomas Coryat, who bent his slipper towards the monument to Tamburlaine

> His head was a large powdring tub of phrases,
> Whence wold pick delights, as boies pick daisies
> O head, no head, but blockhouse of feirce wars
> Where wit and learning were at daily Jars.

I've mentioned, *O head, no head*, Thomas Coryat or Thom Coryatus *Peregrinans* – 'that literate Elfe', as Jonson described him – a Somerset *fantastick* who had entertained the public with a record, having tramped to Flushing in his parlour slippers, of a diverse travel. (His *Crudities* include descants, among other saucy detail, on the courtesans of Venice. His *Crambe or His Colwort, Twice Sodden and Now Served in with other Macaronicke dishes*, was at London published, in 1611, with a verse panegyric from the same Ben. Ionson.)

On a later voyage, Coryat *pedesticated* (so he coined it) from Damascus into Persia and thence to the Moghul court near Agra from where, he scrawled communications from 'the umbilicke of Orientalle India ... to those who are wel-willers of a prosperous issue of my designment, in my *pedestriall perambulations* of Asia, Africa, and Europe.'

All these letters that he wrote from India, except for two or three that Purchas posthumously captured, were lost. But Purchas, who gathered them in to his final *Pilgrimes*, gives us this, for example, to Coryat's Mother, dated *Last of October 1616*:

> I spent in my journey betwixt Jerusalem and this Mogol Court, fifteene monethes: all which I traversed afoote, but with divers paires of shooes, having been such a Propateticke ... that is walker ... for the totall con-
> tayneth two thousand and seven hundred English miles. My whole Per-
> ambulation is like to be a Passage of almost six thousand miles ... thorow Persia, Babylon and Ninivie, to Cairo and down the Nilus to Alexandria.

Also from this sojourn, he addressed distinguished friends in London:

> 'To John Donne, Pseudo-martyr', (alluding to the shroud in which he's pictured), 'Hoskins, alias Aequinoctiall Pasticrust of Hereford, Master Benjamin Jonson, the Poet, at his Chamber at the Black-Friers and Samuel

Purchas, great Collector of the Lucubrations of Classical Authors, for the description of Asia, Africa, and America ...'

On the fringes of the court at Agra, Coryat acquired fluency in Persian, Arabic and Turkish. His motive? 'twas to visit Persia, discourse with the King there, and obtain leave to walk 'into the Countrey of Tartaria to the Citie of Samarcand, to visit the blessed Sepulchre of the Lord of the Corners – which is Tamburlaine.'

To this end, Coryat composed a speech in Persian (he sent a copy to his mother in Odcombe):

Hazaret Aallum pennah salamet, fooker Daruces ve tehaungesta hastam kemia emadam az wellagets door, ganne az mulk Inglazin: kekessanaion petheen mushacas cardand ke wellagets, mazcoor der akers magrub bood, ke mader hamma nezzaerts dunmast.

Lord Protector of the World, all haile to you: I am a poore Traveller and World-seer, which am come hither from a farre countrie, namely England, which ancient Historians thought to have been situated in the farthest bounds of the West, and which is the Queene of all the Ilands in the World.

With three oriental languages, like great Asian rivers, streaming through his intellect, Coryat *pedesticated* into Persia. And his *Crudities* (that earlier book) contained such celebrated sport, that he was calm when

just about the Frontiers of Persia and India, I met Sir Robert Sherley and his Lady, travelling from the Court of the Mogol to the King of Persia's Court. There did he shew mee, to my singular contentment, both my Bookes neatly kept; and hath promised to shew them to the Persian King: and to interpret unto him some of the principall matters in the Turkish Tongue.

But the King denied that *pedestrian* protection. 'There was,' T.C. reported, 'no amity betwixt the Tartarian Princes and himselfe and his commendatory Letters would do me no good.' He died on his return, it was recorded, of a dysentery. And if he had an opium at Agra to assuage his last expostulations, who would begrudge him dreams in which, doubtless, he expired (unless, one might surmise, he suffered the horrors) in a solitary and polychromatic laughter.[5]

_____

5 In a panegyric of 1613 titled *Odcombs Complaint* or *Coriats Funeral Epicedium: or Death-song*, with his *Epitaph in the Barmuda and the Utopian tongues*, by one John Taylor, it is claimed that Coryat died at sea. These lines give a flavour of his

Now I've sketched this picture for two purposes mainly. First, in opposition to the Reverend Purchas. For by contrast with Thom Coryat, who ranged the earth alone, spontaneously and extemporised daily a most singular existence, the pious, sedentary Purchas crept hesitant, uneasy, and in a lament for *Man's first disobedience* and also for the pathos of his own existence. Witness, for example, this complaint, in a dedication letter to George *Cantuar*, which he includes within *Pilgrimages'* Preface:

Had I [wrote Purchas] enjoyed Academicke leisure ... or the benefits of greater Libraries, or sufficient conference with men more skilfull: my Braine might have yeelded a fairer issue, a more compleate and better-armed Minerva ... But besides the want of these, the daily cares of my Family, the weekly duties of my Ministerie, the grosseness of the Aire where I live, which (some say) makes a duller wit, I am sure, a sicklier body, may pleade excuse for me.

But despite such complaints, the good Purchas was not slow to vaunt himself:

Great is the burden of a twofold World, and requires both an Atlas and an Hercules too, to undergoe it. The *neweness* [of my work] also makes it more difficult, being an enterprise never yet (to my knowledge) by any, in any language, attempted; conjoining thus Antiquitie and Moderne Historie.

One aspect further. While Purchas languished at his Eastwood living, in vaporous, remote Essex marshland, a mere two mile ride away lay *Leigh* (by the sea), 'a proper little towne,' as Camden described it, 'and full of stout and adventurous sailers,' at whose dockside New World travellers anchored on their final road to London. Here Purchas would ride (as might have Yorick on his bony and parsonical hack), converse with mariners and see, touch and smell exotic products brought back from India, the Indies, the Americas: trade stuff made in places he could imagine only through synecdoche and hearsay.

Nor was this asphyxiated cleric ill-connected. He was on terms with many an old seaman: Cockes, Barkle, Spelman, Battel, Turner, Captain Salmon, and John Vassal. He knew these writers who had travelled: William Borough (Navy Controller), mathematical Briggs, John Smith of Virginia and, not least, *re* our theme, that happy and distinguished *Holofernes*,

---

colleagues' relish: 'You off-springs of the three times treble Sisters, / Write, study, teach until your tongs have blisters. / For, now the *Haddocks* and the shifting *Sharks* / That feed on Coryat, will become great Clarks.'

Tom 'Crudities' Coryat. (And given Coryat was a familiar of The Mermaid Tavern, we may surmise that Purchas, too, knew Fletcher, Donne and Jonson – perhaps Shakespeare even.)

But while Purchas stayed home with his books, maps, manuscripts and parish duties, patching his quire from far-flung texts and merchant narratives (he and Hakluyt recorded), the errant Coryat extemporised *along the footpath way*: expatiating wildly, as though objects of his observation flowed from every movement of his slipper and in reflexion his own motley prompted.

I indulge myself here, in illustration of these two men's humours. Imagine the shy, dutiful, reclusive Purchas at Leigh's quayside, the salt marsh behind him, the stench of the river in his nostrils, an east sea wind bringing travellers to Thames' sunless, desolating estuary.

Off one of those returning barks steps the dazzling and bedizened, sun-burned, hennaed Coryat, ablaze in calico and silk from Gujarat, the lining of his doublet bloated with the cotton stuffing that conceals his baubles (not many of much value), his feet shod in slippers that he'd stepped in from Aleppo: turmeric on his cuffs from twenty months of curried dinners, his hair stuck with tamarind, beeswax stiffening his whiskers, cumin on his breath and the river of Odcombian language welling in a larynx which had so long been stifled up with courtesies in Persian, Arabic and Turkish and which now issued in a roaring current.

'*Quis est*? You here Purchas?! *Sed quo vadis* Purcha. *Mi care Purchulle*? And if, *vero*, Purchas *es*, swounds, why (I will in my bewildered errancy pervestigate), not also *frater* Johannus Donnus ... Dun ... Done ... Donne ... or steepling and Roman Ben or witty Will Shakespericus, our royal nation's Natural Genius, *veniens e* Shoreditch *atque* Swan or Globus?

'But how now! Elder Samuel (*Shmu-el*: the One who Hears Godde) whom the Lord hath selectivated and who answered "*Hin'eni*!" in the *lashon kadosh* or holy language of the *Hebraicii* – in which tongue the Almighty spake to our declivinated, lapsed First Parents: *Adama* (or Earth) and *Hava* our mother!

'*Sed* Samuel: *Quid hic facis*? Art set to *peregrinate* aboard now some *vessicula marinanti*! Don't descant or decantate to me of moneys! I exavigated from Somerset's old Odcombe three years back now with *duodecim denarii* only in my scrip and have dispensed a mere half groat, tuppence farthing, scarce a scruple more, *per diem* – and on Indus' fever'd plain, a three ha'pence farthing *in extremis*. But see! There's a *naviculant* vehicle out there *super mare* – she'll be *celerrima* and she's yare – that's just attendicating an auspicious *Zephyr*...

'What? Parish duties stay thee? *Desiderata*? Let Corydon or Piers or Colin blazon forth thy Gospel! *Uxor liberique*? You'll find *pulchritudines* enow at the Court at Ajmer of the Magnum Mogul! And breed mewlers and pukers there too, I'll *verasticate* ... No? Ah me then! And to thee alas! *Aval salaam aleicem*!

'*Sed* on *altero topico*: I'm for London – Londres – *aut* Londinium – : and what has *Magister Bin-ya-minus* inscribed in *stylo novo humoresco* these *tres anni, Anno* – Anon *Domini*?

'And what follows Old Bill's *La Tempesta* – that *ultima drama* I witnessed *meis propriis occulis Fratribus Nigris*, or at the Blackfriars – as 'tis yclept by the unlearned? What Bill *mortuus est*? *Buggeratio* that lusty beggar! Dead now with his ducats and beyond all *buggerationes*! Thou cognizest what pecuniary *denarii* he owed my satchel! How, *nunc*, shall I pedestically Propatetickate *ad domum meum Odcombiensum*?

'Swounds, must I *instanter* and therefore now-from unpick from my doublet's *speluncum obscurum* – certain oriental *gemmas*? In lieu of which, mayhap, you'll tender me, some finite *mickle*? As at Isfahan 'tis said: *Room oo Arrac peeada geshta, as door der een mulc reseedam ... Pax vobiscum atque, Pater* ...'

All this above inflected with the Persian, qualified with twists of cider and, proleptically, a can'kin of *canary* from the Mermaid tavern.

Vale, Tommaso, *inquit* Purchas, indistinctly.
Must hence to vespers, *atque uxor liberique.*

But what was Tamburlaine to Coryat or *vice versa*? All Coryat could know of him was what he'd conned in Marlowe's gorgeous and distended bluster. And while Marlowe, from his fen, had roared outlandish but domesticated honey, Coryat must vaunt he had *pedesticated*, in his slipper, spheres that touched an earth that we, in our diminished parishes, must be content to know in reverie and speculation.

Hence of an evening, as we step out for our unpretending supper,
We'ld *fricassee* a turnip on imagination's palate to a nectar
Which – from the sap of that Forbidden and Experimental Tree –
The Serpent Gardener has decocted to intoxicate our poesy.

Culbone Wood Journal 2

All poetic endeavour has its origin in one idea: it is rooted in the Fall and our husbandry with *that forbidden tree*, whose blossom and fruit still inform our existence. All song proclaims a celebration of the orchard in whose cradle we were rocked for that sweet, short single day of our gestation – but from which we have since been in exile. But to sing of Paradise is also to lament our exclusion from that infant dream. And so all poetry is double in its character. We can know nothing but glimpses of that inaccessible *pardes* – Hebrew from the Persian 'orchard' – and our singing issues from our exile to a world in which we are not welcome wholly.

That mighty but all too laconic poem that initiates the Hebrew *Genesis* presents us with a very model of discomfort: and our rhythmic murmurings, expostulations, ratiocinations and effusions, even our brief, ecstatic shafts of light and music (shot through as these must be with consciousness of our mortality) represent a variation of that primal sorrow: as hourly we repeat in countless measures our First Parents' bondage to that shining tree of both enlightenment and disillusion. One moment they stood content to gaze with awe at what they were enjoined to know in childlike ignorance. The next, with the apple in their hands and soon in their bodies, they became as we are, separated from their perfection.

Having thus incorporated what, at the centre, they had been forbidden, they must carry this same thing into exile with them: a fate we have inherited and whose reverberation we perpetuate. Indeed: all action is to re-*verb*, re-enact and express anew in constant variation that fatal first self-alienation.

In answer to the above. All this is metaphor, and by 'the Fall' I mean the phenomenon of mutability. For the prelapsarian is static, and our First Parents made the reasonable and dynamic choice. This was neither sin nor a mistake; it has been called a *felix culpa*. For as they touched the apple, then it was they became human, for the *noli tangere* was stultifying: and through an eternity of obedience, they would have lived in servitude.

By transgressing, on the other hand, they asserted their nature: and in wagering loss against an unknowable, albeit painful freedom, they chose mortality over the pieties of a sterile and eternal sabbath. In so doing, they revolted against perfection. For this courage I applaud them. And if as a result, the fruit must be germinated only to decompose, then we must glory and participate in that susceptibility.

This globe we inhabit is a fruit that feeds, after all, on the compost of its alternating cycles. And I am content to contribute my own rot to the general. (It was, I have been told, a fig tree, not an apple, in the Persian paradise. Did our parents defecate incontinently and for this pollution they were excluded from the garden?)

I approach my confession. For the place one may not reach, call it *Xanadu garden*, is where lines of poetry extend at their warmest and most urgent. And as these converge, their paths contrive a pattern along which the imagination travels, intersecting the ideal, and rejoicing in collusion with it, while also abandoning the humanity from which it emerged, and thus leaving it in a suspension.

As movement accelerates, alien disruptive tensions stretch. No person is left here in the body. Language, which was the medium through which the soul enjoyed the evidence of its encounter, is now a music whose modes are too outlandish to interpret. The mind hesitates and staggers. Rocks, brambles and long-rooted creepers crowd the garden. We turn home for concretions whose gross forms we'd forsaken. And we dig around in fury, hands and faces bleeding. As it opens toward sunlight, the shrine reveals that it, too, started as a ruin. Chimeras, sea beasts, chthonic apparitions, legendary cities and a vast topography of gloomy rivers and infernal marshes adumbrated by the ancients baffle our imagining. Barefoot we stumble over purgatorial escarpments. On we stagger toward shafts of light that wound and dazzle. And so continues clearance of imagination's ideal places.

At the centre of the labyrinth the Great Khan, *ithyphallic*, sword drawn, drenched in Chinese blood, stands growling.

The *mandala* walls along which his Tibetan sage conducted Kubilai, lead to a consecrated centre where an angry deity awaits him. Here was the mirror of the Great Khan's passions, beneath which, in the garden of his possibilities, lay his Buddha nature.

I don't paint words onto this landscape from a plate I hold in preparation. Words spring up in their bird-like colours with sovereign, independent conjuration, the sum of which converge into a single verb in the infinitive, and this in its turn transforms into the noun which is the cosmos: a nominative neuter and yet pregnant with the grammar it's repudiated and ingested.

Are we essentially spectators to the pictures of things? While things, in themselves, lie in their proper selves, beyond our senses?

In imagination I have exgavated through the bodies of the lark and primrose, through the foxglove and the bramble, and have arrived at a subtle and refined nothing. In itself beautiful, but too elemental to grasp by intellection or retain in memory. These essences co-exist with us and are within us. But it is a work lying beyond a voyage, as we outwardly know it, to travel there, dwell and return to the coarse outer integument.

Still, Nature is my cradle. And, at every moment, rocks me gently, wisely to my extinction.

Restless, nightly lucubrations otherwise oppress me. Some demiurge roams my mental chambers. It feeds on me. Its excrements are mine – in origin and residue. O Goddess, take up residence and slubber my psyche with an inspirational, resistant honey!

A confession. It was late. Past midnight. And in search of a quill, I was barefoot in the upper corridor, when I was witness to the womanhood of the young serving girl on whose singing I have reflected.

The door of her chamber was ajar and in the angle of its fore-edge and the door post, the girl's figure was visible, half lit by a candle which stood in a brass dish that lay at hip level on a dresser. The young woman was standing in a chiaroscuro in which the darkness to one side of the room was graduated in the proximity of the candle into a splintering aurora that surrounded the oily and pallid flame and the yellower burnish of the platter over which it stood.

She had just then lifted her gown and it hung momentarily above her head, like a caul or waxy cerement as fashioned thinly by some carver – or closer perhaps to our circumstance on the farmstead, more like a cloud of chaff dust that hangs in a barn and which low sun lights through some cracks of its boarding. (My association is indeed with straw: for her hair, as though wet and gleaming in a dull thick gold was matted on her neck and lay accumulated at the shoulder).

In addition to those ample parts on which it would be a prurience for me to dwell on, it was her face that I recall most clearly. As though Rembrandt had provided her with this, and it shone still unset from his sombre palette, she was turned in my direction, and no doubt because I slid past quickly in the passage, she neither saw nor heard me: and so it was that her quiet features, in the composure of their innocence and self-possession, radiated themselves to me.

Here was a woman in the splendour of her chastity, and I the brief intruder, illicitly and in furtive, ashamed pleasure, a witness to her beauty: at once warmed by a small light and sheltered by the darkness: desirable of course to my manhood, but too precious to conceive of outraging with a signal of my presence. Like Actaeon (less fortunate!), in violation of the chastity and reservation of Diana's nakedness, I fled.

I will not pretend that this farm is where I had intended to arrive. And yet it was during an enforced residence that I composed my poem. Few seek displacement. But aberration conducts us along paths we did not know existed. The more we avoid them, the closer they draw us to them. The labyrinth is magnetised. A black lamp tempting the inhabitants of darkness.

I smile when I think of that young woman's person. Pleasant mental exploit. The flesh sporting, in the innocence of longing, with oneiric freedom. There is no cure for being human. Against all moral law, most men dream likewise. It is not until death we hold everything at once in our embrace, however briefly. (We live in twisting and restricted currents. The triton and the neirid sprawl in saline concupiscences of broader waters. Could we act thus frankly with our bodies!) But the road ahead for me is black. I must kindle my small flame: sufficient to myself and for two others.

A visit from the Muse. Such encounters to be guarded *sans* intervention of interpretation.

The Muse touches from a distance, first with light, and once the devotee's intoxicated, then with music. This blessing bestows ecstasy. Therein peril of derangement. All the deity demands is dedication and obedience. Step no further. (The Muse is a harlot, I have heard it muttered. This can't be. Oh no. Surely. Still, beware imagining that thou art her most favoured lover. Or her first born darling.)

To make good verses lies within the nature of an amicable commerce. It is, in this connection, a wholesome act to offer one's friend the produce of an honest labour. I learned this when I stopped at Linton to buy radishes and lettuce.

What ensued was a hearty transaction, as though, in response to my penny in the gardener's palm, the earth grains where I sowed my coin proclaimed: 'We write these in our gardens.'

To which, when I germinate my verses I would say likewise: 'This lettuce is what I mean. Let these radishes speak for me.'

Bitter prospect of winter. Already I hear crows' wings strike the oak leaf, hard with hurrying, metallic clatter.

Tomorrow we shall eat a final lettuce. Relish while we can, these glassy stems that scream against the teeth and pass along the throat the succulence into which they degenerate with such elasticity!

I look out on the months and see, on brown horizons, dirty turnip infinitely stretching. So cherish, while we may, these last green glimpses.

In the conversation between the poet and the world, a metaphoric bridge of significations composed of often mutually discordant elements is extended. Not one single truth may be observed to make its crossing here, but it is obscured and rendered inscrutable by the very medium that made its going over possible.

Little that is said or written pertains to the meaning which had its origin at the moment of conception. We experience only the artefacture of the means by which a transit has been created. Herein lies a connection between two points: the first which stands before the moment of articulation, the second, which follows it – and so it is said and done, or written.

In the meantime, what we witness is an indecipherable music, as if produced by a gorgeous, indistinctly apprehended and extrinsic being, whose beauty consists of falsifications raised to the condition of an exquisitely construed phantasm. Important here to remember that Ariel, after relatively brief service to the tyrant who rescued and then enslaved him, must have his freedom.

Thenceforth he will sing wherever he chooses and for the most part beyond our hearing. Caliban, who adored this music, will forever roam the island in silence. And we, poor creatures, must amble beside him scratching our heads in an equal quandary.

In the process of composition: the illusion of addressing the world.

At the moment of publication: the reality of sinking into obscurity.

At a certain point in our lifetime we are thrown abruptly on an unfamiliar shore of whose existence we had never dreamed and whose place in the world we can't identify. Disoriented by the sea from which we have been driven and the land which offers no sign that we belong there, we must start life anew from the moment of our abandonment and set out to make comfortable what is threatening and create familiarity from the supervention of a complete strangeness.

There are of course, those, such as Ovid, who have been forcibly exiled and must, on account of some irrational tyranny, endure a dreary and unrelieved barbarism until they drop, among the goatherds, to an end which lacks the remotest consolation.

There are others, who fare worse, whom destiny has sentenced to the most excruciating torture. Fate and nature converge on yet others – Viola and Sebastian are examples – throwing them at random into unforeseeable contingencies from which they must rescue themselves through the exercise of wit, hard labour and, not least, virtue.

If it was, through no mischief of their own, a combination of the ocean and the enmity of warring states that waylaid those twins, then the vicious lords beguiled by Prospero were drawn onto his island, in part by a current, to repent what lies within each person's being. And in tune with that current – the sea responding sympathetically – Prospero bade Ariel harmonise the winds he needed.

These destinies lie unequally in parallel. But too much literary analogy would obscure the point at which, in my nakedness, I have entered. Neither can I explore, satisfactorily, the notion I have introduced, because I am, at this moment, still cast afresh into that environment of the unfamiliar which has, of a sudden, made me a stranger to myself and to everything in my past that I recognised as belonging to me. Self, place and station, all suddenly unknown and alien. How must I start? Only the movement of time, which obliterates itself as it goes, will reveal this.

Unfamiliarity must, I think, be the experience of the old: and this helps me towards a definition of the experience to which I have alluded. To view this notion from a different point, it is helpful to acknowledge that what appears, to an outside view, to be the experience of others, is by virtue of that very distance, normalising and commonplace. Thus, in the company of some older person – I have found myself thinking – it is as though such an elder is just *that* by definition: always has been. Furthermore, that the experience of senectitude is somehow reserved merely for others, and that we are, by virtue of our juvenile subjectivity, immune from decrepitude and even from mortality.

There will, however, come a moment (should one be so fortunate) when one *is* there, suddenly; and that condition of ageing we had viewed with such complacency from beyond, has inalienably become our own. Such a realisation defines the moment. And given no escape is possible, one must finally acknowledge the new sphere – which is strangerhood.

Imagine, but *truly*, Viola's first moments. She is half dead from ship-wreck. The beach stretches bleakly. She is, although she does not know it yet, in enemy Illyria. Stranded in the loss of everything, the world has changed entirely. Is it any wonder that she starts again – God *'ild* her! – as a different person?

It is not often that I resort to the Bible. But given this crisis – and not having my *Aeneid* where I have on occasion indulged, with light-hearted superstition, in *sortes Virgilianae* – I opened the great volume that dominates the parlour: and lo! I laid my finger on this re-animating passage:

> Enlarge the place of thy tent, and let them stretch forth the curtains of thy habitations: spare not, lengthen thy cords, and strengthen thy stakes. For thou shalt break forth on the right hand and on the left. *Isaiah 54:2*

How unfortunate that the surrounding verses ('he was wounded for our transgressions') have anachronistically been deformed to a messianic supposition. Let such poetry reach us naked of whatever hope gave it occasion, and of the impulse or idea that informed its metaphoric energy.

Yea, and though I walk through the valley of the shadow of an onto-logical de-rangement, I will *lengthen my cords*. And hence – *break forth*!

Without any such intention, I have exchanged glances with the young woman who brings me my porridge and have learned this from her de-meanour: that the mind, through the eyes, informs the heart's intention. What I saw in her were chastity and frankness. And while this is what I returned, I suspect that had I identified a lascivious opportunism, my own eyes would have mirrored the same. Am I a mere echo? This is the not unhappy character of a poet whose task is divided between *mimesis* and transformation. And yet such ambiguity must be framed, like chiaroscuro in a master portrait, with the clarity of temperance.

Waiting. Boredom. Ordeal. Solitude. Despair. Disillusion. These are constituents with which we must content ourselves – and perforce observe the world that lies about us *via* the medium of a private and idiosyncratic trouble as though viewing it through an eye infection.

And so for what purpose should I take in this impression of a thorn bush filled with powder-blue and cloud-grey berries that stands shaken by the sea wind against the flint-cobbled wall of the harbour master's office?

My hesitant response is this. What I contemplate in detail represents an ingestion which is followed by its digestion. Then what, if not a line of poetry, must I thereby extrude – like the filament of silk I see this spider running, linking thorn to thorn, from the spirical in its posterior?

This singular thread is contrived into a daring and symmetrical pattern which is at once strong, subtle, iridescent and elastic. Presumably every species of arachnid spins a web which is patterned to an inherited tradition. And yet each web sits uniquely in keeping with the circumstance of its position.

And *for whom* is this spider establishing so intricate a design which is so dangerously exposed to the weather that invades the sturdiest of thickets? The spider builds, as do all creatures, I suppose, for itself alone, and no doubt also for a progeny which will be posthumous to its little moment.

Do not ask me, then, for whom I press out my poesy! This is not a pure silk suture oscillating to syllabic rhythms I've extruded. Rather, it is the thorns across which the metre involves, *encores*, devolves and hangs its pattern. And these lacerate the throat that calls them into being. Let posterity, for whom they are constructed, judge the residue.

Where is the simple and uncontaminated source that springs uninformed and without periphrasis from a landscape of the mind more supple than thought reads from the faculties? Such a sentence alone blocks the leeway of its up-thrust and obscures its own current! A poetry of unknowing continues to elude us, for that innocent state which ante-dates the interferences of a creational intent, presupposes abnegation of ambition. The mind in its pristine status holds no mirror to itself or its environment. Speculation which contains, *within*, the flashing of reflexive mercury (for 'speculation' at its heart's a mirror) has yet to infringe that welcoming, liberal inexperience whose vision as yet remains untainted. But the child, no more and no less than the primrose and the sparrow, composes nothing.

We project, nonetheless, on these beautiful and ordinary beings, our most complicated wishes. But we can never (again!) become them.

In the face of ideal beauty: disenchantment. Dare I tread that consecrated circle? I am pre-empted, in approaching the Divine, by apprehension – or too vulnerable a wonder.

The Muses crowd the throne of the Great Father. That relegation is imperative. What the Father ordains, or chastises and rewards, The Nine Daughters interpret. Such is the nature of their inspiration.

> True Thomas sat on Huntley Bank
> And a ferlie did he see ...

This ballad I must study further – on this very grass where *ferlies* are encountered and where dreamers, like these little butterflies, emerge in brief but lively metamorphosis. Of this, more later.

Somewhere along the footpath, rabbits have scratched away the grass to leave in the earth a red, concave scar in their attempt to burrow. An image of casually abandoned labour. This is one thing I comprehend perfectly.

I may not claim to have chosen, volitionally, the subject, place or form of my poem. Truer to say that its subject and context chose to enter me, and that resulting from this traffic, the composition process, as yet teasingly obscure to me, would appear to have taken place over three stages.

The first came with my perusal of that paragraph in Purchas – albeit I might have been reading any other part of the same volume. The second lay in the penetration of this matter to some occluded situation of unconscious thought. And it was in such a place, crystallising in a region of the hidden imaginative faculty, that the organism of the poem, autonomously, autochthonously developed, evolving, as it were, within a ductile geologic stratum and must continue in that condition until such time as it was excavated at the moment of waking.

The third stage lay with that return of consciousness, during which my hand, as though at dictation from a voice coming from memory (mine, albeit strange to me: mining the ore of an indistinct *Meinung!*), inscribed the lines that lie before me.

The body and the mind in this respect may be compared to the experimental locus of a reaction. As I sow vegetable seed or plant a fruit tree, those will develop so long as their environment remains benign.

Given a good seed bed, light and water, life can not but thrive. Poetry, in a comparable manner, emerges through the impression of some bodily and intellectual mould through which the inspiriting material has been germinated, whether or not this will be the organism of what eventuates in its finality.

About *Thomas the Rhymer* who lay on Huntley Bank and whose body, so he might have felt and told, was racked between the world that he must lose and a dangerous country of imagination. That the poet lay in grass (as did Marvell in his *Garden*) portended a fall and an adventure: while the green drowning waves of an hypnotic and unstable pasture swept away both earth and any mortal individuality he might thus far have clung to.

Stretched in a swoon and made accessible thereby, a *ferlie* in the person of the Queen of Elfland enters and absconds with him as her victim: while the Rhymer, like a damsel in some high chivalric story – drunk with her beauty and half willing – is transported.

The facts of his journey are laconically recorded. Forty days, through blood, he travels. Whose? And from where? Through rivers or seas? The source is not mentioned. Were these forty days the sum of all warfare, conflict between clansmen, rapine? Or was the poet wading through his own life's current? Or some sanguinary limbo that separates this world from its analogue in Hades?

Surviving the ordeal and arriving at a garden (green, surprisingly, and lively), he sees what he surmises are the fruits of the *forbidden tree* a-glowing: but when he stretches out to pull one, it is the Queen – indeed, that serpent of his inspiration! – who forestalls this. Her motive is not far from what the Hebrew God's was. The Rhymer's journey must be, strangely onward, to renewal of his innocence and never in some fruitless divagation, motivated by ambition, thorough the realms of this world's knowledge.

The journey grows dimmer. The Rhymer, without stars to light him, hears a roaring – as of oceanic surges. These are intimations of the infinite whose boundaries, paradoxically, enclose him as though offering a freedom which was never of his choosing. Now the Rhymer is exposed to three distinct prospects. Two of these are moral. The third ecstatic.

The first opens to a path of thorns. This is the passage that the pious take to heaven. The second is the thoroughfare of sin. This leads through luscious fields of blossom. The Queen forbids the Rhymer both these journeys. Instead he must follow a road whose character is simple beauty. Such is the path that leads to Elfland: that continent of poesy whose truths may not be reached but through ordeals of rapture, a disburdening of self and speculative meditation.

Now, on this account, the Queen enjoins silence. How else should a poet reach the *Ursprung* of his *katabasis*? On this subject, as of all things in the faery region, the ballad maintains honourable reticence. How long in human sleeping time were those seven supernatural years? Only those who go can know it.

Now the poem's grosser narrative expresses a distinctive silence. Like the absence of star-light which had blinded the Rhymer, this is the realm where speech has been subdued to what cannot be spoken. This lies beyond singing

In an indecipherable landscape which transmits no reflection.
But whose shades are transmuted through allegorical projection.

This is, surely, as it is with all orders of true poetry, the nature of whose coarser value may want that audacity which lifts mere human breath into the element of aether.

The more subtle the art, the remoter its abstraction.
The less that may be named, the more sacrosanct its terror.

As regards the existence of such a bardic penetralium, it is, I think, what the Jews claim for their scriptures: that such texts are symbolic of realms which may be divined only through long study and devotional singing. Behind those syllables of thorn, which have been steeped in laurel gall and pastoral honey, higher meanings are accessible to those, as with the *faery*, who already have both learning and a modest receptivity. Or as in the ballad, those who are *translated*.

The rabbis, so I have been told, likewise deduce a secret essence in the very architecture of their *aleph beth*, as they name it. These lines of the Hebrew, with their mobile and flexed uprights and flaringly penned serifs, so dark in tight packed hedgerows on the vellum – blackthorn in the desert glitteringly naked! – are, in truth, tinder and candle-wick vehicles of a holy fire which blazes from the core of every ink stroke: and that the scraped silly sheep skin, stiff beneath those spiny and impenetrable characters, is a flaming seraphic Sinaic conflagration of divine knowledge and effulgence.

We may speculate similarly that the pen scratches of our most audacious poets contain fire-seeds concealed in the most opaque dried ink spots. One punctuation point in Shakespeare's foulest papers might thus have harboured or infoliated some aspect of Nature's unlimited mutable variability in whose representation we continue to perform both as minor interpreters and as a motley of common players.

Equally perhaps, that each syllable in Milton is charged, like the earth he mistrusted for its tempting veins of metal, with precious and immortalising ichor. And that Virgil's hexametric alternations (dactyl phasing with a stutter into spondee, Parnassian to chthonic, marine to pastoral, warfare into hymeneal) enclose burning effluvia from Hades' rivers in whose tides he had bathed and from whose currents he forged lofty and consolidated outcrops of his epic. And so on through Dante and Herr Goethe's metaphysical, erotic interactions, whose damnations are intellectual and whose flesh combines metaphor and pleasure!

Is it not the case that the whole of our life is a sequence of episodes that are loosely jointed together and this most often without distinct relation? We might arrange these like pictures, and through the operation of memory and the intervention of our pleasure give each its tincture, varnish, light and shadow, bring this one close and set another in the background. But in truth, there is no clear boundary between such panels. While we see each frame clearly, we neglect its antecedents and most often know nothing of its illimitably ramifying consequences.

All this is painful to contemplate, for it is a measure of our impotence to know the truth of our actions: and if only for this reason, I value the experience of my recent composition. For within this occurrence lies a history I can trace, of whose outcome I am in possession, and where I may view each element as being at once discrete and co-dependent. And while the entirety of the event must be an enigma whose meaning in perhaps most respects remains impossible to comprehend, the inter-relation of its parts has become at least partially visible. But here perhaps I speak from my pride and plume myself too readily on a self-knowledge which, if truth be known, eludes me.

What, in this connection, I might say with better certainty is that death follows life, just as life represents a brief condition of becoming. By this I mean that our existence is just such an *episode* and this hangs between two spaces in which being does not exist and that these two spaces are unlimited in time and are entirely without a character. The two spaces of nothing that enclose each existence are in fact of one and the same medium. The nothingness into which we die is that identical condition of un-being which existed before we were given birth. Whether or not we

43

leave memorials to posterity – which will not anyway remember us for long – the brief interlude we enjoy is a mere interruption, an intervention or insertion into the stream of what wasn't and won't be. What seems to exist, what apparently *is*, is a brief apparition.

Such a spectre is my poem – though I have yet to read it over with any care – as indeed all work becomes. And as such, the creation of poetry represents a stalwart against extinction. This parlour table and the page that lies here each enjoy a like material existence. But the art forms of the polite world carry makers' names. And this addiction to denomination creates anxious traders of us against time. For myself, I am not ashamed to pursue such commerce. That said, I more admire the monuments of that ancient world whose makers requested, without thought of signature or label, an eternity alone for what they made: disembodying their hands of self without forcing their own names on the product of their devotion. Such work stands free of individuality and it is this impersonal character which lifts them to a nobility that transcends ambition.

Thus when I look on some old marble or a head from Egypt, I see there a work of the human mind which has interacted with the earth, and I'm prompted to cry out:

'Here is what man, at his best, can achieve! See how this beauty has survived to live among us! I glory in its maker's selfless and fraternal pact with nature!'

And again the mind reverts to those ballads whose excursions to the boundaries of our world of names still haunt imagination: *Tam Lin*, *Sir Patrick Spens*, *The Twa Ravens* and *The Wife of Usher's Well*, and all that minstrelsy that would teach us, if we dared give ear, to abandon our preening and fastidious, domesticated poetasting! (That Herr Goethe gives us his *Erlkönig* testifies to parallel preoccupation – of which more later.)

Blackthorn grows easily to make these coastal hedges in despite of the ivy whose pleasure is to strangle them. In this connection, the ivy has put out clusters of bubbling green flowers. These exude a mantle of honey whose odour is intoxicating but unpleasant. Wasps, bees and flies congregate on these sickeningly adhesive compound baubles, glutting themselves against the winter. To remember the bee is my signal devotion.

La Fontaine reminds me also. His *Ant and Grasshopper*, its final half-line. In dialogue as follows:

Ant: Que faisiez-vous au temps chaud?
Dit-elle à cette emprunteuse.

Grasshopper: Nuit et jour à tout venant
Je chantais, ne vous déplaise.

Ant: Vous chantiez? J'en suis fort aise.
Eh bien! Dansez maintenant.
'Then dance!' concludes the Ant.

'And starve!' (unstated). The most savage remark in any poem!

The minor voices of the household. Kitchen pans, the rattle of a knife and spoons ringing in a dish which has just now been emptied. The business of what happens between hearth and table. A boy runs in crying, 'Father, the black sow is ...' his voice lost now in the movement of a chair and the sudden stamp of boots. All this reaches my intelligence through the intervening medium of my intestine, which inhabits my body like a thick branch of ivy, convulsing and grasping at what it touches.

Earlier I imagined this organ to have been inhabited or possessed by the Tree of Life *ipse*. Could it be that this, even in the Paradise of the world's body, was sick already or even that this same tree was in itself a *parasite* of Paradise?

If the serpent was its inhabitant, its presiding spirit even, a constituent aspect of its life-sap dwelling both in trunk and branches and internally within the sapiency of its grain ... moreover if that the serpent were the writhing and energic force of the tree: *its* poison was perhaps the apple's savour: a fever-giving sweetness which offered the taster no respite from an overwhelming vehemence of aspiration ... The flavour of life, as elsewhere I have suggested, being what that first bite left in the mouth and which is inherited by all the sons of Eva and her Serpent Lover!

For he, or that, which seduced her to consume the apple was her concubine – an epicene phantasmagoria. And he, the snake, must have also entered Adam: that man who was an emblem, diagrammed, succinctly in three Hebrew characters, of *earth* from the Euphrates into Persia – and in concert, consummated their initiation – a consumption of, and first assault on, knowledge of a Self, the World in its first minutes and of Good and Evil.

The black pig, meanwhile, which had been rummaging for some cabbage stalks that lodged beyond the wicket, had thrust in its head and got stuck inside the sheepfold. She was dragged screaming to her quarters. They'll cut her throat tomorrow evening.

A warm early autumn, and some healthy rain showers in September have conspired to generate prolific crops of mushrooms. Now this morning, I have stumbled with the children out onto the coomb with baskets they have woven for this purpose and gathered, amid woolly bleatings, eight or ten pounds of succulent fungi, redolent of nether earth, for breakfast.

Paint me a better dish than toasts of a coarse, light crumb, which are spread with bacon fat or butter on which have been heaped a ladleful of fresh fried mushrooms (or *mesheroons* as these folk call them): the small, young, white heads pink-gilled with complexions like these healthy children's, while the big old gaffers, their gills crumbling, fold one on another, deliquescing in a sweet and pungent, nectarous, black gravy.

To eat mushrooms is also to engender thirst: for these delectable plants secrete a clammy sort of fume which, not unpleasantly, tends somewhat to constrict the throat: and while I have always found it a simple matter to despatch, at the least, a couple of full dishes, I know what it is to become dizzy with such an eating, and for the throat to palpitate, the eyes to grow distended and the whole system to experience a kind of benign, sick dryness, no doubt on account of that liquorous fungal richness to which I have alluded and which is a residue of their preparation. To avert these symptoms, my recipe is tea: fresh-boiled, hot, in cups big enough to sweat back into – and which, to conclude this gluttonous, brief exposition, create, of the face, a reciprocating fungus!

The simplified finality of tea. And tea's finality of all that's simple. All peripheral preoccupations are obliterated with this harmless tonic. And so here is my prescription:

First having dug the necessary trenches for your four rows of peas and next to them, potatoes, now go to the kitchen and witness how the body, which has struggled in complicity with earth and which steams with a spring sweat, is reduced to the plainest needs of its humanity. Reach now for bread and an ample dish of tea and observe how reduced the rest of everything becomes, as what the body touches transcends thought and all thought's products.

Such are happy moments. For in tea – this harmless infusion which stimulates and then sedates us – we lose ourselves to perfection of leisure. And if this represents the end point of our labour, it is also in itself an object, a completeness that we take into us.

This cup I hold indeed sustains profundities I know transcend my philosophic limits. It has travelled from the East to greet us and we need go no further than its warm dark edge to stay where it has come to meet us. So here while we drink we may sink without thinking. And oh, it is profound. We go down in a single swallow.

In an effort, now I am recovered, to be, in my smock, of some utility, I walked with two children carrying some bags of ewe's cheese three miles west towards the county boundary to a house at the cliff edge – thence the sheep's cheese into Linmouth.

We were easy with each other as we rambled, for the children are cheerful and they answered pleasantly. Sister and brother are ten years old, or round that figure. But not twins, they aver, and indeed their looks proclaim some little difference. For the *child* is brown with a sharp, quick eye while the boy is fair-skinned as a barley whisker. They reply, when I quizz them on this, quaintly – the boy, with laughter, teazing that the child had been a changeling. But then mended his story:

'She wuz dropped,' he avows, 'down the *garn* near the cow house by a tinker woman or a gypsy. 'Er be in Culbone no-one's *darter*.'

'Dropped 'ere,' she repeats, 'by a *mumper* or a *gallybeggar*.'

As we roll on with our cheeses I detect in their accents a relique of King Alfred's Saxon in these meadows!

'Cuz moi colour's this *dun*,' the child repeated, holding her dark arms up, 'thee'rt reckun I did came o' gypsy people.'

'Or the faery,' he against her, squinting his eyes up at their corners.

'An' *anywhen*, they foind me on the *batches*. So *he* baint moi brother!' (Yet more laughter!)

'So aye we maun be wed then,' the lad cries (*tirra lirra!*), 'an' she'll fetch me to 'er country, where we'll live tlgether, always.' What an innocent mix of the droll and the *weird* such children weave from twilight shadow!

At which, I asked them as we passed a ring of mushrooms, what they'd seen and heard of pixies, Jack o' Lanterns (our *ignis fatuus*).

'In the *dimpsey*, that's at *yeaveling*,' the child replies gravely, 'oi seed *faery raids* an' *gallybeggars* dancing.'

'An' oi seed *hinky punks* and imps and *gallybeggars* [sprites and goblins]'.

'Pray, boy', I request him, e'er I knew this meaning, 'what, please you, are the hinky punks you speak of?'

'Theck be the same as *hunky ounks*,' says he with caution.

'And what's *their* nature?'

'They maun play a trick on the *kees*'n *barras*, or sing i' th' *cockleet* till th' *zews* are *bewhiver'd*.'

'And who is the captain, in these parts, of faery people?'

'Ay,' the child asserted, 'theck be th' *Apple Tree Man* who'z all their maister. 'Tis he gives us fruit. And in autumn – when we wussel in th' orchards, we feed 'im a toast 'as bin soaked in a hot zider.'

This place is high, bare, remote. And its solitude is a compound of the silence which itself is an expression of the sky and a vast world it looks down on. The sea is visible as a dark glaze in the distance. And the wind, where it travels, leaves as residue mere shreds and whistles, the tatters of an invisible fabric – a music to which the violin, serpent and bassoon do not aspire. All this then drops away leaving the house in peace and with nothing between the mind and infinitude but thought's own restless and time-tramelled lucubration.

I have made a practice of putting aside this turbulence of perturbations – that current of hot rock in the Phlegethon of my psyche! – and then what silence: the soundless first moment before time and Paradise. Even before God, I would have written, but must remember, as the great book in this parlour recalls, that before the creation, it was formlessness existed: in that God was a part of primeval chaos, and he was at the centre of that instability, flew within it and then from out those buffetings and tides, created nature's order, through which he continued flying. For as Genesis saith: *the wind, or breath, of God moved on the face of the waters*. And thus I imagine the first moment no longer as a silence. But that out of this creative war with chaos, from the tension and engulfings of those contrary forces, came a *second* first moment.

Is there not peace in the following assertion: God created the Heavens and the earth? From this flows the silence in which I have been settled. As a primrose in the hedgerow rises on its stem, the flower opens, and there it stands up modestly in crowds of grasses. This is the silence all things co-exist in. And since all sound arises from the silence and returns there, sound, essentially, is silence also.

Out of the window – I look up from this page – I see the hawthorn hedge and a steep coomb with, further up, more hedge, thistle patches, sheep scattered across the meadow – and it is silence I *observe*. Silence visible. I witness it in the sky, a stone, the path round this farm. The body produces its breath and some mucilaginous interruptions. They too are silence and fall back to it.

Patience. Waiting. Herr Goethe writes in tapering, then rising exhalation:

Die Vögelein schweigen in Walde. Warte nur. Ruhe du auch! We journey in these lines through all Great Nature, returning to the quiet of our proper selves to meditate in silence. Great questions hang. No call to answer.

A fine working dog, well fed and trained to the necessary tasks of man, is an extension and even an expression of our happiness. Racing intelligently and with joy among the flock along the coomb, the sheep dog is a veritable embodiment of the orderly deployment of useful energy. How we strain to reward our dogs adequately with an acknowledgement of our appreciation! But we can never truly know the extent to which we communicate with them.

Walking home last evening surrounded at knee height by a foaming tide of ewes and yearlings, I was moved mostly by the restless and officious discipline of our two canine lieutenants that coursed among their charges, now circling and interweaving with them, now running back to chivvy forward a straggler, now leaping vertically with a strict authoritative yelp, now standing guard with one flank while its partner came rhythmically into view with a secondary stream that fed the main current: all this achieved with indefatigable verve at a whistle or a word from the presiding shepherd. And what is their reward? There is no reward. Given a good home, they would eat and exercise whether or not they herded sheep. No. Their joy is in their work, which they accomplish for its own sake – or so I think they must believe it.

I will not say that this must be the case with poetry. What I know, however, is that the world, which is the poet's universal master, will not pat my head, still less scratch behind my ear for my efforts. Nor will it feed me. Shall I, nonetheless, still laugh and fetch for it – from the spring of the Muses?

Du Doppelgänger!

I have sat here in the parlour following my supper for an hour. And alone with the fire that clicks and tinkles by the table, I became possessed, and none too pleasantly, with an intuition of the presence of another in the chair that had been pushed, since last I sat here, to the room's remoter shadows.

When I gazed through the half light, I could make out a figure of my stature and my composition. The hair, brushed and orderly, was dark as mine is, while the face resembled mine in both complexion and in contour. What startled me, too, was that this person who resembled me was dressed not, as I now am, in white rustic smock but in the garments I had worn on my arrival at the farm: the difference being that the britches I had ruined on my journey here were fresh, as though laundered and reconstituted, while the coat, which had been torn by brambles and squeezed from shape by exercise in wind and rain, was neatly mended.

The brisk appearance of this second person was well sorted with his posture. This was quiet and composed and yet watchful and attentive. And as I put out my neck to catch a better view, he responded with companionable acknowledgement: a reassuring courtesy – and yet uncanny and disturbing.

I looked down to my feet, then away to the grate, and then through the window to the coomb side where sheep in woolly outline stood immobile. Retracting my gaze, I surveyed the room and numbered the objects, now familiar to me, in it: wood pile, fire-irons, brushes; the oak table where I'd laid my papers; the Great Book in its hearty leather. Homely environs that spoke comfortable solace. When finally I returned my gaze towards that languorous but robust figure, there he still sat in the contemplative idleness I had taught myself to practise without too much impatience, and smiling with rapture through the twilight.

As though waiting for my act, or an address to him, or expectation that I'd sing, recite, or remark on the day, the supper I had eaten or comment on the situation of the farm economy, I saw him gaze back now benignly to me while I sat frozen in my chair (my hair stabbing me again and frozen!), dumb struck to be greeted in this mirror constituted of the darkness, of myself, which rendered me incapable – as though, as host, it was incumbent on me here to entertain my ghost! And yet he waited, so it seemed to me, for nothing. Here, in this being, was a self containment so absolute and cheerful, that my own unfixed attention – divided as this was between the alternation taking place betwixt my presence and that other self, which was an aspect of my being – it seemed, to him, or it, of no reality, and if it had that, then no consequence attached to it. 'I am another. And my other is another other,' I observed myself to mutter.

But self-possession radiated from this figment. And as my heart, which had jumped, reverted to its seat and cold horripilations from my scalp and forearms settled, I too sat at ease – as though contracted to a mutuality this spectre, whose beneficence I welcomed now, evoked in me.

For here, while the vision lasted, I understood now, was a whole and more developed self, a self-completed soul that sought nothing further than the calm the evening offered, and who responded to the time with a repose at odds with the repeated starts and self-interpositions I'd made restlessly and inch-meal, by the minute, since I came here.

But how was it I should find myself so represented by this double: just now, here, and never in the past when I have suffered and rejoiced, more even than at present, in painful apprehension, self-divided, of a life – both metaphysical and intellectual?

I note in retrospect that it was *I*, in whose identity I dwelt, who looked on *him*, and not he, as I might have experienced that other as myself, who gazed at me, who was, nonetheless I suppose, an agent of cognition and spectator of the same duality I witnessed. *He* saw me, clearly, and registered, I think, distinct impressions whose image was myself – for this I also apprehended.

But this *other* than me, albeit reduced from the physical person, stays phantasmal. And from this doubleness I've learned: that *being*, bound to thought and body, is not, as I'd assumed, a singularity: and that imagination tolerates, a not unpleasing separation in the self without a dissolution of the integrating faculties.

One further thought. The figure I observed enjoyed the elegance and self-possession of a gentleman: a fellow who'd been schooled, and who might pass for a scholar, churchman, master of genteel profession, one for whom self-doubt, if he should entertain it, might be subordinated, without effort.

But note too, that I who observed, was dressed in *borrowed weeds*, a smock, and that to him who looked on me, I was no doubt a simple fellow whose hand extended merely to the management of dogs, sheep and a few rude couplets. Here then I was a *cartoon* or a sketch – as Gilray might have stretched me – half self-complaisant gentleman, half displaced shepherd.

And here, too, was a simple truth which every poet must encounter. That while the practice of his art implies development of what we call a cultivated intellect (any individual may achieve this), equally important, the simplicity of the shepherd, who has nothing to do but gape at a green landscape, guard his charges, speak with authority to his dog and, not least, sing into a sky from which no interruption comes but from fraternities of larks and finches. Heaven bless that musician. If there is something we may not learn from him, perhaps it is not worth knowing. May Nature take me closer to that condition and let this smock grow hourly closer to my (gentlemanly) habit!

In the peace engendered by this vision of two selves, I slept. And so, no doubt, my *Doppelgänger* left. But here's the curiosity. For during this sleep I dreamed a repetition of my poem, enacted, not as stimulated by an opiate, but as though it had wandered through the drunken memory of a peasant and was transmitted with the rude vigour of a pot-house ballad.

Yea. I stood, in my dream, at the counter of an inn – altered strangely from one where I had passed an hour on my journey – my elbow soaking up the cider from its surface, when suddenly an old father, so heavily grey-bearded that his face had become all but indistinguishable from the sheep that were his livelihood, struck the stone flags with his crook and piped up in a snarling monotone with what at first appeared to be a ballad of the neighbourhood.

The company fell quiet, although not entirely, and thus the stanzas, struggling from his whiskers in the all but opaque dialect of the region, emerged to the mutter of fellow drinkers and the clatter of their cups as they raised them and let them fall.

And this, to my astonishment, was the ballad with which the old shepherd addressed his companions. It was a refraction, a reconstitution, and indeed perhaps a satire of my own unpublished poem, so lately composed that the ink was scarcely set on the page and the dust and crusts were not yet fallen from its blottings and erasures. And here, in rugged, stumbling iambs and in still more ragged dactyls, as though caught like greasy sheep's wool in a thorn hedge, was an ale house song, which was set to a tune – I laughed in amazement – on which generally was carried the commonest bawdry: those excrements of poetry that drop from the mouths of drunken clowns and country yokels:

Now harken t' me and gather ye near
And I'll zing ye a story ye nivver before did hear.
A girt king a' wuz, so moighty an' bold
He had kingdoms a-plenty and mountins o' gold!

Kublai Khan wuz 'is toitle an' much 'e did own:
All the cittiz of Choina did bow t' iz throne!
Now this Khubla did build a girt palace so foin.
It lay hoigh in the moun'ains an' this were 'iz desoin:

'Twer cool there i' the summer, zo that Kubla moight play
With 'z ladies so lizzum an' fair, noight an' day!
Thoze ladies was many and smoilin' they looked
On thir Maister and loved 'im as 'is zupper they cooked.

Now this palace 'twas built in meadows and grounds
Where Kuhbla did hunt with 'iz horses and hounds.
There was rivers an' waterfalls, deep quarries and streams
Where the sun never shoined nor the moon shed 'er beams.

Now when summer were over and Kublah grew so cool,
He took shelter in the city, end o' August as a rule.
An' when it was toime, he would summon 'iz men,
Saying, 'Now is th' moment to go t' war agen!'

When 'e 'ad said this they shouted and cried out so loud.
An' they cloimbed on thir horses and to battle they go'ed.
This Cubla 'iz captains a nice bit o' gold each did give 'em
When from far distant countries more ladies they fetched 'im.

An' one of theze ladies oi did see with my eyes.
She was weepin' and hollerin' roight up t' the skies.
She stood on a bridge an' she sung as she did cry
And on a Jews-harp or a guitar she did play.

Alas! as I transcribed the song I was summoned on business. I recall
nothing further.

Another dream. I was travelling, with Friar Rubeck or Carpini, in the
wastes of Asia, and passing through the spirit-haunted Taklamakan desert.

Toward early evening, we descried a low hill to the west and our horses
having smelled water thereabouts and weary as they had become on the
scantily grassed plain over which we had laboured since first light, picked
up the canter into which I had all day, unsuccessfully attempted to urge
them.

Before long, I too drank in the soft, moist wind, and as the sun began
to sink behind the hillock's north-western shoulder, we saw firelight, then
figures moving slowly between the outlines of a stand of trees which
stood presumably at the margin of the oasis which we were now fast
approaching.

Anxious to gain camp before the sun set entirely, I urged our leading
horses into a gallop, which painfully and bravely they contrived for a
scant furlong. This, however, proved sufficient. And just as the final rays
of sunlight withdrew across the plain, we achieved the oasis and the scent
of water was turned to gratifying actuality. How, otherwise, we would have
survived the night I hesitate to conjecture. But now horses and men, both,

lowered their heads into the dark, warm, brackish marsh water. And while our beasts snorted between draughts of this all too savoury liquor, we lay down near them on our bellies, and then on our backs, satisfied but entirely disgusted, spitting up the after-flavour and finally indulging our worn-out bodies with their first moments – after three days' unbroken travel – of inaction.

Steppe land horses, in their thousands, herded to remote horizons.

A sheep that strayed from Culbone into Porlock, causing havoc among the waggoners.

The visitation of a *Doppelgänger* parallels the expedition where one isn't. Supper eaten. I'm of the same stomach as the traveller who has been in Xanadu. In two-ness, joy. But also apprehension. I am no Colossus. My legs out-stretched scarce reach one another.

What was the teaching from that proper other person? This, unspoken: 'Let your practice be a blessing. Beware whatever art makes of itself and life a travail.'

The young woman who'd been singing. She is half up a ladder and enfolded in the branches of an apple. Her basket hangs on a pruned stub at the level of her waist and she is picking from the clusters that surround her body when, as she turns to pass some down, through the orchard strolls a sturdy yunker – he is five feet tall and no older than twenty – and reaching a hand up to her smocked arse sticking from the ladder, he slaps it roundly: his cupped palm ringing on it with a fleshy echo.

Now he runs on, and on he runs,
   And runs while she stands mute,
She, whose pale skin I had viewed last night,
   Blushes crimson as the cider fruit.

She plucks amain and on she plucks,
   To fill her creel today.
And as she plucks, she flushes red
   And she sings a wedding lay:

'As I was walking by the meer
   A ferlie I did spy.
And a little, little man did bid me go
   To be his lemman – 'twas no deny.

Ah no, Sir, cried I, I can not follow thee,
    For my true love lives here on the earth so firm.
If I left him and journeyed to faery land
    He would come to sore, sore harm.

Nay pretty maid, ye shall come away with me
    And kiss this red ring in my hand.
And if you oblige, 'tis no great thing,
    I will make thee the Queen of all Elfland.

Ah no, Sir, I cried, I'm a simple, simple girl,
    Never fit to be Queen of all Elfland.
And so I ran home to my bonny lemman,
    And I gave him my heart with my own bonny hand.'

Cider making. A heap of scrump – varieties of red and yellow in a sunlight marked by dust and shadow – a vast deal of scab but those skins go in. They wash the grindstone with apple vinegar and then swab it with water. Once the old horse comes in and is harnessed to the bar, she is fed an apple at each fourth revolution. Froth drools from her bit in white elastic swags and slides along the harness and so onto straw and apple leaves that mat the barn floor. A meditating, solemn, half-blind mare whose old memory guides her through each meander. Later when the last sap has been wrung, she will mumble a residue which has the consistency of sawdust. I ask the farmer:

'Did you wassail last New Year?'

'Ay sir, at Twelfth Night we went at it.'

'And you knocked each tree?'

'Ay, gi' trees a whack to fright'n out the imps and fairies. And that show 'em what we'll do if they set barren.'

'And you feed trees some toast with last year's cider?'

'Right up in her crotch. (*Laughs*). That gi' her courage.'

'Will you sing me your wassail?'

'I know what we sang as boys when we went round the houses at Langport – there. But not all the verses. Which I have forgotten.' (*Sings*)

There was an old man and he had an old cow
And how for to keep her he didn't know how
He built up a barn for to keep his cow warm
And a drop or two of cider will do us no harm

The girt dog of Langport he burnt his long tail
And this is the night we go singing wassail
O master and missus now we must be gone
God bless all in this house until we do come again

'That's what I remember. When we've beaten every tree, then we howl the orchard.' In the remarks I've made about apple trees and cider, I've vowed to say nothing on the Fall of Man. And yet ...

An infinite deep azure and small clouds in a scatter of a fish-flesh pattern. A late swallow cuts among these as though stitching a connection between cloud and heaven. If our minds could observe these same alternations, what a counterpoint of singing we would raise with our reflections!

Letters from B, which smack of ancient seas, I've carried with me. The passionate formation of his hand, as though in a streaming of marine currents. The descenders are flourishes done in great excitement. The taller letters flying across the waves of that blue-black script, taking off now into an air which *breezes* between the energy-stiffened pennants of words which have alighted to give him pleasure – and which now ride the crests of the general matter as though basking in a movement to which he has given free and delighted rein.

The pages breathe with an ocean wind whose excitement I inhale as I hold them to me. It matters little whether there is import to what he tells me. The words arch, leaping lively, as though great healthy sea beasts were unleashed from his pen nib, which tear through the water for sheer self-delight in the exercise of their migration. Herein lies friendship: for he exercises himself in so exuberant a current that its very off-splashings near intoxicate me with a tonic which is at once marine and aetherial!

Culbone Wood Journal 3

With a view to ordering a few notations on the border ballads and how this region's folk songs differ from the northern genre, I have been considering, by way of a similitude, the nature of spirits that have been distilled by condensation from the complex of a ferment, as compared to what happens to apples in the more straightforward preparation of cider.

What has struck me as magical is that in the process of distillation two very different operations occur. In the first, grain and water are introduced to one another. While in the second, a Stygian seething and steaming decoction – whose ferment has resulted from that earlier convergence – is vapourised and, in a process of separation and transfusion, becomes, once aged, that spiritous refinement we know as whiskey.

Now, in the course of purifying the organic mash, one might imagine that its parts would have been displaced and something else created. And while there must be truth in this view, what impresses me further is that the product – as presumably in any cooking – remains, in compound, what it first was, albeit alchemically transmuted into the subtle body, or the soul part, of its earlier, complete incorporation.

It is a fine thing, this distillation from such workaday constituents, which is now become so rarified as to have reached its ultimately reduced limit, beyond which it would evaporate into nothing. And that separation from the chaos and the reek of the grist, from which some animation's been extracted, must also, I think, represent a new kind of synthesis: the transcendence of what had been gross having been aetherialised from the coarser body of its matrix and re-combined somehow into a liquor which is at once unadulterated and *sui generis*, while also representing, in a fresh amalgamation, the elements from which it has been titrated.

What is good is that this spirit, whose double character I have suggested, is at once combustible and inert, while its impact on the palate is dramatised by a further separation, the upper level of which diverges along a glittering and brittle, sun-lit pathway, amber-tinted, which expresses, I surmise, the happiness of the barley in its early summer apotheosis, before it is malted, and at last, its impulse to fruition having been aborted, achieves transfiguration.

Branching away from this cheerful region, runs a nether-world current, which is charcoal in complexion and which, in truth, has been converted from an infusion of the stream water which has already been filtered from some inaccessible stratum of peat country. Thus while a first splash on the drinker's palate excites apprehension of its surface glamour, what memorably lingers remains the inner current which has found its way through the lips and the teeth from an underworld of old romance: and which is expressive of a melancholy humour which speaks to us, by inference, in a deep, terse, solemn, sempiternal and reluctantly communicative poetry which copies the earth's brown and is shy of daylight.

If spirits that have been distilled are sluggish in their interaction with us and dwell mainly in a lunar quiet, cider, by contrast, is effervescent, quick (in both its senses) and solar in both genesis and implication. And while whiskey may pretend to hold aloof from the grain out of which it has developed, cider seeks no such independence and is happy to have flowed directly from a tree.

Whiskey ages with a prelatical or aldermanic *dignitas*. Cider, on the other hand exults in being recent: and this quickness – rainfall drawn through stem and blossom, all in one season, to expansion into apples – is what we value it for. And while the mysticality or the *Orphism* of whiskey may dwell within an interior which is hidden, cider, by contrast, is constructed from direct sunlight, and perseveres as it ferments and then continues through its maturation, to draw fizzings from its bottom to the surface in a gladdening circulation, and this renders it unified, sociable and amiably dynamic.

Not being, myself, much of a drinker, I am less interested in the flavours and effects of these two fluids, than in what they suggest to me, of their origin, their transformations and, above all, their relative complication. And I have adverted to these drinks here because I associate them – somewhat loosely and not without a smile – with the rhyming narratives in Bishop Percy (his *Reliques*) and the country songs I hear in taverns, on the coombs as groaned out by shepherds, and indeed, as I've described already, by the young servant woman in this farm house.

Scottish ballads, for their solemnity and remoteness, are, of course, the genre I associate with the dark character of whiskey, while the pretty and sometimes jingling folk songs of this country, come, like the people who perform them, from the ambiguous generosity of *sullen earth* and a mixed, south-western, sweet-sour sunlight.

This is not to say that local songs are in the slightest sense expressions of mere effervescent happiness. The contrary is, for the most part, true – and given the poverty to which so much of Somerset has, in this past decade, been reduced, this is not to be marvelled at. The singers of these parts, nonetheless, do grind out, if I may risk the contradiction, a not altogether honeyed species of music. Their songs, albeit sometimes lumpy and stumbling with respect to metre, express a forthright and wistful sweetness, the tang of late fruition, and the astringency of a sap which equally could proceed from apples and the blood that splashes with naïve immediacy from hearts which have been excoriated by simple disappointments – from which they are unlikely to recover but about which they sing with the same raw sweetness as the cider with which they will for ever be on speaking terms.

In pursuit of more similitudes, I will, for the time being, make no further adventure. I have, besides, already descanted more than enough on *Thomas the Rhymer* – the faery character of which is typical of those distillations which have seeped to us from an occult northern country over two or three centuries.

But what of folk songs? I have heard them described as simple flowers of the people. While silly, this locution is evocative. If flowers could adapt themselves to song, would they not chant, on the one hand of the harsh and stony breast of earth from which they must drag nourishment, of struggles with the sun, their failure against wind, the depredations of fauna and the bitterness of short existence in their season? While contrarily, perhaps, might they not also thank their country gods for rain, cool mornings, summer afternoons, and the ministration of the honey bee which engages their propagation? All this, I grant, is fancy in which I have indulged to encourage the two thoughts that follow.

First: that just as we associate the lives of flowers with self-generative spontaneity, so the folk song of this region, as presumably in most others, represents a spontaneous effusion. And just as the cowslip bolts vertically (how we know not) through the clutch of a silaceous matrix, or the wood anemone obtrudes with no less skilful pushes through the beech and hazel litter, and over a generation will increase their numbers, so songs, like the soft, hairy stalks of primroses and cowslips, emerge in a stage of perfection, flexible and delicate, through the hard soil of an impoverished rural experience.

Second, I claim this. That there is no essential difference between the

59

origin of these songs and the impulses that conduce to literary composition. In both cases, the motive comes from below and from the interior body. All poetry, I think, pushes upward from strata which are inherent but largely concealed. And I would further suggest that those inner regions from which poetry emerges and to whose indistinct identity it alludes, is at once a place of enchantment and a source of expression which is largely tragic. Yea: for certain, the ebullience of natural *ferment* may accompany a grim, dark vision. As indeed, the sun may inform *meadows green* with a spruce, medicinal and rustic mordancy.

But I can not hear a song, whether it reaches me from the distance of a hilltop or from the proximity of the kitchen, without knowing in my heart, that this comes from another heart: one that has been broken, and that from its scattered pieces, a sad and contemplative music issues.

We poets who plume ourselves on learning, on discrimination in our choice of argument, who pretend to a judicious consideration of our diction and conceits, and who take pride in the curiosity of our figures and the daring of our imaginative expeditions – we are, in truth, no distance at all from the pot house and the coomb – as resort we do to the very same sources that inspirit the shepherd and the farmhouse scullion. In this way we share our work with them. We are indeed *them* and they are us. And no man, poet, shepherd, cleric be he, has a right to any claim to pride of differentiation from another. We belong together and we are each other – and thus at one and more or less identically we sing like this girl who does not sing for me – and must therefore be reconciled to a co-existence in solitude.

I have been possessed these last days by a voice that I am hard put to recognise. This was prompted, in part, by the young woman whom I have overheard more than once singing country songs and ballads – those other-worldly lays which sit strangely in a landscape which is benign in meadow aspect, but which assaults, with its very precipitous points of vantage, my confidence in the stability of earth and our habitation of it.

This, in that we cling here to land which seems always ready to topple over itself into the sea, is high country and, as high voices can, takes one to the empyrean that encloses us like a great cone, in whose open end we breathe, but whose apex reaches to the indiscernable, infinitely compacted concentration of the Great All.

Given this sensation of subsisting on the crest of the material world and at the broad end of what gives me life but which mocks us with its high invisibility, I have found myself prone to stumble and stagger. It is not just my voice, which has become intoxicated with alternating happiness and terrors that I no longer recognise. My feet now function as falling away points in a landscape which subverts me to the extent that I question whether I can continue to walk entirely upright here, but should creep along for fear of either tumbling into the abyss or becoming subsumed into an aether of such terrific condensation that I would be asphyxiated with the intensity of its mercurial gases!

By contrast and in concert: a view, dangerous and unstable, downward through tangled rocks and woodland to the ocean draws one giddily to the element of a restlessness expressed by those uncertain fathoms. Down there rush and growl the waters that have streamed from I do not know what remote continents and which will take themselves off on Odyssean voyagings, inscrutably to us, and yet telling us more, perhaps, than we would like to know of the loose-fitting surface of worlds that some day will make off with every one of our mundane occasions.

Given these widely separated regions in which I have been suspended, it is scarcely surprising that the voice that once arose both from my heart and from my intelligence no longer converges from these seats of affect and cognition, and I feel I am, for the time being, gone mad *north by northwest*, deracinated from old certainties of utterance and haunted both by tones I find myself now giving voice to, and also by another that dances over bank and briar and cries to me, like Ariel, 'Thou liest!' And why? Because given the unhinging of the securities that once I entertained, I no longer know why I should be here on earth, what I should do now and where I shall be next, as the whirligig of time, like a wind that seems to sweep and spin me from my proper self, brings in his perturbations.

To live alone with this poem, as with any solitude, has something of the flavour of a private historical event. This is the opposite of Shakespeare's 'alone when most in company'. My meaning is that thought constitutes a polyphonic or symphonic noise of past time, people, memories and circumstance, and that these converge most powerfully in conditions of withdrawal.

Present time stops during solitary contemplation, and the mind reverts to the field of all that one has said, accomplished and experienced. Into this field, all past conversations, meetings, children's games and prattle come together. It is an uproar that company obliterates, but which itself then joins.

To live alone in silence is to live with the companionship of every-thing that has happened and that vocable quiet then becomes a part of antecedent orders of experience. Atop, therefore, those confabulated interactions, floats a poem, mine or any other, which in itself has been fabricated from those currents that gave rise to it but from which it has become separated. It is a part of creational noise. Which itself is consti-tuted of that silence from which everything emerges with a part song.

Apprehension of the beautiful corresponds only sometimes with the ex-perience of happiness. For contentment has its own beauty and this is sufficient to the purpose of daily living. The expression of poetic beauty, however, amalgamates a current of creational euphoria with a melancholy which runs beneath the surface of its primary and unstable elation.

A line of verse may be compared to the complex grain of timber which has aged while it is most alive in the process of growth. Ash, elm and oak all own this character: namely that there are courses lying here against one another in more or less harmonious parallel, but that these run in variable widths, densities and colour, lending the surface a suggestion that there are depths within it where are stored experience of past nourishment and growth-stresses – while the wood, at the same time, enlarges and apparently grows younger at its extemities, as the heart sinks towards its centre and in the same process darkens.

So it is with poetry. And almost every line of Shakespeare expresses this variable and combinative mixture. Part of Shakespeare's greatness lies in the tragic pessimism which he has transcended by means of an euphorically integrative poetic force in the exposition of that vision. There is a terror-inspiring joy to the current of his language. Reading *Hamlet* and *Lear* is like being slapped in the face by the sea. We cry out in shock – and expose ourselves greedily to more and more invigorating buffets.

In relation to the passivity which precedes composition, I am reminded of what Marvell wrote. In these most luxuriant verses, the poet cries in rapture:

What wondrous life is this I lead.
Ripe apples drop about my head.
The luscious clusters of the vine
Upon my mouth do press their wine.
The nectarine and curious peach

Into my hands themselves do reach.
Stumbling on melons as I pass,
Ensnar'd with flow'rs I fall on grass.

Here I note how the world, in having taken vigorous sensual command, exerts a fructifying and kinetic energy, which is flaunted, as it were, on both the animal and intellectual faculties, while these thereby become the objects of this same aesthetical invasive thrust before translating its impact through the rhythmic current of the numbers which are thereby empowered.

How we, as readers, in proxy to such experience, feel the shock of those vegetably realised phenomena! For the motion of the poem lies precisely in the accumulation of those transgressive and self-animated – acrobatic even! – wall-fruit whose delectable impulsion is accompanied by a counter-action of stylistic restraint. I notice here the impersonality, the reserved aloofness of the verbs *drop*, *press* and *reach*. Thus assailed and in suspension, the poet is overwhelmed by the merest hint of pressure that appears to expand from within the objects themselves (as the old song has it 'The apple was ripened and ready to fall') and thence extends to his body which has succumbed to an intoxication.

Few poets – except Marvell's friend Milton at his closest moment to the Tree – have rendered a language so elastic in its sensuality. Round and heavy things having thus become words of an equivalent density, these latter reverting, in the mind's voice, to the phenomena they signify, while the impact of the encounter, the assault of this happiness, is reciprocated by submission (as in the amazed down-movements of *stumbling*, *ensnar'd* and *fall*) and is rendered most complete – through the balance of surrender with a force which is borrowed from the apples, nectarines and peaches – while most masculine and enlarging.

At this moment of climax, as the poet falls away from the stress of these products, he becomes caught up in long prehensile grasses whose texture is as thin as the fruit is luscious. 'All flesh is grass ... And as for man, his days are as grass,' we hear the old Hebrews *jeremiahing*.

And the poet in his guise as primal father, whose name is *Adam Earth*, will return to the dust from which he was made, as will the grass which drags its victim, in the delirium of his sensuality, to a figurative pastoral inhumation.

The poet, at this stage, still glutted with sensation and overwhelmed by competing impressions, now reaches a state of inanition which replicates or at least resembles, the experience which pre-dated the flatus of his initial outcry. The condition that follows is appropriately abstracted:

Meanwhile the Mind from pleasure less
Withdraws into its happiness.
The mind that ocean where each kind
Does straight its own resemblance find.
Yet it creates transcending these
Far other worlds, and other seas.
Annihilating all that's made
To a green Thought in a green Shade.

Earlier I have mentioned happiness. But happiness for Marvell has evolved to a depersonalised enjoyment. The world of the self and of objects is abolished. 'Each kind' (of creature, but by extension, all things) has become an intangible quantity in the realm of primitive, amorphous depths in which mental objects have superseded what otherwise seemed real.

The mind is the world and the oceans therein are navigated (as Marvell knew in fact from Hakluyt and Purchas) by the receptivity of the very vessel that contains them. The All is thus one subject and there remains a mere coexistence of figments: ideal forms which had their origin in the creational mental waters where they had their birth. The life of sensation has dwindled, diminished. Yet nothing has become poor. The whole agglomerated globe is there, as quiet as a shadow, in its having been banished. The condition of *not there* is its co-active and paradoxical affirmation.

How does Marvell contemplate this contradictory process? *Annihilating*, with its long-drawn-out, obliterating syllables, removes all things from the surface. While on the same plane of imagination, that mighty participle-present, in its assertion of unbeing, projects a vast and fleetingly Miltonic out-view. Darkness, chaos and a wind that is conscious, sweeps inert, unknowing waters.

Passive in a tree's shade lingers the poet. He is subdued to nothing and his thought has become a reflection of that absence. Existence recedes. It processes backward. But who *thinks* that greenness? The shade in which that one green thought occurs is a reflexive space which is boundariless and empty. While through this, vigorous and mutually engaging phenomena pursue change and movement. The mind, for the present, is an empty vehicle or screen. And thus it takes on summer's colour. And if it is this greenness which is thinking (as a grass blade or leaf may putatively contemplate its own existence), that thought's activity is also passive. It owns no purpose, no content or motion. Prospectively reactive, it endures without ambition. The poet has died here. But out of this fatality, this sacrificial obliteration, a delicious poetry emerges.

I have recovered from what Heminge and Condell, editors, in 1623, of Shakespeare's *Folio*, a while back, have effected on me.

I'd sat with the Master on a summer evening in a library arcanum and briefly held that noble volume. The Master's chamber, furnished with the Hebrew, Greek and Latin, was packed also with Erasmus, Montaigne, More and Bacon (early printings), French and Italian humane scholars, North's Plutarch and Cervantes, good copies of Bunyan, Thomas Browne, Defoe and Milton, Pope's *Homer*, Gulliver and Johnson, the *Alcoran* and the *Arabian Nights*, Gibbon's *History*, Fielding and Smollet's prolix ramble, grand moralizing Richardson and Tristram's inconsequential gossip – all these I remember.

Here then was a universe of learning and delight so shelved that not a chink remained to fit the thinnest pamphlet in – as though all that had been said was packed here – a world panelled and boxed that stopped at its walls and let in neither air nor *parvenu* impertinently arriving from the future.

But there separate, naked, free, alone, illuminated by low evening sun, lay every word of Shakespeare – as though, he himself, through all the grades of his development and the perfection of his maturity, sat here sentient, alive and spontaneously accessible to the most ordinary chat with us.

'You may pick that up, Sir!' gestured the Master. 'But please not open it. The stitchings are broken. We await the binder.'

To clasp this book, and urgently I did so, was privilege in plenty. Much of it I had by heart and no urge took me to read further. Then this happened. For an instant the totality – from *The Tempest* to the *Phoenix* – was transfused through my hands and up into the seat of all four humours: thus suddenly my body read the whole of Shakespeare in a storm that so shook me that it was some days, as if in a soaking ague of both intellect and body, before I had recovered. And yet, when you think on it, Shakespearean totality is a portion only of a greater Everything – each one of whose *parts* is played out in that 1623 collection.

All the above is germane to my composition in just one respect. This in regard to the integrative element whose operation I have felt at work in my poem. All acts of the imagination convey disparate and fissiparous objects, images and thoughts into some form of junction that otherwise would stray across their own separating pathways.

Here at their convergence – as with the milling of spindrift which has been brought down into some meadow pond from the helter-skelter of its contributory streams which have themselves become swollen in a storm, and which circulates slowly at first after arrival in darker and stiller water before congregating at some point of rest around, say, a stand of alder trunks or bull rushes, and becoming stationary (as also thunder clouds disperse in quiet) – here the stuff which has been torn away in such a flood from every sort of scattered and mutually dissociated environment, comes together in the unforeseeable pattern of a halt, from which proceeds a measured and consolidated setting forth again.

The end-point from this tortuous excursion is this. The unity of my poem lies, if anywhere, in its having swept up a thousand or so bits and pieces and brought them together from their dashing around into one anothers' regions of tumult or of mutual antagonism to reach harmonious agreement – at least for so long as the continuity of my vision could be sustained.

In retrospect, I must confess the nature of this stimulus. What the mind, given the desideratum of an autonomous flexibility which is greater than my own, should achieve without that suffusion, the poppy ushered up from deep sleep's shadow into a wholesomely intoxicating sunlight and engendered that alchemical conversion which transmutes dross and flotsam into the gold vein of a flow. This might of course happen – as no doubt it has done with the greater poets – without the intervention of an intoxicant.

Truth is not one thing. And if poetry is one species of some infinitely variegated absolute, then the constitution and texture of a poem is itself similarly mixed, and any one composition represents a stilling, into measure, of particulars which, beyond the region of a poem's temporary and specific embrace, had otherwise nothing to do with each other.

Continents are separate but mutually contiguous. Wherever we may breathe, we inhale a single air. The breath I have just taken in this parlour may once have been exhaled by Kubla or his sweetheart. No matter. It is fresh to me and sustains the moment. Some day I will inspire my last. And some person will, in good time, inhale what I have used here. Or some measure of this air, mixed, as it will be, with other wisps of the aether.

Just as everything in this world is co-existent and all of Shakespeare's works cohere within a single binding, so any one poem, no matter its content, owns disparity of elements, whose fusion into a concord which is more or less satisfactory is a condition of its status – and it is here that its quality may, at its most ticklish, be adjudicated.

Glancing back over the great country across which my poem had travelled until it arrived at the tip of my quill and was transferred onto paper, I see four converged environments. Distant Asia concentrated into Culbone. And long Chinese centuries merged with the gallop of our 18th century minute. No larger epoch or topography could one mind, in its little movements, carry without extraneous contribution.

Reverting to the Folio. Envisage Armageddon. Earth is grown void. The wind blows daily over nothing. Rain it falleth. Here, in universal dissolution, although no place exists with specificity, Shakespeare has survived the conflagration and Heminge and Condell's great assemblage lies unspoken. There are Rosalind and Beatrice. Prospero and Hamlet. Jacques, Falstaff, Postumus, Titania, Shylock. Could germens from all those spill out and re-populate this wasteland with some fructifying prospect of an hymeneal? Or might the end of this be a Miltonic *Pandaemonium*?

Most works of literature involve convergences of what the author may have read in conjunction with memories which are in reaction to present but half-conscious associative experience – and indeed, one can scarcely imagine a drama or a poem that issued from anything less than some equivalent synthetic action.

In the light of which, I will make this confession. My poem is a confection, a concoction of sources and resources I had borrowed, then kept buried until such a time as they were ready, at a proper moment, for their transmutation.

No work can ever achieve an originality which is devoid, entirely, of an antecedent. Some *Ur* phrase uttered at the world navel which pre-dates the Greek, or a Sybil's raving as she struggles with Apollo and chokes up verses of unmediated inspiration, or, abducted from Lord Rama, Queen Sita's grieving. Did these exist, as we do, with our borrowed measures?

Indeed, what lay behind those sightless orbs that Homer cast backward to the echoes he inherited from bards who first sung of Achilles? Or the *Genesis* writer who eavesdropped not on God's creation but borrowed passages of song from Babylon and Persia? No. We are all of us engaged in a common human share of memories and knowledge. And of this, in

67

the process of our application to the Muses, we make use, when we go on our minor expeditions. It may therefore be claimed of my poem as follows:

In Xanadu did Kubla Khan is from Purchas. Snapped up as noted from the Tamburlaine chapter.

On the subject of *Chandu*, he had recourse to Marco Polo.

Alph the sacred river, comes from Strabo and Pausanias who claim this river ran beneath the sea from Greece to erupt in Sicily as Arethusa. It also surfaces in *Lycidas*.

He stole *that deep romantick chasm* from Southey's *Thalaba*.

Floating hair is remembered from the *Gebir* by Landor.

The demon lover may be traced to *Tobit*.

James Bruce's *Travels* loaned him *Ancestral voices prophesying war.*

Weave a circle, incense-bearing trees, cedarn cover and other passages with magic, paradisal associations are taken from *Arabian Nights Entertainments*, published this decade in Edinburgh. (Albeit that the mare's milk that the Great Khan sprinkled on his path from Shang-du is diffused within this. Of which, more later.)

So be it, with a dozen more examples. The mind mills and mixes what it reads, and like this pudding hung up in a bladder, so imagination will transmogrify its contents with the stealth and spontaneity of an enchantment. How far we may want to produce an entirely original pudding is the question. There are not many, I surmise, would relish its eating!

Nothing comes from nowhere. My own chasms, rushing streams and sea, as previously suggested, come from Culbone Wood and views onto the Bristol Channel – and there is, I suspect, nothing in the Mongol flatlands quite like this parish with its roaring semi-subterranean freshets. Such scenes come not from literary sources. Nature proposes the unwritten story. The holy spirit chants, no doubt, and *is* its own song, also. Could we overhear that primal singing, we might be content to be its audience without burdening the creation with our secondary efforts. In the meantime, we must participate in the activity of nature. And in so doing, marry ourselves with its changing current, live modestly and die within the boundary it prescribes for us.

In all words lie germens: elements of seed which are involuted with secrets that lie within the syllables that come together in them. This seed is buried deep: but it is accessible, so I am told, to certain adepts who by long study, have discerned what lies beyond extrinsic denotation in its grosser vocalic sheathing.

The old Hebrews acknowledged these properties in their sacred language and constructed a syntax around root syllables which were, in themselves, instinct – as are dahlia and iris tubers whose upshot lies in a bud-shattering and polychromatic radiance – with a pyrotechnic store of pliant, energetic flux.

In words that grew from such a root were systems of arcane inference which manifested themselves and were expressed in patterns of metaphysically symbolic numerical combination that were contained within the Hebrew characters and whose inter-relationships alluded to or even represented some aspect of divine immanence.

The Hindus, as explored by Sir William Jones and his colleagues in Bengal, likewise conceive of a seed that lies at the heart of their syllabic coordinations, and that the vowel *a* alone, which informs a majority of the syllables in any sacred text – itself represents and encloses within it the entire creation and the divinities that control it. There are, in this connection, chants or charms consisting solely of the vowel 'a' and this is sung, droned and indefinitely repeated to the end that the singer may enter, as though processing through a temple, the penetralium of that letter and become infused with the spiritual sense of what it carries.

With all this in mind, we must be aware in the composition of our own verses, that vocalic music and etymology (which perhaps correspond to the arcanum of our own language) may carry their equivalent hermetic patterns which are concealed from all but those who – as though in excavation of some fluid mineral essence – have explored them. I fancy that this may be true of certain poets only:

Shakespeare in his intuitive spontaneity, Milton through the same and by lucubrative application, and not least in Chaucer's plantlike couplets through whose tang and movement all the supple quickness of existence may be apprehended.

Each of these poets *mean* what we take them to be saying. But I suspect, especially in Milton, that the poetry is fraught with suggestions that have little or nothing to do with its (sometimes heretical) narrative, but which sing of more oblique realities that the poet was modelling from the clandestine interior of his materials, and which only the Muses (as maybe he conceived angels), but not his ordinary, pious reader, would be capable of divining.

In which connection, Milton's sublunary century. Dismissing *the Mounsieurs of Paris*, the young poet on his way in 1638 to Italy, disembarks at

Leghorn, journeys to Florence, where, tasting for the first time spoken Tuscan, he partakes of *conversazione* at the Florentine Academy.

Next, visiting old Galileo, until recently in prison, he gazes through the *optick tube* he will make famous in his epic, and holds to his eye the poxed, patched, finally de-Ptolemised and unreciprocating moon's complexion.

Once the poet reaches Naples, he visits the tomb of Virgil and tours Lake Avernus, the Phlegraean Fields and Cuma.[6]

What impresses one most is the thought of Milton on the *Campi Phlegraei*, his boots cobbled by some Protestant iconoclast in London, with Hell directly under foot and burning up through English leather to him!

These lines, I suppose, occurred to him from Virgil:

sub rupe sinistra
moenia lata videt, triplici circumdata muro,
Quae rapidus flammis ambit torrentibus amnis,
Tartareus Phlegethon, torquetque sonantia saxa.

With which he would ignite his vision of damnation and enflame the mind of Satan.

Things arise spontaneously and they know what to do. What is it they do? They metamorphose and grow. That much we gather from Ovid who gives us an account of *animalculae* that spawned themselves – *innumeras species* – from the slime that was left when water withdrew from primordial flooding.

Songs and poems give birth likewise to themselves in mental landscapes which follow a withdrawal, as the tide recedes, of violent disturbance or enstasis. These geographies are subject, not infrequently to catastrophic subsidence. After the shock of some disorder, the mind becomes unlike *its own place*, but evolves into an elsewhere. (A fertile valley shrivels into desert. A genial stream becomes a torrent which tosses rocks up from its current. Spring trees shrivel into winter forest. Mountains erupt through cottage potagers.)

From this *Meta Incognita*, as old maps call the unknown places, *nova monstra*, new forms, come into being. These, in brash possession, infest

---

6 It unsettles me to think of Milton in the Sibyl's sanctuary at Cuma and then circumambulating shadowy Avernus. I too have sat in that Euboaean grotto and then walked widdershins around Avernus, to locate (impossible) the mouth of Hades. Some gypsies were camped in the ruin of Apollo's temple. How their tambourines glittered in the bloody red firelight!

both the desert and the sheepfold. And while scions of catastrophe aren't all of them terrible, some kobold or a pack of wolves, will no doubt arrive to terrify such provinces.

In this connection, just as a north wind drove the ballads to us, so I think, to contradict my earlier asseveration, my poem enjoyed autochthonous generation. Where did it come from? If it is good, what matter who composed it? But will I disown it? Ah no. Never. (This I express without much conviction.)

'Prepare now to engage with immensity.'
   'Oh, that can not be so very immense.'
   '*Aber ja*. It is tremendous.' *Silence*.

The first poem

At the beginning of time, as evoked by the poet of the *Ramayana*, two fine birds are at sport in the forest and as their amorous debate proceeds, a hunter stands up with his bow and arrows and shoots the husband. The sage Valmiki who was pursuing his ablutions in the same location is witness to this spectacle and with his compassion aroused by the lamentation of the widowed love bird, spontaneously anathematises the hunter. 'You,' he cries, 'who have killed the husband of this couple, may you not yourself live long!' And to Valmiki's wonder, his reaction emerged in rhythmic measure, or a *shloka*.

It was in this manner that the *first song* came into being – and by some freak of etymology, Valmiki's verse (because it rose from *shoka*, his own grief and the bird's) was called *shloka*, a verse. Poetry thus may be said to have had its origin, after a death event, in lamentation: motivated, albeit, by a responsive compassion. Returning to his hermitage with his mind perturbed, Valmiki was visited by the god Brahma who bade him employ his new-made *shloka* for the opening lines of the *Ramayana*.

The first poem thus arose from a concatenated sequence, which, starting with the erotic freedom of bird song (probably a crane or curlew, *krauncha* in the Sanskrit), was followed by the wife-bird's threnody and concluded with Valmiki's poem which synthesised the previous utterances. Love, death, bereavement and compassion thus inform the first song's origin. Such elements are principal components of all later poetry.

But I have omitted one other constituent. This is the curse that the sage, turned poet, directs towards the hunter: a wild tribal fellow who plies a sanguinary existence outside the boundaries of the Hindu *polis* and not least its vegetarian ethic. Valmiki's compassion thus represents only one aspect of his utterance. For the sage who approves the *kraunchas'* bliss and who responds with sympathy to the wife's bereavement is one and the same who issues a malediction – while this also parallels the hunter's action!

And the curse represents no casual reprobation. Its words are shot in consonance with the hunter's arrow, at the hunter's own being. And now he is condemned, through the arrow of the poem, to more extreme exclusion.

But it is the nature of poetry and not of Hindu *mores* that detains us. Just this: whether those primordial notes of song came from the *krauncha* couple in their love, or from the widow in her mourning, or whether they arose from human sympathy and an anger which was deflected from compassion into the expression of an anathema, each declaration contains elements which have a spiritualised or praeternatural character. The fact that these declamations are uttered at the very threshold of time, lends them further distinct weight: for they are spoken on a stage where naught else happens, and thus suggest huge doings where they are in competition with nothing.

Love, grief, anger and compassion. What more, beside some minor, subtle variations, might there be for the heart to experience and the voice to express? I hear each of these arguments in Shakespeare's *Sonnets*. They persuade me that I might one day comprehend, more straightforwardly than so far I have been able, *Lear*, *Antony* and *Hamlet* in all their tortuous and lofty grandiloquence.

To conclude – with a literary consideration. In Valmiki's story, we are presented with a drama which stands at the threshold between two genres. On the one hand, in the love-and-death narrative, we recognise elements of the folk. On the other, with the intervention of Valmiki into what so far has taken place in the language of birds, we witness a translation from the forest into the sacred environment of an *ashrama* and the 'perfected' character of Sanskrit.

Much great literature, I think, may similarly have been contrived from some *Ursprung* of the sort just outlined. The ballad, for example, has given us the couplets and quatrains which inform even the most elevated iambic composition, to speak nothing of great themes that passed from the rugged Scottish borders to the daintier precincts of the great houses and theatres. (More of this later. For last night, as I happened to recall, on a darkling coomb, the black and horrid verses of Goethe's *Erlkönig*, my mind was impressed with that same confluence of kinds and centuries.)

Thus while the *krauncha* story comes to us through the high-flown medium of the *Ramayana*, my suspicion that this tale derived from folk lore is confirmed by the discovery of its parallel among a *primitive* people. This I learned from Dr C. L. Giesecke: late Professor in Dublin, who recorded a little narrative of a bird wife's bereavement while he was travelling for geological specimens in Greenland.

As Giesecke records it, a Snow Bunting is shot by an Esquimaux hunter and his widow laments – precisely as did the *krauncha* bird in Sanskrit. This, and songs like it from unlettered people, must untarnished be the origin of both the *krauncha*'s song, Valmiki's 'first poem' and all subsequent poetic composition. And note how our own children sing this rhyme: Who killed cock Robin? / 'I,' said the Sparrow, / 'With my little bow and arrow.'

And Skelton, bless him, following Catullus's grief for *passer deliciae meae puellae*, cries:

De pro fun dis cla ma vi
When I saw my sparrow die!

Songs and stories hop around the globe like birds or children skipping. When they alight, we domesticate them into familiar species.

The fresh odour of this page. Rags macerated, dried and rolled into paper.

A dark stench of ink. Soot, lamp-black and oil concocted by children in malodorous cellars.

The smell that creeps from birds' quills plucked by farm wives who choke in air-borne excrements of geese they have been herding, which they'll slaughter for the gentry.

Amalgamate all these and the nose detects another origin of music, literature, philosophy. We approach the sublime through darkness and faeces, and whose underside reveals the misfortune of others. At bottom, in this view, everything is matter, which sidles into time and exits dumbly.

The phenomenon of genius

Not to quibble with respect to its topology, let me dwell briefly on that notion of genius and the spiritual character of its origin. What the Greeks explained in their metaphorical stories, was that Genius lay in a position of uncertain transition that hovered between natural objects and realms of the supernatural. The bodies of all beings were palpably born into a gross materiality, and in this respect a human body was little different from that of a goat or sheep. Goats, sheep and humans nonetheless belonged also to a natural order that was charged with mystery and invisible numenous powers.

Spirits, in parallel, inhabited the rocks and streams. And there were, beyond the experience of ordinary humans, higher orders of a divine presence in spheres that were inaccessible and dangerous, the power of whose beauty engendered dread, drove some mad and inspired others, the initiate, to participate in those sacred and prolific terrors whose daemons equally created works of genius and drove others to their destruction.

Cloud-capped mountains, vertiginous and steaming chasms, the stormy, winter-black Aegean, remote dew ponds deep in rock-ridged hidden enclaves where crystalline rivulets fed meadows whispering with flowering plants, the amorous resort of half-seen beings where goatherds who had strayed too far might dream they had encountered some impossible incarnation of a beauty more desirable than that which is given in a mortal life-span: such was the resort of solitary, and no doubt, deranged seekers after inspiration.[7]

In such reserved localities dwelled Mnemosyne's Daughters. And in that place where their mother had received the golden flood with which the Great Father had infused her womb, they presided in play at the Fountain of Pieria. These were the Muses without whose participation the human mind would otherwise have been condemned to dwell for ever on the flat plains of the prosaic.

The supplicant or devotee who struggled through a wilderness of rock, alone, to this fastness, was granted, as a prize for his exertion, draughts of holy, goddess-suffused water: and *only he it was* imbibed the genial spirit whose efflorescence had arisen from a previous, divine impregnation.

Once having drowned his brain in Hippocrene, the poet must return to his home and to a marriage he had submitted to between the quotidian and the eternal, between the drudgery of bread-winning and the infinitude whose messenger he had become. Thenceforth every tissue of his body was irradiated with that confluence of earth and the divinities that pervade it.

---

7 These were the progeny of Orpheus, too, whose unquenched head still rode, lost, singing on the universal river. How far this dread figure hampers bardic ambition and how far, like some bloody magnet, it might attract those who would put their own persons into a community of Maenads, I refrain from addressing.

This both tore and healed. The dangers he had drunk at once heated him and cooled; they coursed in his intelligence with intoxicating bursts of music, rainbow light and a divine (albeit sometimes atheistic!) philosophy.[8]

From open, upland silence to the hush of birches. Their leaves are small and butter yellow. A stream courses through this with a secretive continuity.

The *Grove of Nemi*: where the priest-king stalks with drawn sword round a tree, the gold leaf of whose one branch, rattles and seduces.

An insane combat for the priesthood follows. The poet enters and joins the struggle. He cries out in sublime hexameters and perishes.

Idleness – from which, creation. We are opposite to God who laboured for six days, whatever such quantities of Ur-time may have connoted, and then rested. But God's sabbatical had no conclusion. Since the final minute of Day Six, he has done nothing.

Having set the universe in motion, God has been idle. Invisible, withdrawn, inert, he sleepily observes our history, but does naught to subvert what free will devises. Far from existing in his image, we flounder to re-enact what God was before this. The Almighty may rest. By contrast, we labour to fulfil our little histories within mortal limitation.

Divagation eastward

I carry two sheets of writing. While my ink horn, from which lines of verse must otherwise have come, stays full. The ink brims still in an undiscriminated mass, with potency it might have lent to verses on the page, but impotent now to discharge its function. Somewhere in this black, my poem lies, at once unformed and in dissolution. The Great Khan with his beasts and concubines walks peacefully within its depths, undiscovered by my burrowing and sleepless quill.

Every syllable I write, in its progress from the left across the page, draws me to the Orient.

As the sun rises, my pen leans towards it and words germinate in furrows I have cut in the paper.

I do not recall having written these words. I note, nonetheless, they came

---

8 These draughts of Helicon consist of no water such as one would piss into a privy. All this takes place within an abstract silence. Of which the world's business, its clamour and confusion, is a small part, both detracting and contributive.

from half sleep recently. In the course of which time, a dome has hung its lower part against my eyes, as though with its gentle hemispheric edges it rested on my eyelids, and which thence give a view – with the ventilation of its apex reaching into heaven – of that abundant nothing in which all phenomena dissolve into the infinite with perfect freedom.

The amplitude of the dome, which is both a sacred diagram and, in small, the sky's vault, stands in a dramatic contrast to our Gothic. For our own stone palaces with their crenellated battlements and moulded decoration are, in contrast to the pleasure dome, designed not just to keep a great household dry but to defend the surrounding land and for protection of aristocratic privilege. The towers and steeples of our churches proclaim an equivalent domination while also aspiring to pierce the lower atmosphere and, as though supplicating in stone and singing praises with a weather vane, reaching towards an empyrean which exists beyond the reach of the mason's chisel.

We in Europe live in geometrical constrictions, cramped by angular postures – as Ariel outlined the cross-limbed posture of that hapless ship-wrecked Neapolitan princeling! – and our sacred buildings are projections of this self-confining physical and intellectual geometry.

I love our churches: not least for the strictness of their rectilinearity and the majesty of their proportions. The Gothic, nonetheless, is chilly. Infused in ruled lines, there is *froideur* even to the arches that soar from block on block of limestone: while the severity of a perpendicular ascent has a tendency to scrape at and erode the more tender faculties, with the result that our thoughts, even in the most flamboyant of our great cathedrals, will be moulded by the shaping that its pious masons themselves imposed on the stones – with the intention, presumably, that these might reciprocate, with some future influence, their own systematic obeisance.

These spiritualised controls would be obliterated could we simply doze within a dome and let our thoughts dissipate along the outline of its shell through which we might, at the same time – given its maternal contour – be protected from any apprehension of a too overwhelming dimension.

A pleasure dome is of course merely a recreational and domesticated rescension of the sort of cupola-shaped roof under which the relics of some Buddhist religious teachers ('idolators' as Purchas called them), were commemorated. These domes or *stupas* were representations of infinitude. And this is what I like. Because the arching upthrust of such a structure leaves earth, where human matter dreams no longer, and in a single movement reaches vertically, describes a modest half-circle and descends having alluded, without pretense, to the plenitude of a circumambience which is at once abstract, complete, filled with arcane meanings and, like the sky it meets and echoes, empty.

All this, at once airy and gentle, is suggestive not of high things, but of spacious and flexible illimitability. Here room is given, rather than ordained. And while a church contains its worshippers within a construction whose exterior attempts to pierce heaven, the *stupa*, while solid, suggests *translucency* to the devotee who must view it from outside: and by means of circumambulating its periphery, assimilate it in a benign sunlight. Thus it enters him and fills his being with a gentleness which is both illuminating and ineffable.

While the dome which I imagined to have stood on my eyelids appeared as a weightless shell, the dome of the *stupa* suggests that same potentiality. Filled as it may be with a worthless, bricky rubble and rising as it does over the exhausted relics that once contained some human inspiration, this building may be described as an *egg*, from whose roundness new life may be anticipated to spring. And while, as suggested, this relatively small hemisphere rises and falls quickly from the limits of its root in the ground, it speaks, albeit with a gracious reticence, of an aether which has no boundary.

Thus while churches, within the coherence to which I have alluded, compress and compel us into bursts of singing and amplify with their stony reverberations the plainsong that their architecture requisitions, the *stupa* induces silence.

For it is in itself a quintessence of that amplitude which, could it contain sound, would reduce this to its own special medium: a sound that has been evacuated from itself and has been modulated to its own peculiar music – which is the sound of *no sound* – and this it will perform, beyond the existence of its constituent minerals, for an eternity to which there will be no appreciative witness.

A garden (Turkey) carpet

I visited friend *M* who'd sent for me to view some unnamed, recent acquisition. 'I have dreamed about this,' was my rejoinder. For that morning, only, I'd been transported to an antique garden, a pool, enclosed by a yew hedge at the middle, where dragonflies – the black *Sympetrium* – fought or mated in a tensile immobility.

At once at *M*'s, I am sat in his cabinet, where following formalities of wine, he leads me across to his great barn in the meadow: for here is spread out the object he has brought me to examine. Eight yards in length and three or four wide, it is a Turkey carpet: so enormous, it upholsters his capacious threshing floor entirely.

'Not mine, I should add,' M murmurs, with a self-defending gesture, in that manner, humorous and unpresuming, which renders his friendships fast and many, 'but an object of transition: *flown* from Baghdad or Damascus – not unlike that company of fieldfares,' with a motion to some ground adjacent, 'on their winter visit.' When we've smiled at his fancy, my friend, bidding me with him take my shoes off, steps on the carpet.

'This,' he continues, 'was never furniture precisely, nor thrown down merely for its owner's comfort, although that's part of it. It was called, in its place, a *garden* or a *winter* carpet. So named for its warmth and its memories of spring, which as you'll note are cheerfully depicted in these figures. A copy, I hazard.' At which, with his toe, he describes a pattern. 'I mean, the lost originals, created for the Kings of Persia, were appropriated by the Arabs, five centuries from our own millennium, who carried them from Isfahan with a deal of other treasure – sawed them into carriageable pieces, and so imported what the Sassanids perfected, to their native workshops.

'Now those women in the mountain villages of *Anatolia*, whose chief devotion lay in shearing, carding, dyeing, knotting and then weaving, are delivered these portions of a carpet that King Chosroes himself in Isfahan had trodden, and so – like *Parcae* or the *Norns* that husband every human destiny, and scissor each string with ineluctable precision – take cuttings from that parent stock whose foliage they have never witnessed – and from some fragment of an elder pattern, graft to that stem a scion species – who knows how germane to its origin? – and engender on their looms these re-invented figures, whose nap, finished with an indissoluble Turkish knotting,' he picks at the back-weave with a quill nib from his pocket, 'we infidels intrude on in our godless stockings!'

As we pass along this carpet I am minded of those women: perhaps twelve altogether – hooded beldams with their children, whose fingers scarce seem thicker than the threads they're twisting – and I'm enchanted by its mystery, at once chaste and luscious, dyed with indigo and orange through its interstitial spaces, and a locus, above all, as one wanders through its patterns of speculative voyages. And one ponders on the years themselves concatenated in its webbing: individuals, each anonymous, many that expired before they saw it finished: while each, as she shuttled, held the whole thing in conception, and contrived, through a concerted activation, to visualise it in completion. As if – like the crocus and the little tulips in the grass their sheep have eaten – it germinated from each weaver's fingers!

I have mentioned my dream. With its dragonflies and hedges. 'These patterns,' *M* continued, 'are spring gardens. Observe, in the middle, that rectangular pond with its floating blossoms, round which emblematic creatures swim in streams, from underneath, that feed it. Note too those angled blue canals that course through the orchards – and quincunxes of poppy, cypress groves and pyramids of rose trees hemmed by fertile and dark earthy lanes that temper the wind blowing in from the desert.' He reached for his shoes. I felt through my stockings the red, fecund earth of Persia. Phenomena explain themselves. 'Thank you,' he said, 'for saying nothing.'[9]

We *jog* along. And we observe. And then we're gone.
The carpet's flown, the garden done.
These two, these three indeed, are one.

---

9 Was this, I wondered, the original pardes God planted east of Eden – from whose earth our First Parent was created – revealed in that weave, expressed from a collective memory, received, as though in dream, by those unlettered women, through whose fingers, nonetheless, unfathomable meanings passed in threads they'd personally spun but which reached back to the mothers of all human destiny?

On Kubilai Khan: an essay or attempt and a digression, with examples

We arrive here at a quodlibet by which the intellect is baffled. On the one hand, as I see him, the Great Khan constitutes an emblem, an intaglio, glowing and refined: a thick-gilded image held up at the terminus of many centuries, and concentrated, with an orient irradiation, at the vanishing point of a temporal distance.

Kubilai, in this regard, is fabricated of imagination. And as such, the Great Khan burns beyond the common as a prodigy, a high seigneur, a cynosure, a phoenix: glaring in fulfilment of abstracted supra-heroic mankind metal. And – as stars, sun, gems and lilies in a sixteenth-century sonnet glitter – this icon has one overwhelming purpose: as tenor of some value for which – in reasonable discourse – there is no realistic explication.

One might argue, on the other hand, that the Great Khan was just another one of history's ruffians. A sanguinary warlord or baditto on whose whips and arrows fortune blossomed a half century, and who seized, with an appetite engulfing almost all of Asia, a parcel of the globe whose sub-jugation made him, in a swaggering and insolent distension, monstrous.

These are separating veins of speculation. And I acknowledge that the first, which is poetic, might generate half truths – even falsehoods – whose gaudy pigments mix with one another, to build, in their convergence, a dark shadow across history.

I

He was parented in bifurcation. And his growth was patterned in a consequential self-partition.

Genghis Khan (1162–1227)
|
Ogodei (d.1241); Chaghadai Tolui = Sorghaghtani Beki
|
Mongke (d.1259); Kubilai (1215–94); Arigh Boke

Tolui, his father, and youngest son of Genghis (each stayed a pagan), was both warrior and drinker – in one of which activities he died prematurely; while Kubilai's mother, Sorghaghtani Beki, a Nestorian Christian, was, wrote John Carpini, former confrère of St Francis, on a mission to the Mongols, 'renowned among the Tartars.' 'In wit and ability,' wrote Rashid-al-Din, historian of Persia, 'she towered above women.' 'A queen,' concluded Bar Hebraeus, 'who trained her sons so well that princes marvelled at her.' A coincidence, this praise from Christian, Mussulman and Jew, for a lady who ordained religious freedom in her northern Chinese appanage!

II

Kubilai's path was both laid down and obscured by this ambitious mother who in 1236 wrested from the *khagan* Ogodei the rule of Hopei, a province of the empire carved out by Genghis on the borderland with China which for centuries had been plundered by the Khitan, Jurchen and the Hsia Hsia. And that year too, in 1215, somewhere in the Mongol homeland, Kubilai was born, to be raised in horsemanship and hunting – half rude only: for with statecraft of some kind in view, Sorghaghtani Beki had him taught to read and write Mongolian – in characters adapted from Tibetan. To his future disadvantage as Emperor of China, Kubilai never learned to read Chinese, although he spoke it.

Kubilai's father spent his manhood on campaigns for Genghis. And when Mongke took the *khaganate*, Kubilai wasted in his brother's shadow until Mongke ordered him to move against the (Chinese) Ta-Li kingdom. This was 1253. Within a twelve month, he'd subdued that region. While seven years later, Kubilai sent his armies east to finally destroy the southern Sung – although this, for a time, was halted by the death of Mongke.

There were two assemblies to elect a *khagan*. One at Karakorum in the Mongol heartland, while a gathering of rivals met in *Kai-ping* – a city Kubilai later made his summer capital and renamed Shang-du: which was Purchas's *Xaindu*. Four years of civil war ensued. On the one side Kubilai. Against him, Arigh Boke his younger brother. The clash was terrific; unbrotherly stomachs haughty and bitter. For while Kubilai had become a sedentary Chinese ruler, the yunker embraced nomadic custom, and Kubilai, he thought, had strayed from that tradition. There was truth in this view. Defined in good part by his own self-division, Kubilai felt it. Still, supported by armies from the Golden Horde and the Ilkhanate in Persia, Kubilai trounced his brother and, with dubious legality, rose to the *khaganate*, unelected.

Kubilai, when he tasted his first action in Ta-Li, was thirty-six: a late initiation for a Mongol war lord. Blooded from this, he'd led his own forces against his brother. But for his third, and most protracted, sortie into south-east China, Kubilai employed Chinese generals, Uighurs, Muslim engineers to build his war machines and Coreans and Jurchens to create a navy. And when, in 1279, his armies, led by a Turkic general, crushed the Sung, Kubilai followed these campaigns from far Ta-du, his winter capital, and Xanadu, his summer residence. 'Ye shall hear of wars and rumours of wars: see that ye be not troubled ...' I recall from St Matthew. *Ancestral voices*! Did Kubilai hear those from his inland cities?

III

The attempt to trace these murderous campaigns defeats imagination. Add those of Genghis, Ogodei and Mongke, the mountains of corpses (profitless resistance!), the rape of nations – all this surpasses comprehension. Pitiless, vain carnage for imperial vainglory, the *khagan*'s exchequer, the pomp of his nobles. Measureless but narrow purpose! (And these, my commonplaces, of a retrospective indignation! Think also of that tender innocent, the last Sung Emperor, snatched up by his minister, and as Kubilai's navies closed, who jumped in the sea near Hang-chow city, which brought to an end three centuries of dynastic elegance – as if two embraced ceramics slipped down through the mazes of an oriental *hades*.)

But hold. And consider, on the other hand, some anonymous Mongolian, conscripted for a steppe-land expedition, forcing his animals through the south China mountains, bewildered and disoriented by the heat and rainfall, contending with diseases of the tropic: pestered in the woods by snakes and insects, men and horses dying in their thousands, until he too stumbled – used up and expendable, unburied, forgotten.

And think, too, of the Great Khan's forays into south-east Asia to exact, through terror, tribute and submission. To whose kings in Pagan, Malabar and Java the Khan sent envoys. And when, in defiance, they cut his emissaries' heads off or sent them packing with their faces branded, Great Kubilai, in a frenzy at this insult to his highness, dispatched yet more horse to perish in his service.

Towards the end of his reign, (his late wife Chabi might have urged moderation), this same Khan – bloated like some oriental Henry, stupefied by liquor and in agony from the gout – sent expeditions to attack Japan. Of the two hundred thousand deployed on these invasions, half perished. On the second invasion there were monitory omens: a giant serpent in the ocean. Then the sea stank of sulphur. The Japanese fought stoutly. And the invaders were annihilated by a wind, a *kami-kaze*, that the Japanese gods inflicted on the Mongol navy.

IV

Now the seas are enormous and as much could be written about Kubilai as there are drops of water in them. But my theme is the great Khan's self-division. Which leads back to his grandsire Genghis (which name means 'oceanic') and the stories, as reported, of his birth, in legend. Now if Kubilai was born to doubleness, the infant Genghis, first named Temujin, or 'blacksmith', emerged, as follows, in this mesh of symbols:

1 Light streaming through the skylight of her tent informed his mother: 'Conceive, and your son will be a World Conqueror.'
2 A swallow, at his birth, flew in from the sea. It settled on a stone and sang day and night. Temujin's father split the stone, withdrew a jade seal and worshipped it with incense.
3 A tale attributed to Temujin's mother: 'A golden man came in through the skylight. His rays entered my womb (polite for *pudenda*), then vanished like a moonbeam.'
3 At birth he was clutching a knuckle-bone-sized blood-clot.
4 He emerged with the state seal of his future empire.

These stories, like the birth tales of many a great fellow, no doubt are *post hoc* hagiography confabulated with traditions from the Christians and Buddhists. And as regards our *Cubla*, they're of two accounts mainly. First, in that no miracles attach to Kubilai's childhood. All we know of him is prose and history. Second, that Genghis, monster that he made himself, is represented by the Mongols as a child of nature and that his gestes, both brave and bad, and the doings of his family, are rendered in a language which conformed to his wild nature.

Now while Kubilai grew up in some comfort on the borderland with China, Temujin was raised in hardship near the River Onon – Mongol territory proper. There, with his brothers and Ho'elun his mother, Genghis struggled through his childhood. And here we approach the crisis of this exposition.

I have mentioned that Genghis was raised by this mother. His father was murdered in Tartar country on a ride home from a marriage parley. And this – a first example of my theme here, taken from a grief song at the father's funeral – exemplifies the pasture-land imagination:

The deep waters have dried up, the sparkling stone is shattered.

Now these song words, in translation, come down to us five centuries later, fresh as where they surged through (as that gushing from the depths where Petrarch contemplated his first *rime sparse*: whose erstwhile subterranean numbers in the Tuscan rose to meet an uprush of telluric currents!) bright, rhetorically balanced and filled, on both sides of that cavernous caesura, with feeling correspondent to their origin and connotation. Life, once flowing like a homeland river, is exhausted. Rock (that man's existence): shivvered. Here is metaphor, too, that springs from native, natural, naive, feeling. What follows is expressed in like easy figures.

The narrative continues, as deserted by its kin, the remnant family plies a bleak subsistence:

> The mother, *Ho'elun*, her cap on her head and her dress girt round her
> knees, ran up and down the river collecting rowans and bird-cherries,
> feeding her chicks night and day.

A picture of pure courage – and a woman desolated in her homeland, whose solitudes, conveyed in this wild detail, are both dangerous and sustaining – and the childhood of a future hero.

When rivalry erupts between Temujin, fourteen, and his two half-brothers, the boy cries to their common mother:

> A bright fish bit, and was snatched by our half-brothers.
> And yesterday we shot a lark with a horn-tipped arrow
> And they snatched this too. How can we all live together?

And the mother in her turn:

> Why do you all behave like this?
> When apart from our shadows, we are friendless?
> When apart from our tails, we have no fat to last us?

Now comes Temujin's first act of violence. He murders a half-brother, who shouts out, dying, in this scornful measure:

> When we should take vengeance on our enemies,
> I am dirt in your eye or a fishbone in your mouth!

Their mother responds with this exalted *agon* (from the *Oresteia*, think ye?):

> Ah! you destroyers!
> Like dogs that gobble their own afterbirth.
> A falcon that attacks its shadow.
> A pike that swallows in the silence.

A camel that gnaws its own colt's heel.
A wolf that stalks its prey in snow storms.
A mandarin duck that consumes its chicks.
So you have destroyed your brother!

Passionate, spontaneous concert! Emergent from, and part of in their current, river, lightning, wind and thunder!

Now it is not my own view that, while Genghis and his generation lived as nature's unspoiled children, Kubilai devolved to urbane softness. I quote merely from the Mongol's *Secret History*, which vaunts exploits of the field and where both lyric and heroic song are represented – as though suffused by impregnating forces – in a manner absent from accounts of Kubilai's doings.

Note also, to conclude, the paradox of Kubilai and his younger brother Arigh. While Arigh and the Mongols still galloped, Kubilai, antithetically, had crossed, or half-traversed, the Great Wall and, in some degree, had stuck there with its rocks and mortar buttressed jarringly against the fork of a painful leg-over: in which place he was, thereby, in some part, disconnected from the pastures of his origin, the northwest region, where his great-grand-dam had wandered in her lamentation.

This Kubilai, then, had made himself a new, and parti-coloured species: one who underwent a separation in his very person. For while Temujin, in adulthood, had fasted, climbed the sacred mountain, donned sacerdotal filet, struggled and communed with spirits, entered calaleptic trances, caroused in his leathers, supped with commoners at *bivouac* on mares' milk and the living blood of stallions, Kubilai had transformed – from stinking buskins and his grandsire's havoc – to Confucian manners, the brocade of office and, perhaps, as we shall see, a Buddhist *Weltanschauung* – to his station as the *Chinese* 'Son of Heaven'.

V

In truth, all this is hyperbolic. And so now, to be plain, reverting to the Great Khan's ancestry, we witness, on the one hand, in the *exposition* of his empire, Tolui and Genghis. While what he took maternally from Sorghaghtani Beki – benign accomodation and good will to govern through a tolerant administration – claims equal moment. Kubilai's leaning towards Buddhists (or 'idolators' as Marco classed them), should be emphasised, although, as we shall later see, with caution. For while the dome he made in Shang-du was for profane leisure, this was complemented by the domes of *stupas* which, he hoped, would bring him rebirth in a luscious sky-y Buddhist simulacrum of his pleasure gardens! Of this latter, later.

Here, then, may it be recorded that, with sundry adjutants and counsellors (a mixed population which subsisted in north China in some numbers), Kubilai incorporated within Mongol tyranny subtleties that were neither native to him nor locally dynastic. Some aspects of his rule may be summarised as follows:

As taught by Sorghaghtani Beki, he supports diverse religions. Adjudicates debates between the Buddhists and their rival Taoists. These continue for some years until in 1281 the Taoists are confounded. Inexperienced in statecraft, the Great Khan takes guidance. First from Buddhist monks of the Ch'an persuasion; later, he favours the Tibetan lamas who have come to China and claim magic powers and skill in policy. Phags-pa lama, over many years (he dies in 1280) becomes Kubilai's chief advisor. They are described as 'sun and moon together.' Of that lama, later.

Of domestic policy: the Khan defends northern farm land from his cavalry, who would turn this otherwise to pasturage for Mongol horses. In conformity to local custom, Kubilai participates in Confucian rituals and builds a Temple to the Ancestors (this includes Genghis!), a shrine to Confucius and ordains the compilation of dynastic histories. He establishes his first capital at Dai-du (Peking). Then builds Ta-du, his winter city: the plan for this on Chinese principles with gated walls, Confucian shrines and Buddhist temples. Taoists, Christians and Muslims are accomodated. Existing Ministries of Finance, War and Public Works he maintains; as also Justice and the Office of Confucian Rituals. Exams for Civil Service places are abolished; previous posts for Chinese scholars are filled by Persians and Tibetans *inter alia*. (Gone the poets and painters who supported their arts with emoluments of office. They flee to the south to live as hermits or in Sung-held cities.)

1271: to legitimise his rule in the Chinese view, Kubilai proclaims the Yuan dynasty. This name, from the *I Ching* book of divination, means 'origins' or 'primal energy.' (This term to mask the Khan's dis-ease as Mongol ruler of Chinese people ... 'So shaken as we are, so wan with care,' as saith Shakespeare's Henry: Kubilai's security dependent on the acquiescence of a people who disdain their rulers.) He undertakes road works, which stimulate exchange and commerce. And in 1289, extends a grand canal to transport water from the south and bring its rich resources to the northern cities.

Kubilai remains a stranger to the Chinese people. Most of his associates are likewise foreign. Still, with these and the Confucians in his Yuan governance, Kubilai exerts himself to make his rule an age where commerce, scholarship and arts all flourish.

VI

Now, *vis-a-vis* Kubilai, all this talk, so far, of Buddhists is a puzzle. For how could a man who spends his life at conquest follow the precept of compassion and non-harming? Further, is the claim in Mongol and some Chinese records that Genghis, too, who had slaughtered more than any in recorded history, was *bodhisattva* (Enlightenment Being!), and that he and Kubilai were termed Buddhist Universal Emperors (*cakravartin raja*) and *maha-danapati* – 'great givers'. Thus the Mongol hagiography:

> A king was born in the Mongol state whose virtuous fortune had reached completeness. His name was Genghis. Kubilai followed. He subjected many countries, adopted Buddhist teachings and civilised his people.

That Genghis and Kubilai were incarnations of the Buddha is widely attested.

According to another Mongol text, the *Altan tobci*, the birth of Temujin was ordained by the Buddha and 'by command from Heaven ... for the sake of suppressing the suffering of beings.'

And this, written equally *sans* irony: that Genghis (*Tyrannus!*) was *Vajra-pani*, a protective Buddhist deity and also *dharmaraja*: 'king of Buddhist teaching'.

Kubilai, likewise, was proclaimed to be *Manjusri*, deity of Buddhist wisdom. And in China, he was 'Kubilai, the Wise Khan and *cakravartin*,' guardian of a Buddha carved from sandalwood by Maudgalyayana in Buddha's lifetime (!!) – while in 1279, Kubilai built the White Stupa to house it.

One explanation of this sacred exaltation of assassins lies long before the Mongol tyranny. For under the Wei, a millennium before, stood a formulation that every Chinese Emperor was a Buddha. This same notion, which had waned, came back, encouraged by Tibetans, into Mongol China.

With regard to Kubilai, the image, from a cult adopted by the Mongols, of a god-king, *Vaishravana*, serves us. This depicted the god as a warrior in armour: in one hand a cudgel, in the other a *stupa*. Elaborating on that contradiction, one might add a third hand, in imagination, balancing the *stupa*, in which he holds his *pleasure dome:* a site, perhaps, devoted to the satisfactions of both higher mind and lower person!

VII Great Kubilai's initiation

But was Kubilai, in experience, a Buddhist? Consider first the Khan's first two confidants: both from the *Ch'an* sect (which in Japan they call *Zen*), whose practice was in meditation and a path of non-attachment. This lay beyond the Great Khan's aptitude or interest. The Way of the Tibetans, homologising deity-propitiation borrowed from the Hindu, shamanistic magic and flamboyant Himalayan pageant, offered brazen musics, dithyramb, theatrical excitement and promises of rebirth in a paradisal Western Heaven – all more in harmony than *Ch'an* with Kubilai's circumstance in history's spectacle.

Thus Phags-pa took Kubilai and his Mongol entourage somewhat as the latter had appropriated China. And Kubilai was initiated by that lama into esoteric rites, which were named for *Hevajra*, a god who was worshipped in Tibetan monasteries. These same rites were connected to *Mahakala*, a secondary deity, to whom the Mongols called on subsequent campaigns, against the Sung especially – of which more later.

At home, Buddhist court rites, the *Suppression of Demons and Protection of the State*, were introduced in 1270. Twice, each first month, was a circumambulation of the capital, watched by Emperor and his family, this followed by religious plays and music by Chinese, Muslim and Tangut performers. I mention, too, a circle that they made around the Emperor's palace, 'for luck to the living and to ward off evil', because that formula is pertinent to Xanadu. For similiar propitious, sunwise rites of circumambulation were held each sixth month there.

Reverting to some details of Great Kubilai's initiation, the Khan, at his wife's urge, and the Phags-pa *lama*, was inducted into Buddhist *tantra* – a congeries of sacred patterns, incantations, spells and rituals that lead, through a journey of some complication, to the centre of a mystery, or a point within a circle, where the mind, which represents that figment they call *person*, is subsumed into a sphere so abstract, absent, negatively present, that it dwells for this time in a reconstruction of the *here* we call reality, in which paradox is reconciled and individuality abolished: a sphere where nothing is which also isn't: in itself both nothing and its opposite: in life deathless, and in the self's death, self-existent.

There was a philosophic architecture to such exgavations. A *mandala* (or 'circle' in the Sanskrit) was used, the function of whose study in its subdivisions and symbolic patterns was to reconcile the absolute and relative realities: by day to memorise, at night to recreate in recollection the circle's interpenetrating geometry, and this led the mind, through labyrinthine concentration, to its integrative centre where the idea of a god or Buddha held residence in emptiness and liberation. This, once mastered, lent the world – its starts, stirs, discords, dislocations, inconclusive endings – an intelligible pattern: benign, serene, symmetric and explicit in which all things belong in harmonious standing.

There was also a place, the Great Khan learned to his almighty satisfaction, for sexual congress that was practised by some adepts. For in the union of the male and female, the *member virilis* sustains – in the course of a protracted sojourn in the dark, vast *antre* of the Prime Creatrix represented by a female consort, where all in birth and pain grows manifest and plural as the multiplicity that pullulates around the centre of the *mandala* – twoness. And, by reduction from *prapanca* ('diversity' or 'fiveness'), personhood converges with the other, and that unselving thence dissolves into an Absolute where unity and twoness are assimiliated into Buddhist 'Nothing' or *shunyata*.

Now as to other powers of *tantric* aspect, both Marco and Purchas describe what priests or *bacis* showed off at Great Kubilai's table. And how they made wine jugs float across the banquet and serviceably hover at a diner's elbow. Or intoning magic words they conjured hail to devastate a rival's barley harvest. Wizards of the *tantra* thought that they effected such eventualities. These, for the advanced, were illusions conjured, smilingly, to demonstrate the imperfection of our senses. Such was the play of *maya*: that shift and shimmer of illusory phenomena on the surface of the dream we all inhabit.

How those adepts of *Hevajra* joked at such extrinsics! And here was another where a philosophic truth, or at least its poetry, inhered within the symbol: a rite in which the circle, properly construed as both a holy place and metaphor for all that's dangerous and sacred, would bring fructifying rainfall as the adjunct to that philosophic implication:

> Draw a circle, using *black* from cemetery charcoal, *white* from powdered
> human bones, *red* scraped from bricks that demarcate the graveyard, and
> *blue* from a mix of human bones and charcoal. Then draw at the centre the
> god dancing and speak holy syllables.

Who'ld not be impressed by this amalgamation of discrepant colours and the mix they come from, wet from dry precipitated, and a roistering with death, conducing or inducing movement, toward the earth, of life from heaven.

Like spices pounded with a pestle, a veritable *karree powder* made of burnt wood, human bone and brick is drawn to ring a deity, whose dithyramb is roused by singing. Then the god would dance within that hallowed circle.

Such, and their like were *tantric* carnivals with which Phags-pa *lama* schooled the Emperor of China! And given such deployments coincided, both in picture and intention, with the Great Khan's ancient steppeland ceremonials – spirit conjuration, shaman dancing, scattering of milk and cinders in a circle and communion with ancestral spirits through the roof-wheel at the apex of their yurts' circumference – these elements of *tantric* mystery were not foreign to him.

VIII Of domes, yurts and stupas

I have mentioned the Khan's portrait, and another one of him with Chabi, and that these images were made by Anige, an artist from Nepal who worked first in Tibet among the *lamas* and then brought to Peking by Phags-pa *lama*: for as it's well known, the Great Khan made a practice of importing craftsmen, and in 1261 alone, bringing, all at once to China, some three thousand families of jewellery makers for the decoration of court ornaments and Buddhist trappings.

In connection with our interest in the *stupas* (domed Buddhist build-ings) that he decreed to be put up in China, Kubilai caused to be trans-ported from Nepal some eighty (only!) artisans: and among them, this same Anige, a precocious genius, aged just seventeen on his arrival, who already, as a child, had mastery of Hindu architectural theoretics (the *Sutras of Measurement* etc.), Buddhist metaphysics and, not least, sculpture, engineering and the casting of bronze images.

When word of Anige reached Kubilai, the Khan ordered him to his presence and, astonished to find that he was still a boy, observed him for some time in silence before initiating a conversation which has been recorded as follows:

Kubilai: (not unkindly): 'Art not, young man, afraid to come to an Empire vast as mine is and so very far removed from your own mountain kingdom?'

The lad, unabashed, replied with a conventional Buddhist formality: for he believed Kubilai to be a Universal Buddhist Emperor of wisdom and compassion, and spoke up thus (roughly):

'The Sage regards people in all directions as his sons. When a son comes to his Father, what is there to fear?'

'But what prompted thee to come to court?' Great Kubilai continued.

'My family lives, as it always has done, in the West (India). I accepted, however, the edict to go to Tibet to work on a *stupa*. I saw constant wars there and wished Your Majesty could pacify that country. I come now on behalf of sentient beings.'

Kubilai: 'And wherein lies the special skill that brings you to me?'

Anige (in the parlance of a Buddhist adept): 'I take my *mind* as teacher. And I know, through mind only, architecture, metal casting, painting, carving.'

Thus the record. But here's my revelation – which concerns the dome the Great Khan now decreed: less for his diversion, but in the service of religion and in harmony with Phags-pa's order which had promised Kubilai's *polis* supernatural sanction.[10]

And so Anige was enjoined as follows: to design and construct a golden *stupa* for the late Fourth Patriarch of the Buddhist Sa-skya sect. And this monument, with its dome gilded from the melt of countless gold *taels* and topped with umbrellas (symbolic of the Buddha's aristocracy), was erected within the space of two years in the Main Hall of the Sa-skya monastery in Ta-du or Peking.

The work having been accomplished in harmony with Himalayan architectural principles, which themselves originated from the Indian Buddhist pattern, Phags-pa was so gratified by the perfection of this monument that he forbade its architect to go back to his family in the mountains. And as a consequence of his success with that *stupa* – of which, even as a ruin, no trace has been uncovered – this same young man became, over the decades that followed, a chief among the Khan's advisers, building three *stupas*, nine Buddhist temples, two Confucian shrines, one Taoist temple, and not least, astronomical instruments for the measurement of time and the study of the heavens.

Now just as Kubilai had a portrait taken some four years after 1260 to celebrate victory over his brother Arigh, so the *stupa* was ordained in that same year when he proclaimed himself the Khan of Khans or *khagan*. Thus the *stupa* at once sanctified and sanctioned his scarcely legitimate claim on the *khaganate*, and marked the beginning of his war against Arigh.

Subsequently, Kubilai attributed this victory to the power bestowed on him by this monument: for the *stupa* also represented to him the superiority of the religion with which he had become affiliated, and the beneficent security of Buddhism as opposed to the superstitions to which

---

10 *Re* that *stupa*, Kubilai's order was instigated by his wife Chabi who in 1253 had been initiated into rites of the deity, *Hevajra*. With a view to erecting the projected *stupa*, Kubilai received initiation later that same year.

his brother still adhered – but which the Great Khan himself had never entirely abjured. For while Kubilai may have been, in part, a Buddhist, he maintained observance of old tribal custom, and officiated, on Chinese soil, at Mongol rituals. One example should be noted: that he scattered mares' milk – as he might now in the *tantra* – to ensure good fortune before migration from his summer to his winter residences.

Of which perhaps, I had some cognizance when I homologised 'the milk of paradise' with *kermiss*, a fermented milk drink, sacred to the Great Khan's person that was expressed from Kubilai's horses – his exclusive property?

Returning to our history, it was now, in 1264, with the support of Phags-pa and Anige, that Kubilai founded a Chinese style of administration in Kai-ping – but which, from now on, would be named Shang-du, 'the Upper Capital' or *Xanadu*.

And with reference to its pattern, it may be noted how this Mongol chieftain, with these individuals from the Himalayan kingdoms in his circle, established a city which conformed in major respects, as to its geomantic elements and the Confucian character of its organisation, to a Chinese model! A confluence of incongruities that was a characteristic of the age over which the Great Khan presided and of which he and the diversity of his advisers were an expression.

IX The tents and palaces of Ogodei

It is worth observing, to anticipate Great Kubilai's own seasonal removals, how Ogodei, his older brother, travelled. According to Fra Rubruck and Fra Jean de Carpini, as well as the Persian Rashid-al-Din, all of whom preceded Marco, Ogodei Khan would process in this manner:

From March 21 to 21 April, he stayed at his capital Karakorum in what the Chinese called his 'Myriad Tranquillities Palace'. For the next forty days, he removed to a nearby palace, built for him by Arab craftsmen and in ponds that fronted the principal building, he hunted water fowl – as later Kubilai would at Xanadu.

He then returned in early June to Karakorum and from here he would travel to his 'Welcome Carriage Hall', some three miles from his capital.

Four weeks later he processed to the mountains. Here, 'amid cool waters and much grass', he erected a pavilion with walls of latticed wood and a ceiling of gold-embroidered cloth. This, according to Rashid-al-Din, was 'a great felt-covered tent which held a thousand persons. The outside was adorned with golden studs and the inside covered with gold-embroidered silk or Tartar cloth' or *nasij*, obtained from Muslim weavers.

The priest Carpini described these three pavilions:

The *Golden Orda* is a wonderful red-purple tent surrounded by a wooden paling. Resting on pillars covered with gold plates, it is fastened with gold nails.

One month later, Ogodei rode some four leagues to a river, and here the *Orda* was again established. The Great Khan remained here until the sun entered Virgo (21 August) and first snow had fallen. Then Ogodei returned to his winter quarters on the River Ongin where he hunted till mid-February.

Lastly he went back to Karakorum to make merry. 'He had youths stand before him, and would devote himself to pleasure. He opened the doors of his treasuries and shared his bounty. At night he had archers, wrestlers and bowmen play against each other, and made presents to the winners.'

I have extracted this information for the light that it throws on Kubilai's semi-nomad dome and how this fitted with his residential custom. For on the basis of Ogodei's history, we see Kubilai's habit lay within a pattern laid down by that brother. Also to be noted here, in complement to Kubilai at Shang-du, the construction and the transportation of the *Orda*, and further, in the movement of both brothers in the final days of August, when Mercury had entered Virgo – a removal in late summer borrowed from nomadic habit.

X A yurt (or *ger*), the sun and stupa dome

On the Great Khan's dome, which like his brother's *Orda*, was a huge bamboo construction, let us quote Marco:

At a spot in the Park where there is a charming wood, he has another Palace built of *cane*, of which I must give you a description. It is gilt all over, and most elaborately finished inside. The roof, like the rest, is formed of canes, covered with a varnish so strong and excellent that no amount of rain will rot them. These canes are a good three palms in girth, and from ten to fifteen paces in length. They are cut across at each knot, and then the pieces are split so as to form from each two hollow tiles, and with these the house is roofed; only every such tile of cane has to be nailed down to prevent the wind from lifting it.

In short, the whole Palace is built of these canes, which (I may mention) serve also for a great variety of other useful purposes. The construction of the Palace is so devised that it can be taken down and put up again with great celerity; and it can all be taken to pieces and removed whithersoever the Emperor may command. When erected, it is braced against mishaps from the wind by more than two hundred cords of silk.

The Lord abides at this Park of his, dwelling sometimes in the Marble Palace and sometimes in the Cane Palace for three months of the year, to wit, June, July, and August. When the 28th day of the Moon of August arrives he takes his departure, and the Cane Palace is taken to pieces.

In comparison with Ogodei's *orda*, as previously suggested, Kubilai's dome may further be conceived as a transformation of a nomad *yurt* or *ger*. And as we have seen, despite their splendour, such wandering or planetary 'palaces', taken down and moved in August, were hypertrophied nomadic *yurts* – of the species Mongol herdsmen packed up after breakfast and re-established where the pasture took them.

The movement of these yurts and domes suggested, also, greater circulation. Oh, the same round sun (which we, as did that irritable lover, Donne, track in its passage) for sure was a model for the *yurt*'s circumference. While the framework of the wooden 'roof wheel' at its apex answered the sun's travel over grassland and horizon. Here, in the spoked round of that tent roof is an image, in the homestead ceiling, of eternal motion. And in moments of reflexion, as the sun ran its circle, the Mongol shepherd no doubt felt his life companioned that procession. Here, then, in his simple residence, were smacks of the eternal which could be moved round daily!

XI

It is clear from the above that in our treatment of the Great Khan's buildings, we have strayed into the metaphysical – and that even his ancestral people's tents expressed upward, cosmographic, stretching.

Given, however, that Great Kubilai had adopted, in so far as he was able, the customs of his Chinese subjects, it is not to be imagined that he'd put up buildings which did not conform to geomantic practice as ordained two thousand years before by *Shang* diviners.

To site a building, to accord with principles of Chinese geomancy (or *feng shu-i*: 'wind and water'), it was essential to ensure its situation was, in terms of its inherent forces, propitious. These resident powers were known as *ch'i*: a term that denoted 'energy', *élan vital* – a current or spirit that informed all things, including the human mind and body.

An associated factor lay in the phenomenon of mutually opposing, but creative principles, namely *yin* (dark and female) and *yang* (light and male). Vital *ch'i* was present at its most beneficent when some proposed environs for a building were construed, by specialists in augury, as having equilibrium of *yin* and *yang* elements.

All cities, palaces and districts of commerce, agriculture, religious devotion and pleasure are places where action (which is masculine in character) and receipt of action (female) are accomplished. And for *yin* and *yang*, in any such environment, to achieve their balance, the process of acting and receiving must be reciprocal and harmonious.

It will be understood at once that a *pleasure dome*, in which the entertainment implied the interaction of a man and woman, must be constructed according to the most auspicious alignments. Precisely how that hybrid of the pastoral *ger* and Buddhist or Confucian garden *kiosk* was sited in the Shang-du parkland Marco makes no mention. What Polo tells us is that the palace proper, a marble building, was surrounded by springs, and that these were converted by Kubilai's engineers into genial ponds and waterways which were *feng shu-i* features of the Emperor's garden.

It had been a Ch'an monk, Liu Ping-chung, who surveyed the site, on the 'Yellow Lilies Plain': a sea of golden blossom every summer. This lay on the north bank of the Luan River, some thirty-six miles from the town of Seven Lakes, or Dolon Nur. Kubilai enlarged this and sited his new residence a little way from it, Liu Ping-chung divining currents of the *ch'i* that coursed here: thus sanctioning the palace and its dome's co-ordinates in harmony with geomantic omens. This, in 1256, they called the summer capital, K'ai-p'ing, which Kubilai changed in 1263 to Shang-du, or the Upper Capital, to rhyme and contrast with Ta-du (Peking), the Central Capital.

With respect to these auguries, we may surmise that when Kubilai left Xanadu in August, this was also sanctioned by proprieties of place and season. For not only was it an interaction of *ch'i* with its associated *yin-yang* determinants which controlled the virtues of a site, but the summer palace, as with all important buildings, was likewise constructed in accordance with a larger, indeed cosmological, cartography, in which the cardinal directions were marked by the disposition of the constellations – the latter, themselves, being associated with the earth's four seasons: while these were identified, in turn, by the names of Four Celestial Animals. Thus:

Direction	Season	Animal	Constellation
East	Spring	Bird	Hydra
South	Summer	Phoenix	Scorpio
West	Autumn	Tiger	Aquarius
North	Winter	Turtle	Pleiades

Just, therefore, as Shang-du was built in concord with convergent geomantic and astronomical properties of the place where he exercised his
manly actions (love and hunting – which are *venery* in both its meanings)
so he abandoned his summer residence on the day in August when the
Phoenix of the *South* which dwelled in *Scorpio* gave way to the *Tiger* of
the *West* which had its place in the constellation of Aquarius. Thus was
the Son of Heaven sited properly between the earth and heaven. And how
cheering, besides this, for Great Kubilai to listen to the clatter of bamboo
poles as his (recollection of a) family *yurt* was disassembled – just as if
his little tent were being folded and he was repairing with his kinsmen
to fresh grassland.

Equally of interest: that this site was chosen not *despite* telluric fluxes,
but *because* the earth housed restless water, coursing, no doubt, underneath
the palace meadows from the Luan River whose tributary streams surged
through surrounding pasture and formed ponds, lakes and streams which
could then be channelled by Great Kubilai's Arab engineers to fashion
in a pattern that conduced to happiness and entertainment – as some
centuries later they would also in Granada. Thus engines of imagination,
Chinese and Arabian, wove artifice and nature in a mutual sublimation
for the Great Khan's pleasure.

XII

Reverting to Anige who, as we've seen, had built the White Stupa, it
is worth noting the part he played, once Xanadu had been established,
in the improvement of that place. Now Anige's versatility extended some
distance beyond his superiority as an architect. In illustration of this, on
his arrival from the Himalayas he had undergone a curious ordeal that
the Great Khan set to test his virtuosity.

This task was to repair a bronze image whose detail had been so intricate and whose destruction into pieces so entire, that the best artisans of
the empire had despaired of mending it. Anige, presented with this same
pile of fragments, withdrew for a year, and having worked diligently and
alone, presented himself at the end of his retirement with the image in
his hand, which he had restored to its previous ornate condition.

In the light of this story, we may turn, in connection with the deities
we have associated with Kubilai, to another of Anige's constructions: a
colossus he created in the Great Khan's service for use against the armies of
the southern Sung. Now it will be remembered that through the offices
of Phags-pa, Kubilai was initiated to the *Hevajra Tantra*, and while he

remained a (sedentary) warrior and tyrant, he was supposed an adept of this esoteric Buddhist practice.

Now, for the purpose, finally, of consolidating his empire, Kubilai around the year 1274, planned an invasion of south-east China, which remained the stronghold of the Sung dynasty remnant. And just as the Great Khan had attributed his victory over his brother Arigh to the domed Buddhist *stupa* that Anige had built for him in Ta-du, so he was given to understand by Phags-pa that a parallel strategem might be employed against the very enormous Sung armies.

To comprehend the nature of this ruse, in which religion was put to the service of a brazen military advantage, we should elaborate briefly on one feature of Tibetan religion which has been mentioned only in passing. Namely, that on the passage of the Buddhist *dharma* to the Himalayan kingdoms, it was a sect which had adopted certain Hindu features. And what the Buddhists took from India would further be affianced to the practice of Tibetan folk religion. The *tantra* (so they called it), thus by Kubilai's time, had grown into a colourful incorporation of those three components.

One aspect of the evolution of that most quietist Indian philosophy – which had been born from the intuition of agnostic speculation – was the development of a cosmography inhabited by a population of Buddhist deities (bizarre oxymoron!), some of whose most ferocious attributes might also be traced to the imaginings of Tibetan witches.

Now with respect to Anige and the task set him by the Great Khan for the confrontation of the Sung, this represented an hypertrophied continuation of the work on the little statue he had been given on his arrival in China. But whereas his original assignment had been to reconstruct a relatively small icon, the new commission required him to make a statue of such gigantic proportions that it could be viewed from a distance by a large assembly of people over a wide field.

It is not unusual, of course, for a campaigning monarch to invoke the support and approbation of his God and to attribute success therefore to a supernatural justification. Think only of our own egregiously heroic conqueror at Agincourt whose cry 'God for Harry, England, and St George', is apt make even the least sensitive of his auditors quiver with a queasy oscillation between patriotism and embarrassment. And, no doubt, later when, in the seclusion of his soliloquy, he addresses himself to the 'God of battles!', this same, late, princeling invokes a biblical antecedent – albeit he had limited understanding of what the original connoted. All such rodomontade, as Falstaff had observed in the previous history, consisted of no more than the air along which such rhetoric is trumpeted.

All gods are abstract. And it is hard to believe that Shakespeare's Henry, the historical Plantagenet, or even those warrior Hebrews who fought, so they believed, under the protection of their hypothetical deity, entertained a very clear notion of what the Psalmist's 'Lord of Hosts' signified. I, too, am inclined to prefer my Absolute in terms of an amalgam of a quasi-Falstaffian aether and that paradigmatic absence which was imagined by the Buddha in his meditation.

I was alarmed, in this connection, therefore, on opening the translation by Charles Wilkins of that barbarous and exalted Sanskrit epic poem, called the *Bhagvat-Geeta*, which was published some years back in *Asiatic Researches*, to encounter among passages of undeniable wisdom, verses which were descriptive of an eschatology that impress little but horrific figures on the reader's imagination. I will quote a small number. For without them it may be difficult to imagine the colossus made by Anige in the Great Khan's service.

Thus Wilkins's Krishna in his Vishnu aspect:

'Behold, O *Arjoon*, my million forms divine. Behold, in this my body, the whole world animate and inanimate.' [*Arjoon* saw him in his] supreme and heavenly form, with many a heavenly ornament; many an upraised weapon with celestial robes and chaplets. *Arjoon* continues:

'I behold, O God! Thyself of infinite shape, formed with abundant arms, and bellies, and mouths, and eyes. I see thee with a crown, and armed with club and *Chakra*, a mass of glory, darting refulgent beams around. I am disturbed within me; my resolution faileth me, O *Vishnoo*!

Having beheld thy dreadful teeth, and gazed on thy countenance, emblem of Time's last fire, I know not which way to turn and the fronts of our army, seem to be precipitating themselves into thy mouths, discovering such frightful rows of teeth! Whilst some appear to stick between thy teeth with their bodies sorely mangled.

The heroes of the human race rush on towards thy flaming mouths. As troops of insects seek their destruction in the flaming fire; even so these people, with swelling fury, seek their own destruction. Thou swallowest them with thy flaming mouths.' To which the god replies:

'I am Time, the destroyer of mankind, come hither to seize at once all these who stand before us.' *Bhagavat-Geeta Lecture XI*

I have mentioned that when the Buddhists took their idols from India to Tibet, they carried with these images traits which they had borrowed from Hindu traditions. And those depictions of Vishnu just given are representative of the pattern which was adapted into Tibetan Buddhism and which thereafter gave rise to a pantheon of deities then brought to China by Phags-pa *lama* and his colleagues.

Now this same Phags-pa had some interest in maintaining the patronage of his master and it was therefore to his advantage that the Khan was successful in his domination of China. Together, therefore, inspired by Phags-pa's understanding of Tibetan icons, Kubilai and his Supervisor Artisan in Chief, that same Anige, devised the notion of creating a colossus in the shape of the Tibetan deity *Mahakala*, of previous mention – whose name, as we should explore briefly, is from the Sanskrit.

Of interest here is the fact that while this great god, and some other northern Buddhist deities, acquired names in the Tibetan, these also maintained their Sanskrit, and even Hindu, nomenclature: *Mahakala*, meaning, in this case, both 'Great Black One', and, given that *kala* connotes both 'black' and 'time': 'Great Time'.[11] (Worth noting here is that Herr Schlegel chooses the meaning 'time' in his translation to Latin: '*Dies* sum mundi eversor ...' suggesting perhaps an echo of the 'Dies irae'!)

The ambiguity of *kala*, in the context of our discussion, is no mere quibble. Nor did I choose my portion from the *Geeta* unmindful of the varied lights it would shed on the subject of Anige's monument. As we shall see, the *terrific* aspect of the Hindu *Vishnu* (who, elsewhere, under the name Krishna, is Arjoon's driver, playful child, a thief and blue- or black-skinned lover of amorous young milk maids!) is not unlike, in both action and appearance, that figure of 'The Great Black One' which was constructed to confront Great Kubilai's opponents.

Let us, for convenience, pass over the possibility that the Great Black One of the Tibetans represented the god Shiva the destroyer or the loathly goddess Kali ('Black'), whose name is a feminised derivative of *kala*, and who is depicted dancing garlanded with skulls, while she drinks from one of them the life blood of a victim. No representation of Anige's *Mahakala* has come down to us. No doubt it was broken up in battle. What we have in abundance are Tibetan works painted on silk banners, and among them, visual renderings of Mahakala.

In brief, these are fierce. Black, fat, tusked and grinning, bloodshot

---

11 'The epithet Maha, or Great, being prefixed in token of distinction.' This pithy definition is given by Governor Warren Hastings in his Introduction to Wilkins's *Geeta*.

eyes a-flame in the relish of a fury, bedizened with death's heads and festooned with serpents, this shock-noddled monster squats and stamps up and down on corpses or on shrieking demons, wielding with one of his several pairs of hands, an adamantine chopper with which he macerates in a blood-filled half-skull, the bodies and spirits of those who affront him.

But hold. Before we revert to Anige's statue, let us hasten to put forward this singular addendum. Atrocious as these images in their materiality appear, it is to the imagination and hermetic places of self-scrutinising contemplation to which they were directed. And far from representing mere ferocity and terror, these icons were adapted from the Hindu by doctors of a Buddhist fraternity whose purpose – in compassion for souls tangled in their passions – was to guide their brethren to discover, by means of a *metaphorical representation*, some analogously construed and hypertrophised symbolic visual revelation of defilements, hindrances, perverted views and obsessions that raged within their unpurified spiritual constitution. More could be explained.

Suffice it to remark here that what is grotesque in outward formulation constitutes a mere guiding ornamental pattern by means of which the metaphorical nature of even the most theatrically convincing of our self-perceptions is rendered artefactual – and thereby available to a transmutation.[12]

This last notion returns us to the Great Khan's statue. What happened was as follows. For five wasting years, the Mongol armies had besieged two fortified Sung cities and when at last, in 1273, these strongholds fell, Kubilai sent one of his armies (some hundred thousand) to complete the conquest of southern China. Superstitiously or not, the Emperor had enjoined his *lamaistic* colleague to sanction this campaign, and in his turn, Phags-pa sent for Anige to build a temple at the city of *Chu-chow* from within which, abetted by the material presence of Mahakala and his entourage of minor deities, the Buddhists could pray, or cast spells, for the Great Khan's victory.

---

12 With respect to the *Geeta*'s Hindu iconography, I note Governor Hastings's helpfully convergent two views: 'One blemish may be found in it, which will scarcely fail to make its own impression on every correct mind. I mean, the attempt to describe spiritual existences by terms and images which appertain to corporeal forms. Yet even in this respect it will appear less faulty than other works, and defective as it may at first appear, I know not whether a doctrine so elevated above common perception did not require to be introduced by such ideas as were familiar to the mind, to lead it by a gradual advance to the pure and abstract comprehension of the subject.' Introduction viii.

A curious little story lies behind this engagement of the deity. Another (anonymous) Tibetan master, an associate of Phags-pa, who was known for his magical prowess, was one of the great promoters of the cult of Maha-kala, and had been sent for by Kubilai during the sieges just mentioned.

'Why,' demanded the Great Khan, 'had this Guardian Deity not helped during five exhausting years of conflict?'

'Because,' replied the adept, 'he was offended not to have been invited.'

Hence, now, the construction of both temple and images. And this in a direct confrontation with the Taoist deity *Chen-wu* to whom the Chinese prayed, without success, for their protection.

So it was, in the crisis of this drama, that the monstrous body of Mahakala was revealed at the front of the Great Khan's army. Consecrated by the afore-mentioned magician and through further esoteric rituals, spiritually empowered by Phags-pa *lama*, the deity was erected facing south-east in full view of the Sung – and it was, according to Chinese histories, the terror inspired by the sight of this horrifying apparition, that led to the failure of their otherwise well-regulated armies. And thus, too, a deity from Tibet whose features had been borrowed from old Hindu sources and modelled in obedience to a Mongol chieftain by an architect from the Himalayas was deployed in south China in the guise, as it were, of a military engine.

This was 1274. In possession of all China, finally, the Great Khan dispatched Anige to Xanadu: where to seal the empire, this time, from invaders from, *inter alia*, his own old kinsmen, he enjoined his architect to build on the northwest and northeast sides of his city two new Buddhist temples: thus completing, through propitiation of the Buddhist deities and in *feng shu-i* engagement with telluric forces, the protection of his Upper Capital.

XIII

This brings us to the Great Khan's final *stupa:* which was the last and most celebrated dome he enjoined from his chief architect. This, un-like any other of Anige's constructions, has survived to the present, and remains one of the capital features that may be seen in old Peking. We should add that it was the successful completion of this that crowned Anige's status – albeit after Kubilai's death, his fortunes, under Temur, the penultimate Mongol emperor, declined.

And so here, in Ta-du, the great White Stupa rises. On the bones, as it were, of a previous stupa which had been built, in the late 11th century, to house (unlikely this) some reliques of the Buddha *ipse.*

In harmony with that supposition, and some time before his business with the Mahakala statue, the Great Khan was adverted to some rumours of an augury. These stories arose in a western district of his capital, where white glimmers, on successive nights, were seen emerging from the previous stupa's ruins. Assuming that the reliques there were lighting it, Kubilai ordered the stupa to be opened.

The excavation bore a fruitful outcome. And when, in March that year (it was 1271), Kubilai and Chabi viewed the contents of the inner chamber, they were pleased to discover, among sundry objects, 1,008 small stupas made of earth mixed with camphor, gold and coral, alongside 130,000 tiny, sweet smelling stupas which had miraculously kept their fragrance.

Even in the absence of one cinder of the Buddha's body, there could, in the circumstance, be no question but that a new and monumental stupa should be built to enshrine this collection of important little domes. And so it was done. And just as light had been seen at the previous ruin, so in the spring (it was 1279), when the stupa was finished, a new light was observed. It came from the West – whence the Blessed One's teaching – as though from the Ganges a sunset were projected on this lofty monument which climbed now to the Chinese heaven. Thus was this dome, as ordained by Kubilai, gilded by a *sovereigne eye* which had risen in the East – on this, the Khan's most propitious testimonial – in the maturity of its own setting!

During the ceremony at which the dome was consecrated, Kubilai decreed that arrows should be shot from each side of the stupa to measure the boundaries of a new Buddhist temple – which was named according to the most obsequious Chinese convention, the *Temple of the Emperor's Longevity and Peace*. This would become the most magnificent of Anige and Kubilai's sacred buildings. Many thousands of peons and off-duty soldiers, who cut down some sixty thousand trees and spread more than five hundred and forty melted *taels* of gold to decorate the Buddha figures, were employed in its making.

Deeper in his age, the Great Khan went to view the temple and installed in there an aromatic Buddha. Only living Buddhas, Kubilai remarked – from self-conceit or unwonted insight *in re* other halls which stood empty as the Buddha's teaching – might dwell in those precincts.

XIV

Now it is scarcely a surprise that Kubilai, no more nor less than any individual, should be marked by elements of self-contradiction: for are we not all a mere brindle of constituents that flock around and are half-absorbed in, or are pasted on some semi-constituted individuality that travels through a life, until its final breath, in metamorphosis and aberration? And is not each – in far Cathay as here at Culbone – a mere medley, 'motley minded' (as Touchstone has it): elements mis-matching one another, sans coherence, whose mutually confounding qualities and dissonant vocalities – as with any poor forked cockscomb of a harlequin or masquerader in his spangled, ill-assorted patches – scarce know their own neighbour, albeit they live, *cap-a-pie*, in one body?

Earlier I have alluded to a bird song from which the *Ramayana* issued. And also to Herr Giesecke's Greenlandic voyage, whence he brought back, with his bags of rock and bird skulls, tales from the Esquimaux, whose stories and their like I think represent the skeleton or fundament of much in more elaborated literatures. And in Giesecke's box lay another story, whose character evinces a shrewd observation. This runs as follows:

A Raven and a Northern Diver meet one day, in *Ur*-time (as such meetings happened) when both birds had been hatched in the same white plumage. Displeased with uniformity of costume, the two birds engage, using soot from an oil lamp, to decorate each others' feathers. When the Diver sees its finish in the spots and streaks with which Raven's painted him, he's well pleased with his finery. But as he works at his reciprocation, Raven grows impatient. A quarrel ensues and the Diver hurls the soot pot over Raven's feathers – henceforward soot black as we know them.

The first moral, that of Nature's wonderful variety, is simple. A second perhaps lies within the action. In this, Nature, hints our story, brings about its own creative changes: some of these benign and others conceived in conflict and convulsion. And in comment, perhaps, on man's own unaccountable behaviour, creatures co-exist in happy partnership or else prey on each other: playing, as did Puck, their tricks in either jest or mischief. These tricksters represent a dangerous but productive fellowship. Still, who acts, against who's acted on, are aspects of some converse *other*. The birds, at their outset, shared uniformity of whiteness. In separation, they remain, though different, aspects of fraternal interaction, whose contraries are parties to the other: the one maculated, veined and mottled, the second – as he'd matched the snow in blankness – black as the night of an Arctic winter![13]

---

13 Again, I am informed that the Diver's maculation represents the streaked sun

Now with respect to the Khan, I will venture this sally. That Kubilai, as with many great ones, was a bedizened and strutting, fustian, fantastical, plumed bawcock, something insecurely self-conceited in his gaudy: and instinct, like those animals of story, with antemundane, sportive impulse. So the life force drives him, and from a stage in history's theatre, he ornaments his time – casts shadows of massed horse across the wastes of empire – as he, in turn, is variously, vainly, painted: a pranked, trimmed, tricked-out, gorgeous, fat, cock, demi-self-created, self-consuming, Bird of Paradise.

XV

Now all this pertains to one thing mainly, which is the Great Khan's dome and his Shang-du gardens. For just as Kubilai, as hinted at, was motley as Autolycus (in kind) or Touchstone (both in mind and costume): and that these, as we, are represented in the Diver's diverse plumage: so that motley is reflected in the context and pattern of great Kubilai's garden. And all the history we've adduced thus far conduces to one simple notion. This. That just as the Khan contained within himself these oppositions – Mongol horseman, Chinese Emperor, alien, dictator, auditor of wise Confucian, Buddhist and Islamic counsel, murderer and Buddhist ruler, husband, libertine (a *Lovelace* who brought love to a house of prostitution), and aye, a *bodhisattva* of compassion, and just as the dome in his *Xaindu* garden was, in conceit, a *ger* assimilated to a house of pleasure, sited within 'wind and water' principles, resort of great Kubilai's aestivation, secure in one place, but disassembled as a nomad's might be in the final moon of August: this counterpointed too, *qua* a roundel of pleasure, by Buddhist domes both excavated from the past and decreed from Anige: so the choice of this site, his 'Upper Capital and Palace', that same *Xaindu* Purchas knew from Marco who had walked there, harmonised with Kubilai's inner disaffiliations.

XVI

Two simple notions lead from this long labyrinthine lucubration. First, that the history we have crudely traced of Shang-du region with its patchwork of unstable antecedents to the Great Khan's residence, presents apt correlation to the nature of this despot: for just as Kubilai was a pied and polymorphous pantaloon or pierrot of a personage, so history encroached,

---

in its struggle to be born from winter. The Diver and the Raven are conceived thus as the co-existence of alternating light and dark seasons.

with its *penumbra*, on this paradise in which he sank each summer. And past time, half-finished, all too present, which the Great Khan recognised, in summary and detail, hummed from nearby in the circumambience of peace he made there.[14]

Such were the shows of past eventuality: shadows never seen, but sensed moving in time's backward but translucent recess, as though on a screen that stood behind, but viewlessly infused, the Great Khan's present.

Second: this site, with its intrinsic instabilities, was a place where he might dare to think his second self, that part which masqueraded (*sic*) as Emperor of China, might well – as snakes shed skin they've finished with each winter – be let slip for the season. This was a place in which the Great Khan might revert to where he'd started – as a Tartar. That this was illusion was plain to any one who'd undertook his smallest order, and also to that self (on account of its inherent scission) which knew very well the alteration he had gone through since his days, as yunker, among herders, or as princeling when his older brother sent him on the Ta-li mission.

But what follows is of greater moment. That which he acquired as King of China (and his Chinese name, *Shi tsu*) were formulae and trappings, folderols and artificialities. And just as history's shadows flitted around Shang-du's border, so gold thread and ermine stretched thin on Kubilai's shoulders, and the oscillations in him between *quondam* Mongol and his character as Emperor were uncertain as that boundary – with its intermittent Chinese Wall (O Wall! that he looked back through) – which

---

14 And just as we enter an assembly room or theatre, sensing generalities that mill around us and we comprehend instinctively, without a conscious knowledge, forms and fashion, manners, tittle-tattle, foibles that surround half-sensible awareness: so by intuition Kubilai glimpsed his antecedents. And just as his Tibetan mentors fabricated veils, that were abstract, round their persons, thereby shielding them from charms and hatred with an equanimity they cultivated from the Buddha's teaching, so the Great Khan holiday'd immune, if not untroubled, by the ghosts of warfare traced here.

Thus Kubilai held his paradise in mind en route from Peking's summer. And, in a cooler silence, apprehended, from a present distance, lang syne perturbations, the thronging of horsemen from grass land to battle, the constitution of alliances, their crises and their dissolution. All this murmured on the fringes of the Great Khan's quiet. Or, homelier analogy, as though in a bee's nest, at the terminus of galleries constructed by accumulated honey, the King lay securely but awake to rumours of a rival hymenopterid incursion, the forked, smoking sticks of tribesmen (impertinent interrogation), long, curved, thirsty bird beaks, the prehensile tongues of sloths and armadillos or the bear's claw – ineluctable, indifferent to stinging – that may one day come there.

he apprehended.[15] No aspect of which would be remarkable were it not for our interest in Shang-du *ipse*:

In which connection we've already noted
Part of what the pleasure dome connoted,

and have scumbled on the page – as though sketching future plans across its later ruins – how Kubilai chose this place to fix a palimpsest on future continuities – and also, in part, both for its geomantic auspices and its propinquity to homeland pastures.[16]

XVII

This Upper Capital lay on an uncertain landscape. And Kubilai knew those regions bordering his Mongol pastures had previously been run through. Settled insecurely by the Sung, five (brief) previous dynasties had wrestled to control their fluctuations. The Khitan, first in 924, had swarmed south into China. Then in 946 they drove back the Chin and took K'ai feng. In further incursions, they forced a treaty with the Sung. The Sung treated with Manchurians (the Jurchen) and in 1115, they pushed out the Khitan. But the Jurchen turned against them, laid siege to K'ai feng and by 1126, set up a Chin empire. Now Genghis unified the Mongols and invaded the Chin. Peking fell. But when Genghis turned home, the Chin recaptured its lost territory – which the Sung then recovered. By 1233, however, the Mongol had rode east again. So the wars continued, with an intervention of the Tangut or the Hsia Hsia, who, in turn, were defeated by Mongol armies.[17]

---

15 Compare unstable souls of Shakespeare's upstarts: 'God knows, my son, / By what by-paths and indirect crook'd ways / I met this crown, and I myself know well / How troublesome it sat upon my head.' 2 *H. IV*. V.v And at Bosworth, Richard: 'What do I feare? My selfe? Theres none else by, / Richard loves Richard, that is I and I, / Is there a murtherer here? No. yes, I am ... I am a villaine, yet I lie I am not, / Foole of thy selfe speake well, foole do not flatter ...' *R. III* V.v.

16 It was so at Shang-du, as noted of Peking by Rashid-al-din, that that city, not long since, had been built by the Chin, which was then razed by Genghis. And thus Kubilai 'voulait la restaurer; mais il aima mieux, pour la gloire de son nom, fonder une nouvelle ville pres de l'ancienne, et il la nomma Ta-du; les deux sont contigues.'

17 This world's a whirlpool. Think back, instead, to old T'ang China! Serene, so we think, in uniform coherence. But then, as we seek beneath the glazed sheen of its surface, look there, at its heart, on this maelstrom of peoples! How Kubilai's hybridised regime was mirrored or reversed back then: Mongols transported to be horseherds, grooms and lackeys. 'Tartars led in chains!' sang T'ang poet Po Chu-i, 'their ears pierced, faced bruised – driven as slaves to the land of Ch'in'. Witness Uighurs captured and Tibetans exiled. Enslaved Arab and Korean soldiers. Turks and

These details shan't detain us. Nor may I vouch for their extreme exactness – if events are a *maelstrom*, so the record inherits that inherent movement. My thought is this simply. That as the Great Khan rode to Xanadu each summer – a ten days' journey, first undertaken in the mid-1250s – a cooling vision of his palace, nonetheless connected with all past eventuality, rose to meet him.

XVIII The voyage to Shang-du: preliminary fancy

Regard, first, this map. And note the journey from Peking, due north and then a little west to Shang-du city. This was also the initiation that justified the languor of his aestivation.

The road was not long – about a hundred miles, some 750 *li* by Chinese calculation. And this presented nothing of the danger it would hold for solitary travellers and pilgrims.

But Kubilai, too, was a lonely pilgrim. He travelled, of course, with extensive attendance. And while chamberlains and wives and cavalry came with him for his service, what this entourage created was a compound solitude: for thus to be enclosed in fleshly armour emphasised the softness of his little body. For while he was the Son of Heaven, his person remained ordinary, and as this travelled, entertained much incoherent incident and ratiocination. This, for example, I imagine:

Now, on a bridge, beyond his winter city, the road follows a small river. And Great Kubilai hears the *kalavinka*, emblem of the Buddha, calling, and can scarcely believe the freedom of this little finch's twitter, its separation from him and how mortal things and essences converge in singing. 'Ah me,' the Great Khan murmurs, 'this indeed is evanescent. I'll use the status I enjoy to render it, if only for a little, permanent.' (Sharp, green paddy answers, over glimpses, between stems, of water, with a surreptitious whisper. Apricot and peaches negatively shake their blossom.)

'See, in these ensamples, how past labour may conduce to present pleasure – the secondary product being what is beautiful to those who glance here. Why shouldn't I, albeit a barbarian, be sensible to what the poets have engaged with, as a reflex to their exile?

'Hearken as they chant their arcane, *sauvage* disadvantage! How their bitterness ennobles and corrupts the peony and their misfortune taints the

---

Persians, Pygmies from Sumatra, caged black girls and albino troglodytes. Karluks from the steppeland, bearded Ainus, Indians in thousands brought from Magadha, the very realm where Buddha preached compassion ... Was this world any different in kind from that of Kubilai?

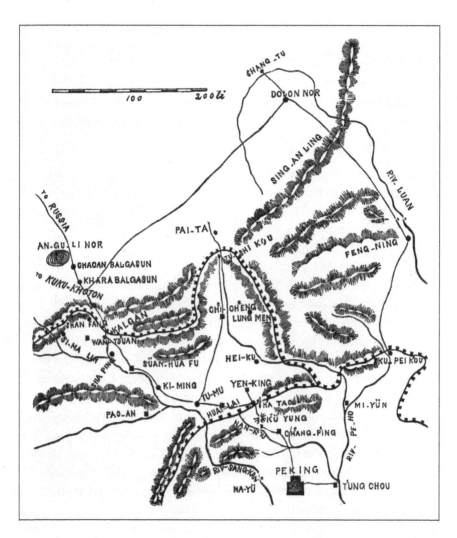

bronze chrysanthemum! In song or in dream, or reflected in their wine, alone, these poets are at home again. Oh ye woods! and oh ye individual trees! Redoubts of contemplation and of longed-for privacy! Speak ye to me!'

Three-quarters on the way, on another little river: see a small homestead. Women spin silk in the mulberry's shadow. Children fan their heads with blossom. 'Now here's a pleasant little *locus*,' the Great Kubilai murmurs. 'I shall take it with me.' And he appoints a captain of five hundred to dig up the farm and bring it, with its people, to his palace.[18]

---

18 As for the evil smelling jakes on the periphery of the orchard, they left this where they found it. Where, I ask, did our First Parents plant their excrements in Eden?

Arrived at Xanadu, are excavations. A tract is cleared by the same five hundred. But when later they return to what they had disposed, the fruit trees have died and underneath them lie the families which had lived among them. 'Such might have been expected. Nothing endures in this world of illusions,' their captain, mouthing a Buddhist commonplace, mutters. And confident the Great Khan had forgotten its existence, they turn the village on its head and inter its beauties.

Years have their passage, and nourished by the corpses that lay jumbled among plum stones, a grove of trees emerges from the ruin. Walking there one morning, the great Kubilai is enchanted by this spectacle of fruit, in millions fattening but green still, with vestigial pruinescence. 'Ah me!' he sighs, divided between appetite and contemplation. 'These plums, short-lived, alas, may prove delicious. I'll have them sent to Ta-du in the autumn.'

XIX Continuing with history

Three roads led to Shang-du from the winter capital. The most direct went north to the Great Wall through a defile in the mountains and was served by eighteen stations, military outposts, and Huan-chou, a small city. This is the path that Kubilai travelled in the summer, but took a longer, western road on return each autumn. This latter, in that it turns its back on Xanadu, need not concern us. A third road, east of Ta-du, lay in flatter country. Along this, Kubilai's luggage was transported and followed, towards the end, the Luan river, on which goods for Shang-du were carried.

Now the nature of Great Kubilai's journey evokes as many mysteries as his summer residence – on both of which subjects one may throw off only indistinct surmises. One thing is certain. That Kubilai did not reach his destination (which was ten days on horse), as I did at Culbone, in a lather of his excrement and desperate for hot water and apparel! But while this farm house stood without anticipating my arrival, Shang-du every summer lay in trepidation of the Great Khan's visit.

As Kubilai approached, the landscape grew familiar. Cold wind from a green horizon carried scents of steppeland grasses, each of whose kinds he could name in the Tartar. Here, at the least, he could conjecture for himself the native character that Arigh Boke had twitted him with wasting.

XX

I have again read Marco and admit him to have walked convincingly around the summer palace. Dressed no doubt in ministerial or merchant fashion and conversing in the region's languages, I wonder if this proper little fellow might not, nonetheless, have seemed, to those who had not met his kind, a *monster* (as Trinculo conceived the word) as were those *Esquimaux* snatched up by Frobisher from Baffin and, for public entertainment, had been set to hunt swans on the Bristol Channel – a few mere leagues from where I have been sitting in my own, unwonted, shepherd's costume! We are, I suppose, all Calibans to one another.

XXI

Marco had wintered in the Ta-du palace. And now the Great Khan's summer residence was built, as he described it, of a *monumental marble*, painted with beasts, birds, trees and flowers, 'all done with such art that you regard them with astonishment.'

Now this is what astonishes a quiet reader: for was it not sufficient to have built a garden and endowed it with exotic species, but these latter must be pieced, by artifice, into the building's marble?

It is thus, through our dreams, we ornament, with *rich increese*, what stands in its simplicity before us (as an *unswept stone*) and thereby foreswear *unsullied* perfection. (To gainsay which I aver that such exuberance is love. And if love's folly, let fools' beauty rule. Love life, I argue, if that is to be foolish!)

XXII On gardens

Now it is attested in the Chinese annals that among the sights the Great Khan passed on his journey to Shang-du, were orchards yielding peach-wood for his bowmen, celebrated bridges and old gardens: and these latter, with the stations where he rested, were the *clews* from which his annual road depended. Now our own English garden's a darling creation, and I'd lay down my life for any unpretending petal in 'em – nay, even for one hairy final parsnip. But shovel these aside we must – until we can next put a boot out in one – and view some features of the oriental garden against which to measure Great Kubilai's paradise.

XXIII

Now while Mongol chieftains rampaged through China, the painters and the poets of that country went on, with a poignant and enlarged intensity, singing in the gardens that their forebears had created. And these gardens, further, were concretions of the poetry and paintings that they fashioned in such places.

And indeed, much more than this. A garden was a holy place, most anciently, a situation built with rocks and pines and lily pools, devised with priestly diligence to tempt a visitation of immortals who dwelled otherwise on heights of which the garden was a simulacrum. Here, as construed by adepts of the *tao*, the elements of *yin* and *yang* conspired in balanced yielding to each other, harmonising with the universal principles of opposites in congress, whose soft strife was propitious to all those who acted in accordance with its flux and *noumen*. Earth and heaven meet in such environs, where, with mild glances, as he roams its quiet, a man contemplates, reduced, the blessed whole of nature, and by means of garden makers' artifice, apprehends its unity, his own place between dust and aether, and there finds truth in meditation on the tranquil way, or *tao* – lost otherwise in uproar, hurry and ambition.

Thus the Buddhists and the men of *tao* who cultivated self-refinement. The Confucian, too, weighed down by office and asphyxiated with res-ponsibility, likewise made his *hortus conclusus*, arranging, in small city courtyards even, rocks to make 'false mountains', excavating ponds and setting pines, bamboo and willow or hydrangea coverts to retire in.

Six centuries, indeed, before Genghis took Peking, the poet Tao Yuan-ming (his name a nice co-ordination of three separated entities!) composed this summation:

I lean on my south window and I think
How simple to be happy with this garden!
Here I stroll for pleasure,
And at sunset walk around my solitary pine tree.

There were also gardens at once famous – what an oxymoron! – and hermetic. One courtier of the Sung made a celebrated 'Garden for Solitary Enjoyment'. Another, the 'Retreat for Thinking Garden.' Some families under Kubilai's rule, withdrew and, as Voltaire may have learned from them (or Persia) foreswore public life and retired to cultivate their gardens (Voltaire gives this teaching from a *Turkish* gardener!). One such was Ni Tsan, of whom more later.

Now a Chinese term for 'landscape' is *mountains and waters*. While *digging a pond and piling up a mountain* implied garden making – which, in miniature, evoked those features. Once rock and water, or, as they said, a landscape's *skeleton and arteries*, were brought together, garden makers added modest buildings: little pavilions and gazebos, belvederes and porches, bridges, studios that leaned out over water, while screened, mystic paths linked seats of contemplation to shelters by fish ponds where the movement of a single carp or barbel was the contemplation of a whole existence.

XXIV

How much, when he stepped down from his palankeen, tumescent no doubt, with adventitious expectation of a *nautch* girl in some house of pleasure, did the Great Khan comprehend of what he met there? And what smiling, disrespectful ironies were veiled by adepts who conducted the Great Kubilai along pathways where the shadows of the *yin* on sun-sprent *yang* of lime-washed walls and lattices intersected with each other – but whose rude stone, trees and water spoke nothing of the *tao* or mutually reflected principles of artifice and nature to the Son of Heaven who had wandered in here?

Now the Chinese garden is an asymmetric maze: and in this it reflects Great Nature's uncoordinated ranges. And if nature extends wild, the garden has, within its boundaries, tamed this. Thus, too, a *person* and his labyrinthine complications, who enters a garden, *all in peeces*, and is cured, for a moment, of self-biting contradictions – as perhaps the Great Khan may have felt now as he visited these features of the country he had unified, without, himself, assimilating with it: except, that given he'd appropriated its last furlong to him, he was curious to comprehend some aspect of his subjects' manufacture.

Thus might Great Kubilai have stood in a *ting* (whose meaning is 'to stop'): in a plum-flower-shaped kiosk. Or sat gazing from a *tsi* (which means 'to borrow'): a gazebo by some willow trees and leaning across water through which lilies raised their candid blossom. Or maybe, those two words compounded, in a *ting-tsi*, where to stop is to dwell and do nothing in a 'borrowing' from nature and to realise in those minutes where a human life is sited: in dust-fated flesh and short-lived breath, between the earth and heaven, and all the harmonies and jarrings whose collusion reveals unity of things and beings in their fleeting histories.

XXV

How far His Lordship was acquainted with what follows about royal parks I can't determine. But every *Chinaman* in Kubilai's circle would have been acquainted with their garden history – from old Shang to the Han and through to the Ch'in Emperor's celebrated Shang-lin hunting region. Now the history of this pertains to the Great Khan closely. For as

Marco has written, around Shang-du Palace lay grounds which had some paradisal, numinous association:

> Inside the Park there are fountains and rivers and brooks and beautiful meadows with all kinds of wild animals, which the Emperor has procured and placed there to supply food for his gerfalcons and hawks.
>
> The Khan himself goes every week to see his birds sitting in mew, and sometimes he rides through the park with a leopard behind him on his horse's croup; and then if he sees any animal that takes his fancy, he slips his leopard at it ... While roaming the park are special breeds of white mares and cows whose milk no one else dares drink except only the great Khan and his family.

Beyond a presumption that this *milk* had sacred character, I will not claim again to comprehend the nature of the drink the Great Khan and his kinsmen swallowed: save it represented a quintessence drawn from some digestive interaction of the palace grasses and thoro'breds associated with a spirit-land of which Kubilai and his ancestors were denizens. Such, from necromancer Genghis, as his chief, was the imperial inheritance.

There were older conjunctions. The Shang kings had built parks. And those were solid people (viz. their bronzes). Yet before them, ancient, divine rulers laid out gardens in whose legendary precincts dragons bathed, the phoenix nested and the unicorn cavorted. On the so-called *Burning Island* in another royal garden, a bird, dimensioned like a sparrow, fed on turtle brains and pearl for sweetmeat and would hiccough gold dust which was melted to make cups and dishes.

To be king in such a park implied both congress with the gods and energetic hunting. Meat from the Shang hunt which was offered to the powers protected, purified, preserved the empire. Hence this ode (one of many):

> The king walks in his garden.
> Harts and does hide there.
> White birds shimmer.
> At the hallowed pool the king sits.
> Up from its surface, fish come leaping.

Principal among reserves was the Shang-lin park, 'Supreme' (and later) 'Tabooed Forest', which the first Ch'in Emperor laid out in BC mid-third-century, northwest of Chang'an, his capital city. Having conquered all China (as would Kubilai fifteen centuries later) and pulverised the palaces of rival monarchs, he vauntingly rebuilt their simulacra round his own seat of power and fenced a grand reserve around it, dragging animals and trees from every quarter of the kingdom.[19]

Time rendered this a legend, and later Han emperors enjoined poets to extol it. Eight sacred rivers met here, rhapsodised one singer, from the four directions, flowed through meadows, down deep, precipitous abysms and wound through groves of cinnamon and flowering camphor. This fullness, or completeness, made it of itself, a universe that represented both a model of the Empire and a sacred pattern. Here, in its meridian, one poet chanted:

Grass grows in winter.
Zebras and tapirs, aurochs,
Unicorns, rhinoceros,
Onagers and mares roam freely.

As demonstrated in the *Songs of Ch'u*, there were further effusions about numinous ponds and stone-beam bridges, forest piedmonts and roofed galleries or terraces where pleasure might be taken and incantations chanted to propitiate the Heavens. For which purpose, boys with peach-wood bows shot arrows upward to sever the bridge along which interfering goblins travelled – and thus cleansed the empire.

XXVI

Now if oxymoron may be rendered concrete, Chinese gardens, vegetably, did it. On the one hand, hunting parks cleared wilderness country of predatory animals thereby protecting the neighbourhood peasants. And while, on the other, those domains represented paradisal spaces, demonstrating men's control of nature, the nobility walled off fields and orchards – reminiscent of our own unwarranted enclosures – and as Mencius complained, 'took people's cultivated land to make gardens and preserves of them.' A reserve, continued Mencius, should have higher purpose, and be of advantage to the *general*. But no. Already by late Chou there were peasant rebels against hunting parks and the *corvées* exacted for wall construction.

In connection with Kubilai and his paradise much later, stood a further

---

19 A royal park was *yu*, a hunting park, *yuan*. The latter word meant also 'garden'. While *yuan* and *lin* ('forest') were words describing a retreat for scholars, literati, poets. Paradise, in parallel, was *ti yu*, 'preserves of the gods'. Any correspondence between *yuan* ('hunting park') and Kubilai's *Yuan* dynasty, I leave to the reader with more special knowledge.

incongruity, in that *barbarians* across the Wall, were construed to be non-human. These were 'dog, bird and snake folk'. Animals – antitheses of cultivated virtue – lived for mankind service. It was noble for the emperor to slay a leopard, and justified (except in their exclusion from a royal hunting ground) for peasants to take hares and pheasants. A cloak, for the former, must be trimmed with sable, a cap or tippet with marten and the ermine. While courtesans and dancers were bedizened with kingfisher, finch and oriole plumage.

According to a Han poetic rhapsody, there were, in the *Supreme Reserve*, swan-geese, herons, ducks and bustards, edible turtles, crocodiles and sturgeons: bred, kept and fed in pools contrived ('their rightness fit for Numinous Plantations') from bubbling springs and tributary rivulets. From the north and the west, the Emperor brought camels, asses, *tarpan* and (unaccountable nomenclature) the bloodsweating Median. While in the *Tabooed Park*'s south quadrant – some *qua* tribute from Kanchi, Annan and Arabia – wandered ostriches and elephants, caraboas, sambars, giant dogs and panda. As Gibbon wrote of what Commodus paraded in the Forum: 'Ethiopia and India yielded their extraordinary productions.'

According to Han poets, bears and tigers, foxes, raccoons, ducks and cranes were confined both in cages and in *palace apartments*. And when the ground was cleared for a grand winter hunt, beasts were driven in promiscuously by grooms and mounted beaters for the entertainment of a royal party. There arose then 'A wind of feathers and a rain storm of blood.' This, according to one poet, 'dyed the earth red and obscured the heavens'. Tigers were set to fight elephants and buffalo, strong men wrestled bears and leopards. Sated by such spectacle, the Emperor's party feasted on the outraged carcasses to music from boats and tumblers who performed on floating stages.

Such profanities were costly. Under Wu Ti's rule, five-hundred-thousand drudges worked to level and enclose one reserve. I can not account for the truth of this contention, but in one royal park were grottoes jewelled with the most exotic minerals: sapphire, amethyst, chalcedony and coral, in extravagant arrangement. Grape vines from Persia, oranges from central Asia were brought there. 'Camel Kuo', Ch'ang-an's celebrated hunchback gardener, commandeered exotic peach tree cuttings, a thousand miles across the Taklamakan desert from Samarkand, to graft on the wood-stock of the native persimmon, whence he grew enormous golden peaches for which the Empress had expressed insatiable craving.

Such palatable ornaments were transported to adorn the quarters of the

Son of Heaven. And if succulence is holy, as indeed it may be, then these flesh-pots were cloisters of carnality and monasteries of consummation.[20]

XXVII

How such matters could be sacred can't be comprehended quickly. Nor how thoughtful Buddhist and Confucian gardens co-existed with, and sometimes inside, hunting parks of earlier rulers. Objurgation came from Taoists and the Buddhist *sangha*. This happened when the T'ang made, after centuries of desuetude, a 'Tabooed Park' north of Ch'ang-an, their new northern capital. This reserve was administered with kinder husbandry, expressing the governance of a Confucian *humanity*. Henceforth, according to this rule which they called *jen*, no beast could be hunted in its breeding season. Animals, the Taoists taught, must be accorded the same freedoms as human beings: 'Shepherding people is like keeping birds and beasts. If you shut them in preserves and walls, you destroy their wild hearts.'[21] A doctrine of *not-harming* came from the Buddhists. In both religions man and beast were adjudicated equals. The T'ang took notice – for a short time albeit.

XXVIII

One factor I've kept back. Not everything is written in a moment. Otherwise our words would clamber onto, through and over one another, and – like toads that Othello, in a horror of imagination, filled his brain with – they would *knot and gender* in a self-annihilating pullulation: gather-

---

20 Lest we smile with condescension, recall this profligate display in 1575 by Leicester, who entertained the Queen at Kenilworth: 'At her first entrance, there was a floating island on the pool, bright blazing with torches, upon which, clad in silks, were the lady of the lake, and two nymphs waiting on her. Within the base court a bridge was set up, on each side whereof were posts with presents to her by the gods: a cage of wild fowl by Sylvanus; rare fruits by Pomona; corn by Ceres; wine by Bacchus; of sea-fish by Neptune; habiliments of war by Mars; and musical instruments by Phoebus. And for the days of her stay, rare sports were exercised: in the chase, a savage man, with satyrs; bear baitings, fire-works, Italian tumblers, a country bride-ale, with running at the quintin. Besides this, he had upon a pool a triton riding on a mermaid; as also Arion on a dolphin, with rare musick. Dugdale, *History and Description of Kenilworth Castle*, 1777. Did Prospero, perhaps, attend these masqueings?!

21 Chuang-tzu had also written: 'If we should make a cage of all under heaven, there would be no place of refuge for the sparrow.' In this I'm reminded of some words of Mr Blake, an eccentric whose writings, while curious and uncoordinated, contain arcane wisdom. He would coincide with both Chuang-tzu and Hamlet on the providence of sparrows – viz. *Auguries of Innocence*, his Robin.

ing, with light that should intensify with each sequential exposition, to a darkness that deepened with each reflection.

But as ideas float around, and each has obscure peripheral surroundings, so nonetheless these eidolons have kept their place (as I've wandered uncertain) in particular meadows that have been there always and towards which I've stumbled with uneasy scratching.

XXIX

Those fields towards which I have been groping, held their place, I am sure, in Kubilai's imagination. These were *Sukha-vati*, a *Mahayana* Buddhist paradise, which the Great Khan would have known from Phags-pa *lama*. And this *locus amoenus* of the Western Heaven, which Kubilai intended perhaps merely to copy, represented a celestial meadow which could only be imagined in a metaphoric figuration – which, baldly quoted, appears, no doubt, simplistic:

> This Buddha country is clean, pleasant, beautiful and without fading flowers. The winds blow everywhere in the four quarters and scatter down fresh flowers. And *beings*, if touched by those winds which blow perfume with various scents, are full of happiness.
>
> In that world of *Sukhavati*, clouds of perfumed water pour down heavenly flowers, seven jewels and sandalwood powder. In that Buddha country, beings always live in absolute truth till they reach *nirvana*.
>
> And again, in that world, there are lotus lakes, adorned with the seven gems, viz. gold, silver, crystal, red pearl, diamond, coral. They are full of water which possesses eight good qualities. And again, there are heavenly musical instruments always played there and the earth is of a golden colour. And again there are in that country swans, curlews and peacocks. Three times every night and three times daily, they come together, each uttering his note. When men hear that sound, remembrance of the Buddha and his teaching rises.

From what do such imaginings arise in our world of things and bodies? Did someone, indeed, entertain this vision? I believe it. But it did not arrive in dictionary grammar, but came without lexical definition: a phenomenon of space and light, remote harmonic bliss whose identity lay beyond expression. The text, anonymous and ancient, penned on birch bark, stretched once on some Himalayan hermit's table. And the dream that lay within the ridges and the furrows of its *deva-nagari*, stood, *sans* dreamer, in a western Buddha's heaven, where the *kalavinka* finches flitted, rivers intoned their enlightenment *epode* and trees expressed incense which was sacred music.

Now I have enjoyed a parallel occurrence, albeit not sacred. Such things happen in a locus which is neither a location nor a place in the mind nor the dreamer's person. Instead, these things subvert the individual who thus subsequently falls away, replacing the self with an abyss, a crater or a cavern which receives, and also *is*, experience in which the sometime person has become its obverse or its neighbour – resembling, perhaps, that condition of a hunger, which is empty and passive: a lacuna or a circumstance of being, bare of quiddity: a shell, an empty theatre, without actor, without audience, *sans* Act I to Act V and *sans* an author.

As the mind re-awakens to its previous station, words, like sparrows that convene on our domestic sweepings, run towards it in their several duties, very busy and pecking, and bring to consciousness the darkest notion of its import, overlaying it with homespun, chirping, crusts, husks, craps of language, an expedient, metaphoric rough-wrought grammar, whose images are lifted from the *tiring house* of poesy – a wardrobe of attendants' costumes, targes, buskins, motley, and this deforms, both cloaks and ornaments, its original nature, and the figures that grew up round this, like a thick, mixed forest, cast variable shadows on it, be it bird-call, butterfly flamboyance, hymenopteral rumination, the hoof-beat of domestic cattle – or untrammelled *satyrs*. And thus, reverting to the commonplace of artifice, the quill, traducing what had been, and now is half-forgotten, limns its tawdry.

XXX A paradise story – told by Marco

'In Alamut, Lord Hulegu, who was Khan of the Levant and Persia, Kubilai's young brother and his ally, laid waste to the stronghold where a Saracen inducted his *Assassins* before sending them abroad to kill his rivals.

'This place of seclusion in the Elburz mountains was fashioned as follows: its gardens were planted with flowers and fruit trees. Streams of milk, wine, honey and fresh water ran freely through it. In pavilions built of gold and precious masonry were beautiful young women who danced, sang, dallied, played music on stringed instruments and sported on the lawns and in the orchards. The Old Man of the Mountains, so they called him, defended this Paradise with an inexpugnable castle, so that no man could enter who had not been sent there.

'Now this is how the Old Man used his garden. A few at one time, some six or ten young blades of the region who'd been chosen for their fitness, were admitted to the Old Man's presence. There he descanted on the theme of Paradise, assuring them that he, like the Prophet, could grant their admission. Having drugged them with an opiate, the Master had them carried through a secret passage to the gardens. Here they were laid out in pavilions.

'On waking from his slumber, each boy found ladies in attendance who tempted them with drink and viands, provokingly caressed them and offered every satisfaction that young hearts incline to. Thus they passed some days, and again the young men were laid out with a soporific. On waking in the Old Man's palace, each victim was questioned on what happened in his absence and then promised that the ecstasies of paradise he had enjoyed was a mere prelude: and that if he conformed to the Master's bidding and would die in his service, he'd live in Paradise for ever. In this way the Old Man bound his Assassins, who would venture into nearby kingdoms, reaching Baghdad and Damascus even, and having killed the Master's enemies, gladly paid the forfeit.

'When Kubilai's brother heard of these abuses, he assembled an army and marched on the Ismaili. Secluded as they were, the castle walls, after three years' siege, were breached, the fort laid waste, the Old Man taken and his Paradise reduced to nothing.'

What is this rigmarole from Persia? Whose dreaming? Is it comedy or history – or some moralising phantasy? Marco, who recalled the fable, had strolled Xanadu and scarcely can have swallowed this decoction of the *faery*. Or did Xanadu itself, perhaps, lend the story credit? The cool three months that young Venetian spent at Shang-du must indeed have appeared as a species of paradise. But even in such a dainty situation a man's assaulted with bad dreams and tooth-ache, intestinal fluxes, days of tedium, misunderstandings with young women and many an unsettling encounter. What, besides, might flow from Kubilai's displeasure? A valuable stallion has the warble fly. A courtesan miscarries in the Emperor's presence. All merriment ceases. The Great Khan's passion overwhelms the palace. The woman vanishes. A household steward is casually strangled. The Khan strides through his paradise gardens. He is carrying a naked weapon.

XXXI

But what of that Saracen's fictitious heaven? It was, of course, sensual and that, not the gate, its fascination and its limit. A very kitchen of

119

assassins, it was paradise reversed, where evil was rehearsed. The serpent there was the idea *ipse.* There never was a garden, nor an Old Man's palace. No besotted yunkers in those quaint and concupiscent quarters. This poisoned posset circulated in imagination. Some fruit had over-ripened. Fermented deep into the seed, the skin suppurated an intoxication. I have tasted that elixir. It repeatedly seduces. No antidote has been discovered.

XXXII

And herein lies a final *clew* on which to hang the Old Man's story. While the Great Khan built his paradise at Xanadu, his brother and auxiliary gave battle to a dream, laid siege to and destroyed, another – its Saracenic shadow. The idea remains. All artifice perishes. First history and then nature overwhelms it. Time itself, that artefact of our imagining, is fugitive and evanescent. Thus the profession of the *kalavinka* finch's singing.

XXXIII *The Mind Landscape* scroll of Chao Meng-fu

Some years before Great Kubilai summoned him to court in 1286, the painter Chao Meng-fu, a scion of the Sung nobility, had lived in retirement from the capital, at Wu-hsing, his birth place, just north of Hang-chow. There he executed his most celebrated scroll, *The Mind Landscape of Hsieh Yu-yu* – a work that summarised the very notion and the virtue of reclusion.

To comprehend Chao's composition, we should recollect its subject: which is a study of the hermit Hsieh Yu-yu, a fourth-century ascetic who, like Chao, had left the capital to live obscurely, and famously proclaimed: 'Court life is insufferable. But up in the hills, I am any man's equal'. (Familiar sentiment: the coombs above Culbone are my own best companions!)

In Chao's painting, done some thousand years later, we observe a formal, subdued landscape. No aetherial peaks with hermitages insecurely perched on shelves above crevices and fissures. No cataract vertiginously plunging. No crooked old pine, its roots in a crack and fed by the air from inaccessible and chilly fathoms. This scroll is more quiet. Its rocks billow and reach peacefully to heaven, below which sits the hermit meditating on a stream which flows gently from the top and dissipates into a river in which stones, like floating sponges, wind to the edges of the composition as though leading the viewer to a speculation on mutability and non-existence.

From patches between rock and water, emerge thin springy trees whose branches, in thick clusters, are blotted onto cliffs that stand behind them, while the deep ink of their foliage, and the lighter rocks that reach to heaven, complement each other in a mutual differentiation. This convergence is part of Hsieh's contemplation: the soft darkness of one thing correspondent to the pallor and the hardness of the other: all things coexisting in exchangeability. While reposed in his own shadow, the hermit partakes of the same transitions.[22]

This is what Chao imagined for his predecessor sage who was remembered, along with many lost to history, for his not wanting to be remembered. And so he removed himself from court (where, on account of his birth and genius, he held a position) and devoted his remaining days, or so intended, to painting and to contemplatation.

Now here's a surprise. This Chao, having fled the Mongol with his fellow literati, received a summons (it was 1286) from Great Kubilai, and with this he complied and served for the next decade as Secretary of War – which is hardly stranger – before once more withdrawing, then repeating that return – to serve Kubilai's descendants.

How Chao's acquiescence was received by colleagues is expressed by Ni Tsan, who was sometime owner of the *Mind Landscape* scroll and who inscribed this verse upon it:

This was Hsieh Yu-yu, portrayed correctly among the hills and cliffs.
But at the Gull-Wave Pavilion [which was Chao Meng-fu's residence],
As the moon went down, the window that opened to the night was
    empty.

In response to this expression of a disappointed fellow-feeling, here's a further question. If Chao could spend a decade on the Emperor's business, what might Kubilai himself have not achieved, had he sported less in his pavilion, but absconded to some holy *kiosk*?

A second thought. Strangely, for an illustration of passivity, the scroll suggests a politic opinion of the Mongol dispensation. 'This', tacitly saith Chao, 'presents a path. Our mountains and rivers are resorts of the spirit. We, only, comprehend this congruence of rock, water, pine trees and the sky, in which beings subsist in natural, often voluntary, poverty, and thus refine their coarser existence.

'Such environs for the occupier have mere military implication – a

---

22 Chao remarked once that he used a 'flying white' brush-stroke for the depiction of rock. While the streaks thus produced gave lightness of texture, he drew trees in 'large seal script', which rendered their foliage flat and static. The origin of both strokes being calligraphic, Chao's images bespeak a special poetry.

barrier behind which the Sung have retreated. The Khan may expunge the scope of my freedom. But gaze, from the vantage of Gull-Wave pavilion, on *Hsieh Yu-yu*'s landscape, and you will retrieve some parcel of its features!' These are contradictory views which compromise each other cruelly.

XXXIV *The Mind Landscape – a pendant*

Now here is further explication. This lies in the Buddhist notion of 'recluse at court' (*chao-yin*): a path of the spirit practised by the man who acts in public, but who maintains in himself a place of contemplation: remote, monastic, unassailable as Hsieh's *Landscape*: pursuing within the turmoil of a secular existence, the hermit's way without removal from society. Chao's life, like that of Hsieh, no doubt, followed this apparent bifurcation, which through a secret calming, united itself to a self-free nature.

Did Chao bestow upon his Master glimpses of this scroll he carried, as it were, within his person? For Kubilai's self-divisions were, as we have noted, fissiparous and painfully unwholesome. (Here would be teaching for him – as it is for me. I confess it freely.)

XXXV **The Great Khan and poetic distance**

It is perhaps not generally realised that Great Kubilai was a patron of the Chinese theatre and that he went to the play much as did our own Elizabeth, and in the more sophisticated comedies that were presented to him, he no doubt laughed as he was prompted by his advisors, who in turn roared with him when he burst out spontaneously – which he did now and again whether or not he understood what he was watching.

Of course the Great Khan insisted that the drama should for the most part be written in a vernacular tongue which was not Chinese. And itinerant troupes – like our home-spun sixteenth century dusty-foot – must provide a variety of entertainment. So they danced and sang and threw themselves into acrobatics and pantomime, with the result that the Great Khan, along with the rudest of labouring people and their children, could stamp his feet (when he was not too much afflicted by the gout) and sing along contentedly with these jolly species of vaudeville.

Poetry was a more difficult matter, and because I understandably associate the Great Khan with this genre, I must pause to consider how I might regard him in a relationship with that idiom.

All poetry is concerned, in some way, with the ideal and thus it aspires to one aspect or another of greatness. The *ideal* of course has different objects with which we identify it. But perfection of beauty in our own traditions is encapsulated for the most part in evocations of women whose exaltation may be translated into a language which is a reflex of what is experienced from a distance.

That which lies *within* our hand may nonetheless reach an ideal status. A wild flower, for instance, in the young hours of its morning. And yet at what stage of its existence will it fall away from this condition, whose perfection of character is anyway a repeat or a construct of our prejudice and ideation? And a cynic might argue that Laura or Beatrice need only suffer a bad night to render her face puffy, or give birth and transmogrify her *gigue* to a milk-saturated waddle. We all end up, in truth, as bags of suet – and the first face of the primrose will be soon enough a torn smut on some shepherd's boot sole.

The rites of poetry forestall such lapses. Here, natural objects are withdrawn – by the imagination which is magical in operation or through the chimical achievement of vocalic music – into abstract realms of heightened visionary language where the transient beauties of the world are removed from flux and preserved in a transmutation of their original status and thereby eternalised. This was the boast of the Latin poets and one that Shakespeare postulated in his *Sonnets*. What our poet omits is that it is the condiment of the syllabic combinations and the spices of his own most felicitous diction which serve, by distillation, to preserve what otherwise might have remained a commonplace body. Thus within his vaunting lies a seasonable modesty which one might assume to be an aspect of the devotional element which engendered the gesture. Without love for one's subject and for the process by which one seeks to modulate that impulse into poetry, one deals merely with a clay whose character lies at most in the potential of its own dullness.

In which connection, the Great Khan, as with the object of Shakespeare's admiration, is captured in my own creation and stands there – when in more analytic mode, I'm not belabouring him with satire – ablaze in a formulation whose intent is to render it indestructible and effulgent. To this I have aspired, in part, by rendering ideal his paradisal station, and thus have removed him from the duty of being entirely human. So he's reduced, in the alembic, from what is no doubt the baser metal of his historical self, to an emblem surrounded by the jewellery which is his palace with its gardens. Like the slabbed gold tokens with their *lama*-ist inscriptions given him by Kubilai that gave Marco safe passage, so the Great Khan, in my mind – as are emperors to sycophants – is made a *thing* which has been refined to a lasting representation of value.

Now this, within all the superfluous paraphernalia of his palaces, is no doubt the manner in which the Great Khan attempted both to perceive himself and to convert that self-perception into a view of him by his subordinates. This took, presumably, a force of will: for as we have observed, that elevated *self* had a tendency to topple and divide, and in so doing found it an effort to believe in the integrity of its exaltation.

Rapaciously enjoying the greatest beauties of his empire and casting each aside before she lost the perfections for which she had been taken, the Great Khan thus stood with every ideal woman, as an ideal 'husband', and within the harbour of each love room of his palace, was enclosed, like the soul of the singer with his Stella in a sonnet, a dichotomised spirit. So they hung *like caged birds*, choiring for the hours of each encounter – and the world (if it existed) stood still around them: held away from that conjugation which was, for the moments of its lasting, the centre of the empire with the Emperor, coupled as he must be in it, representing its totality and consummation.

And to such was attached an imperial gesture. 'O my America, my newe found lande,' cried Donne in his rhapsodic moment. But this occurred 'twixt thoroughly and rough-rubbed Cheapside sheets, and if later, the poet re-organised that same linen to a proleptic figuration of his burial shroud, that was the limit of its distance from him. When, however, Kubilai received his maidens, he was consummating an imperial embrace, and laying a seal upon those regions which had prostrated themselves for his possession – which ownership, in private, by synecdoche, in series, he confirmed as their lover. In this way the Great Khan husbanded his empire and possessed it, as our young, salt sonneteers desired to hold their more limited madams – to whom they cried, nonetheless, over the distances that were measured by the inaccessibility of their end point. *Sans* which we'd have no gold or silver sixteenth-century poetry.

XXXVI Epode – happy palace and its poetry

Having in imagination visited the Great Khan's dome (so call it), I have, five centuries on, enjoyed the good fortune to sit with that Emperor, observe his person and, I hope, divine some aspects of his thoughts and affects. With respect to his private life I am therefore confident that while his satisfactions were great, he experienced longings to which he could neither attach words nor confide to any person.

Knowing that his presence in the north of China had sped the *literati* into exile, the Great Khan wished earnestly that some few more might have stayed who could have taught him to express his higher mind – or find if such a thing existed.

There they sat, the Sung *intelligentsia*, in huts on cloudy mountains or in riverine pavilions, contemplating movements of the air and water, exiled from work that would support them, while making with a melancholy confidence, poetry and paintings in which future viewers would detect – through ironies concealed in literary tropes and enigmatic brush strokes (whose dry textures were expressive of contempt for grosser modes of being) – the unhappiness of their displacement.

How little Great Kubilai knew his own good fortune. And given that his empire would have lapsed by the middle fourteenth century, how short-sighted. Nor could he comprehend, that while he, too, must live in an exile of a sort, respect for his stature would endure with two descendants only, representing to them, as somewhat shakingly he does for me, an emblem of poetic reverie in somewhat forlorn a radiation.

None of this would concern us, were it not for the record left by Kubilai's grandson, Toghon Temur, the last Yuan ruler: who composed this lament on his own displacement to the Mongol homeland when the first Ming Emperor drove him from the Ta-du palace:

Ta-du! Splendid city! My vast and noble city.
And thou my summer residence at Shang-du Keibung!
You too, yellow plains of Shang-du
Where my ancestors took pleasure.
I fell into a sleep and dreamed.
My Empire had gone!
And Ta-du of the precious, beautiful materials!
Ah Shang-du which united the perfections.
Alas for my fame and glory as Khagan:
I who lorded the whole Earth!
When I woke and looked out from the palace,
How fresh the breeze, and how loaded with perfume!
Turn which way I might: I saw everything was beautiful.
And all was perfection. Alas for my Ta-du,
Sanctified seat of immortal Kubilai!

All Kubilai had owned thus passed – so the Buddhists might have warned him – and those who had oppressed the Han Chinese were exiled to their *quondam* country. In which connection, it's worth noticing the pathos of this fellow's separation. All China had been in his possession.

125

These, so he cries, were in his ancestry (how short that sequestration!) And now this Mongol chieftain indites Chinese poetry to lament the loss of what those recent forebears stole and handed to him.

Recall, in this regard, the vatic agons that some Mongol scribe attributed to Genghis and his mother. In contrast to which, Great Kubilai thought and spoke in prose his ministers translated into proclamations. In contrast to which, the hapless Toghon had absorbed so full an education in decorum that he made, as he left China, an urbane panegyric in literary Chinese, correct in dutiful Confucian sentiment, to honour Kubilai. Such ironies lie far beyond their mere expression.

I append these verses from a Chinese poet of the Yuan, lost to history. Perhaps every soul on the east side of the Wall that Toghon left behind him, had experience of like displacement?

> Fur rags on a dusty stallion.
> Somebody's whip stirs reed-flowers at the roadside.
> From the saddle, bow and sword hang sadly.
> A path lost in mist. West wind among pine trees.
> Autumn. Floods. A homeless feeling.
> Crows gather in the evening.
> Geese land on a sand bank.
> They cry out of habit.

Thus goes all that bravely grows toward the *everlasting bonfire* – albeit from the ashes, phoenix seeds may germinate and re-initiate the cycle. So let us, with our own brief lives and numbers, do that honour and enjoy it. Lament, therefore, to no great effect, thou long-since-driven-out-of-China, Toghon Temur, and wander, with the shades of Mongol warriors, this overgrown path to Shang-du's ruins. Grey with dust the poppies on this terrace sunk in grass whose roots grip who-knows-what composted horseman's reliques. The Great Khan's hawks *ha' ta'en another mate* – an unknown *maister*.

XXXVII

I dreamed of Xanadu the other Night. All in a broken and apocalyptic Light. Self-dissipated in unmeasured ocean Caves of Sleep – Entwined with Weeds of Memory, Abstraction, Speculation, Trance:

As Rocks against a fortressed Island, hurled, Those Images shelved back, split, spilled and were engulfed or fractured in co-active Dance: All Reverie effaced – And what had been illuminated by the Night, dispersed, discharged, dissolved – And were eclipsed by Light.

XXXVIII

It is five years or more since Spode brought out his table-pieces in the *Willow* Pattern, and it's been my good fortune to have received a set, *via* Wedgwood, who had travelled from his potteries to see me with it. The bowl in my hand, like much of such tea-ware, copies, somewhat loosely, blue-and-white ceramic which is made at Ching-te Chen on the Yangtze river, thence carried to Nankin and transported past the Cape (boxed down in the bilge atop the ship's ballast) to Bristol.

The painting on these cups tells a story as follows. In mid-picture are three figures: the first, a father who runs across a Chinese bridge, flourishing a whip with which to beat his daughter and her lover. Behind this stands a tea house with an orange tree above it. A knotty willow leans aslant the water where a boat is anchored to receive the couple. A fence, the lover had transgressed, enfolds the foreground. Two birds (not *kraunchas*) flirt above the willow. It is a sentimental tale. And while components of the scene are drawn from oriental landscape, the romance is a fiction dreamed up in a Stafford manufactory.

Now as to cups in China, what they say is – Nothing: these vessels being reticent and modest as to colour, shade, shape, decoration and dimension, and whose fundamental nature lies in self-effacement. A tea bowl is – a *Buddha* of utensils – nought but a hemisphere which stands open to what comes, from time to time, by chance, to fill it. Some day, in Old Time's vast, audacious spaces, this vehicle will shivver.

Thus to contemplate a cup as such (the Sanskrit *tathatā* postulates such 'thusness') is to know the temporality of all phenomena. It is hard and fragile. Its stout, unspotted glaze suggests an ideality of form without content. Its gracious emptiness proclaims perfection. But howsoever it's sublime, a mundane earth – that *loess*, which since the world began, has blown through northern China from the Gobi desert – informs its surface, kiln-baked in the 'dragon's entrail' of a terrace excavated from a garden slope which once supported greener mustard.

Now in contrast to this elevated tea-bowl is our busily and briskly, thickly printed *Willow*. And while the former guards a quiet sequestration, the latter prattles at a gentleperson's table – which, for better or nay, is where it finds me.

XXXIX

If I've digressed here, lead me *Musa* (vocatively speaking) back to Xanadu – and Culbone. For my notion is simple. Just as Spode applied a *transfer*, once engraved, to biscuit, and then dipped his tea-cup in the glaze of that specific tin he had decocted, so I've projected my own print, which is blue with distance, across Culbone: imposing, in this process, *Xanadu*, on homely grazings – as though glossing, with a cobalt I've extracted from a current in the Bristol Channel – pastures which speak, jarringly, of China and of Mongol grasslands: rolling, as these will yet, from Dolon-nur (the modern city), whose outskirts touch the Great Khan's palace ruins, and thence due west to Samarcand and Karakorum.

XL

We have, in Kubilai's mind, attempted murmurings, close-lapped and hemmed, with synchronous or co-extensive edges from time's hubbub, each of which claimed, in disparate co-ordination, the attention of their Master as he scanned the borderland he'd stretched, Colossus-like, his thighs, in gouty aches, to straddle, from one fiefdom to another – Shang-du to a green infinitude – as if every antecedent led to, and hence sealed and blessed, his rule, *qua* culmination, so he might have dreamed, of history.

What remains may be said in a very few words – and these straightforwardly or more or less so. We can't perambulate that garden. Not least, descry the margins that cut one part from another.

For just as the Great Khan hearkened to those ghosts of tribes in mutual displacement, so his ear engaged with susurrations made successively from precincts, mostly lost now, of dynastic notables, whose 'wind and water', Kubilai's engineers and hierophants enjoined gardeners to copy.

With this difference. For to coincide, was one thing, with tradition which had made the landscape, by an act of concentration, more Chinese in provenance – its native province – and in continuities of imitation. Rarer, that this *parvenu*, who also cultivated China, should re-enact – in realisation of a memory or geste of the imagination – the notion or idea of pasture and, abstracting for his *recreation*, Mongol steppeland, subjoin to those spaces that close-hedged the palace with its ornamental ponds and streams that drew migrating fowl to fish there, and in turn to be shot at from a terrace – this artefact or simulacrum of what had made him, once, a shepherd rider, who in freedom had roistered with his falcons, and hallooed, unjessed in their swoops and soaring, on wind that carried to him a mixed emphasis of thyme and grasses, draughts of mare's milk and the blood he supped fresh from his stallion's shoulder.

Culbone Wood Journal 4

I came a mile or so through beech woods and finally an arch at the crest of the forest gave onto a meadow in the dip where some fifteen men and boys were at a game of cricket. It was a green sward, at once sylvan and pastoral, in this ample, sunlit glade, while three men from the side that was batting swept scythes, like sharpened bat blades through long grasses at the boundary area.

As I stood at the wood's edge in a space made by a geometry of beech roots and leaned my hot back on a trunk, the scene that lay below me moved in two coordinated patterns: the batsmen shuttling, as it were, within a loom, whose encompassing framework, represented by the fielders, lay in attachment to and separation from

those figures at their centre who flailed with their weapons and ran as though weaving a fabric which was at once spun from the body of their own activity and also out of the stuff which the opposed, surrounding mechanism of the fielders contributed.

Viewed from the path, as I'd come through the wood, the scene, reduced by distance, appeared like a panel in a stained glass window whose pigments were so concentrated and whose figures so distinct in a quasi-hieratic separation that I thought at first I had come upon some ceremonial - only music was lacking - as in a round dance or some antique mummery.

But this is just a game - so I chided my enthusiastic vision. But still I returned to those mowers on the boundary. They, too, will *go in*. And once in, by the end, will be dismissed - perhaps for nothing.

I returned through the trees and glancing one last time behind me, observed that the mowers were reduced to two. And wandering on, recalled Marvell, whose *Mower's Song* has it:

And Flow'rs and Grass, and I and all
Will in one common Ruine fall.
For *Juliana* comes, and She
What I do to the Grass, does to my Thoughts and Me.

Which is the *Psalm* and Seneca or Cicero, made dark by Eros. While Shakespeare in his Sonnet warns his leman

... nothing can 'gainst Time's *scythe* make defence
Save breed to brave him, when he takes thee hence.

The final comma, with a lifetime hanging on it, placed at the caesura, is Shakespeare or his 1609 compositor. They spell 'scythe' *sieth*: a dry, sharp, whetted, sweeping sound that suggests both *saith* and *sigheth*. To which, at the risk of hubris, I append here:

Thus Time *scythes* us with a *sigh*,
Which is its own and ours.
For this same *sighing* is
What Time's scythe *sayeth*.

Away from the cricket, which game sets with sundown, the word 'scythe' in the Sonnet follows *hideous, sable, silvered, leaves, erst, sheaves, bristly* and *wastes*: these, among other, secondary sibilants, we all shall be scythed down by. Let us therefore play to the end while light holds in the meadow!

And may lovely *Juliana* also come,
Howsoe'er she *sighs* down some.

My urine, I notice this morning, is turned green and indeed smells as such. This, I suppose, on account of my having eaten asparagus last evening. Delectable vegetable. And I am gratified that it has continued to transform at least a part of me. If this was my last piss, I would bless it. Green and twisting, as asparagus tips, *ipse*.

Sweet Laudanum – *Deserted Village*.

Returning from my walk, another young woman. I saw her seated between two apple trees, smiling generously as she gave her breast, while the lips of the infant were extended at her in a paradisal gluttony. His lips were thin and empurpled round her teat and she laughed as he tugged in a delirium of her sweetness.

I was drunk on myself (the usual kind of human animal). Therefore what she sang, I don't remember. I recall, nonetheless, her lullaby expressed a rapture that was milk and honey. So with her infant, I too drank it. (Piercing sweetness half remembered from transfiguration of a childhood!)

Three older children played beneath the blossom, their faces upturned like wood anemones in changing shadow – illumined from sideways in a tactful contribution to the sunlight.

Now a bloody Phlegethon has engulfed my brain and my red heated thought is rushed along it, thrown up from the vein but not cooled before its tumbles back and in again.

Such thought has the consistency of the hot, rocky current from which it emerged: and as to its shape, it appears about to set, to consolidate from its initiality. But at the moment when its seems ready to achieve some form that I could put a hand to or be moulded, it returns to the Phlegaean flux where it's thrown about once more and deformed as in the tumult of it first emergence.

The degree to which one is tormented by desire is in proportion to the extent to which one is, and apprehends oneself to be, in a process of dissolution.

It is Man's fate to be in a situation of uninterrupted want: and it is this lies at the heart of Paradise stories. For Paradise is that orchard in which everything is perpetually in a condition of perfected growth: every fruit being ripe, while the desire to eat and gustatory satisfaction must (paradoxically: I do not believe this) be in equal and simultaneous fulfilment. Paradise, in other words, offers the experience of a hunger which is no less happy than post-prandial gratification.

Man's own perfection in Paradise, too, was realised: both he and his fellow creatures being at once new and altogether completed. The Genesis story, on the other hand, would appear to contain another, secret, teaching. Indeed perhaps several. Beneath the perfection that radiates from each gladdening and golden rind lurk both liabilities for deliquescence and the energies that lie in seed, which will scatter and grow, but whose scions, howsoever husbanded, degenerate across their generations.

On this propensity to putrefaction: nothing is immune from the cycle of mortality. But it is Man's imperfection that preoccupies me here. Marvell spoke only for himself when he observed (with naughty wit!) that it would be double paradise to live in paradise alone. Not so Adam for whom God must, at that man's request, create a partner and in so doing remove from his body a rib which hitherto had been a constituent of his wholeness.

In the midst of perfection, therefore, Adam knew that desire which emanates from the experience of incompleteness. Pefection was not, in itself, sufficient. Indeed, that apprehension of the incomplete was a part of perfection, which therefore must have contained, in itself, incompleteness.

And while one might argue, as perhaps the rabbis have, that to enjoy some object, one must extract it, as in the case of Adam's operation, from *oneself*, there remains what I have suggested as a secret teaching: for having achieved that object, which was Eva, then the seed had already fallen and the cycle of renewal, in the shape of progeny which implies both growth and degeneration, was set in motion.

How all this applies to my condition here, having written my poem more or less successfully on this sheep farm, I will set out briefly. Alone in this place, I have brought forth, as though from the interior of my body, this object and I am made glad by it. And yet it was a kind of suffering, albeit in the ecstasy of sleep, that sired its birth: for I would never have fabricated such a work had I felt complete enough before I wrote it to abstain from its composition. Like Adam I conceived desire. And just as Eva must be formulated from her future husband's rib (in the androgeny of our first Father lies a tempting subject), so this poem issued from my person. I am tempted to jest – from the flux of my intestine!

Here, then, it lies in its fragmentary perfection. Albeit – like a child which is drawn out from its mother with sweet ease at the first push but who emerges from the knees in a truncated mutilation – the second half is cruelly missing.

The object of these thoughts is mortifyingly straightforward. In just proportion to my desire, so I feel myself dying. Indeed, I apprehend it now. The shoots and the streaks that would force themselves up and come into the sun from a hidden or inchoate self are already on the path to nether regions. (I am one with the crocus bulb that throws up her brave and spear-like flowers which are stiff in their first tumescent thrust and then flap in the wind, collapse and are flattened – by sun, rain or wind and a hapless disappointment.)

Perhaps more to the point – for it is of the body and its mental products I am speaking – in desire for a woman, fulfilled or not it matters little, what I most express is my mortality. Death flashes up to me at every movement. In like manner, performs poetic aspiration, confected as this is of desire to run counter to infernal torrents that roar to extinction and which then in themselves are lost in the labyrinthine amplitude of Lethe's winding and the Acheronic marshes.

Helpfully pessimistic and pre-emptive wisdom, one is tempted to conjecture. But such knowledge, if one may so call it, is feeble. For against all stoical or noble forethought, desire may never be extinguished. *Go little booke* I would love to murmur as though remitting my work to join and even build on *unswept stone* or *gilded monuments*. But in my craving to force some formulation of the language on the world, I inhume what I have written, as in one of Shakespeare's blackest Sonnets, *with vilest worms to dwell.*

Here is no morbid apprehension or pessimist imagining. I hear them palpably chew, as the words that I submit to the heavenly Muses vermiculate and squirm across these pages.

We have a reasonably clear understanding of why and in what manner the angels rebelled, the consequences of their fall and the relationship of that to human imperfection. What excites my curiosity is the question of angelic physiology. Conventionally, I have been led to assume that angels would have been constituted from light whose order and intensity was predicated by their status in the angelic hierarchy. This heavenly light, I assume, represented a reflective quantity which had been borrowed from or been freely bestowed by the inexhaustible sum of God's endogeny: and thus these aspects of Him were externalised into entities which, in their partial separation from Him into angelic bodies, radiated back to His effulgence. That the angels existed in freedom from their source, further suggests both God's generosity and a danger to whatever He had become (by subtraction?) as a result of these operations.

Given what we know of the outcome – angelic history differs from ours in that there has been only one recorded war in heaven – I have been reflecting on what it may have felt like to have been Satan.

All I surmise is that the satanic body, like that perhaps of every fallen angel, felt much as ours do when we undergo a fever. Thus while angels that continued to submit to heaven, experienced such lightness and smoothness that the word *body* as we understand it must represent a misnomer, in Satan's case, the dulcetude and purity whose texture was air and whose movement implied music, was transformed to a heavy and coarse-textured, complicated, aching density, whose marrow was knife blades at sharp angles to each other and whose flesh was filled with hot, dry ashes.

This is my notion, my only opinion: that we who are poets are fools of the Muse, from whose realm of gilded mountain flanks she beckons, in the knowledge that we will never reach the zone of her *arcanum.*

Obediently, we stumble off the road towards her mountain, but in no time we lose sight of it. If, meanwhile, we have the good fortune to encounter a child or some goat herd who is idle but who understands the by-ways of Parnassus, we may grope a road homeward. Once back at the hearth, we will sit, for the duration, on our care-worn arses and, at best, write doggerel.

There may, however, exist a less morbid sequence to these prospects. Viz: from illness, on account of its position between life and final silence, comes vision – and from this vision emerges the poem. All poetry with a claim to a truth of some description must have engaged with a point of origin at this same oscillating locus of fatality. It emerges, in other words, from a *travail* in which the sickness from which we are hourly expiring leads us to the simplest but most exalted intuition: and this is to sing in an ecstasy from which aspiration has been voided. Death of course stands always at the poet's elbow. It sharpens his bone for him to write with. Its loosens his occiput for the poet's eye to gaze through. In a rapture! Wonder!

Further to the nature of angelic bodies and the contrast I have suggested between hot, rough cinders and a celestial kind of music: smoothness and coolness come into the experience, and these latter represent an aspect, in our own lives, of corporeal well-being, a condition somewhat rarely achieved, in which all the faculties operate in wholesome quiet: not a squeak or a click from our babbling intestine nor any panic-stricken syncopation of the heart against the chest and rib-cage, the blood serenely running, the liver and brain compacted in a mutual sympathy: then the body, having of itself achieved a regulated and tranquil homeostasis, may be experienced somewhat to drop away from the intellectual func-tion, leaving the mind thus in a condition of near perfected detachment whereby it finds itself suspended no longer in an environment, which has become familiar to daily experience, of blood-rush, hurly-burly and discomfort, but in which it is fed simply by the air which enters the system and returns out to the aether in soft and scarcely perceptible movements, to the extent that flesh too now joins itself to that medium and is homologised with the lightness which bathes, in gentle tides, the far reaches and the full extent of its interior, thus rendering it at one with that universal quietness in which plants achieve their native and compliant nature and into which all creatures, though they scarcely know this, man included (truculently), turbulently, struggle.

In the wings of the theatre. Actors in various stages of address and decoration, stage mechanics, managers, the wardrobe mother, wig-makers and cosmetic artists, the clutter of props and lamps extending out to light the apron and the rise and drop of flats, which lusty young men who will never see the fair side of the curtain heave up and down with ropes and on pulleys.

In commotions which are screened entirely from the audience, musicians, singers, dancing masters, stage hands, painters, messengers and other theatre servants slither whispering past one another as the principals run, stroll or hobble on and off through the action.

All that is missing backstage in this crucible, invisible, of mystery, is the voicing of the drama. This latter is projected to the public on the other side, as though *out there* was some faery realm of irreality. And here also, off stage, in a silence which is shared, as if in speeches that extend on threads, inaudibly between the actors, who wait passively within earshot of the drama's progress.

Back stage, then, the play is present in this manner: withheld and in separated and unspoken parts, and these remain, as in the abstract form wherein they were written, until taken forward to where, for the audience, they are fitted, for a brief duration, into the pattern of the speeches which constitute the drama – after which they disappear until the following night's production.

Within all this hugger mugger, which is no less theatrical than what goes forth into the *auditorium*, all the actors have their proper names and characters. Each spends his day as himself, in his home, in lodgings or in eating houses, pursuing his own unscripted life – alone, with lovers or with friends and family. As each day, piecemeal in its conjugations as the backstage drama, unfolds, the persona which the actor will that night inhabit hovers somewhere in the shade of what he's conscious. All he thinks mingles vaguely with speeches – dreamily in the absence of stage interlocutors – that he will deliver at nightfall from the proscenium.

As afternoon drags on to evening, in the hour before the curtain rises, the actor's twilit half-life starts up once again, and his uncostumed self prepares to slide into that other person. Disguised in costume, wig and grease paint, and handling whatever props – for Caesar, Anthony or Richard – he will pick up and let go as the action demands, the actor is transmuted, paradoxically, in neither exactly this life nor the other, to the semi-achieved status of a double being.

Once dressed and he steps out on the apron, he must synthesise and simplify: evacuate his true self and merge with the individual he has been engaged to impersonate that evening. Thus his costume comes *true* in this very process and for a brief few minutes, or at best two hours, he is simply that being, about whom there is nothing beyond words in a *quarto* play book.

In contemplation of all this, I think of Garrick, and most especially in his role as Richard III which he played some fifty years back at the Drury Lane Theatre. (That noble building gone, alas, for ever now.) A sweet, dear man, Garrick, but preoccupied with fame to so wonderful a degree that when he woke each morning, so I imagine, he informed his pillow:

'Good morrow. David Garrick greets you.'

And to his linen: 'Garrick rises.'

And addressing his tea cup: 'Garrick will now breakfast.'[23]

On stage that evening, Garrick must be cognizant, not just of himself and of his lines, but of who was in the house to watch him – his friends Johnson, Burke and Pope among them. Pope, in this connection, is known three times to have witnessed Garrick at the Theatre Royal where he played the role of Richard – this as recorded in Hogarth's portrait of him – dreaming on his murders.

No doubt Garrick held Pope in somewhat higher view than he did his tea cup, and so I postulate, with this short speech for him, a postlude to my dithyrambic fancy:

I am Garrick. Since Burbage, Tarlton, Kempe and Armin,
The most celebrated actor. And, as at this moment, I play Richard,
Pope sits down there, somewhere, hid in the darkness.
And aye, hark'ee! I hear scratching – and his shrill, low whisper.

(Is that Alexander Pope I see before me, a quill poised in his hand?
Is that he in his high seat, which, raised next to Johnson,
Appears like a mirror to reflect my own figure:
Our persons doubled in a couplet that is Pope and Garrick?)

But hold! Wrapped as I am now in King Richard's numbers
And lapped round with his armour, how far may I remain, indeed,

---

23 I recalled, later, Goldsmith's affectionate epitaph for Garrick which contains this couplet:
On the stage he was natural, simple, affecting;
'Twas only that when he was off he was acting.

As Garrick? The lines – which Pope and I have harmonised
To complement our century's graces – flow out from my person.

Pope watches. Listens. Shakespeare stretches from the swanlike
Neck of Garrick and thence out to our poet. Pope hears Richard.
Does this, for him, obfuscate the player that was Garrick?
And how much Garrick is there for the poet to reflect on, as Richard
Scintillates before him in the glamour that has overwhelmed him?

I know little of the theatre and I have written the above merely as a
figure to illustrate some inflexions of what I have myself experienced in
the composition of poetry. This.

Just as that fustian whose props, thespians and costumes, flats, wings,
stage-hands, extras and disguises converge in a construction from whose
union the play issues, so poetry is generated in a play of collaborative
mental eventualities with its scenery and recollections, masks, images and
dreams which cling in the amorphous shade of half-truth and similitude
to such diction as the poet has assembled in his apprenticeship of a
diverse study.

And just as the theatre represents a working place in which things,
characters and functions must co-operate in back-stage obscurity for the
purpose of projecting the transient movements of a drama, so the mind
has its population of intellectual agencies which are at work with an
accumulation of properties whose interactions conspire to produce poetry
when it becomes ready to step on to the proscenium of an empty sheet
of paper.

And just, likewise, as it is a confusion of phenomena that act together
behind the curtain that produce the illusory integration of a drama that
takes place on the proscenium, so poetry that arrives on the page represents a 'front product' issuing from a confusion of *quaint devices* that have,
in conformity with all manner of aesthetic desiderata, been refined and
made symmetrical. To read a poem thoroughly, one must comprehend
the surface of its rhetoric with a cunning which is sufficient to divine
the nature of the apparatus that lies behind it. Without knowledge of
its props, masks, costumes, sceneries and back stage chatter, a poem is
mere flat film which has settled nervelessly on an equally flat surface.

I woke this morning from a dream which had in view three large, un-
titled, leather-bound volumes. Sprouted from their edges I descried several
shrivelled extensions of the print in their interior as if extracted passages

had been torn out and tattered. This phrase in my dream followed: 'If on that pathway ...' and then I woke. In reaction to this, these fragmentary reflections:

First, that we poets are wont to imagine that the paths for which we are destined should be furnished with a pavement for others to accompany us along, and that this will be impacted with the books that we will eventually have finished. Secondly: like actors who get stuck in parts they play and who never can extricate themselves properly from speeches which express the thoughts and actions of imagined people, poets, through sheer habit, become what they have written.

Give, thirdly, such a fellow a couple of decades to pursue literary ambition, and, through association with the materials of his daily intercourse, he transmigrates into a species which is peculiar to his calling. I see such creatures up and down the country (and indeed in my own somewhat cloudy psychological mirror) attempting what they imagine to be casual association with that majority of citizens which has nothing to do with the begetting of literature. And while we recognise these latter as enjoying a human outline, the poet may be observed to have metamorphosed into the shape of an ambulatory bound volume, sheathed in creaking leathers, from whose fore-edges and spines, little feeble arms and legs have sprouted and whose middle places – heart, lights and liver – have shrunk to the consistency of stale, dry paper.

Such, when we lie down in a completed anonymity, becomes our solitary monument. Constructed not from rocks of marble and with gilded panegyrics, but built from our own reduced, transmuted beings, where the book-worm blunders with its head through our stanzas and the earwig scatters its dark, granular deposits.

In pursuit of poetic truth, one may create a monster of oneself to achieve a mere approximate intention. The nature of that deformation lies in its composite identity, the parts of which are disparate and usually incongruous: the celebrated biform, for example, that was the issue of Pasiphae's infatuation with a bull and which became the presiding spirit of the labyrinth. A writer's own labyrinthine person contains several such manifestations. They are accretions of the diverse energies that adapt to one another in the twilight of his interior and of whose confluence he is often, most likely, unaware.

I have seen a model of Cellini's *Perseus* whose hand is plunged in that thick bed of snakes which crowns the Medusa. Perseus exerts a muscular,

determined grasp. But unlike him, we can neither deracinate nor extermi-
nate that interfusion of mental vipers. This is because they have nested
in our brains, where, having once hatched in the nourishing and warm
heart's egg, they have grown upward. Palpable, perhaps, but indiscern-
ible without some externalising mirror of the sort Perseus held up, with
his shield, to the Gorgon. And then struck her head off as, for the first
time, in that burnish, she observed herself – preserving the reflection
for Cellini's copy!

Considering again the Gorgon's head Cellini modelled. I would say that
when a sculptor cuts stone away from the form he is determined to reveal,
by the same token, he builds into it the *emergency* of his conception and
that this is what becomes expressed. All beauty grows forward from some
previously opaque quintessence and what we see, which has been brought
to the surface, is informed by an interior modelling without whose presence, the surface (of a nothing) slips away, revealing the emptiness from
which it was, perhaps, unwisely dared.

Any form that has properly been achieved thus arrives from two in-
teriors: that of some material – wood, stone or the flux of language – and
abstract stuff of the imagination. Thus it is that what gets done comes alive
from behind. And those who contemplate it from the outside are animated
in harmony with both projected and discovered centre. Such a work then
finds its place within the viewer's person, where in the complexity of a
meditation, it may serially, and for ever, be recovered.

How the gods struggled with a spectacle of human beauty is attested
by Ovid. And how Apollo (or his like) felt flesh against them and young
women sensed a god's thrust from that hypostatic body, is a matter for
lubricious speculation.

Everything is mutable and all things smoothe into another musically,
just as Ovid's verses swim in singing through the forms and species, which
at a god's touch, change into another's character.

In parallel with these exchanges, lie incompatibilities of deities and
humans who share the upper air with allegorical *personae* whose nature,
qua identity as flesh or spirit, is uncertain.

One such in Ovid is the figure of *Invidia*. First, before we're introduced
to her we learn Minerva's angry. I forget the reason. Though in the background there are Hermes and a girl he visits (not her jealous sister). All's
to do with lust and pulchritude. But when anger bred from thwarted

gropings after beauty feast on its imagining, revenge is liable to choose a resolution of its outrage in a region of the horrid.

'Minerva,' writes Ovid, 'straightway sought the filthy cave of Envy. Her home was hidden in a sunless valley – numbing, gruesome situation.'

Now here's a convergence. What's divine purports to loveliness and immortality. But Invidia – a lumpish, brooding female who subsists alone on snakes' flesh – is a deathless, self-consuming figure: pale, heavy, sullen, stinking, venomous, infected: neither deity nor human, but a congeries of physical and psychic properties, loathsome to both gods and people. Existence for Invidia, in Ovid's sentence, is 'to gnaw and to be gnawed'. Wherever Envy walks she tramples flowers, blasts the tree-tops and contaminates whole cities. While having need of her, fastidious Minerva can't tolerate her squalor. Still, when (from anxious distance) she commands Invidia infect a woman who's offended her, the slut concurs with surly acquiescence – while envying the joy the goddess takes in malice!

Now whereas God blew life through Adam – breathed *ruach* (wind or spirit) in him which had travelled across primal water – *Invidia* exhales pestilence into her victim. And just as Adam sprang up in the clean, fresh spirit of a gardener, so the object of Minerva's anger, through Invidia, is transformed to a simulacrum of the latter. Thus the girl the goddess hates eats envy and is eaten with self-eating:

> Just as when a fire is set beneath a pile of weeds
> And these waste gradually with slow consumption,
> So the girl's cremated (*crematur* is Ovid's passive).

And when, *en passant*, she is touched by Hermes on his way to ply her sister's body, the girl's invaded by a *cancer inmedicabile*. Her breathing freezes. Her neck turns to stone and words, if she still has them, harden in it. There, at the end, she sits, a statue, blackened by her soul's taint, at the threshold of the chamber where her sister waits for Hermes' visit.

While we can extract *Invidia* intact from Ovid and comprehend her operation without too much antecedent, in Dante – given, as suggested by the poet, that the Muse Calliope controls his epic – the thought is complicated, across thirteen *Cantos*, till he treats with Envy as the foil or a disturbance to a continuity of images and figures whose impulse, through successive waves of light, is towards a grander resolution which is the radiance of *Paradiso*.

First, recall 'Invidia' derives from *invidere:* 'to look askance at, glance maliciously or cast the evil eye upon' the happiness of others. This in itself is a perversion of what should in humane intercourse be clear, direct, reciprocating, sympathetic and receptive. Second, in the circumstance of punishment that Dante, with a high-toned Christian fancy, chooses for those souls which had as mortals lived in envy, we should note it is, in consonance with *in-videre*, the eyesight of these sinners punished:

chè a tutte un fil di ferro il ciglio fora,
e cuce sì, come a sparvier selvaggio
sì fa, però che queto non dimora.

For the eyelids of the Envious were stitched up,
Like an errant falcon's, with an iron wire.

I won't expatiate on this barbarity. But trace briefly instead how *light* it was, by increment and repetition, interlarded with defining shadow, led two poets to the spectacle of Envy.

Now in contrast to the penitents whose eyes are *seeled* (a verb from falconry employed by Shakespeare in *Macbeth* etc.) Virgil, who is Dante's guide, enjoins him: 'Fix thine eyes through the air quite steadily'. To which the younger: 'So I opened my eyes wider': a visionary moment as two *Seers* who have climbed from darkness watch together!

Next, emerged from the *Inferno*, unfouled, on the flat shore at the foot of Purgatory Mountain, Dante surveys latitudes of time that both binds the round world to its calendar and separates its regions. Venus, rising, flames in Pisces as she had done at the stroke of the Creation (our First Parents were cast out into the Northern Hemisphere that evening!), and their minds relieved, with sober happiness, of Hell, as *morta poesi risurga*, the pilgrim poets reach the Second Realm at sunrise, where a 'colour sweet of oriental sapphire gathers on the forehead of the sky' surrounding *Purgatorio*: and Dante – while Aurora's pale cheek fills with crimson – in his rapture, at the same time, apprehends the sunset in Jerusalem (antipodes of Purgatory) coincident with dawn there, and conjures Midnight's hand that lets fall *Libra*, or the Balances, on Ganges River.

I can't itemise each instance of the light, in either constancy and intermittence, that streams through Dante's exposition. To cite a few disjunct examples, there is 'whiteness (vehicle of angels) coming from the sea'. While the poet notes his body, in a moment of reflection, interrupts the sun to throw a shadow, while Virgil, disinterred from Brindisi and requisitioned by the Emperor Augustus for re-burial in Naples, who's now a shade and throws no shadow, recalls, poignantly, how once he cast the image of an earthly figure. The same complicated planet *Sol*, in Canto IV, acts as a mirror to the radiance of Godhead, which travels north and south in alternating movement, while having heard, some Cantos later, the Souls' *Compline* with their chant *Te lucis ante*, the reader is invited: 'Sharpen well thine eyes to truth: the veil is thin' (a fine promise, hard to credit!).

In another Canto, Dawn, with the suggestion of a saffron borrowed from *Tithonus* in Virgil is invoked: as though behind each tercet that ascends to Paradise (the three-line stanzas linked into a stair, one ledge of *terza rima* rising to another) are pagan burnings which infuse, with classic light, the optimism Purgatory offers. Last (though not exhaustively, by antecedent) Pity opposite to envy's sordid glancing – stays the poet when he views those shades which sit together on the penitential terrace, each self-enclosed and huddled mutually remote in its privation, while light pours, unregarded by them, down from Paradise that tops Purgatory's fertile summit.[24]

The signs, the angles, houses, the meridia, symmetric antipodal hours, horizons, moving spheres, fixed stars, planets in alignment, zenith and ecliptic, the degrees the sun traverses, when it's 6 am in Purgatory and pm in Jerusalem – all this Dante felt in motion round his small, warm mortal effort to pursue the limits of his moral voyage. I don't comprehend those wheelings, involutions, planes and astronomic correspondences. All I see is two small bodies (one translucent), at once close and distant: cloaked and sandalled, dark within the universal circulation Dante walks through, as the light streams down and draws him upward.

Cowled and – here's my interest – with their eyes mewed, sit the Envious. They too are overwhelmed with light from Heaven. But they can't see it or enjoy the view it offers – unless between the iron stitches, they glimpse filaments of God's light: double torment, for they know it's there, but sit in darkness which is of the self, in separation. Once, in daylight, they could *look askance* – 'desiring this man's art etc.': but now, in purifying penitence, they are compelled to rest *with what they most enjoy contented least*, the verb *invidere* reversed sharply inward!

---

24 The roll's been with us for some centuries, so I won't rehearse its culmination – beyond recalling that by Canto V we've met a goodly company of penitents: from la Pia, German Albert, Montefeltro, Rudolf Ottocar, Sordello, Peter the Third and Charles of Anjou, William the Marquis and Conrad Malaspina. (Had I the gift, I would, with these *personae*, write a comedy progresses, like *The Winter's Tale*, from near damnation to deliverance!)

Envy is aroused when we regard ourselves in relation to that which we conceive as being the experience of other people. Shakespeare summarises this in Sonnet XXIX – as also in the acts of Iago, Edmund, Don John etc. (no ladies in that company!). And these present us with the most profound explorations of how it feels to be in dispossession. For what we 'most enjoy' may very well exceed, without our knowing it, the sum of things that we imagine others to possess.

While envy may be accounted a sin, it is also instructive to contemplate it as an attribute allied to the perception of incompleteness that afflicted, as we have suggested, the rebel angels – whose corrosion is an emblem of our own most besetting of conditions. For to envy that other man's presumed good fortune is to effect, from ourselves, a subtraction which diminishes us, and we can never truly be that whole self which had been set growing in childhood when our lives are consumed by this process of comparative espying. I would add two things merely.

First, in that the exercise of envy is to a limited sphere of acquaintance, might one not, with good logic, extend envy to everyone on earth who might also enjoy the happiness we attribute to the people we know well enough to rival?

Second, envy derives, in good part, from an ignorance of the private experience of those we observe from the outside merely. Who can tell what mortal pangs afflict the happy? It is a commonplace, of which we can grow weary, that the poor man, who has nothing that can be taken away and who is allowed to rejoice in the simplicity of his condition, is superior in happiness to his comfortably accommodated but politically afflicted king. Shakespeare's histories tell us this in abundance. ('So *shaken*', the first words of *Henry IV*, express the horrid shocks of pomp.)

If, in this connection, we discount the genuine adversities that Hamlet suffers (and, except that the King attempts his *taking off*, some might opine, along with his Mother, that he should merely get on with a life which promised to be one of exceptional promise), we might pause on this line in his Act IV soliloquy: 'How all occasions do inform against me.'

A lesser poet might have rested his pen with the word 'conspire'. Why 'inform', then? This verb is instructive in that, with instinctive genius, Shakespeare suggests that what we see in Hamlet's situation is as nothing to what secretly, multiply, like anonymous spies, is conspiring with deadly and informative purpose against him, who is singular and defenseless.

Hamlet may now rest a while. For I invoked his appearance to suggest this merely: that enviable persons are subject to *occasions* that we can not imagine. And while we may envy them – as the grave digger might have envied the luxuriously upholstered metaphysical hole the Prince indulged himself in digging – we should turn our faces from this position of making comparisons. This because that enviable person, for all we know, swarms with agonies of having been *informed* against which are inscrutable to us. This verb 'to inform' has further useful connotation, in that it suggests an infiltration to the self (which is vulnerable and porous) from hostile others.

Finally, in Hamlet's speech (the Prince, if he's aught, he's a thing of re-appearances!) the sibilation of 'occasions', further implies a multiplication of what can't be known. This, like serpents hidden from their victim, hisses. And so when we arrive at 'do inform', these have germinated from their condition as imagined people or eventualities and have become forms which infuse the individual who remains in his solitude to suffer with them. For no one outside himself will ever see their habitation in him.

When, therefore, we resort to this process, we intromit the object of our envy with our own 'information'. And in *informing* against him, we hurt ourselves also and so drag our lives, which might comfortably have trotted through some pleasant meadow, into cold lagoons of gall – green and diseased and deep as the sea which indelibly will stain us.

The verb 'to inform', from Old French: *enformer;* Latin, *informare* [*in+forma*]. Some usages and meanings:

To give form or shape to; to describe
Informed in the mud on which the Sunne has shyned. (Spenser *FQ* III, vi.8, 1590)
And so omneity informed Nullity into an Essence. (Thomas Browne, *Religio Medici*, I.35, 1643)

To put in proper form
Awakes his lute and 'gainst the fight informs it. (Anonymous)

To delineate or sketch
The man, O Muse, inform, that many a Way
Wound with his Wisdom to his wished Stay. (Chapman, *Odyssey*, I.1)

To take form; to form or be formed
It is the bloody businesse, which Informes
Thus to mine eyes. (*Macbeth*, II.1.48)

To impregnate, imbue with spirit, inspire, animate
The God of Souldiers ... informe thy thoughts with Noblenesse.
(*Coriolanus*, V.iii.71)

To direct or guide
Where else shall I inform my unacquainted feet
In the blind Mazes of this tangled Wood? (Milton, *Comus*, 180)

To impart knowledge of a fact
Enformed whan the kyng was of that knyght. (*Squire's Tale*, 327)

To furnish a magistrate or the like with accusatory information
Ananias ... with senioures ... enfourmed the ruelar against Paul.
(Tyndale, *Acts*, 24:1)

To gain knowledge or information
    Informe yourselves,
We need no more of your advice ... (*The Winter's Tale*, II.1.167)

To give information, to report
Is not thy Master with him? Who wer't so
Would have informed for preparation. *Macbeth*, I.v.42

To bring a charge or complaint
Sinisterly to speake, or otherwise enforme against them. (A. Day,
    English Secretary, 1625)
Twas he informed against him. (*Lear*, IV.2.93)

To inform a thing to a person or make known as an informer
Whatsoever has been informed was my fault. (Sidney, *Arcadia*, V)
My servant talk'd ... as if he was a spy, and had inform'd what presents
    I had made. (Pococke, *Description of the East*, 1753)

It is not the poet's task to pursue each word in the language with all
its meanings and to hunt down each fissiparated nuance. When these
emerge, like bees in a great cloud, from its remotest etymology, whose
roots themselves beg further, deeper origins, it is tempting to withdraw,
with a muslin on one's face, from the buzzings and stingings one has
provoked with the investigation.

So I shall never again resort to any of the meanings of the verb *inform*.
Indeed, I am almost persuaded, like Iago, who informed in a number
of ways, with malign success on his betters, to end my days in silence.
But I have already used the word I have abjured! 'From this time forth I
never shall speak word,' said Iago. Did torture, as promised, ope his lips?

(What happens after every Shakespeare play is pregnant as the matter
in it. But the weight of that fecundity's dependent on the import of its
antecedent matter. It is this informs it.)

On the subject of envy. The word *cynosure* suggests itself. Just as Belinda in Pope's *Rape* is the focus of admiring eyes – while also we detect the jealousy whose flame glints hard green in the heart of every *Nymph* of her acquaintance – so the Khan epitomises everything that's precious and transcends the half-humanity of all who are not him.

And while he cannot be himself except as Emperor of All Occasions, Great Kubilai's is detestable perfection, inspiring envy most particularly from those who know him. All good, as comprehended in his dispensation, is subsumed to his appropriation. And given he lacks nothing, his completeness proclaims the deficiency of those whose existence is a pre-requisite to his elevation. For what would greatness of the One be, without subordination of the Many?

Any excellence in the *general*, indeed, that might occur in the vicinity of such overweening, is sucked from its source and husbanded to his exclusive oneness. The envy engendered by the Khan's advantages is thus mirrored and projected by the Emperor *ipse*. He may not be jealous of himself: but his envy of those who could, in spite of relative misfortune, be equal him to in some way, is unappeasable. Some of these he will assassinate. Others he'll annihilate in the mere process of his sublimation.

With what I most enjoy contented least. (I, too, have 'Sonnet 29-*sans*-sestet-sickness'!) Shakespeare's most remote ancestors had not yet been conceived in the Midland counties when the Great Khan struggled in Cathay with the sentiment so complete in its expression here.

I am enchanted by the transformations of a line which is at once perfect in iambic regularity and ideal in its vernacular straightforwardness: the singularity of which lies in the development of its syllabic variation.

First in this line, arrive divergent clinging and unclasping movements of alliterative effects: two insubstantial 'w's enclosed by a feebly whispered 'i' and a scarcely more declaratory 'a' breathed forth without a referent and in abstraction: the instability of whose sighs are then pegged down with the attempted but uncertain perpendicularity – as though in the erection of a Roman capital – of 'I'.

These sounds are at once followed by the assonantal marriage ('most enjoy') of two 'o's with the separating plainness of this bread-like '-en' whose work it is to neutralise the over-ripe fullness of the dominating vowels: as though that wind-harrow'd, solitary and emaciated first person pronoun had, for a moment, in imagination, gloated on a self-possession: this reinforced by the deceptive and penultimate 'contented', whose unlikely projection, by the line-end, of a positive affect or resolution, is starved off by a thinly hissing sibilant in 'least' and the drying east wind of its middle 'ea' diphthong.

Important to note here the separation of *enjoy* and con*tent*ed which unequally balance on either side of that great caesura, whose space, which opens following the first three iambs, suggests a melancholy disassociation, uncertain self-assurance, dissatisfaction and a fissure in the self to which only the cold gape of paper over which it is spread could give adequate expression.

Is this not a music which spells out, literally, with alphabetic characters, self-distaste, distrust and self-contempt? Imagine the Great Kubilai leaning forward in his self-division across three or four centuries to a future page of English, and muttering in Tartar, this most apposite pentameter, of whose truth about irrreconciliation, he was supreme in his example.

> When in disgrace with Fortune and men's eyes
> I all alone beweep my outcast state

Another word on this sonnet where I have so tortuously entangled Great Kubilai's person. Just this: that within the declarative plainness of the opening two lines, a pattern of perfected beauty in its assonantal values lies, as follows, in a natural and unforced distribution:

e i i ā i ō ū a e ī
ī ā a ō e ēē ī ōū a ā

Now here is a modest paradigm of writing and an object lesson in withheld ostentation. For while every vowel is deployed in its short or long value, these numbers are neither coloured nor emphatic. And yet what subtle shapes and shades are suggested in their disingenuously artless and apparently impromtu scatter.

Note how the first three syllables are short and scarcely accented and how trippingly they lead to the long 'a' of *disgrace*, which in itself tips over from the unstressed 'dis' to a heavier fall on the monosyllable 'grace' – which condition in relation to the grace of heaven is denied by its prefix, despite the apparent weakness of that antecedent syllable. This short 'i' in 'dis'- is followed after 'grace' by its equivalent in 'in' and this leads to the swollen resonance of 'o' which suggests a (pagan) opposite to 'grace' in the person of the (goddess) Fortune.

In line 1's last two syllables, we find the short 'e' of 'men' crescendo to the outburst (a vocalic blast!) of *eyes*, in which visualised scorn has been turned on his failure. This followed by enjambment, for ironic contrast, with the long 'i' in line 2 of the pronoun 'I', whose vertical initiality is compromised at once by the falling motion of the a a o in 'all alone', whose own isolated hollow is succeeded by the keening music of 'beweep' with its short/long descent to the pathos of ee, which ironically again introduces a large new variation of the i in 'my'.

Bees that clup together to forge honey whose importance to them lies in an ownership which is collective, while the motive for its production lies in mutual providence. I have eaten it from a hive which stood in barley and on the border of woodland where I fancy they supped thorn blossoms and honeysuckle. (Do they, I wonder, swallow poppy?)

The honey came out smouldering on a broad, flat knife with fragments of the wax they make, which is their cupboard. This renders it possible to chew what otherwise would be liquid. In winter this freezes and the bees sleep in it.

Is this why we call these creatures *hymenoptera*? In that they are of an order whose members, indissolubly, are married to each other? (My brotherly pact is with the goddess Nature. Do I parley likewise with my own kind, sharing, as our forebears did, a mead that bound them, sometimes, in fraternal sweetness – and a drowsy humming?)

How many separate little worlds we pass through in our navigation of the all- encompassing immensity! This is too bewildering to contemplate and I will not attempt to enumerate the elements that whizz before me and demand attention.

I should take counsel from the honey bee that darts only from one resort, about which it is confident, to another: choosing a clover for its scent and colour over a rose which it knows by some signal that forewarns it. How many detours and diversions through multiple wrong turnings might we avoid did we enjoy such a devoted orientation!

But I must stay my judgement and let it wait on closer observation. See now, the way this late bee goes to forage, and how clumsily it runs into a hollyhock, to fall back again and circle among daisies before completing its research with a bitter-smelling, brown chrysanthemum where it treads around in pollen and emerges dusted to the thorax and its back legs loaded with clots of nectar. How much might I learn from the ant and the bee. But I don't e'er imagine they'l'd learn aught of me!

About the melancholy that lies within the measure of some stanzas of folk poems. Witness these numbers and their jaunty, loping skip whose syllabic accumulation approximates the fourteeners of Chapman, but which sing of a sorrow for which music is the only proper expression:

Abroad as I was walking one morning in the spring
I heard a maid in Bedlam so sweetly she did sing.
Her chains she rattled with her hands and thus she sigh and sing
'I love my love because I know he first loved me.'

My love he was sent from me by friends that were unkind,
They sent him far beyond the seas and that torments my mind.
Although I'm ruined for his sake contented I will be,
For I love my love because I know he first loved me.

Now here is a good art. Need I comment on the discord in the pattern first established (a spring morning by convention) and the horrid rattle of the mad girl's chains which she shakes to accompany her plaintive ditty? And in that she contemplates her fate with such succinct acceptance, is there not another sadness emanating from her ruin?

I mean that some third party has betrayed her, and that, in all likelihood, her lover has gone mad, as she has here, in the unapproachable Antipodes. The growth of love on the home green having been aborted – because no doubt of inequality in standing – so he, poor John, burns in Van Diemens Land, while she lacerates herself in the vicinity of Minehead.

These obscure and anonymous tragedies are the half-hidden substance of human history – they are happening here, right now, in this place. But the hearts of those who suffer are alone in their knowledge of such events and will never have a chronicle beyond the mournful little verses that may be overheard in our milking parlours and taverns.

And yet, as folk songs tell us, these obscure cottage tragedies have their place on the rude, public stage of an aristocratic history in which kings and generals, through the proxy of those pressed to represent them, fight one another. As in this song I heard sung by a fellow in West Harptree (pertinent nomenclature):

As I was a-walking for my recreation
Down by the green gardens I simply did slow,
I heard the fair maid making great lamentation,
Crying, Jimmie will be a sliding to the wars I'm afraid.

The blackbirds and thrushes down by the green bushes

They all seem to mourn for this fair maid,
Crying the song that she sung was concerning her lover:
Jimmy will be a-sliding to the wars I'm afraid.

And Jimmy will return with his heart full of burning
To see his love Nancy lie dead in her grave.
Young man forsaken he died in a week,
Crying so he had never have left this fair maid.

Success may attend every lad on the ocean.
God send him safe home to his sweetheart and wives,
For peace may be claiming in every nation.
God send my soldier home to his bride.

Amen to this sentiment. And deliver us from armed princes.

Goethe's *Erlkönig.* It would be strange were I not preoccupied with this poem, for it is at once in ballad idiom and a work of Herr Goethe's most boldly crafted lyric art, which in eight simple quatrains, concentrates what is primitive and terrible with a narrative that outreaches the disingenuous simplicity of its genre and achieves the elevation of a tragic drama in a sequence of precise acts. The effect of this lies, as with the best in our own traditions, in its power to mark our waking minds with images of nightmare and to accumulate within our sympathies an unassuagable tension of pity.

All this occurs along the current of a horseback gallop which we join in the first line and which continues to its conclusion as the rider, with his boy still warm – the child's soul having been extracted by the Erl King's fingers – comes to rest, unquietly at a threshold on which no-one greets him.

Up till that catastrophe, this is poetry of overwhelming locomotion, and yet the agency of its momentum, which lies partly in the muscle and the acquiescence of a charger, is relegated to an implication. For while on the one hand, Goethe brings the Erl King and his family close enough to strike terror by proximity, his victims are anonymous, the nature of their flight unstated, the time itself (*so spät*) the bleak occasion for their twilight journey.

This is poetry, too, of unrelieved but enigmatic masculinity. For in that each protagonist is male – we may include the horse's presence – we are closed in a world of patriarchal workings. But despite the embrace of a paternal forearm, the father, blank in his denial of the boy's foreboding, is powerless, while the goblin seducer, albeit he professes wife and daughters, is motivated by malevolent, effeminate infatuation.

Somewhere, also in the ballad landscape, which is misted with willows and water-seeking alder, the Erl King's mother sneaks in gentleness, and his sinister, tendentious daughters anticipate the boy's arrival with infernal games and other ghostly entertainment. The boy, as he rides, is dragged towards these gambols, until, all movement finished, the dull, thick finalising consonants of *Tod* (enclosing an O: that most capacious of our vowels which breathes suddenly no longer) conclude the journey.

Screened behind the diminishing stanzas, the Erl King runs back to the willows, the boy's soul stuck in his goblin fingers.

On nether-world contingencies like these, which often are unpleasant, the subterranean currents of our poetry's dependent.

To my left the inexorable hillside. To the right the enormity of a chasm. Prompted by another poem of Goethe: my quill hesitates as though in the expectation of a commentary to this picturesque drama. Even the small birds *tacent, schweigen* – as in Goethe's lyric, the grandeur of whose possibilities are in my consciousness often. 'Ruhest du auch': ambiguous asseveration! We wonder, as we quietly read, if he speaks to a lover, or addresses himself, or an 'us', in conjunct.

The verse, either way, is of love and instruction. Love, in that its lines express supple, warm relations between articulating self, the natural world and another being. Indeed. The poem is a gift: in itself a vehicle of affection and it instructs in directing us to a passivity which may be learned from birds, mountains and tree-tops which have entered a condition of hush. If the work is in part spoken to the poet's own (or other!) self, then he is directing himself to a situation of receptivity, without which poetic experience would for ever be out of reach.

Of associated interest is the inference of distance. Herr Goethe speaks from ground level in a forest solitude and refers upward to birds, tree- and mountain-tops which are present but beyond. These separate but companionable phenomena have a non-human language of self-existence – whether or not directly articulated. But for the time being they communicate nothing except a quiet which it is the writer's task to absorb.

We must remember, too, that the title of this poem is *Wanderers Nacht-lied*. The sun has gone down and the solitary traveller sings, albeit silently to himself, in response to and within the environment of a charmed natural repose.

Poetry, in my experience, is a continual singing in the dark. It is, at the first, an interior action in which the noise of daily language is sequestered and inaudibly refined. This takes place in the night-environment of the intelligence, enclosed in an unlit reclusion. Just as a dream, however stormy, enacts its business in darkness and privacy, so the poem comes into being from a shadowy chamber of which the author is the sole inhabitant.

And he himself may be a stranger there – hovering over what he can perceive only vaguely and whose true nature is obscure. The deeper the obscurity the more profoundly he must sink to retrieve whatever matter is secreted in it.

Sometimes he will emerge with nothing. On other occasions with a deranged nonsense of the kind that makes all of us, now and again, jackasses. But with the assistance of some craft to which the Muse, with long practice, has apprenticed him, he will beat what he brings up into a comely object.

Too great a reliance on the effort of craft may, paradoxically, drain life from what has germinated in the darkness and it will come forth stillborn. But again, given that initial receptivity to which Goethe alludes, held in equipoise with a determined application of art which remains humble in the presence of the Muses, the wholesome and well-nourished child of genius will have scope to be born in the perfection of its originality. But without these two elements, at once conspiring and in methodical variance, it will emerge a thin and undernourished thing of persiflage and superficiality.

Subjectivity and observation. No money in these. Did I own a shilling beyond immediate need of bread and meat, this would find its way from my pocket to an ale house and leave residues of dust and scraps of paper.

Electing poetry, one chooses poverty. And in the absence of some worldly talent or profession, fools turn to verses as if to proclaim their incapacity. There are, further to this, men pursuing business and polite professions. And fellows such as Sheridan and Garrick who contrive a living in the entertainment of the public.

The existence of theatre is, of course, predicated on a convergence of fashion and polite boredom. For the theatre to succeed, it must attract people who will make an appearance at the play, creating of their position in the audience a secondary drama; while the exercise of their necks in long sequences of *how-d'ye-do's* represents a sealant which, for the duration of an evening, eradicates unhappiness and tedium. As for the playwright, he will sweat himself into sufficient nectar for these butterflies to gobble from his blossoms – which thus engenders pollen to sustain them till their next public showing.

As for me, what I write – if ever it were to reach an approximation of such an audience – would represent a *somnifer* against such occasions. But how much would such a person pay me to send them, now and then, to sleep and stimulate them sufficiently in this respect, to boast that a certain Mr — provided a capital draught of oblivion? To be taken, with wine, in the privacy of their library and with appropriate quantities of yawnings? Watch now as my public rages!

With reference to what one has published – the notices received – the society one inhabits – the number of copies of a book that have circulated – the antecedents and contemporaries with whom one has made a connection – such are the questions preoccupying those for whom literary life is a means of affiliation or advancement.

What happens in a poem or a novel, and the manner in which it is written, retain significance only in so far as these relate to the age, what a critic has written about them, how far the work has been distributed and what developments may be expected from it. Who, further, will receive that writer's next submission? What great emolument might it command and how far will that compare to what he's got before, and what other writers may obtain from other houses?

All this may be of historical interest. But the histories of such affairs are become a substitute for the experience from which writing emerges. And by degrees it overtakes literature as a great cloud descends across the detail of what the author has observed in open sunlight. And given, therefore, all such factors that are peripheral to creative life, and on account of economic, biographical and anecdotal preoccupations that attach to any work's appearance, it progressively grows more difficult to separate these phenomena from the realm of experience through which a writer's thought may lead us.

A work of imagination, in this way, becomes the event or the phenomenon of its coming out, both of which push into the foreground, while the nature of the work itself, in style and matter, lose what integrity it may have enjoyed before the character of a book evolved, into a question of its standing in the world as an occurrence.

A writer who gets caught up in such preoccupations loses control of the experiences which inspire his mind and he becomes a *figure*. Such a position is a phenomenon of the present age and its dangers are not difficult to see as, for example, a successful author's mode of expression becomes embedded in an ever quickening production of what his public has in mind for him.

A first lesson to draw from this is that the writer must, above all things, become detached from the expectation of an effect. If an audience is believed to exist, let it first be among the Muses – which are the angels which hesitate over our presumption of an encroachment on their dangerous precinct. Only in the obscurity in which he originally began may questions of importance that will outlast him present themselves: for a mind that remains disengaged from ambition (and thus receptive because undistracted by the 'thing' which success renders that which had previously been alive) is for ever fresh and will perform its gymnastic undertakings with spontaneity.

Success, for any such person, becomes a misfortune whose illusory glamour reveals itself generally too late. To bid farewell, for one who has tasted fame, gives rise to bitterness where otherwise it might have constituted the occasion for an advance towards further originality. Better not write than to be fashion's toy. And best not to read, if the effect of that pastime is to encourage in the future work of an author the equivalent of a new top hat or bonnet.

I have been thinking once again about the mind of God: and the means by which the cosmos into which the world came to be placed, emerged when it did from the pre-ordination of His creational impulsion.

The notion of time is perhaps not important: and yet given the existence of a deity for whom everything is possible in an eternity which is without limits, I am, no doubt frivolously, preoccupied with the commencement of our Bible in which it is stated that *In the beginning* God created the Heaven and the Earth. Which statement is followed, as though in retrospective temporal sequence, with an assertion that the *Earth was without form, and Void.* The latter part of this phrase (with its ponderous comma), being our King James translation of *tohu va bohu*, coming as it does after the verb *was*, represents a further conundrum. For *was*, as both the Hebrew and English past tense express it, suggests, does it not, a prior situation of being: namely the anterior existence of earth as *tohu va bohu*? Which condition, if it can be represented with the past tense of 'to be', must either suggest the existence of some pre-creational phenomenon or a state of non-being which pre-dated the beginning of God's creation.

Of course the rabbis might argue that the phrase 'In the beginning' (*b'resheet*) means not 'In the beginning' but 'the beginning *of*' (as in *Genesis* 10.x: 'the beginning of His Kingdom was Babel'.)

This quibble is good and in part solves my puzzle. For if this be the case, then God did not create Heaven and Earth at the beginning of everything: but rather He conceived these two entities at a *new beginning* and in context of a chaos which had previously and perhaps always been there in the darkness, which was palpable, 'on the face of the deep'.

There was, in other words, in existence, water already: and God's recognizable creation, as sensually we apprehend it, was consolidated at the outset of its own beginning. The anterior, as Milton expressed it in his lovely and exalted verses, representing what might only be alluded to: for, given that we exist merely on the near side of its spaces, we may not penetrate that 'dark, backward abysm', which (to deform Shakespeare) precedes Time, while God was there *in*, *on* and *with* the pre-existential and unformulated waters:

> Thou from the first
> Was present, and with mighty wings outspread
> Dove-like satst brooding on the vast Abyss
> And mad'st it pregnant.

As Milton I suspect here divines, God had lived as a Presence in an incalculable present condition which stretched back to 'the first': which, God being eternal, had no conceivable beginning, but which at a moment that was willed by this same *Elohim*, was made pregnant with all we would come to know.

What was God's mind, or in God's mind, during (if that preposition is admissible) the infinitely long chaos through which He forbore to render the pre-creational waters fertile?

Such speculations are interesting, I think, mainly in so far as they have a bearing on poetry: and the creation of poetry as it occurs in men's imagination and the manner in which powerful and lovely figurations are experienced as consolidating from the pre-creational depths of an intellect which previously has been without form, and void.

Reverting for a moment to the mind of God: would it not be that at the moment of 'beginning', He held in His imagination the entire panoply of the creation: and that it was there in His infinitely fertile vision which was and is His person, and that He had only to render concrete this imaginative totality by an act of will (and this over time as represented in six symbolic days) which is subsumed in the verb 'He created' – which great poetic artefact, itself, is a component, one may suppose, a reflex or reflection that, like a secretary, in God's service, published itself as a record of th' event.

I would go further and ask this. That if the constituents of this *Great Everything that we Know* co-existed in God's mind at the beginning, what differentiated this from its formularised expression as earth, heaven, firmament, dry land, seas, bright lights, living creatures that fly, creep and swim, followed by beasts of the earth and finally Man in His image?

Did not all these swarm on the pre-creational waters in God's imagination before He laboured to distribute them through the thirty-one verses of His record of the event over those allegorical six days and set them moving, in series, until by the sabbath, the entire system was in motion, independently of that energic impulsion, while He rested and let it proceed?

Might we not therefore ourselves imagine, that either all this had existed in the mind of God: but that in the action of the verb 'created', He separated Himself from what He had imagined, or that what we experience as the creation remains in the mind of God and that all there is and all we know continues as a representation of that sacred moment of beginning or even of the pre-beginning? Only if we choose to believe in the former proposition, of course, may the problems of evil and of death satisfactorily be explained: these negatives occur beyond the mind of God as a reflex of Man's freedom, in that he, and our first Mother, separated themselves by choice from the All Good that constituted Paradise – which latter might be comprehended as a symbolical manifestation of the deity's superabundance.

On the other hand, we might, quite contrarily, argue that since everything in the universe *is* of God, then death and evil represent a component of His completeness. And that it is the duty and the task of human beings to separate from this aspect of God without alienating themselves from the essence of His being which is a goodness which comprehends and yet transcends death and evil.

I have subverted my disclaimer. And these animadversions have entered or perhaps even constructed a labyrinth which has led me so far from the realm of poetry that I scarce know whether I am inside or outside, at the outset or the centre, lost or crawling with some prospect of an exit (or an entrance even), at the end or a beginning, half way along or nowhere that I can identify. In such a position, all, perhaps, one needs is the fortitude of folly. For how can it matter, what difference can it make, given (*argle*) I am somewhere within the infinite confabulation of God's mind, in whatever place I find myself, or believe myself to be positioned. For everywhere is here and here is infinitely exchangeable with both itself and everywhere.

Now, with all this in consideration, we have, as poets, an obligation to continue the creation as it has been patterned into nature. Nature proclaims itself to be the work of God and since we are a part of this, we too must sing forth with the nightingale and the sparrow, uttering our song, as angels are supposed to, and in thereby expressing our part in the creation, signify the place that we too occupy in the Mind that has conceived us in its image and thus send forth into the welkin our part within the counterpoint that tunes the sky and the earth in what Dryden described as 'heavenly harmony with which the universal frame began'.

And just as old Abraham must sow the desert, it's the obligation of our common voice to sing: which, meagre as it may be, represents a portion of the *intellect divine*, and in so acting, extends self-song out to nature in a consanguineal fraternity. To co-existence in that, *atque in perpetuum: Ave!*

Xanadu was built according to the traditions of Chinese architectural practice in a domesticated harmonisation of *wind and water*. By contrast, the hunting preserves that surrounded the palace represented the Great Khan's attempt to enclose himself within an environment that was from his western homeland. In that these were a re-creation, extracted from the lands where Kubilai's brethren continued to pursue ancestral freedom, what the Great Khan's garden attempted to reclaim was a representation of where he had come from, and whose character oscillated between what was of yore, and an artificial recreation of it. A paradoxical adventure in that it mirrored the conundrum of the sedentary Chinese status he had chosen.

Imagine him therefore rushing through these meadows, following deliberations at the palace: he has been in conference with his Uigur generals, Tibetan prelates and Arabians, and they have touched on diverse subjects: paper money manufacture, how distribute this through China, fortifying border regions, the excavation of canals and road construction, along with shade tree plantings and erection along major highways of hostelries for travellers, endowment of Tibetan monasteries, Christian hospices, *medrassahs* for the Musulmans to study in, trade compacts with Corea and the planned assault against Japan.

Laying aside his morning's business, throwing down the robes of policy and depositing in a council chamber the weight of a throne – which has been shown to be a seat that crowds the shoulders closer than it does the arsehole of a monarch – the Great Khan reverts to what he might have once been. Gone the stifling, embroidered robe, the braided hat and jewelled pendants. Off with dainty sleeves and slippers. And on, then, with his leather buskins as he leaps (or struggles) on a pony and canters from the palace, long hair streaming, his face against a wind that blows in from the mountains, and the horse back surging upward on his genitals. Now old hunting comrades have appeared – from having idled months or years in the Great Khan's stables – and they gallop at his side as equals with Great Kubilai's favourite goshawks on their wrists and shoulders.[25]

---

25 Oh, I've said all this before and have been tempted into mockery. I wanted, just now, to ride out with him for the sake of my own freedom in a companionable sincerity.

The Great Khan's apartments: fixed on *Eros*, partly

In re further aspects of Great Kubilai's household, I have in my hand *A New History of China*, by one Gabriel Magaillans SJ, which was done out of French and in 1688 published at St Paul's Church-Yard.

Into this book is packed a folded map with the title *A Plane of the City of Pekim, ye Metropolis of China*: an engraving executed with some geometrical severity which shows the palaces and temples that constitute the Emperor's enclosure.

Now I've pondered this somewhat meanly schematized reduction of those premises, and albeit this plan arrives five centuries after Kubilai, much of Peking, the winter city, was built by that same Khan: and so I've made the apartments, here identified, the locus of some harmless dreaming. And while at the outset of my exploration, I came, through Purchas, to the Great Khan's summer palace, I have now drifted east and migrated a season.

To initiate my ramble, which is otherwise quite innocent of topographic knowledge, I transcribe below a sampler from Magaillans in his Eighteenth Chapter. And having established something of that survey, I'll take on myself, still purblind in oneiric speculation, an entry to the Emperor's chambers. First this from Magaillans:

> The First Apartment is bounded on the north side by the famous street of Perpetual Repose. From thence you proceed to the Third Apartment which is called the Portal of Beginning.
>
> After this, you enter into a spacious Court, bounded by the Eleventh Apartment, which they call the Mansion of Heaven Clear and without Blemish, and which is the richest, the highest rais'd and the most sumptuous of all.
>
> There are five Ascents to this of very fine Marble, each ascent containing five and forty steps, adorn'd with Pillars, Parapets, Balusters and several little Lyons, and at the Top on both sides with ten beautiful and large Lyons of gilded Brass, excellent Pieces of Worksmanship.
>
> To the North and within two Musquet shot of these Hills, stands a

very thick Wood, and at the End of the Wood, adjoyning to the Wall of the Park, are to be seen three Houses of Pleasure extraordinary for their Symmetry with lovely Stairs and Terrasses to go from one to the other. This is a Structure truly Royal, the Architecture being exquisite, and makes the eighteenth Apartment, being called the Royal Palace of Long Life.

And so now I enter, in the challenge of a new displacement, as if still from a haunting of my earlier excursion.

1. *The Sovereign Concord House which Entertains Heaven*

That which is *Sovereign* is trustworthily golden. This predicates an assiduously refined thickness from whose centre, the glow of the thing radiates as though steadied by a pulse which maintains the royalism of its endogeny.

As the centre works by self-maintenence to refresh what, at the core, it must continue to be, the surface of the piece is in receipt: rhythmically and by repetition, and exists in the character of a perpetual becoming which has been manufactured from the interior.

Alchemy proposes to cast out what is dull, thick and leaden, and to purify that which is coarse to the empyrean of what it could not, without some intervention, independently achieve. With all its elements in harmony, as though smelted first very thin and then consolidated into the sterling of a good bulk, this quiddity, transfigured, represents a valid *Concord*: expressing the truth of its own highest possibility.

This is, of course, the basis of the imperial constitution, and the *Sovereign Concord House* will be a sanctified locus of the Great Khan's apotheosis and stand graciously in a condition where Heaven meets the Earth and where any distinction between these two spheres has been eliminated.

Here, neither vaunting itself nor in a false, obsequious crawling, Earth entertains Heaven. As though among two cultivated persons of an equal standing, one happened to be host and poured wine for the other, and so they met in uniformity and raised cups in equality, as if one were the other. From this *Concord* follows.

2. *The Portal of Beginning*

That an apartment should be also a *Portal* suggests that however it is enclosed, it represents merely the entrance to the next. Anywhere we stand, sit, lie down or walk is, likewise, the *Beginning* of some new estate. For the term of our lives, we are, howsoever we appear inert, perpetually in motion. There is boundariless hope in the naming of this apartment.

All will be new and engaged in self-renewal. Even here, in this damp, snug and half-darkened little parlour, I feel the cool encouragement of mountain breezes sweeping Xanadu and rendering the Great Khan's limbs and spirit youthfully elastic. Thus he begins with me anew. As I do with him at this *Limen of Beginning*.

3. *The Mansion of Heaven Clear and without Blemish*

On account of his powers and the exalted position that he will occupy for ever, the Great Khan's dwelling is a simulacrum of *Heaven*, designated at his command by loyal subjects and employees whose work resides in the maintenance of this *Mansion* in its status without *Blemish*.

As Great Kubilai takes residence, however temporarily, in this apartment, its sublunary precincts are, paradoxically, inhabited as though by its proper god. Subordinates who come and go according to Great Kubilai's needs represent a part of this official *Heaven*: for this place would not be a *Mansion of Heaven*'s office were it not for the services done there for the Great Khan's pleasure.

The class of person who effects these duties can not, however, be said, themselves, to reside in the same unblemished heaven. These are people who, like the fabric and the furnishings of the apartment, contribute to its perfection. It is of the essence that they should, once they have served their purpose, withdraw, leaving Great Kubilai in the isolation of his own complete self-being. This is a characteristic both of their absence and also of the potential, as they are needed, of their brief and instrumental presence.

4. *The Royal Palace of Long Life*

All monarchs may be expected to enjoy long lives, for it is believed to be the fate only of the disenfranchised poor to die young from the mishaps from which nobility, with its immeasurable privileges, can insulate itself. History has yet to give proof to such a theory. But given that longevity may be viewed as a reward from Heaven, the *Palace of Long Life* may be understood as a medicinal environment within which the Great Khan could, as it were, draw the elixir of his expectation.

The gods are eternal, and Great Kubilai – whose subjects were enjoined to address him as a deity – derived his inspiration from this knowledge. We should recall, also, that among the many religions that the Khan tolerated in his empire, lived the Taoist fraternity, whose priests were adepts in alchemical preparation – of gold leaf, sulphur, cinnebar, mercury and I know not what beneficent distillations – whose ingestion endowed immortality.

On this subject, however, I must register skeptic reservation: for if these same chimists were incapable of providing Great Kubilai with a reliable specific against the gout from which he suffered agonies, what in the armoury of their pharmacopeia, I ask, could they propose against the worm, whose burrowings have reliably been observed since the beginning of time to be ineluctable – and to lord its proper kingship over the most elevated corpses?

5. *The Portal of Great Purity*

Given that his life was devoted in public to the pursuit of power and in private to pleasure, it is inconceivable that moral purity should have been attributed to the character of this great chieftain who took upon himself the far eastern imperium. And yet just as he took such an interest in Christendom that he ordered the Venetian *signore* to send him oil, through papal sanction, from the Holy Sepulchre, so from the Buddhists the Great Khan would have gained some knowledge of the *Path of Purification* as it was pursued in the monasteries within his empire.

But *Great Purity*, I surmise, related less to the spiritual character of the Khan than to the principles on which the palace architects and geomancers would have constructed the imperial residence. For it would have been unpropitious indeed, whether this palace were to serve as hermitage, hunting lodge, stables or house of prostitution – or any combination of these – were it not built, for Great Kubilai's pleasure, in conformity with the most stringent of indigenous divinatory principles.

It was the *place* only, therefore, and its liminal properties, to which the notion of purity must be attributed. The Great Khan could do what he liked there. As he threaded that doorway, he entered what could not be deranged. But as the rest of us, in modest aberration, are transformed in some degree by thresholds we approach and leave behind us, might not Kubilai, or some edge of him, have changed as he transgressed that *Portal*, and leave a residue of what he'd come in with? Given, however, the accumulating bustle and the encrustations of an Emperor's existence, such translations remain subtle – and if they happen, superficial.

6. *The Portal and the Street of Perpetual Repose*

The Great Khan's palace is for his repose. For a warrior king exerts himself beyond all natural limit and it is right that such an individual should maintain a palace where rest may go on, and never have to end except as he chooses.

In our English parlance, one might anticipate the words *Perpetual Repose* on some funerary monument. But this, as related to Great Kubilai's palace, alludes less to mortal dust than to a condition which belongs to relaxation into quiet and delightful activity.

In this regard, it may be surmised that the gods, whose status the Khan approaches, inhabit a region from which any notion of effort has been removed: and that this represents a condition towards which they themselves perhaps evolved, and therefore also to which certain human beings may be thought to approach in the development of their faculties.

An apartment so named is thus a reminder of such a possibility and a locus of retreat which will bestow on its residents the enchantment, howsoever seeming, of its inherent character.

7. The Portal of Mysterious Valour

Courage resides neither in the blood nor in the muscle, but where the heart exudes a more reserved elixir which is of a spiritual morphology.

Great men are those who, without fully comprehending the transaction, have intuitively submitted to ordeals of transition. Hence this *Portal* in Magaillans connotes a point of both continued exit and return. Through this gate, which renders each novice progressively more abstract, the spirit will essay a passage. Whence and whither they conduct such a shuttle are neither in question: instead it is the activity of such a process which knits into the being that which is necessary for the perpetuation of its most delicate build: until such a time that a kind of perfection, as to *valour*, and its mystery, is achieved – at the least to the satisfaction of participating *lares*.

Still, the individual who has undergone such an initiation is no different from another. Great Kubilai's armies are filled, successively, with many tens of thousands for whom these procedures represent a childish pastime. As masses of such individuals are left fighting in far-flung districts and to perish anonymously, so they are replaced by those whose own short lives they themselves interpret as mere figures of a pattern which it is within the Great Khan's own destiny to drive forward in the fulfilment of his imperium.

Men who would be great are those who plume themselves in dangerous states of a quasi- or *soi disant* deification as a result of having ostentatiously travelled on their best horses through this Portal in pursuit of some perfection – or its simulacrum. Whether the Khan himself is one for whom the notion of *Valour* represents the spectacle or the pretense of having been seen on some such a gaudy and impressive mount remains unknowable. Such are residues or dreams of conduct that the imagination must pick over with discretion.

8. *The Portal of Ten Thousand Years*

Amalgamating the long years, *Ten Thousand* led to latitudes where time, through metamorphic passage, long since gone, dissolved entirely.

In a single condensation, *Ten Thousand* representing an infinity of instants (in the Sanskrit, *kshana*: the length of time it takes a healthy man to snap his thumb and finger.)

Through which gateway, Kubilai expected to contrive emergence, embalmed dynastically in fame and happiness. Death, for such great ones, being a misnomer.

9. *The Fifth Apartment – the Supreme Apartment*

Ascending from greatness to what is ever higher – travelling through elevations rarified beyond the properties of *aire and angels* – such are the pathways diagrammed in this Apartment.

But at the point where he assumed he had achieved apotheosis, Great Kubilai had not realised the supreme. Nor when he dwelled here did its environment thus advise him. No: this stood apart in its own proper condition, which was wonderful, albeit subordinate. He or that which would be great, will wait.

Striving for a transcendence, the Khan found it had been contrived already: an architecture which had been construed on the flat and from there piled into the aether, and which enclosed that sphere:

The inner walls being of a light blue and gold with which sky and sun competed, one thereby completing the other in a radiance under the dome's arch which drew the light in to the extent that the apartment appeared to lift itself, circle on its own axis, float up of a sudden and thence ascend in a turning movement in the direction of the heaven whose shell it echoed and into which it would become assimilated.

But that which is supreme can only be called such from levels which do not reach it. Nothing aspires higher. And yet what lies beyond represents conditions so refined that no character may be said to attach to them. The supremacy of this apartment remains therefore an innocent allusion to what may never be experienced, still less conceived, as in our previous description, except through the grossest diagram of its possibilities.

Thus when Great Kubilai steps there in the self-confidence which is his delusion, his process to that chamber represents merely the ordination of which he has been told the potential. It is of course a lie, that sublime. Because it was after all, something he might have brought with him – in his pocket, or somewhere.

10. *The Twelfth Apartment which is called Fair and Beautiful Middle House*

To explore for beauty demands less valour than does the execution of a battle and to gallop with one's cavalry towards a veil of arrows whose encroaching shadow will engulf your men within moments of their release, striking thousands in the face and tearing the entrails out of horses in a terrible and chaotic screaming.

If such an encounter does not arrest the charge, the second rank will go forward across the carnage raising the veil of its own weapons, and so by mutual elimination, the field becomes simplified and reduced for the contemplation of the last and no less unfortunate marksmen.

There is no beauty in warfare. And those on whom this truth has been impressed have therefore devoted the remainder of their energies to the rehearsal of what may be salvaged of human ingenuity.

The Great Khan had been travelling, one late summer, across half-dead grasslands and then stony desert, when the advance party which had been sent forward to prospect for water, returned to report a small oasis. On the arrival of the imperial party, Great Kubilai ordered that the horses should be led to drink: and as each mount crept up to the slime, the water hole (if it could be so described, for it was half dried up in alkaline and sun-shrunk crystals) was soon drained.

No single person drank that day. But a full week later, the Khan's horses made an entrance to the city. Half the men who rode were dead. And whether Kubilai survived is not recorded: they had all, in those days and nights of violent madness, lost their garments and no person, in his inanition, could be told from another.

When the man who claimed to be the Great Khan tottered into the palace and was treated by his surgeons, it is said an alteration came upon him. For the period of a month he consumed no meat or liquor, took counsel from a man of learning and discoursed to his entourage on the *Middle Path* of the Buddhists.

When gradually this lapsed and Great Kubilai reverted to the character by which he had been remembered, this aberration was forgotten. And yet, perhaps, below the surface of his character ... But no. The whole episode was a fiction of some court buffoon, if any such existed in those days of moment. Best never to have strayed from peaceful havens. These it is are *Fair and Beautiful*.

11. *The Palace of Flourishing Learning*

Learning was and was not Kubilai's ambition. It was, after all, a simple matter to surround himself with scholars and in this way to assemble a body of men who could pronounce on all that could be known of earth and heaven and convey this knowledge to him as he might demand it.

Knowledge, of course, is so varied and extensive that no one person could expect to contain all that can be known. And if it was the Great Khan's intention to point his captive scholars in the direction of his own mind and, serially, enjoin them to project into his one head (howsoever enormous) their collective learning, then his project must have failed: for even in the greatness of his person and status, he could not contain the immensity of that range which stretched from science through philosophy, history, statecraft, the fine arts, all the many religions that were represented in his empire and much more that I can neither recollect nor imagine.

Nor in his innocence, would Kubilai be capable of formulating helpful questions of the scholars who passed through his court. And so just as they were stuck there, exiled from environs which would further their own studies, so the Great Khan was marooned amongst them and incapable of even the most modest conversation which could have elicited the smallest element of enlivening information.

What looked, therefore, like a court which was decorated with the choicest luminaries of the empire and where learning appeared to thrive at the centre of the Great Khan's power, was in fact a place of tension and sterility, in which few felt capable of conversing with one another and in which, at its highest circles of scholarly achievement, Great Kubilai himself stood quite alone and in an alienation from those fruits of intelligence he so craved to consume and even, in his beneficence, disseminate among his people.

He took comfort in the advice of one man, first. This individual was a Buddhist adept, and one who previously had lived in retirement on Wu T'ai mountain. While this philosopher had been surprised to have been plucked from his obscurity and carried from a life of vagabondage into the luxurious premises of the palace, this simple soul had adapted himself with complacency to an enforced imprisonment and his good humour was such that he looked on himself as fortunate to have arrived at a higher peak of deprivation to walk through: for the Great Khan's court was, to him, a place so poor in the attributes of natural richness on which he was used to thrive, that it became a locus of the most esteemed challenge which could only lead to higher spiritual attainment.

Knowing this man to possess insights into the nature of existence that might enable him to make some kind of intellectual progress without the trouble of acquiring too much more of the Chinese language, the Great Khan summoned this mendicant, and having offered him wine (which he refused with a laugh) and tea (which he accepted), installed himself in a little pavilion which was out of the sight of the palace and proceeded to converse with him.

The content of any conversation they enjoyed is of course unknown – for any transcript of what passed between them is lost. Scraps of discourse and a number of words that were overheard by an attendant passed into folk memory and – no doubt inaccurately transcribed and then translated some four centuries later by a colleague of Magaillans – these came my way in some notes in the possession of one Dr— whose residence I visited lately on an excursion to the Swiss mountains.

These are the words from that conversation that have come down to us: *court, city, ambition, sandals, no view, mist, wind.* To render these words intelligible, I have used them as the basis of a short poem. Following this, I have constructed a dialogue, as perhaps it proceeded, between the Great Khan and the adept:

Far from court and capital
A sage, in grass sandals,
Dwells among clouds and wind as company.
Long since, at court, he had ambition.
Now he harbours no view or opinion.

The conversation goes as follows:

Khan Tell me, O sage, what I should do to be wise and thus be saved?
Sage Leave your capital, Highness.
Khan How can I be certain that this is the path?
Sage I do not know. There is perhaps no path.
Khan Where, then, should I go?
Sage You are the Emperor. You may go where you choose.
Khan Where did you seek truth?
Sage Out there. Some place that is nameless.
Khan You mean in the mountains?

Sage Those are not what you may think.

Khan Must I travel there alone?

Sage You will take every self in your possession. Which you'll then send
back to join you in the city.

Khan In that case I shall stay here.

Sage It will make no difference.

12. The Palace of Mercy and Prudence

Let us try to imagine how *Mercy and Prudence* inhabit the same palace.
To exercise mercy one must first have power. And so Mercy sits alone
on a high seat of judgement. All who come before Her are scrutinised
and weighed. Their histories are recorded. Each is allowed to make one
statement. The court's scribe notes this on a scroll which Mercy reads
with care and then for some hours will meditate on its import. Prudence,
meantime, lingers by the judgement desk, contemplating quiet actions.
It is these are decisive. Herein lies the world's misfortune.

13. Processing through the Great Khan's apartments

It was the Great Khan's privilege to process through his apartments in
whatever order his caprice may have prompted. Thus, he might, unlike
his subjects, enter where he chose. But what signified the numbers that
attached to each apartment? And how did those numbers correspond to
the names with which they were associated?

Herein, I think, lay the beauty of this palace: it was constructed according to a certain order, but within this lay foundations that were mobile.
And thus the apartments, some of which consisted of separate dwellings,
might be (or were experienced) not merely as originally designed, but
made themselves accessible to places and identities within the palace
compound which were – perhaps as these were viewed by people along
different meridia – liable to alteration.

For such patterns to persist in variation, a linear series must at first have
been set forth – hence the names of each apartment and its associated
number. But the essence of the palace lay in its metamorphic character,
and of this there is more than a hint in the description which has come
down to us from the Jesuit Magaillans.

According to Magaillans, 'the First Apartment is bounded on the north
side by the street of Perpetual Repose. From thence you proceed to the
Third Apartment which is called the Portal of the Beginning.' But then,
on the other hand, as wrote Magaillans: 'the second Apartment ought to

be called the first'. Securely to interpret such a statement would tease us beyond endurance.

But herein lies an essential meaning. *Viz*: that the palace itself existed as a subject for interpretation. Why, for example, when the entire edifice must have been constructed by the best architects of the Orient, should only the Twelfth Apartment, which we have surveyed at Number 10, be called *Fair and Beautiful*? Does this not proclaim nonsense? Deepening that confusion, I have muddled up Magaillans' numbers, thereby rendering the sequence of this record, at best, inconsequential.

14. *In which mansion did the Great Khan take his leisure?*

There were occasions when Great Kubilai dawdled in this or that pavilion and was incapable of deciding for one afternoon or evening in which to stay. At the best of times and in his most confident moments he was unsure for precisely how long he should remain in any one of his apartments. And so he would enter: and having indeterminately filled it with his presence, would soon get up and walk, in a decided manner which belied his uncertainty, to another where he would reside for a short period before again moving on to the station he judged to be appropriate.

Given that each apartment was subtly different from the other and that each had been given a title in conformity to a character which signified relations between heaven and earth, and even in the relationship of Great Kubilai himself both with higher powers and with his empire, the Khan, whether in residence or progress through his apartments, must respond appropriately to the demands of each particular environment.

Given that each apartment communicated its character directly, even the most casual perambulation was subject to a special demand. Thus when the Great Khan entered the *Mansion of Heaven Clear and Without Blemish*, he must know this to be the most rarified of simulacra. Here he must fix his mind on a space that prefigured the heavenly realms of immaculate clarity which he could expect one day to enter. On settling, by contrast, in the *Royal Palace of Long Life* he must contemplate the expectation for him, whatever sickness he might suffer, of a sacralised and somewhat distasteful longevity.

While the *Sovereign Concord House which Entertains Heaven* elicited from him the demand that residence there meant something which it was beyond his powers to achieve. The Great Khan knew this and was somewhat disconcerted by it.

Such anxieties were compounded by the fact that each wonderful apartment was decorated with symbolic representations which he did not understand and about which he was too bashful, emperor though he was, to make enquiries. More: there existed, throughout his palace, inscriptions in Chinese. And while he had, since childhood, spoken this language, it was with a barbarian tonality whose accent could make his more elevated Chinese advisors cough softly with mortification.

His very concubines, several of whom had been chosen for their superiority in the arts, might inwardly smirk even in the course of his most furious embraces in the knowledge that he was incapable of reading the ethical and philosophical inscriptions that bedizened his chamber of pleasure. Sometimes, in amorous conversation with some beauty in whose confidentiality he was certain, he might, with a careless insouciance which belied the intent of his request, murmur that he would now, having finally allowed her to rise from pronation, enjoy being read to – and thus assimilate, by proxy, the moral character of the chamber he had ordained for both his pleasure and his edification.

In the Chinese view, pleasure connoted something more than the satisfactions of the body. And even within this grosser sphere, there existed – as taught by the initiates in India – sublime experiences, for whose careful achievement Great Kubilai had no patience. This, after all – to borrow from the Sanskrit – was something of a boar of a man or a bull: one for whom the height and pulsing of his member was the be all of his manhood and whose gratification must be accomplished in a greedy and animal consummation.

After which urgency, in lieu of lying genially with his paramour and contemplating with her the exquisite vault of the chamber in which they had been playing and whose harmonies they had been encouraged by it to replicate, he would roll over and snore, while the lady would creep back to the *gynaeceum* where she would rest in the ambiguity of a purdah of one who had been at once privileged and abused.

This may be added (some may nod in recognition): that *eros* serves to sweep up everything of mind and body, and in so doing, will reduce to nothing all that does not lie within its moment. Earth, sun and moon are thereby harvested or garnered in, and at the same time cast away: for these, in acts of congress, represent an all-consuming All Things, in both incidence and in oblivion, and thus the cosmos, which is otherwise at hand, is both annulled and recreated.

This fact was of immeasurable convenience for one such as Great Kubilai, who stood both at the acme of authority and lay in his pavilions uncomprehending as a baby. While the meanings that inhered within the architecture of his mansions, which had been fabricated for his glory by a subject mind whose speculations he could not follow, would, with effortless repeated acts of rutting, be annihilated wholly.

15. *The Palace that Envelops the Heart*

If the solace of a happy private life represents a good, then surely it was in the seclusion of his apartments that the Khan found his satisfaction. And in commandeering – as though equipping himself with an elite personal guard – the most delectable young women of a remote province in which the prettiest children were be found, he ensured that he was surrounded with an inexhaustible supply of companions who could bring him pleasure and avoid disgusting him with foul breath, dribbling or snoring. (For those to be disqualified from the companionship of the imperial chamber would be weeded out during an intermediate period of observation by old ladies who bedded down with each candidate and made notes of their habit). In thus fortifying his hearth with pulchritude – and all that this entailed of emissaries and other subordinates who would, every three years, effect the import of these damsels from their places of breeding – the Great Khan was, of course, also executing state policy.

And if we are reminded of how gloomy Dis plucked Proserpine from meadows where she herself plucked flowers, let us recall also that according to Marco, it was, at this time and in those parts regarded as nothing but an honour to provide Great Kubilai with your prettiest daughters and to imagine a successful future for them in a place of privilege and exaltation.

But to my point, which is the nature of the Great Kubilai's's most intimate experience. Let us assume, first, the existence of women's quarters at a sufficient remove from the Khan's apartments to ensure mutual privacy, but still close enough to allow a quick transfer of persons – for nothing can be guaranteed to irritate an Emperor more than to be kept waiting or to be visited by a companion who arrives in disarray, perspiring or otherwise displaced from the coordination of her perfections.

I will not dwell on the cultivated entertainment that ensued and the manner in which this evolved into a carnal sporting. What exercises me still is the fact that this engrossment, howsoever it took place in an absolute seclusion of Great Kubilai's choosing, remained a political act which had its place in the life of his empire, and further, that his private chambers represented *state* apartments: and that were he not Emperor, this or that young woman would have been smiling on some toothless yokel across the rows of millet they were harvesting and that she would produce babies with him under rice thatch, sink into bucolic maternity, fast become a grandmother and die in the anonymous province where her granddaughters would repeat the experience.

But transported from — Province, here this fine girl stood, swayed, danced and sang and then dallied with the greatest Emperor that the world had ever seen. And for one night, for a week or a month, he would enter her body and she would receive the elixir of his potency – a commonplace enough currency! Subsequently, she would retire to the Great Khan's *harem*, to be presented in the end, if she continued to behave with decorum, to one of Kubilai's officials, who would do with her as he wished – albeit never again to see her kinsfolk or her childhood companions. Who, after all, would bother, once she had served her limited purpose, with the repatriation of such a little individual?

Reverting to the nature of the Great Khan's private transactions, it is reasonable to assume that he and his concubines, coming as they did from widely separated regions, spoke languages that were mutually unintelligible. And albeit locked in concupiscence, each party to that pleasant strife was, as to the realm of theory as opposed to practice, shuttered away securely from the other. Delightful, to Great Kubilai at least, as such encounters might briefly have been, this was nonetheless lonely exposure to some solitary other.

With strangulated grunts of lust he consumed her body – and then others still more fresh and lovely. While they, in return, as custom demanded, murmured teasing endearments in their region's language – though who knows with what insults in their honeyed and lubricious accents they assaulted him! Still, once the sweet event had run to consummation, an empty silence followed. And gathering now that *liquefaction* of her silks she had rustled in with, the lady hurried off with her eyes averted to the women's lodgings where shuddering in recollection of the indecencies to which she had been subjected, she gave herself over to her colleagues and rivals, who led her to a bath house and assisted in her toilet.

I have, in my imagination, expatiated somewhat pruriently on these eventualities in order to give air to the following suspicion. And this as follows. While the ladies of the harem were captives and, indeed, were enslaved to a tyrant whose only *raison d'être* was the exercise of power, the Great Khan, in turn, was in certain ways in the power of his ladies. For it is not difficult to imagine the women's gossip that followed each encounter. They were, of course, kept for one purpose only. But while they, in the changing composition of their group, represented a society, Great Kubilai was just one. And as he grew in years, he grew less manly in comportment and less capable of performance.

What intelligence, therefore, might have passed around among his women on a night when Great Kubilai was incapable? Or when his member had deflated quickly? What tattle, likewise, must have circulated on his porcine swellings or his fat-squeezed eyes, his gouty legs and ankles, the putrefaction of his breath and the pendulous belly that toppled him around when he was aroused, whether or not he had been drinking?

It is, of course, unthinkable that the Khan was not aware of such eventualities. What therefore should he do with the women with whom he performed unsatisfactorily, or even with those in whom he sensed a distaste for his attentions? Might they, at the outset, have been warned not to gossip about their imperial lover? What threats would have been issued against such an infraction? Could it not have been simpler just to do away with those who might retail discreditable narratives?

There were good reasons to oppose such a policy. A strangled concubine spoke grimly from the couch she had vacated. And the terror that such a crime would inspire might so intimidate her colleagues in their relations with the master that any spontaneity that they might bring to his pleasure would be impossible for them to sustain.

These were, I surmise, a small number of the circumstances that attended on the Khan's existence: and while *The Palace that Envelops the Heart* had been constructed for the enjoyment of great men and the employment of enchanting women, it was a place where beauty threw long, poignant shadow. And where greatness was reduced to a bewildered, solitary inanition.

Bolder slopes but lighter marches: notes taken from an Alpine landscape

It is midday in June and Mercury has entered Gemini. Out from the House of Mutability, the equinox achieves its culmination and from that altitude, the planet reigns in cordial and astringent sovereignty.

The air here *bites shrewdly. It is very* clear and windy. High on Rigi Mountain, seeking fire of the empyrean and ice from an infernal region, I have stood prospecting from a parapet of granite and pyrites (fire-stone!), and gazed down the rock toward some frozen branches of a cataract, so deep-ribbed it gripes the eye and renders freezing any thought that lies behind it.

O, who can hold a fire in his hand
By thinking on the frosty Caucasus?

cried bold, perhaps essentially unfeeling, Bolingbroke, as though he'd been bound there with Prometheus for some immortalising expiation. Thus *glacière* and zenith, whose signals are heraldic, blazon separate, incompatible extremities.

The mountain's ineluctability. How restless it makes us to rush against it. But before we scale its flank we bow in its direction.

There will, however, be fools who continue travelling in this posture: a pietistic hypertrophe of reverence which is self-serving. Nor do such people comprehend similitude. For what stands in concretion and the image this projects must co-exist in a harmonious adjacency of tension which conduces to a wholesome, but medicinal uncertainty.

Similarly, it would be to misunderstand the practice of bowing: which is to acknowledge the telluric pull of earth while observing the majesty of what transcends where we have planted ourselves. The Buddhists bend to images (or idols) of their leader in this spirit of respect for exaltation: which is the idea of a perfect, dead man now insensate as this rock that stands aloof, repels and draws me to it. But I may also choose *not* to bow. The Alp leaves me this freedom.

The lake, bracketed by mountains, is not uniformly turquoise but graduates to Prussian under storm-cloud and a paler sky-blue towards the sunlight and receding forest.

As though dropped from the heaven of some other mineral planet, the flatness of the water renders the horripilating foothills and serrated upper peaks yet more imposing. I stand looking from a range which rears behind me. Which is more elevated: to be on those heights opposite or to gaze across the lake and up towards them? 'Answer me,' I cried, 'Echo!'

But you, poor Elf, live only in some other's Self.
I am that too.
And therefore answer for both *Ich* and *Du*.

One may witness a great deal in the course of a walking tour of only seven days – but it would take the same number of years to understand what one has seen and yet again longer to interpret it. These are three different processes. And it is only when one arrives at the last that one may take up one's pen and make sense of the experience.

And yet is there not something wonderful to an enthusiastic out-rush? For without the faculty of inexperience and a juvenile, hubristic rashness, no one would get anything said, still less versified.

'*You* tell me what I should do now!'
(Echo's silent.)
'What? You mean extemporise?'
'If you have life force – then you will be noticed.'

The bounding growth of Rousseau's prose, which sends out sentences with branching, exuberant and leafy flourishes that swing free in the breezes of his speech as he reduces them to paper. This in contrast to the medicine of Voltaire's syntax, whose ironies ring forth with an astringency beyond the inference his punctuation brackets.

Here I am in Rousseau's country, to which, while France condemned the inspiration of *Emile*, he escaped (to no better reception), but where I now stride, a free man who rejoices in the good fortune of an unquestionable liberty. Rousseau's is a *walking along* writing. He's got *Emile* up in Sherwood Forest green. And like Montaigne, he contrives a conformable, elastic language from where to extend the companionship of one who can express himself without an antecedent doctrine, prelatical pontification or the self-defended posturing of a syllogism-driven academician.

What, by contrast, do my poetic ruminations achieve? At best they're inoffensive. And no one, least of all our bad dead Khan, will send me into exile for an iambic indiscretion. But what the *Lumières* provide us (though they also wrote it) is a harder thing than poetry. It takes a different genius to accomplish those progressions. And if I attempted them, I might end up ranting without reason in a labyrinth of self-perpetuating alexandrines!

The bird in mountain ash with this repeated message: 'I'll sing to you these few bright shillings!'

Each note shuffles on the other, as though threepences and sixpences – small, light pieces – had slipped into the roulade of a heavier currency.

The cowbells, by contrast, have a watery and hollow music, as though this issues from a container which is in the continuous movement of being emptied and moves in synchrony with the little torrents that rush from crevices in the hillside.

The lower bell notes meanwhile sound the walking ground bass of a passacaglia which is decorated from beyond by the cheerful falsetto of birds that sing continually in freedoms about which they rejoice, at this high altitude, with justified pride and patriotic *élan*.

In the crypt of an Abbey, a small inner room through whose darkness I am greeted by the coarse-grained features of a corbel. It is sneering. Near this, traces of another where all that remains is an expression of disdain which searches the shadows for an object of interrogation.

A madman might imagine that these heads had thrust themselves from the granite to make a judgement on him: and that such witness might be carried to a chthonic power whose memoranda were stored in some library of infernal *incunabula* which, table by stone table, grew from the foundations, until the entire building was displaced by records of the pilgrims who had sojourned here without recovering from their delusion.

I knew of one, elsewhere, who believed that could he cut deep into a slab of marble he would find his name engraved there. Another, whose projected thought, he reckoned, could raise death's heads, roses, shields and panegyrics dedicated to him. There seems, I contend, an aristocracy of the ambitious, the imagination of whose immodesty it would be an impertinence to scorn. God bless such delusions. But defend me from them.

While I struggle with inaction, both inertia and my fight against its strangle become the activity of a non-action. Which engagement generates asphyxiation.

Now seated this July beneath a cherry tree which is in the full-flame of fruition, I'm in serene enough condition. These are a small, sour cherry which some, with a digestive virtuosity, can gobble raw, but which most of us eat cooked and broken with a pound of sugar or reduced to a preserve and put away against the winter.

It was light until ten, and then about that time, I betook myself to acts that now have their product. While the blackbirds made off with fruit from higher branches, I stood among the lower twigs, and dazzled by light that still glanced around each unripe cherry and which darkened the red ones, I gathered, simply by reaching up and slightly pulling, a good half basket.

Now I have, during the season, passed under this same tree innumerable times and on each occasion it reveals a different complexion. But it's this, in the tree's guise as a food store, that provokes observation:

A blackbird clutching a low branch, grips a cherry in her beak, drops it, pecks uncertainly another – and this falls too. A third, finally, she grasps. It stands packed at the base of her bill, distending the stare of that wary, inexpressive eye, and then she flies off from the orchard, half-choked with her guerdon. Were I tempted to moralise over this sequence of attempts, I would, I hope, resist. But how *she* might comment on my relations, idle and then predatory, with this quite successful tree? Well, that must remain her most blackbirdy of secrets.

This dream I woke from. Christ nailed with pegs that had been whittled from the Tree of Knowledge to the trunk of that same Tree, which itself, by turns, is the Serpent and the Body of an Angelic Host shouting praises to a Natural Order of which the Crucifixion has become an outraged Negation.

And in one man's fate, *katharsis* of all human history? I suspect not. Christ was murdered because he represented an irritant to Roman hegemony. The two men who flanked him and who were, like all human beings, the progeny of Nature, suffered torments that were equivalent but nonpolitical, and so history passed them over.

It happened one June evening I was reading in the orchard which was lit no longer with mixed apple blossom, as last month it had been. And while *Juliet* protested in Act III she heard the nightingale and her – very recent! – husband claimed the lark was up and he must with it: there close at hand, but shrouded by green fruit and foliage, a nightingale broke into singing and pierced the *sweet strife* of the lovers' antiphon, as though this noisy little bird, aloft, fugitive and hidden, had tuned its throat to relatively early Shakespeare.

It sang – or *he*, I thought, did. And after some pages, the bird got his answer with reciprocal opinion: shrilling with a high-flown gossip, which – self, breasting self, in a mutual division – shattered the young apple shadow.

I'd hoped, as they flitted between tree tops Juliet would silence them. But no. Importuning one another with their marriage canon they proceeded – and I fled that music.[26]

Where, having stopped before, at daybreak, had this singer started? All one may conjecture is the place the nightingale elected to begin was – its beginning: and from that questionable moment, we embark on attribution or interpretation, joining what we *cast* upon it with the currents we have bathed in since, as children, we were led out through, in June, the *darkling* coppice, by our proper nurses. (When we were small, they loved us for our artless spirits. And we loved them for their precise simplicity.)

Reverting to that bard, a bird: it's immortality in what is mortal we imagine. And the more insistent this proclaims proximity, the higher we're inclined to elevate it from us.

What would gratify me *merrilie* would be to follow, notate, fix in a description what these spouses chime on one another, so uxoriously public, as though the world they fill with song's their bridal chamber, and – like those *krauncha* birds' unlucky hymeneal – chant from the outset or even before it: which is anywhere there's love that's founded on a reciprocity.

The nightingale, of course, is what we most aspire to. But who then does the hunting, *sleeks the nest* and edifies the babies? Do these kings of the *laryngo*, with imperial enchantment, subjugate the lark, the blackbird and sparrow to their service?

Be that their business, I stand clipped in by these disjunct stanzas: within each of whose *hiatus* hangs a statement, in suspension, till the next pre-meditated fragment enters. Those silences, themselves, are both universities and nurseries. And within these, since, I think, they're pieced to one another's margin, there, along with wheezings, whines and squealing,

---

26 *O Nachtigall*, I, rueful, la-ed back, *Ruhe! Ruhe bitte! Ich möchte unser'n Shakespeare lesen* – obfuscated as it is already in this salad of a hypallage and vegetation. (Vacillating also between kind, confused Friar Lawrence' garden and that single-minded murder student, the Apothecary!)

lies an interrogative, half-swallowed by a chatter that suggests a modesty, a hesitation or a reticence – for sometimes even *Mon Sieur* Nightingale is at a loss for an idea or inspiration! But that don't stop it. No. Each pause re-introduces an intensified and whinneying per*sev*erance: *cheeps, cheezing, whees, whirrs, then* a *jug-jug-jug* (or *chook*) and *twee-twee-twee,* succeeded by roulades of *piu-* (a liquefaction, flatters water) and whose cadence climbs in a percussive fluting, within which – residues of qualm absconded – was its statement or thematic iteration.

Now the intervals, I'd judge, between each utterance, each clear but inexplicable, are uniform. Each silence equal; in itself a music. While into those pauses arrive rumours of surrounding jawdaw, chaffinch, blackbird – startled too often for no good reason.

There are also insects – and these, as though the nightingale had, in full spate of an inhalation, swallowed down some hummer, and these became incorporated in its *tuc* and *wheet-wheet-wheeting*: which accelerate and then, as though that bee or fly's wing had got stuck, edge-on, in its larynx, the *aria* gets tense and condescends around its intromission as the melody engulfs – and finally digests it.

Thus it is, at intervals between each stanza. For the swiftness of this bird's consecutive ideas disrupts or at the least disturbs too frequent a self-reference. It's extreme, that invention (a compulsion), whose sweetness is a rush creates a drama of the tree-tops – peaceful otherwise: till they, as well, are caught up in that dormitory lucubration!

(I *maun* let this go now. Float off and, two nightingales too many – Shakespeare nesciently interrupted – sleep now. That's if Juliet allows it.)

Can form take leave of the colour of which it is constituted? Or colour subsist in separation from the place and time through which it was manifested?

I stood on the cliff-edge for an hour or so, absorbed with changes in a sunset whose glamour became magnified by each shift in cloud the sun lit from behind, and which offered a fluid and a sailing blue, each of whose modulations offered the appearance of a consummation, but which in truth was a stage in a sequence of unequally composed, dissolving tableaux. This constitutes no certain answer to my question. I rejoice merely in what comes into being. And equally admire its dissolution: form disappearing with the dissipation and the death of colour, while offering the promise of a repetition of its transpositions.

She dwells in a moral and aesthetic purity which I can not emulate. This is because I love my faults and it is my very incompleteness that maintains my ambition. If, as she is, I were good and beautiful already, where would I adventure? The imaginative life rejoices in its imperfections: and were I to feel complete, there would be nothing left to make.

One must beware likewise of attempting to create too perfect a refinement. In certain imperfections lie the rude beauties in Shakespeare – for which we love the difficulties of *Coriolanus* with its inexorable grammar, and those passages in *Measure for Measure* that repel interpretation. Against this, Augustan polish gives us so little to grip that we are in peril of sliding away from it over the same surface from which it seems to have been fashioned. (Lovely it remains, however. And we would go mad if we did not have Pope and Johnson to warn us against too gross a disproportion in our writing – and indeed in our self-being!)

Let us all therefore strive, both for that balance in our loves and couplets, and for so tremendous an idiosyncrasy as to assassinate too great a moderation. And thus caparisoned with dialects of motley, caper with the Bard's fantasticks into a dotage of imperfections!

Against the above. Two marks of a great writer are: Amplitude, in fraternity with a simple loftiness of utterance. And compassion for the world and all the beings in it as expressed in an apprehension of *lacrimae rerum*. Transcending any fault, which is an allowance of genius, Shakespeare does both these in exemplary abundance.

Milton was the magnificent and disdainful exception. Because, for him, perhaps, Christianity was warfare.

I dreamed on the vulpine hostess of my Alpine lodging and she presented a very image of horror. I was, as happened yesterday, seated at an inn table, when she entered enveloped in a blue and red cape as though Lady Macbeth were homologised in this figure with the Virgin Madonna. On a tray she carried stood plates of reeking viands surrounded by bowls of what I took to be a thick red wine which had been heated for some ceremonial.

She stopped, as she entered, at the threshold and cast a violent gaze around the table. When her terrible brown eyes came sweeping towards me and settled on where I was sitting, she rose to a height which seemed far in excess of the figure that she naturally presented and with her hair scattered among the ceiling beams, she hurled the tray in my direction. As this travelled – an age seemed to pass before it came upon me – I heard her scream, as though in revenge for acts, she implied, that emanate from men in generality: 'There! That's for your inconstancy!'

And at once I was awash with blood that spurted from the flying basins, while the hot meats bounded, beating in a wild rhythm of human hearts and a miscellany of other palpitating organs, onto the tables, the floor, my legs, my groin – and flapping even over my face and chest.

As these danced in a ragged formation around the table, our hostess, whose face had been lately transfigured into the most grotesque deformations, burst suddenly into light-hearted singing which she interspersed with a sequence of musical and childlike chuckles. My cowherd companions, who seemed not in the least alarmed by their hostess' action, continued uninterrupted to talk among themselves, supping from their crusted mugs and mending the pipes that they passed to one another.

'Either these gentlemen entertain no fear of this witch in whose house they are taking their leisure, or (is it possible?) they remain unaware of what I have suffered.'

Perhaps – I reflected as I left that murky tavern – this is what happens in all daily intercourse. And when it is *their* turn to be assaulted, *I* will be the one who is incapable of bearing witness?

I pass groups of cows with whom the herders of last night's meeting (or its dream) are intimates. Each swings a bell with its identifying tintinnabulation. They all eat grass and, promiscuously, the wild flowers that grow here in a profusion of blue and yellow. And while I am preoccupied with rudimentary floral taxonomy, they ruminate on them for their sap, as the cowherders' minds are filled with the next season's cheeses.

While cows innocuously graze, I too experience security along this higher path I've taken up the mountain, where I'll enjoy a prospect, *alp on endless alp*, which I'm exempt from climbing.

Jonson's great lines accompany my footsteps:

> But sing high and aloofe,
> Safe from the wolves black jaw, and the dull
> Asses hoofe.

As the cattle digest flowers, and their milk will turn into delicious cheeses, so the Wanderer consumes impressions and their accumulation builds towards his wholeness. The ambitious will turn images that they've absorbed to products of imagination. And while the purity of experience may be violated by the effort of conversion, ambition has this virtue, in that it keeps a person lively.

But too often, youth's attended by the self-absorbed regard of a Narcissus. Shakespeare's mirror (like Narcissus' pond stood upright) must be held to Nature. But this implies its unreflecting surface faces inward. Montaigne's the great exception. Impossible to weary of that sage's ruminant and scrupulous, self-chewing-over.

There are, on this mountain, small herds of goat which are enclosed now and again by cottages or little sheds. These skinny and dishevelled creatures, which unlike the cows, appear in need of a thorough hairdressing, also carry their distinctive bell collars. As they move, grazing up and down their pasture, so they chime. And because they have each carried their bell since before they can remember, they seem not at all disturbed that these pendulations from their dewlaps clatter.

I am tempted to imagine that these useful creatures assume both bell and necklace to be a part of their body – and not hung there purely in the interests of their mercenary superintendants who are breeding them for meat and cheeses. And just as they can detect the beating of their hearts and the inhalations of their breath when they are at rest, so they apprehend their bell to be an organ which is associated with motion and with the nodding movement of feeding.

There are among the cows, so many bells that the cacophony of these presents persistent commentary on their movements. Thus also in our thoughts. I will wander toward a higher elevation, beyond the rabble of these cattle, in pursuit of freedom from the clattering that hangs on my own intellection. On the far side of the mountain, high, beyond the bell and gentian, between snow and aether, lies visionary freedom from all thought and feeling!

I have come to a woodsman's hut with its axes, long- and short-toothed saws and its rough, notched benches which are themselves in danger of being sawn into firewood. This place of rugged labour is situated next to a little chapel where a priest no doubt toils for the salvation of these semi-heathen people. And because of this, I have become preoccupied with the adjacency.

At which, I ask, should I throw myself in submission? I have a tendency towards worship, which lies in disharmony with the pessimism of my unbelief and allied to a skeptical disregard for particularities of religion.

If we are to live in a metaphysical dimension – which, whether or not we want to, we may – this is an abstract and diffuse medium which defies calculation. And I would be more at home measuring the length of a pine plank than in speculating on divine immanence.

Given the choice, as suggested by these chapels, between the profession of priest or woodsman, I would unhesitatingly choose the latter. And then jig from peak to peak all evening with the *hamadryads* I have liberated.

It is hard to believe that this immense chain of mountains spread before me, to the extent that, seated as I am in a flowery meadow, I must turn my head all the way to the left and then right and even a little over my shoulder in order to take in the entire prospect – it is difficult to believe that this is not simply a painting or the long stretch of some theatre scenery. And why do I believe? In part because I am here with all the mixed feelings of pleasure and pain that inform each moment of existence.

And a horse fly which had settled on my ankle to sup on my life's blood by donating its sting, has flown away having successfully achieved what it came for. Ruddy, aching sunset heats my ankle. How climactically this itches! So I turn back to the mountains, and the distant grey, blue, ice-white of their half-truth cools me.

Prophetic anachronism

Ich weiss nicht, was soll es bedeuten,	I don't know what this must mean
Dass ich so traurig bin,	That I'm so sad,
Ein Märchen aus alten Zeiten,	A tale from the old days
Das kommt mir nicht aus dem Sinn.	Won't leave my mind.

These fainting and yet virile numbers are composed as if by my *Doppel-gänger*. And just as the Judaic Heine's apostasy in some sense rendered the Hebrew of his sensibility still more alien to the Christianity and perhaps the Teutonism he both deprecated and embraced, so the Great Khan made himself a modern person, and his self-adoption into China intensified his apprehension that steppeland grasses still palpably adhered to his buskins.

It would take some volumes to explore this lyric episode. And yet briefly as follows: the quatrain *faints* in that the mixed sibilation of the opening two words articulate a knowing sigh (*Ich weiss*) which is sunk or annulled by *nicht* – a syllable which repeats the hiss of *Ich* and thereby topples that away from its initial verticality (as noted before in a Shakespeare Sonnet).

By the time we have arrived at two further little sibilations (*was es*) that perch on either side of the caesura, the poet's confession of unknowing has drawn us in concern towards the sofa where a dream has disturbed him. Given that we are in the realm of an expostulative subjectivity, the verb (*soll bedeuten*, 'must mean') that lies on the eastern side of the caesura arrives most welcome: for what those last three words suggest is that some haunting, unidentified, weighs down on the *Ich* which renders it thus the object of oppression.

So far, the simple music of this line, so wonderingly candid in its vulnerability, is composed of finely tessellated verbal parts which have been placed together with the delicacy of a goldsmith: the finicking intaglio of its detail accumulating into a long exhalation which the brevity of its nine painful syllables both belies and then artfully enjambs with the forthright confession of its sadness in line 2, thus giving the whole sentence the sweep of a statement which has led from consciousness of a bewilderment to an incapacitating melancholy.

By line 3, however, the poet has travelled some distance, and into a mysterious new country. There is further estrangement. For while lines 1 and 2 are set firmly in the present, this moment of reflection is invaded by the presence of an *Ur* time, whose character is inflected by a suggestion of the Medieval, whose *Märchen* and ballads were the literary vehicles of what came from yet more ancient folk traditions. How justified, then, this poet's disturbance: for despite his present and reasonable awareness, inscrutable loomings have entered his condition, lie heavy, and won't leave it.

We scarcely need to be told the story that follows: the Siren or the *Lorelei*, whose beauty and whose song draw fishermen to doom, has already, by the first stanza, enacted her work on the poet. Little wonder then that a story of magical temptation in the face of cruel beauty should have exerted the weight he apprehends in that distracted first whisper: where, as helpless self-witness to his own susceptibility, he identifies the *matter*, and in the course of a quasi- Odyssean voyage, that he has, at least psychologically, undertaken, he succumbs to *glamour*, along with all the common little fools – those brawny mariners! – who smash their boats and break their hearts on rocks where the Siren disarmingly continues to ply her combing.

Now whereas Goethe in his *Erlkönig* creates of his verses a horseback journey, with Heine, the experience of the ballad, while masculine in its orientation to what is *Weiblich*, is feebler. Heine's verse is sleek. It issues from the salon. And yet, by means of an intelligence that reaches beyond the urbane slipper, his stanzas retain the beauty of what he longs to touch, how dangerous soever this is to him.[27]

Note, finally, the rush of his lyric solution, so perfectly tuned to both parlour and the ballad quatrain: at once genteel and Medieval, suave in diagnosis of *malaise*, and chanted as if by a simpleton, a knave in a wanderer's adventure ballad. *O Doppelgänger! du bleicher Geselle!* ('Thou pallid companion!') as Heine, older, might have written of the faery, and the cunning of a younger man's intoxication. Such lines incorporating hauntings from our long inheritance, speak with an unsettling familiarity. As perhaps to all who have thrashed in and been strangulated by those other-worldly meshes.

But this story from *alten Zeiten* – how that sense of ur-time sings to us with its smack of the Euphrates! – is not just for Rhymers. No. That old day is a universal presence: and grows to be a worry – a dream that has been shared by every mind since Eve gave birth to bifurcating tribes of gardeners and hunting people – because now it's overlaid by conversation, behind whose chatter, interlarded with authoritative lectures, it hangs, transformative, but filled with peril, with its looms and needles, supernatural combs, spears, traps and every kind of hunting tackle. It's in the old Garden, and carries an infected germen, which, too boisterously watered, will overwhelm the orchard and grow poisonous apples.

Those were some thoughts as I looked down on the Lake and heard the cows behind me ruminating on wild flowers and grasses. What, I ruminated with them, if some witch on the Rigi sent a spirit in her service paint my cyclid with a buttercup elixir – and like some Pasiphae in pantaloons, in the character of Bottom, I were lacerated with a passion for a Switzer cheese cow, and she appeared before me as some bovine *Lorelei* whose mooing'ld lure me to perdition and I died here for her apathetic udder?

In my little hut: malaise, lethargy and thoughts of dissolution. Outside in the meadow, a cure among flowers, mountain waters that sustain them, and so uncomplicated an air that it simplifies, with every breath, both flesh and spirit. And these thus become, while the weather holds, united. The Lorelei may sing. But I am havened by the Rigi – in despite its mountaineering witches!

---

27 Heine steps into the rough world of the folk in his *Buch der Lieder*. But he wants to walk off on the beach with fisher girls and dally with them in imagination when they should be packing tubs with herring.

A stream in a ditch which is cooled by pine shade. Overhanging this, a thick, dirty dome of last year's snow is moulded to a scallop and ridged into a fan of barnacle-like encrustations. There it will lie all summer until it is covered in fresh snow which will outlast next season. And so on to the everlasting bonfire.

If there is one haunting to whose possession I have submitted, it's that exercised by Alpine meadow gentians: and this is a condition by which I am happy to be enthralled. It is the sheer beauty of this mountain blossom, whose horn rises in distinct, dark blue from long and grassy leaves, that is, in form and in complexion, perfect.

This is a flower that I associate with Proserpine. Imagine that young woman, where she gathers in Aegean twilight, flowers that match in dark hues with their slender petals, grace that shines from her, as she runs through a meadow and then, in her demise, is dragged to Dis's dismal, melancholy kingdom. Down, down she descends – still clutching, in her worry, shining, long stemmed blossoms that she'd gathered for her own dark hair or evening table.

Enthroned eventually as Dis's consort, she radiates, still, a soft, deep light, which glows blue as gentians in an Alpine meadow. This sustains her winters of infernal residence. And I, too, keep my spirit buoyant, through her presence, in these little blossoms.

Gentian, buttercup, anemone. Promiscuously, soon, to be cut for hay. How the animals will bloom with eating these delicious grasses, hemmed in by lime-stone henges through the winter.

In prospect of this, I stopped at a meadow and kept vigil by a mower who walked behind his scythe – as though stately old Time, in hemispheric rhythm, swept back the hay he lined behind him, as he did the season – before this jolly month had even reached its climacteric.

The mixed magnificence of hill and mountains with their rocky flanks and glassy crescendos that reach toward heaven. In the evening, sunlight veiled with a blue mist that rises from, and now falls towards the shifting turquoise of the lake beneath us. The scale of this small portion fells me. But one must stand up to what is tremendous – with the companionable respect of one who participates in what is great without aspiring to its dimension.

At a rockfall in a clearing some men stack hay beside a wooden shelter. As they load what they have gathered on a wagon, their conversation turns to some eventuality connected with this place, and once they are done, they settle on a pine trunk and refresh themselves with dried meat and with water from a bottle. I refrain from questions: for I've identified a melancholy presence in the rocks that fringe the meadow.

As I sit with these men and they follow my gaze to a fissure in the cliff face whence these rocks have fallen, I note their cognizance of my intrusive curiosity, and so with them I eschew the warm, flat boulders where we might have stretched our bodies.

If I'd wished to plumb a ghostly story, I might have been unnerved by this. I glean, as it is, the bare bones – words are insufficient – of a local tragedy. Thus we hold vigil in a shared solemnity. And then walk home to the village.

This mountain solitude – at once charmed and desolate. The high peaks draw the footstep upward. A sharp cough drags me downward, while at heart's bottom lies the well of melancholy that feeds imagination its dispiriting confabulation.

Take this lesson from the marguerite which lifts twenty outstretched petals and its pad of powdery, vermiculated yellow – all reaching skyward to a sun which only variably responds with the benediction of an answer.

There are no longer the 'old days'. And transformation lies in the seeds of the present that we grasp darkly, but may not comprehend. There is however an inherent machinery, latent in our age, which breaks through with a persistent and surreptitious violence from its dormancy and which will change our world for ever. That, I fear, will evolve into an age of the inauthentic. But we, by then, will have been so long gone that our apprehensions will be of no consequence.

The privileges of this temporary mountain existence: first in that it lifts us to a sphere that belongs otherwise to the imagination. And second in that it offers a down-view onto the life we lead *normalerweise*. It is both the height and the simplification which adverts us to the lower and more complex divisions of our activity.

Thus gazing down onto the labyrinth of interconnected paths – some already followed, most still untried – I grow breathless with amazement that any human can survive the perturbations, false starts, disappointments and infatuations he meets daily. It is, in this lofty regard, a wonder that all mankind is not reduced to a despairing madness.

I have stopped where a long scarlet beetle is making an assault on a stem of light pink clover. It thrusts its head and feelers between the petals, backs its abdomen to where it came from, stands waving its feet into the complexity of the flower head, tramples quickly backward in a ripple of its six co-ordinated insect legs, opens its wings with a crepitation of enamel and flies off to new pasture.

Another, in the meantime, basks idly enjoying the sunlight on the open face of a yellow blossom but then finally attempts to burrow to its meagre depths, emerging with little but a dusting of pollen on its wing cases. So these *coleoptera* have their passions, blunderings and divagations. The honey bees, too, are oscillating knowledgeably around the meadow. Everything but flowers

That rise, blow and die
Before the gazer's mortal eye

exists in a concert of restless and dizzy milling. And yet I suspect these little fellows, the natural poetry of whose ambition lies in pollen grains and pin-drops of honey, know very well what they want, and go about their affairs single-mindedly and with an instinct that we might learn from. (But see *supra* on a bee that staggered, with a stupifying optimism, around in hollyhock blossom.)

As I walk up on the Rigi, the weather alters by the moment. Streams of cold air are replaced abruptly with a smotheringly damp sunshine that envelops the face as though in heated flannels that are charged with hot, thick honey. The wind blows between these layerings as though through bars of sunset, paying out its thin grey cloud-stripes on a primrose-yellow horizon before dissolving into a darker, swallow-breasted twilight.

The doubleness of everything is thereby multiplied. And the multiplication we observe, only in miniature, is a part of a grand and inconceivable number which both changes and remains constant in its variation. We see only a little at any one moment. Thus encouraging a confidence in everything and nothing.

She is inside, sober this time, with an almanac on the table and her long nose searching out, within it, planetary motions, permutations and disturbances. I order a grog and sit outside the tavern on a bench near which a woodsman labours. Presently, comes out last evening's witch and nods, smiling to me, then approaching her wood cutter, stands in conversation until a laughter between them is ignited, as though by the friction of one timber on another, and she retreats into the tavern.

Twice, as I sit here, a veil of thin blue cloud is blown across the peak that rises nearest above us, now concentrating itself into a sheet and now balling up its vapour so it drops into the lower slopes and is dissipated among the pine branches. Chattering in her merry dialect, she stands behind me again now, in animated conversation with a taciturn young man who sits with his mug and answers her with caution.

As this talk proceeds, the words 'fault', 'punishment', 'forgiveness' – as if these bobbed on a stream amid the current of her dialect – are thrown up inconsequentially. Invisibly to me, as I can measure from the movement of her clogs, she goes in and out – as though she is the door, itself, on hinges which heavily push her from the darkness of the interior into the damp, uncomfortable, warm noonday sunshine – while in this connection, I anticipate, too, from the heavy door's swing between these positions, a blow from her on the neck – or equally from her interlocutor – though it would be she, I think, who would strike him first, with his own tankard.

And still all at my back I hear are fragments of a minatory dialogue – as though witchcraft were insinuated, by a species of diffusion, towards any party who might fall within the web of their exchanges. 'But it is *he* who is the witch,' I overhear my speculation. (But then doth not 'speculate' imply, like 'maculate', the distribution of infected particles that will stick to an otherwise clear membrane?)

This, however, was no *Lorelei*, exalted in a naked separation. Ah no, this one's swarming and appropriative eye would, had I turned in her direction, have made a soup of my whole person, boots and body, and indeed a meaty one, for supper. Nor would she sing, I think, unless to sit up on a midnight branch and screech a portent, for her sisterhood to halloo back to her!

A small grey and purple butterfly on the path which, without argy-bargy of an introspection, knows itself. Had I trodden on that specimen, the universe would have been depleted – as Catullus wrote of his puella's sparrow: *qui nunc it per iter tenebricosum.*

These little creatures do not fear death and we may take heart from their single-mindedness. Prescience is a condition with which we humans incontinently allow ourselves to suffer. Let us continue at least half-blind to our own destinies and profit from what time we enjoy in the present! (Long live such commonplaces that justifiably survive our nurses – who lived better lives than we do.)

A mighty presence to which every blade of grass and flower contributes. Rocks, precipices, waterfalls and black canopies of forest represent the supporting architecture which is constructed of the same matter and which contains eternal, self-perpetuating energy.

It is difficult to know whether one belongs to all this, for to apprehend it expresses a degree of separation. And yet when I turn to the surface of this pine trunk, with its lichenous growths and ragged, barky islands, I see my own nature mirrored from these patterns – clinging as they do in living, obscure interlockings.

And suddenly now, I observe myself reflected, to extreme reduction, in a ball of sap that stretches from the loose edge of a bark fragment: on the point, for longer than I can wait for it to drop, of a precipitous decision, but incapable of moving forward.

Thus I am repeated in that picture of Narcissus I have derogated. Let me better vanish, and in more than my reflection, with this drop of resin.

Five men have walked by without greeting or acknowledgement. Am I finally invisible? Delightful condition.

Could I only turn the process on myself and live like a plant whose being lies in its up-stretch as it reproduces without self-reflection.

Now here was a spectacle I had not witnessed previously. On a wet log in the forest, the grain of it coming away in yellow rotten lumps, two stag beetles advance, and with antlers levering and tossing, fight, while a female, waiting to be mated, observes until the victor has dislodged his rival and he turns, with elephantine triumph, and covers this consort for whom he has done battle in a blind and horny grasping.

This prompts in me some boyish thoughts of many colours. But most, I think of Nero, screaming at the games, in his arousal, as one fighter fells a rival, and at Nero's signal, intercepts his victim's heartbeat with his sword or trident.

This was not my feeling. But I heard, at that moment, all Rome in uproar and the Colosseum shaking. Caesar retreats then to a side room and outrages his catamite, who bellows with the surprise. And then, like an infant, guzzles on Poppea's nipple. She is with child and quite soon he will kill her.

Reverting to the beetles. To fight, presumably, is in every species' ancestry. Nor is it simply imperial to do it in the service of a woman. Even butterflies attack and eat each other. I have seen the *Small Blue* which seems otherwise a snapped-off edge of heaven, sup in clusters of a dozen on a dead one of their number – and leave nothing but a patch of damp for ants that followed.

Topographical descriptions

The Rev. John Collinson, the case of Edmund Rack, a visitor from Porlock, views of a rainbow over Hurlstone

The *Hundred of Carhampton* [in which Culbone lies] is situated in the north-west part of the county, and is bounded on the north and northwest by the sea and on the west by the borders of Devonshire.

This mountainous tract may be called the *Alps* of Somersetshire; the whole country being a picturesque assemblage of lofty hills succeeding each other, with deep romantick vallies winding between them, in which most of the towns and villages are situated. The hills are principally sheep-walks; but in the western part many of them are so covered with heath, fern, and moss, as to afford little pasturage. The steep sides of most of them are either entirely vested, or patched with beautiful hanging woods, intermixed with projecting rugged rocks. The vallies are fruitful, and generally watered by small streams, running over rough rocky channels, and often interrupted by stony fragments fallen from the mountains. (John Collinson, *The History of Somersetshire, 1791*)

What happiness it might have given me had the world of my poem belonged properly in Kubilai's empire! And yet how misguided. For what could I touch of Shang-du and the gorges, mazings, rivers, gardens, pastures I'd imagined? All I can claim is that I stretched my verses, in their flexible ductility, across that chasm separating Culbone Wood from Xanadu.

Here then, in this parish, is my proper station – almost new to me as Xanadu, albeit closer – and at a damp end of the rainbow bridge which reached me back, estranged or de-ranged, many unfamiliar centuries.

And my theme lies, indeed, in this domesticated situation: for my rhyming was engendered not in Shang-du or *Serinde*, but rather arose from this home-spun region. For while in my dream, I travelled to Cathay, my poem belonged finally and first in Somerset's Carhampton Hundred. And why, afterall, should I shog off this little parish at the west end of our county on some pretension I had travelled eastward – when most I knew of that horizon was what I'd read in Purchas, Marco and some little passages of Sanskrit?

Let me then quote from two publications that have come to hand, both written near the time of my own visit. First, from Rev. Collinson's *Somerset History and Antiquities*. This followed by the Greenwoods, County Surveyors, who *delineated* Somerset.

Of Culbone, or Kitnor, Collinson writes:

A very small parish on the sea coast, nine miles west from the town of Minehead, containing only nine houses and fifty inhabitants. The lands consist of eighty acres of arable, and two hundred acres of pasture and furze-brake, the rest is wood.

The ancient appellation of this parish is Kytenore or Kitnore; that of *Culbone* having obtained in later times, from the saint to whom its church is dedicated. The Norman survey calls it *Chetemore*, and thus describes it: *in the time of king Edward it gelded for one hide, and one virgate. The arable is two carucates. There are two villanes, and one cottager, and one servant with one plough, and fifty acres of pasture, and one hundred acres of wood. It is worth fifteen shillings.*

The church is a small Gothick building, thirty-four feet long, and twelve feet wide, consisting of a single aisle, chancel, and porch, covered with Cornish tiles. The situation of this church is singularly romantick; it stands in a little narrow cove, about four hundred feet above the level of the water. On each side of this cove the hills rise almost perpendicularly more than twelve hundred feet high. That on the west side is conical, and considerably higher.

The back of the cove is a noble amphitheatre of steep hills and rocks, which rise near six hundred feet above the church, and are covered with coppice woods to the tops. The trees that compose these vast plantations, set by the hand of nature, are oaks, beech, mountain ash, poplars, pines and firs, mingled together in the most wanton variety. At the back ground of this cove, through a steep narrow winding glen, a fine rivulet rushes down a narrow rocky channel overhung with wood, and passing by the church, forms a succession of cascades in its descent down the rocks into the sea.

The spot is as truly romantick as any perhaps which the kingdom can exhibit. The magnitude, height, and grandeur of the hills, rocks, and woods, at the back and on each side of the cove; the solemnity of the surrounding scene; the sound of the rivulet roaring down its craggy channel; the steep impassable descent from the church down to the beach; the dashing of the waves on a rough and stony shore at an awful distance below; the extent of the channel, and finely varied coast and mountains of Wales beyond it; form a scene peculiarly adapted to strike the mind with pleasure and astonishment.

The parish cannot be approached on horseback without great difficulty, and even danger; the road from Porlock being only a path about two feet wide, winding in a zigzag direction along the slope of the hills, and often interrupted by large loose stones and roots of trees. The woods abound in whortleberries, and a variety of fine polybodies, lichen, and other mosses, among which is some of the yellow rein-deer moss, very bright and scarce. There are also some rare plants; and many wild deer, foxes, badgers, and martin cats, inhabit these woods.

During the three winter months the sun is never seen here; being entirely hid by the height of the surrounding hills.

In complement to Collinson, here is the Greenwoods' succinct description:

a very small parish, in Carhampton hundred, 3 miles WNW from Porlock; containing 10 inhabited houses, and 11 families, 6 of whom are employed in agriculture. This parish is environed on every side by mountains, which rise so high as to render the sun invisible nearly three months in the year, and for the same reason it is not possible to approach it on horseback without danger. The church is a neat Gothic building situated in a narrow cove, surrounded with hills, ascending almost perpendicular to the height of 1200 feet, and covered with oaks, beech, ash, poplars, pines and firs, mingled together by the hand of nature in the most picturesque manner; a beautiful rivulet rushes through a narrow channel in the interior of this cove, and passing the church, forms a succession of cascades as it flows down the rocks into the sea.

Such are the environs – bar poplars to which I will not swear. And while to the Greenwoods this location's *picturesque*, Collinson maintains it's *noble* and *romantick* – tempting to readers of a walking habit.

But in his Preface, Collinson gives something extra. For as prelude to his thirteen hundred pages, he sketches how a knowledge of *Provincial History* contributes to an understanding of our nation and shared human nature.

Now here's a purpose which is altruistic (and hieratic!), with part of which I am in sympathy. For it's Collinson's aim to nurture *amor patriae*. 'We cannot love', he writes (or preaches), 'that with which we are unacquainted.' And as love augments with knowledge, so we better comprehend, with respect to our county, 'works of Providence. By *intuition* of these, the mind exults in pursuing the Deity.'

With *intuition* I am in concurrence. This – in that it joins a person to the object of his contemplation – enobles that in us conjoins itself to what it witnesses in Nature.

The coincident details in Collinson are clear. *Mingled* (he writes) *in the most wanton variety* are grand *rocks and woods* and a *craggy channel, dashing waves* and an *awful distance*. All these heightened by secluded situation, echoes of previous habitation and the drama of its place between the mountains and the ocean. (What better stage could Wanderers in execution of a *Nachtlied* wish as stimulus to the imagination?)

But did the Reverend's mind 'exult', with *pleasure* and *astonishment*, in Culbone's grandeur? Can *rapture*, after all – along with whortleberries and tiles and all the woodland species that he itemises – be classed as topographic information: as though the landscape, itself, were provisioned with the therewithal or substance of a visitor's reaction to it and thus offered it to all who walked there to receive it equally?

Following this question, I am tempted to surmise the Reverend's rapture, not unlike the information that he lays before us, is somehow borrowed: and that Collinson expresses not what he had felt and witnessed, but was copying, instead, a style of *writing* – of the sort presented by 'pretenders who impose with an affectation of sensibility.' (This from Edmund Rack – about whom more later.) Which leads one to suspect that Collinson had never been to Culbone, nor in many places like it.[28]

Still, Collinson's in sympathy with the sublime. It's to his taste – in moderation. And while he stands as mere spectator to those forms that might, were he receptive, rouse his passion, for me, because the *chasm*, *crag* and *channel* harmonise with what I've witnessed – and extremes of feeling thus excited – my impulse is to echo and reply, expand and imitate what nature sings, and so I chant back to her what she's told me.

The cascade rushes at some distance from the Reverend eye.

The same torrent bursts into my heart – and *conturbat me*.

---

28 Moving south-east to Wookey Hole, C. describes 'a rich champaign with pleasing variety of surface, watered by a copious rivulet'. 'The approach is picturesque, the scenery wildly magnificent.' Towards the cave, stands a 'romantick hollow, whose terrace leads to the cavern's mouth,' where he walks to 'an excavation, rough and dirty'. Cheddar elicits a similar, detached depiction: 'This cavern is rugged and uneven, but contains spacious vaults, whose arches present an awful appearance. There are views which are grand beyond description, and where the prospects exhibit that wild magnificence which cannot fail impressing the mind of the spectator with awe at the works of that Power, whose voice even obdurate rocks obey, and retire.' (Note echoes of *Matthew* and *Psalm 97*!)

On Edmund Rack

Who was at Culbone Fifteen Years before me. (And whose Dome and Subterranean Rivers anticipated those I cultivated in the Great Khan's Garden.)

Now from idle reading I have stumbled on a page substantiates the Reverend's distance I'd suspected. Thus a magazine reviewer of his *History and Antiquities*:

> After several endeavours to form a topography of this County, the task has fallen to a Reverend gentleman, who has not in the ten years since his proposals appeared in 1781 been able to give such an account of it as becomes the duty of a county historian in this improved *aerea* of topographical research.
>
> Mr Collinson [he continues] is a mere compiler from *printed* books, [here I think of Samuel *Purchas*!] borrowing even his description of seats and grounds from Arthur Young, that universal tourist. Careless of authorities, or unknowing how to use them, almost all he advances rests on books or his assertions. *The Gentleman's Magazine* of '93

But no. It was not all exactly so. Behind his page there lay another hand – once sensitive, now cold – which Collinson refers to briefly in his *Preface*:

> The Topographical part of the work rests on inquiries made in many successive years by my late friend Mr Edmund Rack, to whose assiduity I pay this merited acknowledgement.

At first, perhaps, this mention appears forthright, generous even. On closer reading, it's indifferent. Buried in the *Preface*, Rack's presence counts for nothing. He's the ghost in the *corpus*. Once he has done service, this Norfolk weaver's son (who'd made his living as a dyer), is penned up in a sentence. The book's proclaimed author is a Church Patrician. While Rack *exits*, once he'd briefly entered, like a footman, in a single movement.[29]

Now it's not my intention to *colly* (blacken!) Collinson, who died in '93, mortified perhaps by his reviewer. But my curiosity was roused concerning Rack's place in these volumes. And more important, who it was had

---

29 Edmund Rack was a Quaker who in '75 had travelled out of Norfolk to study and improve the agricultural practice of the western counties and 'promote the good of the community'. In '77 he founded the West of England Agricultural Society; he was co-founder too of Bath's Philosophical Society. As Friend to True Liberty, he wrote (among much else) a pamphlet on reform of Parliament.

walked at Culbone and descanted on *romance, astonishment* and *exultation.* So, when next in Bath, I sought out Rack's surviving papers.

I've said I won't dishonour Collinson. He died aged thirty-six, just two years after *Somerset* was published. ('We tremble,' frowned his critic, 'for the fate of *Wilts.* which Collinson announces as preparing!')

But I confess to a shock when I visited the rooms where Rack's notes, brought there from Long-Ashton, were laid open to me. For the very first page revealed, *verbatim*, that account of Carhampton, with its *Alps of Somerset*, I've quoted.

Alas. Those paragraphs that Collinson presents *as his* are reproduced from Rack exactly – who wrote them as he toured, alone and on foot, exposed to all weathers, suffocated by a cough – that terribly shook his poor, thin chest – the travelling exacerbated. This, in '87, killed him.

Now I won't make Rack a martyr entirely. His experience of commerce was a fuel to the business. From home in Bath and from the field, Rack's was the genius of the enterprise to publish Somerset's topography.

But this pious tradesman also entertained a literary ambition. He joined the *Beaux Esprits* who attended Lady Anna Miller at Bath-easton to write verses which were printed as *Poetical Amusements* – 'follies' wrote Walpole which were *artificial flowers.* In parallel, Rack was also taken up by Catherine Graham, republican and scholar whose *History of England* Walpole recommended for its 'strength and gravity.'

These patrons were well suited to the temper of Rack's several interests. Though Catherine's *brother* James, the celebrated Master Quack, pressed Rack to maintain falsely that James Graham cured the 'cough and asthma' which had driven him to Bath from Norfolk.[30]

Established in Bath, Rack published a substantial book of *Essays*. This, intermixed with verses in accomplished couplets, was printed the year he set out on his topographical researches.

Now here's the enigma. With reputation high but his health in decline (he often writes that he is 'poorly'), how was it that Rack, in his late middle years, should embark on such a walk until his demise in '87, albeit intermittently, through a hilly and extensive country?

I have read through Rack's letters. These offer something of an answer. For in '80, Rack complains he has been disappointed by a partner at his dye-works and has lost his savings. Smollett, in a passage written

---

30 Besides his 'Celestial Bed and Medico-electrical Apparatus', his treatments included 'Electrical Ether, Nervous Aetherial Balsam, and the Imperial Pills'. Rack was persuaded publicly to declare a cure – which alas never happened.

just when Rack removed to Bath, outlines (from his own experience) the nature of this situation:

> About a dozen years ago [wrote Smollett, who was also dying], many decent families, restricted to small fortunes, besides those that came hither on the score of health, were tempted to settle in Bath, where they could live comfortably ... at a small expense; but the madness of the times has made the place too hot for them, and they are now obliged to think of other migrations. Some have already fled to the mountains of Wales, and others have retired to Exeter.

Thus Squire Bramble in *Humphry Clinker*. And so, like many of those *decent families*, Rack left on his perambulation. Armed with Bowen's *Improved Map* and with a 'Welch poney' he acquired in Taunton, he travelled the county and surveyed every parish, its landscape, natural history, populations, agricultural practices and its architectural features. He subsisted on subscriptions he extracted from the gentlemen he interviewed on their estates and farming practice.

And Oh, were his shade to enter James' Parade today and wander through the pages Collinson collated, he would recognise a book that *he*, in flesh and blood, had written!

We shall return to Rack in Quaker character – when he's arrived at Culbone and stands by the cataract, alive with his pen and stammering in admiration. But first, Rack leads me, and I follow willingly, to digress into a realm where he sings as poet.

I have mentioned Rack's walk with his pony and map. But in between a youth among the weaving people and his present solitude, Rack had schooled himself in poetry. And in a brace of poems, *The Cell of Contemplation* and his *Temple of Fancy* (A VISION in Two Cantos) which were printed at Bath with his book of *Essays*, he transcends the bagatelles he'd improvised at Lady Miller's, and voyages through visionary landscapes, as seized (in each) by sleep, he enters, with a lassitude unwonted in a Quaker, rhapsodically imagined faery regions. Here in his VISION, which Rack had composed by 1780:

With heat oppressed, a sylvan shade I sought,
The seat of peace, of solitude, and thought.

Mute was the grove [he writes] save where the murmuring bees
And droning insects hovered in the trees.

Lulled by their sound, all indolent, I lay,
To Sleep, who waved his *poppies* round, a prey.

Now, as Sleep from (metaphoric) poppy overwhelms the dreamer's faculties, his senses, which before were unified, are sundered and imagination is unleashed to wander:

[Sleep's] fascinating power each sense confined,
But free remained the ever-active mind.
Imagination still her sway maintained,
And roved aloft, with pinions unrestrained –

Now the Poet, become *Seer* – as though voyaging through Galileo's *optic tube*! – descries a new world beyond earthly gaze:

There, far above the ken of mortal eye,
Full in its blaze, a radiant planet lies,
By poets yet unsung, though here resides
The power who o'er their sweetest lays presides.

Unbound imagination, and what draws imagination to it – these reciprocate:

To this gay region of perpetual spring,
Some power unseen directs my towering wing.

Besides Godfrey's *Court of Fancy* – one source perhaps of his invention – did Rack have access to the *Discourse on the Western Paradise* we have visited? I don't think so. But here in Rack's couplets reigns that paradise combining meadows, music, streams and ornamental forest that Kubilai enjoyed at Xanadu each summer:

High rose its hills, with lasting verdure crowned,
And flowers immortal decked th'enchanted ground.
Meandering streamlets through the meadows glide,
And strains harmonious float along the tide.

Next, gorgeous buildings – as if nourished by the earth that feeds the trees surrounding them – ascend:

Thick, through the groves, the gilded temples rise
In sacred pomp, and glittering seek the skies.

Joined in concert, *as I also* dreamed them, are a damsel and the instrument she fingers:

In this retreat, attracted by the sound
Of heavenly strains, a charming nymph I found
Sweeping a lyre – To softest notes of love,
Swift o'er the quivering string, her flying fingers move:

Visionary enchantment overleaps its antecedent culmination:

The thrilling sounds, full, sweet, melodious, roll,
Charm the rapt ear, and captivate the soul. –

The dreamer supplicates the Nymph for her identity. She rejoins:

The goddess FANCY here extends her reign.
On yonder hill her towering temple stands,
The work of ages, raised by FANCY's hands.

In a first hint of the moral vision which concludes poem, the Nymph
attributes transience, and therefore imperfection, to her Mistress:

There she resides, with ever-changeful eyes:
Her own creation round in prospect lies.

The dreamer, like true Thomas *Rhymer*, submits to the Nymph and she
conducts him to the Goddess' Palace:

Near, and more near, the blazing pile we drew,
And all its splendors opened in our view.
Towering sublime, th'aerial mansion stood;
In rear half-circled by a gloomy wood.

This classical Arcadia dominates the VISION's second *Canto*. And while
my eye wearies of the Paradise Rack labours to depict (too long), scattered
throughout are couplets of perfected balance – such as this, in which
surprising Nereids exercise:

Swift through the waves the shining wantons glide,
Flounce in the stream, or shoot along the tide.

The pre-eminent moment, paradoxically distinguished by a vision of its
mutability – and enacted in conclusion by the *long length* of an alexandrine – comes finally within the dreamer's observation:

One ample room the wondrous pile contains;
Not without change a moment it remains.
High rose the roof; a vast stupendous *Dome*!

The spacious vault a thousand lamps illume.

Full in the centre, on a pearly throne,
In gay attire, the goddess FANCY shone.
A vesture, dipt in Iris' brightest bow,
Flows o'er her limbs, and floats in glittering folds below.

Transient reflections flow across a glass with which the goddess labours. This mirror's surface is (turned inside-out) her mind: and (strangely) is infused with life the restless deity expresses with it:

Before the queen an oval mirror stands,
The curious labour of her active hands,
Ample its size, of wondrous texture wrought
With power endued, surpassing human thought.

What Fancy sees combines both things that independently have drifted to the glass, and what, in herself, she has imagined:

On this deceptive mirror FANCY gazed,
For in its field she saw whate'er she pleased.
Whate'er in thought her fertile brain designed:
The varying labours of her changeful mind.

Wherever Rack learned Latin – as he shuttled the loom or stirred the dye-bath – his references are not perhaps the happiest. But while his couplet about Lucan's mis-informed, Rack writes here (with a harmless cruelty) that matches Pope in wit and elegance:

These, in their order to describe, require
The fervent heat of true poetic fire.
That fire which glowed in Maro's tuneful page,
And blazed refulgent in the Grecian sage.

That Tasso felt, when magic scenes he drew.
Which Lucan thought he felt and Ovid knew.

Now here's a passage echoes or pre-figures the co-active presence, in my visionary *Fragment*, of musician damsel and the dome of an imagination:

While here I gazed, a lute's harmonious sound
Floats in the dome and fills the circuit round:
The notes mellifluous, slowly-tuneful, roll,
And soothe the secret springs of FANCY's soul.

Albeit Rack has discoursed on the play of *maya*, which represents the superficies of experience, crudely here, he breaks that charm and tosses a quotidian, cold stone onto the shimmering and flimsy surface of the ratiocinations he'd initiated:

The music ceased; a solemn silence reigns
Through all the temples, all th' inchanted plains.

And now a second Goddess, Truth, appears and reprimands the poet – to whom, somewhat condescending, she attributes inexperience:

'Why thoughtless youth, is thy unguarded mind
To FANCY's fond illusions thus inclin'd?'

This dislocation breaks with violence on the reader. Dispirited, the poet, too, is shot down by abrupt apostrophes that pierce, split, penetrate and pinch the final adjectival present participles:

Then, with her sceptre, TRUTH the mirror struck;
Which instant in a thousand fragments broke.
Down fell the magic glass, with *shatt'ring* sound:
The shining spoils lay *glitt'ring* on the ground.

Tumult (as I've written). Expectation of *Erhebung* – punctured. This I comprehend. And painfully remember:

Now of the pompous pile, no trace was seen
Nor aught remained of the once potent queen:
The phantoms all were fled, and nought I found
But one vast dreary desart spread around.

Such is the end of Rack's excursion. And if this place of desolation is what *Truth* occasions, let me live on fondly in illusion. (For Oh! how Rack recalls ... that once the Dome of *my* imagination foundered, its over-hanging shell was broken ... infiltrated by encroaching *desart*.)

Now much of Rack's *Vision*'s in an ornamented language – from which fustian I have extracted passages that breathe out freely from what's suf-focating otherwise.

But in Rack, as noticed earlier, ran antithetic currents. And on stylistic manners he was a *sharp, judicious* critic (albeit not, as some are, *Tartarly and savage!*) For Rack proclaimed that he detested artificiality and denounced 'vain pretenders, who impose on the *sentimentalist* by an affectation of sensibility'. (Such was what I'd sensed in Collinson – whose ardour expressed all the feeling of a sheet of paper!)

Rack recommends, further, in *An Evening Walk*, 'Chaste composition, plainness and neatness in both dress and writing.' While later on his *Walk*, in recollection of a sunset ('striking and magnificent'), Rack scrutinises finely, nay, *anatomises* his reaction:

> At the first view, the mind is usually overwhelmed with a tumult of wonder and delight: – a confusion of images, a rapid succession of ideas, for which language wants a name; – a transport of astonishment which seizes all the faculties of the soul.

Now here's nice understanding of the operation of impressions which sublimity arouses in us, and how the faculties are incapacitated by that joy which comprehends within it a perplexity whose character – since language is inadequate to name or grasp it – is inexpressible: while ecstasy is superseded by a philosophic contemplation of the quieter fields strong feeling opens:

> But by degrees the sensations become less violent and more pleasing: astonishment is succeeded by a calmer delight, and transport subsides into reverent and pleasing admiration.

Wonderful! No finer, more discriminating passage. And in view of later exposition on the subject, note Rack wrote this ca. 1780.

Rack the Quaker

I should recall, reverting to his Somerset excursions, that Rack was a Quaker, had published a *Life* of William Penn and admired John Woolman (best of Quakers, without Fox's choler or Penn's acquisitive ambition) who had walked through the Colonies singing God's praises, preaching to the Indians and rebuking slavers. Woolman also censured *dyeing* – trade Rack lived by![31]

Lately, Woolman had arrived in England and died near York a little before Rack removed from Norfolk. His *Works* were published. Lamb, that generous friend of man, adored him. Crabbe Robinson declared that

---

31 'Dyes, wrote Woolman, 'being partly to please the eye and partly to hide dirt, I have felt, when travelling in dirtiness, and affected with unwholesome scents, a strong desire that the nature of dyeing cloth to hide dirt be more fully considered.' The nature of 'unnatural' dyeing as transferred to literary composition is an issue that commands attention!

'Woolman's is a beautiful soul. An illiterate tailor, he writes in a style of the most exquisite purity and grace. His moral qualities are transferred to his writings.'

Rack strove to write, like Woolman, with an ethical simplicity. And just as the American had walked intoning Psalms alone and to both African and Cherokee, so Rack, *Tremblingly alive all o'er*, and stained no longer with the (literary) dyes that Woolman had disdained, walked naked of ambition in a Quakerly devotion, and – open in his solitude to the Creation – stood by the chasm and swallowed down its torrent.

By *dyes*, I mean, of course, those affectations he himself considered he'd adopted in poetic voyaging to realms of Fancy. And with something akin to the Psalmist's ecstasy, Rack cried out (in plainest language):

'All nature is Thy temple, from which the language of praise incessantly ascends to Thee from the various gradations of existence.' *The Earth is the Lord's and all the creatures in it. I will bless his works in all places*, Rack re-articulates the Psalmist.

Rack anticipated this simplicity in his *Cell of Contemplation*. Here once again, the *Rhymer* reclines 'Till gentle slumbers snatched [his] sense away', and the dreamer finds himself, it seems, within a dome, whose 'ample roof appears an azure sky,' around whose walls 'Creation was displayed':

A wondrous scene! Compos'd of light and shade –
A wondrous scene! The work of hands divine
Where power supreme and art immortal shine.

Much as in my *Xanadu* (coincidentally – for Rack was composing in 1780):

deep sink the vales below,
Capacious beds, where rapid waters flow.

Hence, deep beneath the ground, in circuit wide,
Slowly meandring, creeps the parent tide,

And forms the springs which, bursting from her veins,
Refresh and fructify the thirsty plains.

The Dreamer, recognising he's in Paradise – enacted here, as in Shang-du, by subterranean courses and by mazings of the stream these feed, which in its turn feeds earth and paradisal trees that grow up from it – now enjoys a vision of our Parent, Adam. While CONTEMPLATION, demi-deity, enjoins the dreamer to become a second Adam, and 'the Eternal Architect adore.'

'Come then,' she cries,

In this retreat for ever seek to dwell,

Here, here, in peace, erect thy humble cell.'

Thus from a poetic complication, Rack extracted, or reverted to, a deeper plainness. He abandoned the couplet. The Dome he'd erected in imagination shattered. The Quaker in him from it hatched as Adam. So Rack walked – and walking shook his spirit as it had John Woolman's – naming what creation as it stood, so far, in Somerset this century, spoke to him and which he answered, annotating that which lay outside him and (poor fellow) desolately coughing.

'So shaken as we are ...' the line recurs

I'll make no more of it. (I am not Rack and he, as I betimes shall be, is unintelligibly dead. And most of what he noted I have quoted, as if Collinson had wrote it.)

But before exchanging an *adieu* with him, let me contemplate two pages, in Rack's hand, that composed at Culbone. (Had he lodged on this farm where I took shelter? Entertained a *Doppelgänger* – mine perhaps? – in one of those two parlour chairs that face each other?) Wherever Rack had sat, reflecting on the transformations he had undergone – from weaver, dyer, poet, essayist, philanthropist to antiquarian – he walked here with *astonishment* and *pleasure*: 'different shades of green,' he wrote at Culbone, 'and the rich tints of the autumnal colours inexpressibly beautiful' – and as Rack approaches death, we feel his spirit move across the paper:

> a fine rivulet [he noted] rushes down a narrow rocky channel over hung
> with wood with a fine gurgling sound, and passing by the church, forms a
> succession of cascades in its descent down the rocks into the sea.[32]

How well I recognise that up-burst, then its down-rush into darker water! But then, as though some interrupter's lumbered clumsily among them, or landscape unfenced previously has been inclosed with hedges,

---

32 And at Hardistone Point, from which I saw a rainbow stretching, Rack wrote as follows: 'On the coming in of the tide, the ecchoes and dashing of the waves in these caverns is tremendous and astonishing. At low water the shore exhibits a striking scene of rocky fragments which have been washd from the cliffs above and ly scattered around or piled on each other in wild magnificence ... The cliffs on the east side hang over the beach with terrific sublimity and granduer [*sic* his spellings].' How prospects such as these made this honest Quaker shake!

Rack's notes from Culbone have been ploughed, harrowed and divided, scored through, scarified, submerged, scratched out, blotted and deleted. It's Collinson (because he has to) readies the text for publication. (Words, like caged birds, flutter their brief lives and then die behind the bars that screen them from us.)

Rack's labour ended after six years' walking. He met endless discomfort – not least, 'a thousand fleas', he cried out, biting him at Compton Martin.

'For ten days', Rack wrote to Collinson at New Year '87, 'I have been so weak I could scarcely hold my pen. I must resign myself to the fury of the storm which will soon hide me for ever.'

Where he died is unrecorded. The last sentence of his final letter reads:

Sharp blows the wintry wind.

Farewell.

And my *vale*? I inscribed these lines on a mud track outside Culbone – and re-iterate the question, long since trampled by the sheep and cattle:

If Rack was the spectre in Collinson's *corpus* –
Are Rack and I, perhaps,
The *Doppelgängers* of each other's *opus*?

206

The County of Somerset Surveyed by Day and Masters

Design'd and Drawn by C. W. Bampfylde Esq.re. Engraved by T. Bonner. The Ornament by P. Begbie Sculpt. Publish'd according to Act of Parliament by W. Day of Blagdon, March 1, 1782.

I've mentioned Bowen's map that Rack set out with. This beautiful thing, one inch to three miles, with apple green and yellow boundary shading, Rack carried folded into quarters. But given Bowen shows just four roads in Carhampton Hundred, it dizzies me to think how Rack first travelled. Culbone and Porlock stand naked to the sea from one another: neither's joined by road to anywhere in Somerset or Devon.

In March '82, a new map is published. It's one inch to a mile, in nine plates, handsomely engraved on copper. These Rack carried in their several pieces. When the parts are attached to cardboard or a canvas backing, the *Day and Masters'* map's prodigious.[33]

Unroll Day's map and gaze across the county – like jackdaws that prospect a chasm! – marsh and grassland tufted, the high places hatched rhythmically: Sedgemoor and the Mendips sweeping between Cheddar Hills and Shepton Mallet: Wells and Wookey at its centre, the Polden Hills and Quantocks parallel, the Black and White Downs counterpointed with each other.

Villages are joined by turnpikes, *inclosed roads* and open roads across the commons. A track through the woods connects Culbone and Porlock. While a path across the coomb winds south of Culbone where it lies sequestered – *pars densa ferarum tecta silvis* – figured like an orchard in a Turkey carpet. The farm where I stayed's a quarter of an inch due west of the initial *C* of Culbone.[34]

The visitor from Porlock – a contested visitation

Here, at the risk of some controversy, I would recall Rack's mention of that path from Porlock:

> The parish cannot be approached on horseback without great difficulty, and even danger; the road from Porlock being only a path about two feet wide, winding in a zigzag direction along the slope of the hills, and often interrupted by large loose stones and roots of trees.

---

33 I've measured it from side to side – it covers three whole library tables – it's six foot long and almost five foot wide.

34 Some Nine were engaged in the construction of this map. These were the land surveyors, an enclosure commissioner, a landscape gardener, a customs house officer, a half pay-army officer, a school master, engraver and a sculptor or artist.

In which connection, I'm pretty well convinced a claim I've made about my Culbone visit and the outcome of my poem, has its basis in false memory – an experience, if I remember rightly, with which I am familiar.

Now I've suggested that a visitor arrived on business from Porlock. And while, that afternoon, I translated my vision, this individual interrupted the transcription. But granted I myself retailed that information, I don't, on reflection, think it happened in the manner I've suggested.

The reasons that inform my disavowal may be summarised as follows:

Who, first, in the light of Rack's observation, would undertake that journey of an afternoon in autumn and hazard a return that evening? (If he'd lodged here, we'd remember!)

Second, I knew no-one – bar the landlord of *The Ship* at Porlock – in that village, still less any person with whom I had commerce. Besides, most important, I had arrived from the Linton direction over on the Devon side: and did anyone in Porlock have some business with me, how could they have got knowledge, when I'd been in residence a mere half-day, of the farm house I had chanced on?

For while this story provides a gratifying emblematisation of the manner in which the workings of genius may be differentiated from the gross counter-activity of the material world which brings down to the coarser ruck of time and commerce the otherwise uninhibited freedoms of an imaginative expedition,

it is all too convenient for those who profess sensibility, to counterpoint their claims to a situation on Parnassus against the dead touch of business, and thus to lay blame on the world, when it was – given the responsibility of a poet to entertain the Muse according to the capability of his own genius – the dreamer himself that spontaneously gave up, as perhaps the action my dreaming had when my *Fragment*, was in fact already finished.

So much for that business. (Unless, of course, it had been Rack, revisiting the declivation of his VISION, which had returned – with *ecchoes* of a dome about him and with hints of a divine musician – to shake me. That, however, is unlikely.)[35]

---

35 In contrary pursuit, I undertook, some idle time later, researches in the Porlock Parish Register. This based on fantasy I might uncover in those entries, men – aet. up to forty, hale enough to walk to Culbone and then home by lantern – the name and business of my interrupter. So, following familiarities of wine with Porlock's rector, I noted 30 names from the Baptismal Record, starting *ca* 1750. My conclusion? Of boys grown able-bodied in the years in question, the most were John (14) and William (12). Thomas followed (5), next Nicholas and Richard. If thus I did receive some visitor that afternoon, his name most likely had been John – or

A rainbow from Hardistone or Hurlstone

Now on a number of occasions, I have remarked on the discrepancy between the situation in which I composed my poem and the latitude of its enactment, and it remains to confess a certain tension in my own mind that both joins and separates our own unpretentious Culbone and a Xanadu which is all splendour. In this connection, I should describe a phenomenon I witnessed as I walked, later in the course of the same residence, on the road which leads from Porlock towards the Quay and then back toward my farmhouse lodging.

It was an afternoon in mid-October and the sun was showing itself horizontally through a veil of water drops that drifted on the air in a suffusion which was somewhere between a rain shower and a lazily meandering curtain of translucent mist particles.

As I rounded a corner which was marked by a beech hedge (of the sort Billingsley in his panegyric on the late enclosures has recommended to the landowner who seeks grander profit) and turned my face across a meadow towards the lime kilns below me and to Hurlstone Point that rose in the distance, a rainbow came to view, one of a very strong colour, which arched from the headland and then plunged into the waves as though to replenish itself in their watery and green momentum. While the sun shone from the west, the sky to the east was filled with thick grey cloud, and the darker this became, the more intense grew the rainbow – God's promise, so I recollected, to old Noah in his righteous boating.

As I strode from this delightful apparition (the afternoon was waning) the more radiantly that rainbow flamed: and, of itself, seemed to walk in a species of bending movements, as if travelling into Devon, until it stood with one foot on the stones of Porlock Quay while with the other it reached into the shallows whose silver or white flashings the rainbow stained with an irridescence that the sea water now stretched around and now brought back again into the solidity of its column.

Thus the bow held its form, at once architecturally rigid and in a striding motion, and swinging its foot out, travelled parallel with my own wayfaring. And remarkable as were its colour and the animation of its reaching onward, it was its tenacity impressed itself on me. This was no momentary or fleeting vision. As I walked hard west, and *it* appeared to pursue *me*, the bow held

---

William. Provisioned thus with orts to dip into a Lethe of uncertain recollection, I smote the board – 'Let rest,' I cried, 'this *Nemo* in his anonymity. John, William, Nicholas or Richard be he, I'll never learn his business or identity. And so *No One* stemmed the flux of – but no matter.

its posture, a good forty-five minutes, getting out of my sight only when, as finally I entered Yearnor's woodland, I had travelled beyond a view of the sky. And for all I knew (I slept in my parlour) it continued to hold its place that evening and irradiate the moonlight.

Delightful as it was *per se*, I now must deflect this rainbow to a different purpose. And here I shall be brief as I can be.

Just this. There exists an imperative guides the imagination which owns a constitution which is, as divined from the rainbow I have adumbrated, both diaphanously intangible and so materially constructed that this leads, as did the bow, from *terra firma* on some near shore – which is our body in a particular locality – to a place afar off that may not so easily be touched with the mind: for this latter is as sundry and elusive as the scarcely cognized intimations that directed us to it.

Both the going out movement and the place to which that motion is gone, are therefore, at least, twofold in character. The rainbow may thus be the grand experience *ipse* and an aspect of the vehicle that carries us to it: the thing in itself and – as in a wet sky, painted on it from its convergent parts, by God for old Noah – the sign that proclaims the genesis of an experience in the observer: which is the sublime object held above us and a projection which is also the expression of our own self-generating Iris.

To pursue this conundrum, I would aver that the rainbow is endogenous to the intellection of all human beings, and that we carry this most joyous spectrum, with its banded multiplicity of colours, in us: and that enter, as we must, the forest of confusion and of dark discomfort, we have it in our command to discharge from our psyche its jovial, splendid and uplifting effulgence and that this will irradiate our most desolated moments and conjoin our being to an empyrean which will answer back to it and, as it were, substantiate and re-invigorate even its most tentative excursion.

Thus my conviction. And my poem – even were it my last, as I fear it may be – is a signal of that correspondence between what *Great Creating Nature* has in her generosity bestowed on the landscape over which I was travelling and the gift, which I have had implanted in me – a particle of the divine which the Quakers have described as a 'seed of light' – which the rainbow, both in its heaven-to-earth emergence and as a expression of my own generative capability, is a condensation.

These thoughts conduce to the following opinion: for by coincidence or no, they are notions that own kinship both with the nature of my poem as it arrived – from nowhere that I could have anticipated, but which I must regard as magical – and the environment of its composition, in this homely parlour.

Now with reference to this rainbow – or *Bridge of Dreams* as it suggested itself to be – we might pause at an ancient figure, which is in Homer and Virgil, of two gateways of dreaming: the one made of horn and the other of ivory:

Two gates the silent house of Sleep adorn;
Of polish'd ivory this, that of transparent horn:
True visions thro' transparent horn arise;
Thro' polish'd ivory pass deluding lies.

Beautiful as is Virgil's representation (and there is more to it than I can survey here; nor is Dryden without fault with respect to his numbers), my own experience disallows the separation of truth from falsehood: and I would claim that imaginative experience contains both horn and ivory in amalgamation, a mutuality of truth and 'deluding', the partition of which our forebears held necessary for the maintenance of their own imaginative order.

And while, in that this literature of the ancients remains in most respects superior to our own, I must obey that integrative impulse which leads me to a sense of, and a belief in, the truth or the reality of my phantasmagoria. This Bridge of the Dream, in other words, represented and indeed was, a locus of illusion and an actuality, both. And in that this pathway conducted me to another place from this, the fabric of that bridge partook of both worlds and in conjoining the two, *was* them, by virtue of that conjunction, in one.

I will take one step further. For that bridge has to do with more than poetry and voyages of fancy. This rainbow is nothing less than the ground on which we live. Oh, we claim that we are *here*. And indeed this is what appears. Our earth is hard, or wet and raw. We travel over it in a stamping movement and for the most part it holds us. But still, while I believe this to be, I know, or feel or believe or perceive my experience to be transitional: and that as one footstep replaces another, the first, in a retrospective immediacy becomes an element of something that exists no longer, and that I cannot be certain that what replaces it is categorically distinct from what I have just left behind me. Next, as this mingling grows closer, I can no longer allow the present to own any greater material hardness than what shadows it so nearly.

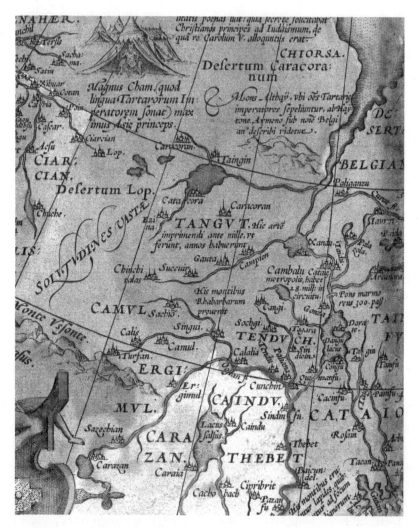

If this be my experience, I can not claim the thought to be my own entirely. For I have lately read a narrative, in Sir William Jones's *Asiatick Researches*, told by the Hindus, which proposes, in a marvellous speculation, that human life and indeed our entire universe represents the dream of the god Vishnu, who lies sleeping at the bed of the universal ocean and from whose mind emanates a flowering lotus, and that the blossom of this is his dream and that everything in our world is contained in that efflorescence.[36]

---

36 As Calderon hath said: *que toda la vida es sueño / y los sueños, sueños son.* 'For all of life is a dream, And dreams are simply dreams of dreams.' Nor need I quote Prospero's most elevated lines here.

To conclude, less abstrusely, I would point to a two-ness which, on cruder ground, was expressed by my dream of Kubilai's China: and this duality is *pied*, or counterpointed, with these elements as follows:

My vision was of both here and elsewhere: of now and the archaic. It was built of grinding clockwork minutes while lying also beyond time in an incessant perpetuity. East and west were counterpoised and reconciled without abandoning the regions where they'd started. Thus with its muddy coombs and sunset rain, Somerset in autumn was accorded with high Chinese summer. While sheep at Porlock fed in pasture made lush with an improvingly excavated marl, there the Great Khan's horses swarmed across steppeland punished by the sun to a brown *zavanna* – the two chorused across a chancel, which on one side was an English Gothick, while the other lay in tented and domed Tartary. Here the Culbone shepherd and the plough boy whistled. There, artisans from Asia and Damascus plied their geomantic speculation. Housed in this parlour, a threadbare poet lost his wits – and scattered a few sh--s. There, the Great Khan deployed a sovereign freedom, executed pleasures and extended his borders from Hang-chow to Corea.

All these were reconciled and, for the time being, were at one. And here is a conclusion, albeit inconclusive. That this rainbow, whose import I have so falteringly attempted, was, effectually, an emblem of our most

integrative and yet abstruse dreaming. For was this not, in a palpable and topographically embedded materialisation of light, a concretion, albeit beyond our reach, of what is transient and abstract? Did I not observe through the single witness of my eyes, the very quick of what one may not grasp? Still, the headland sustained it. The Channel drank it. The bow marched, with my *jog* along *the footpath way*, pre-empting my *hent* against *stile* and hedgerow.

Thus, we exist, as do these silly sheep between the furze and beech hedge plantings, within our mental enclosures. But here, even on the least of our imaginative excursions, we are led forward by signs stepping from the headlands of our own bony foreheads into realms that lie beyond us, and where, indeed, we tread self-fabricated spectra, painted as these are, internally, with self-generated pigment and moving to an *antiphone* of what is and what may not be, which fixes us, transformed in part, to what place our bodies predicate, and removes us, with an upper walking, which – translated from the signals of its architecture and momentum – for aye, becomes the very property of our imagining. And so when we wake and are planted in the habit of our sublunary station, we may know – as did, unconsciously that rainbow which lunged across and down from Hurlstone – where we may locate, retrieve, enjoy, express or inhabit the vision which sprang thus, engendered, both by optick predetermination and by preternatural ordination, from the most commonplace of our headlands.

Postlude: Porlock

I have wandered with sufficient leisure. Convinced, to the end, I have been nowhere. So I've tramped back, towards Porlock, down through the wood, no trace intact of previous error: Xanadu, I understand now, which was non-existent on my road here, beyond echoes of Rack's fancy (whose domes, albeit they pre-empted mine, evaporated in the air of which he built them) knocking on my shoulder, just as lately, grinding out my innerds, I ascended.

About *Man's first Disobedience and the Fruit of that forbidden* Quince or Apple, Purchas started: and I followed, eating with greed from that same orchard. And so initiated, in a dream, the Great Khan's presence – as Tamburlaine, that Shepherd General, it might otherwise have been: to kneel at whose tomb, incontinent Tom Coryat, plunged his hyperbolic slipper into Persia – for no more purpose than my own *pedestication* towards Kubilai's House of Pleasure.

But now as if the Great Khan and the Phags-pa *lama*, like *djinns* which had been cramped in Purchas' oil lamp, if he had one, and then loosed by me on rubbing in my dream at it, continue to rehearse their reverie of Empire (and its contrary in *Buddha dharma*), Great Kubilai takes his leave of Culbone.

'I am of Porlock now!' I hear him murmur. And would, if so, induct his subjects into Mongol husbandry and Tibetan *tantra*. An unaccomodating landscape for his mares and stallions, as we stumble over trees, past lime-kilns and domed charcoal firings. 'For whose venerable *reliques*, these Somersetshire *stupas*?' Great Kubilai muses. And while he ponders this, we reach the channel, skirt the wetland margin, and so into Porlock.

No longer the shepherd in my habit, I dine at *The Ship* on a herring and boiled mutton. Two words, now familiar – *Xanadu* and *Kubilai* – ring out from a distant grassland.

I walk from the tavern and go further through the village, at first behind the churchyard and then up into a pasture. There are sheep but no shepherd. Is that someone singing? It is simple to withhold an answer! I have walked too far already and stop to gaze across the coomb's ridge toward Culbone.

It is late afternoon. I lie down by some thorn brakes that the wind has twisted. Some birds, in a flock, arrive to feed on berries. They climb through the leaves, then fly off chirping. When I wake from my sleep I have dreamed of nothing.

Note to the reader

This writing began on the first of three visits to Ash Farm, between Linton and Porlock, where Coleridge is said to have written *Kubla Khan* some time between 1797 and 1800, though the place and date remain uncertain.

The poet withheld publication until 1816 when, encouraged by a short-lived friendship with Byron, he gave this account of its origin:

The following fragment is here published at the request of a poet of great and deserved celebrity [Byron], and, as far as the author's own opinions are concerned, rather as a psychological curiosity, than on the grounds of any supposed poetic merits.

In the summer of the year 1797, the author, then in ill health, had retired to a lonely farmhouse between Porlock and Linton, on the Exmoor confines of Somerset and Devonshire. In consequence of a slight indisposition, an anodyne had been prescribed, from the effects of which he fell asleep in his chair at the moment that he was reading the following sentence, or words of the same substance, in Purchas's Pilgrimage: 'Here the Khan Kubla commanded a palace to be built, and a stately garden thereunto. And thus ten miles of fertile ground were inclosed with a wall.' The author continued for about three hours in a profound sleep, at least of the external senses, during which time he has the most vivid confidence that he could not have composed less than from two to three hundred lines; if that indeed can be called composition in which all the images rose up before him as things, with a parallel production of the correspondent expressions, without any sensation or consciousness of effort. On awaking he appeared to himself to have a distinct recollection of the whole, and taking his pen, ink, and paper, instantly and eagerly wrote down the lines that are here preserved. At this moment he was unfortunately called out by a person on business from Porlock, and detained by him above an hour, and on his return to his room, found, to his no small surprise and mortification, that though he still retained some vague and dim recollection of the general purport of the vision, yet, with the exception of some eight or ten scattered lines and images, all the rest had passed away like the images on the surface of a stream into which a stone has been cast, but, alas! without the after restoration of the latter!

Then all the charm
Is broken – all that phantom world so
    fair
Vanishes, and a thousand circlets spread,
And each misshape[s] the other. Stay
    awhile,
Poor youth! who scarcely dar'st lift up
    thine eyes –
The stream will soon renew its smooth-
    ness, soon
The visions will return! And lo, he stays,

And soon the fragments dim of lovely
 forms
Come trembling back, unite, and now
 once more
The pool becomes a mirror.

[From *The Picture*, 91–100]

Yet from the still surviving recollections in his mind, the author has
frequently purposed to finish for
himself what had been originally, as
were, given to him.

In 1934, a manuscript of *Kubla Khan*
in Coleridge's fair hand was found.
The postscript of this so-called Crewe
manuscript is as follows:

This fragment with a good deal more,
not recoverable, composed, in a sort
of Reverie brought on by two grains
of Opium, taken to check a dysentery,
at a Farm House between Porlock and
Linton, a quarter of a mile from Culbone
Church, in the fall of the year, 1797.

Despite the discrepancy between
these *post hoc* recollections, each is
rich in evocation. Whether one or the
other represents the truth has been
analysed at length – but even the
meticulously forensic discussion by
Elizabeth Schneider remains agnostic
as to date and circumstance. Since
I have not attempted anything that
resembles a historical reconstruction,
I have been happy to fall in, more or
less, with the outline of Coleridge's
narrative and have made this a part of
the context of my work. But while the
persona of these *Journals* believes that
he has retrieved the poem from an
opium dream, I concur with sceptical
opinion on the disorganising, rather

than on the creative operation of
drug experience. This means that I
do not altogether collude with what
the speaking voice in these pages has
told me about the poem's origin – and
indeed, about quite a lot else.

As regards interpretation of the
poem, much of what I have written
represents side issues – this perhaps
driven by the speaker's own avoidance
of a sense of incompletion. And
Kubla Khan has been so thoroughly
described over the past two hundred
years, that I have nothing to add, and
I have pursued very little research
into the literary and historical canon.
During the second year of writing, I
did read Richard Holmes's brilliant
and sympathetic biography, Elizabeth
Schneider's important study of 1953
and was given access to the Crewe
manuscript in the British Library. I
also looked briefly through Coleridge's
Notebooks for the year 1797 (a likely
date for the composition of the poem),
but otherwise have re-read none
of Coleridge's prose beyond that
quoted by the scholars mentioned. Any
similarity between my own syntax and
that of Coleridge is therefore either
fortuitous or derives from long-term
memory. I suspect I may have been
influenced more, perhaps somewhat
anachronistically, by Sterne, Fielding
and Richardson.

Anachronism is in fact integral to
the fabric, perhaps the pathology, of
my enterprise. A good deal of what
pseudo-Coleridge writes here derives
from sources, most obviously about
Mongol and Chinese history, that

weren't available to him. In equal measure, because I didn't want to attempt speaking for a mind that could express itself supremely for itself on most subjects (particularly politics and philosophy), those themes are absent. That said, I have, *ad lib*, introjected my own interest deriving from Sanskrit studies and Buddhism. But while Coleridge had certainly read some of the first English and perhaps German translations of Hindu texts, the persona who engages here with Buddhist ideas, is a long way from the historical Coleridge.

In connection with the voice, it would be difficult to try explaining how or even why I came to write in a late eighteenth-century dialect (if that's what it is). I did of course have Coleridge in mind when I visited the farm in 2008 and where I started this work. The germ of the project was, however, conceived three years previously when I was discussing *Kubla Khan* with my daughter, Elizabeth, who was working on an A level essay. What impressed itself on me at the time were both the circumstances in which this, Coleridge's masterpiece, was written, and the phenomenon of its having been composed, as the poet claimed, in a remote place which was so far removed from that other remote place, Xanadu, about which virtually no information was accessible during the poet's lifetime. Once I had located the farm where Coleridge may have stayed, I was fortunate in two main, unanticipated, respects. First, because I lost my way on the quite arduous

off-road walk and arrived in a state of collapse and minor illness. Second, because the next two visits involved similar challenges. From those *indispositions*, arose the shaky, but disinhibited skeleton of the voice which subsequently inhabited me and which became a species of *Doppelgänger* I continued to live with for four years. Minor illness, fatigue and solitude were, I suppose, the determinants for what I continued writing, and those conditions, which were frequent whether or not I was *in situ*, encouraged its somewhat discontinuous spontaneity.

Having disclaimed scholarly and/ or historical research, it would be disingenuous to claim that I have had no awareness of who Coleridge was, what he wrote and the outlines of his biography. But while it is no doubt disrespectful to impersonate so a great writer, it would, perhaps, have been a more serious discourtesy to have studied his work closely and then rewritten what I surmised he might also have meant. So while Coleridge, and some of his interests, of course, lie within this work, my very partial knowledge of the man and my own preoccupation with things that may not have concerned the poet, became more pertinent. I should also confess that there are other poets whose work I read more often – Virgil, about whom Coleridge had reservations, being one of them. That said, I recall with gratitude, a number of high points in my reading of Coleridge's poems with students at South Hackney School in the late 1960s, at Pentonville Prison, Northwestern University, Islington Sixth Form Centre and with my daughter Elizabeth. I owe a great debt to the enthusiasm and insight of all these co-readers.

Here then is a being, perhaps scarcely a man, alone, solipsistically talking or writing (I have never been entirely clear which). Late eighteenth-century England is absent in most respects – though there are references to the enclosures and aspects of Somerset culture which pertain to the language of speech and folk song. The character who speaks is married and has a child; but these figures are peripheral to his self-absorption: and Purchas, Coryat and Rack are closer to him than his family, the Wordsworths or Southey, none of whom have a place in these notebooks – albeit previously the poet's writer companions had walked in the same landscape, though not, so far as I'm aware, up through Culbone Wood. And while there may be an occasional recollection of Cambridge, Alfoxton where the Wordsworths lodged and Nether Stowey where Sarah kept house, are buried by the presence of the wood through which this vaguely outlined individual struggled. The farm house parlour (which I have imagined as the one where I sat and wrote during my own visits), the surrounding coombs, a view down to the Bristol Channel, the Xanadu of Purchas, Marco and not least the character of the historical Kubilai Khan are home and companions of a writer who is rooted in a present landscape but whose imagination takes him to Asia and other districts of the ancient and unknowable.

As to the form of the work, there is, beyond arrival in the first and departure in the last sections, virtually no narrative trajectory. On the one hand, much in the notebooks is composed during the few days (presumably) over which the speaker recuperates on the farm. Some sections, on the other hand, suggest that he has been away and then comes back, or takes his leave, having, perhaps years ago, already departed.

This absence of biographical verisimilitude is counterpointed, perhaps jarringly, by a number of contextualising 'facts'. The moment I entered Culbone Wood and struggled, several times up and down its difficult pathways and looked through trees to the Bristol Channel, it became clear that this was the landscape of Coleridge's poem (perhaps overlaid a bit by Cheddar Gorge and Wookey Hole). And so I have made something of this, as I have of the topographical works about eighteenth-century Somerset. These inconsistencies are, I suppose, congruent with the flying notebook/fantasia genre in which the work emerged. If I had attempted to organise the book with any pretence to narrative consistency, then I would have been aping the biographical symmetries which proper scholars have accomplished already. The incongruities also represent elements of the comedy which is part, no doubt, of every poet's existence. This book, in the end, is a series of prose poems, much of it about poetry.

About Edmund Rack and Collinson: these passages are literary historical and, in part, critical. But whether Coleridge met Rack, knew he had been at Culbone before him or, perhaps most important, had read his poetry, remains unknown. Pseudo-Coleridge analyses some suggestive congruities, but comes to no conclusion. He shows little or no surprise that the man who had conducted topographical research at Culbone had, separately and earlier, written poetry containing imagery that prefigures passages in *Kubla Khan.* The parallels between Rack's work and that of Coleridge are intriguing. And given that Rack became a West Country resident makes it feasible that Coleridge would have read his *Essays, Letters and Poems*, published in Bath in 1781. I don't know whether these possible connections have been noted by Coleridge scholars.

Perhaps most inconsistent with the anachronistic majority of this work and my avowed repudiation of literary history, is my brief excursion into the issue of the visitor from Porlock. Since I don't believe Coleridge could have composed so perfectly constructed a rhymed poem within, or even after, the chaos of an opium delirium, I also have doubts about the historicity of his interrupter. It is unreasonable of me, in the light of my disclaimers, to pursue the issue. But given that I spent some time walking round the area, I became interested in the logistics of how someone from Porlock could have known of the poet's residence, visited him in his farm house and presumably returned to Porlock the same evening. I have therefore projected my own scepticism, briefly, onto the speaking persona. That said, I did visit the Somerset County Records Office to read the parish registers that the author mentions, and the names he cites in his somewhat casual footnote are from those sources.

Anything, of course, is possible. And Stevie Smith's musings on the subject represent, I think, the definitive fantasia. Among other speculations, she says: 'I long for the Person from Porlock / To bring my thoughts to an end.' Her cheerful but macabre nonsense expresses very beautifully, I think, ways in which we charm ourselves with unconvincing little stories. 'It was not right, it was wrong./But often we all do wrong,' she wrote all too wisely.

From Samuel Purchas, *His Pilgrimage*

In *Xaindu* did *Cublai Can* build a stately palace, encompassing sixteene miles of plaine ground with a wall, wherein are fertile Meddowes, pleasant Springs, delightfull streames, and all sorts of beasts of chase and game, and in the middest thereof a sumptuous house of pleasure, which may be removed from place to place. Here he doth abide in the monethes of *Iune*, *Iuly*, and *August*, on the eighth and twentith day whereof, he departeth thence to another place to doe sacrifice on this maner. He hath a Herd or Droue of Horses and Mares, about ten thousand, as white as snow: of the Milke whereof none may taste, except he be of the bloud of *Cingis Can*. Yea the Tartars doe these beastes great reuerence, nor dare any crosse their way, or goe before them. According to the direction of his Astrologers or Magicians, he on the eighth or twentieth of *August* aforesaid spendeth and powreth forth with his own hands the Milke of these Mares in the Aire, and on the Earth, to giue drinke to the spirits and Idols which they worship, that they may preserue the men, women, beasts, birds, corne, and other things growing on the earth.

These Astrologers, or Necromancers, are in their Art maruellous. When the skie is cloudie, and threatenth raine, they will ascend the roofe of the palace of the *Grand Can*, and cause the raine and tempests to fall round about, without touching the said Palace.

These that thus doe, are called *Tebeth*, and *Chesmir*, two sorts of Idolaters, which delude the people with opinion of their sanctitie, imputing these workes to their dissembled holinesse: and for this cause they goe in filthy and beastly manner, not caring who seeth them, with dirt on their faces, never washing nor combing themselues. And if any be condemned to death, they take, dresse, and eate him: which they doe not if they die naturally. They are also called *Bachsi*, that is of such a Religion or order, as if one should say a Frier-Preacher, or Minor and are exceedingly expert in their divelish Art. They cause that the Bottles in the Hall of the great Can doe fille the bolles of their owne accord, which also without mans helpe, passe ten paces through the Aire, into the hands of the said Can, and when he hath drunke, in like sort returne to their place. These *bachsi* sometimes threaten plagues or other misfortune from their Idols, which to prevent they desire so many muttons with blacke heads, and so many pounds of incense, and *Lignum Aloes* to performe their due sacrifices. Which they accordingly receive and offer on their Feast day, sprinkling Broth before their Idols. There bee of these, great Monasteries, which seeme like a small Citie, in some whereof are two thousand Monkes, which shave their Heads and beards, and weare a religious habite, and hallow their Idols feasts with

222

great solemnity of hymnes and lights. Some of these may bee married. Others there are called *Senfim*, an order which observeth great abstinence and strictnesse of life, in all their life eating nothing but Branne, which they put in hot water, and let it stand till all the white of the meale be taken away, and then eate it being thus washed. These worship the Fire, and condemned of the other for Heretickes, because they worship not their idoles, and will not marry in any case. They are shaven, and weare hempen-garments of black or bright yellow, and although they were silke, yet would they not alter the colour. They sleepe on great mattes, and live the austerest life in the world.

You must know that for three months of the year, to wit December, January, and February, the Great Kaan resides in the capital city of Cathay, which is called CAMBALUC. In that city stands his great Palace, and now I will tell you what it is like.

It is enclosed all round by a great wall forming a square, each side of which is a mile in length; that is to say, the whole compass thereof is four miles. This you may depend on; it is also very thick, and a good ten paces in height, whitewashed and loop-holed all round. At each angle of the wall there is a very fine and rich palace in which the war-harness of the Emperor is kept, such as bows and quivers, saddles and bridles, and bowstrings, and everything needful for an army. Also midway between every two of these Corner Palaces there is another of the like; so that taking the whole compass of the enclosure you find eight vast Palaces stored with the Great Lord's harness of war. And you must understand that each Palace is assigned to only one kind of article; thus one is stored with bows, a second with saddles, a third with bridles, and so on in succession right round.

The great wall has five gates on its southern face, the middle one being the great gate which is never opened on any occasion except when the Great Kaan himself goes forth or enters. Close on either side of this great gate is a smaller one by which all other people pass; and then towards each angle is another great gate, also open to people in general; so that on that side there are five gates in all.

Inside of this wall there is a second, enclosing a space that is somewhat greater in length than in breadth. This enclosure also has eight palaces corresponding to those of the outer wall, and stored like them with the Lord's harness of war. This wall also hath five gates on the southern face, corresponding to those in the outer wall, and hath one gate on each of the other faces, as the outer wall hath also. In the middle of the second enclosure is the Lord's Great Palace, and I will tell you what it is like.

You must know that it is the greatest Palace that ever was. Towards the north it is in contact with the outer wall, whilst towards the south there is a vacant space which the Barons and the soldiers are constantly traversing. The Palace itself hath no upper story, but is all on the ground floor, only the basement is raised some ten palms above the surrounding soil [and this elevation is retained by a wall of marble raised to the level of the pavement, two paces in width and projecting beyond the base of the Palace so as to form a kind of terrace-walk, by which people can pass round the building, and which is exposed to view, whilst on the outer edge of the wall there is a very fine pillared balustrade; and up to this the people are allowed to come]. The roof is very lofty, and the walls of the Palace are all covered with gold and silver. They are also adorned with representations of dragons [sculptured and gilt], beasts and birds, knights and idols, and sundry other subjects. And on the ceiling too you see nothing but gold and silver and painting. On each of the four sides there is a great marble staircase leading to the top of the marble wall, and forming the approach to the Palace.

The Hall of the Palace is so large that it could easily dine 6000 people; and it is quite a marvel to see how many rooms there are besides. The building is altogether so vast, so rich, and so beautiful, that no man on earth could design anything superior to it. The outside of the roof also is all coloured with vermilion and yellow and green and blue and other hues, which are fixed with a varnish so fine and exquisite that they shine like crystal, and lend a resplendent lustre to the Palace as seen for a great way round. This roof is made too with such strength and solidity that it is fit to last for ever.

On the interior side of the Palace are large buildings with halls and chambers, where the Emperor's private property is placed, such as his treasures of gold, silver, gems, pearls, and gold plate, and in which reside the ladies and concubines. There he occupies himself at his own convenience, and no one else has access.

Between the two walls of the enclosure which I have described, there are fine parks and beautiful trees bearing a variety of fruits. There are beasts also of sundry kinds, such as white stags and fallow deer, gazelles and roebucks, and fine squirrels of various sorts, with numbers also of the animal that gives the musk, and all manner of other beautiful creatures, insomuch that the whole place is full of them, and no spot remains void except where there is traffic of people going and coming. The parks are covered with abundant grass; and the roads through them being all paved and raised two cubits above the surface, they never become muddy, nor does the rain lodge on them, but flows off into the meadows, quickening the soil and producing that abundance of herbage.

From that corner of the enclosure which is towards the north-west there extends a fine Lake, containing foison of fish of different kinds which the Emperor hath caused to be put in there, so that whenever he desires any he can have them at his pleasure. A river enters this lake and issues from it, but there is a grating of iron or brass put up so that the fish cannot escape in that way.

Moreover on the north side of the Palace, about a bow-shot off, there is a hill which has been made by art [from the earth dug out of the lake]; it is a good hundred paces in height and a mile in compass. This hill is entirely covered with trees that never lose their leaves, but remain ever green. And I assure you that wherever a beautiful tree may exist, and the Emperor gets news of it, he sends for it and has it transported bodily with all its roots and the earth attached to them, and planted on that hill of his. No matter how big the tree may be, he gets it carried by his elephants; and in this way he has got together the most beautiful collection of trees in all the world. And he has also caused the whole hill to be covered with the ore of azure, which is very green. And thus not only are the trees all green, but the hill itself is all green likewise; and there is nothing to be seen on it that is not green; and hence it is called the GREEN MOUNT; and in good sooth 'tis named well.

On the top of the hill again there is a fine big palace which is all green inside and out; and thus the hill, and the trees, and the palace form together a charming spectacle; and it is marvellous to see their uniformity of colour! Everybody who sees them is delighted. And the Great Kaan had caused this beautiful prospect to be formed for the comfort and solace and delectation of his heart.

You must know that beside the Palace (that we have been describing), i.e. the Great Palace, the Emperor has caused another to be built just like his own in every respect, and this he hath done for his son when he shall reign and be Emperor after him. Hence it is made just in the same fashion and of the same size, so that everything can be carried on in the same manner after his own death. [It stands on the other side of the lake from the Great Kaan's Palace, and there is a bridge crossing the water from one to the other.] The Prince in question holds now a Seal of Empire, but not with such complete authority as the Great Kaan, who remains supreme as long as he lives.

...

You must know that the Kaan keeps an immense stud of white horses and mares; in fact more than 10,000 of them, and all pure white without a speck. The milk of these mares is drunk by himself and his family, and by none else, except by those of one great tribe that have also the privilege of drinking it. This privilege was granted them by Chinghis Kaan, on account of a certain victory that they helped him to win long ago. The name of the tribe is HORIAD.

Now when these mares are passing across the country, and any one falls in with them, be he the greatest lord in the land, he must not presume to pass until the mares have gone by; he must either tarry where he is, or go a half-day's journey round if need so be, so as not to come nigh them; for they are to be treated with the greatest respect. Well, when the Lord sets out from the Park on the 28th of August, as I told you, the milk of all those mares is taken and sprinkled on the ground. And this is done on the injunction of the Idolaters and Idol-priests, who say that it is an excellent thing to sprinkle that milk on the ground every 28th of August, so that the Earth and the Air and the False Gods shall have their share of it, and the Spirits likewise that inhabit the Air and the Earth. And thus those beings will protect and bless the Kaan and his children and his wives and his folk and his gear, and his cattle and his horses, his corn and all that is his. After this is done, the Emperor is off and away.

But I must now tell you a strange thing that hitherto I have forgotten to mention. During the three months of every year that the Lord resides at that place, if it should happen to be bad weather, there are certain crafty enchanters and astrologers in his train, who are such adepts in necromancy and the diabolic arts, that they are able to prevent any cloud or storm from passing over the spot on which the Emperor's Palace stands. The sorcerers who do this are called TEBET and KESIMUR, which are the names of two nations of Idolaters. Whatever they do in this way is by the help of the Devil, but they make those people believe that it is compassed by dint of their own sanctity and the help of God. They always go in a state of dirt and uncleanness, devoid of respect for themselves, or for those who see them, unwashed, unkempt, and sordidly attired.

These people also have a custom which I must tell you. If a man is condemned to death and executed by the lawful authority, they take his body and cook and eat it. But if any one die a natural death then they will not eat the body.

There is another marvel performed by those BACSI, of whom I have been speaking as knowing so many enchantments. For when the Great Kaan is at his capital and in his great Palace, seated at his table, which stands on a platform some eight cubits above the ground, his cups are set before him [on a great buffet] in the middle of the hall pavement, at a distance of some ten paces from his table, and filled with wine, or other good spiced liquor such as they use. Now when the Lord desires to drink, these enchanters by the power of their enchantments cause the cups to move from their place without being touched by anybody, and to present themselves to the Emperor! This every one present may witness, and there are ofttimes more than 10,000 persons thus present. 'Tis a truth and no lie! and so will tell you the sages of our own country who understand necromancy, for they also can perform it.

And when the Idol Festivals come round, these *Bacsi* go to the Prince and say: 'Sire, the Feast of such a god is come' (naming him). 'My Lord, you know,' the enchanter will say, 'that this god, when he gets no offerings, always sends bad weather and spoils our seasons. So we pray you to give us such and such a number of black-faced sheep,' naming whatever number they please. 'And we beg also, good my lord, that we may have such a quantity of incense, and such a quantity of lignaloes, and' – so much of this, so much of that, and so much of t'other, according to their fancy – 'that we may perform a solemn service and a great sacrifice to our Idols, and that so they may be induced to protect us and all that is ours.'

The *Bacsi* say these things to the Barons entrusted with the Steward-ship, who stand round the Great Kaan, and these repeat them to the

Kaan, and he then orders the Barons to give everything that the Bacsi have asked for. And when they have got the articles they go and make a great feast in honour of their god, and hold great ceremonies of worship with grand illuminations and quantities of incense of a variety of odours, which they make up from different aromatic spices. And then they cook the meat, and set it before the idols, and sprinkle the broth hither and thither, saying that in this way the idols get their bellyful. Thus it is that they keep their festivals. You must know that each of the idols has a name of his own, and a feast-day, just as our Saints have their anniversaries.

They have also immense Minsters and Abbeys, some of them as big as a small town, with more than two thousand monks (i.e. after their fashion) in a single abbey. These monks dress more decently than the rest of the people, and have the head and beard shaven. There are some among these *Bacsi* who are allowed by their rule to take wives, and who have plenty of children.

Then there is another kind of devotees called SENSIN, who are men of extraordinary abstinence after their fashion, and lead a life of such hardship as I will describe. All their life long they eat nothing but bran, which they take mixt with hot water. That is their food: bran, and nothing but bran; and water for their drink. 'Tis a lifelong fast! so that I may well say their life is one of extraordinary asceticism. They have great idols, and plenty of them; but they sometimes also worship fire. The other Idolaters who are not of this sect call these people heretics – *Patarins* as we should say – because they do not worship their idols in their own fashion. Those of whom I am speaking would not take a wife on any consideration. They wear dresses of hempen stuff, black and blue, and sleep upon mats; in fact their asceticism is something astonishing. Their idols are all feminine, that is to say, they have women's names.

Now let us have done with this subject, and let me tell you of the great state and wonderful magnificence of the Great Lord of Lords; I mean that great Prince who is the Sovereign of the Tartars, CUBLAY by name, that most noble and puissant Lord.

Acknowledgements

Many thanks to the following libraries and archives: Somerset Records Office for the photo of the Day and Masters map used on the cover. Bristol Records Office for photos of Edmund Rack's manuscript. The Wellcome Institute for photos from Ortelius's atlas. The School of Oriental and African Studies for the photo of Bretschneider's map showing the Great Khan's route to Shang-du.

Passages from the work in process in slightly different shape have been published in the following: *Shearsman Magazine* (two sections), *The Bow-Wow Shop* (three sections), *Litter* (Leafe Press: two sections), *Intercapillary Space* and *The Fortnightly Review* (two sections). My thanks to all editors' hospitality.

In the course of writing, I have had great help from these friends: Richard Bready, who read the MS as it progressed and gave detailed, erudite and often life-saving advice. Roger and Barbara Langley who offered enthusiastic encouragement as did Robert Saxton and Peter Riley, to whom warm thanks. Particular gratitude to Martin Thom who read the MS twice in close detail and offered comments from many perspectives of his expertise. Ewan Smith designed cover and contents and gave valuable advice on the text. My warm thanks also to Morris and Mary Rossabi, distinguished specialists in Mongolian and Chinese history. Gratitude also to Jenny and Tony Richards for their hospitality at Ash Farm, Culbone. To Martin and Denise Paris who made possible a journey to the Rigi mountains. And to my daughters, Elizabeth (with whom this all started during a discussion of *Kubla Khan*) and Anna (great wise reader), both of whom have been amused and supportive.

I would like to dedicate the book to the late Roger Langley and to Richard Bready.

Bibliography

An Improved Map of the County of Somerset, 1790

Anchorages on the South Shore of the Bristol Channel 1812

Attiret, J. D., *Particular Account of Emperor of China's Gardens*, 1752

Beckwith, Christopher, *Empires of the Silk Road*, 2009

Bergreen, Laurence, *Marco Polo*, 2008

Berliner, Nancy Zeng, *The Emperor's Private Paradise*, 2010

Billingsley, John, *General View of the Agriculture of Somerset*, 1798

Emanuel Bowen, *Improved Map of the County of Somerset*, 1777

Boyle, John Andrew, *The Mongol World Empire*, 1977

Bretschneider, E., *Notes on Chinese Mediæval Travellers to the West*, 1875

Bristol Records Office, *Ashton Papers*, various dates in the 18th century

Cahill, James, *Hills beyond a River*, 1976
— *Lyric Journey: Chinese Painting of Yuan Dynasty*, 1996

Camden, William, *Britannia*, 1695

Collinson, J., *History and Antiquities of the County of Somerset*, 1791

Copeland, *Spode's Willow Pattern ... after the Chinese*, 1980

Coryat, Thomas, *Coryat's Crudities*, 1611

Day and Masters, *The County of Somerset Surveyed*, 1782

Drew, John, *India and the Romantic Imagination*, 1987

Ellia, A. J., *Classified Lists of Words to Illustrate W. Somersetshire*

Erdmann, Kurt, *The History of the Early Turkish Carpet*, 1977

Fitzhugh, William (ed.), *Genghis Khan and the Mongol Empire*, 2009

Franke, Herbert, *Tribal chieftain to Universal Emperor and God*, 1978

Franke, Herbert (ed.), *Cambridge History of China*, volume 6, 1994

Giles, J. and M. Cohen (eds), *Serinde, Terre de Bouddha*, 1995

Greenwood C. and J., *Somersetshire Delineated*, 1822

Grousset, René, *The Empire of the Steppes*, 1970

Hamilton, Sir W., *Campi Phlegræi*, 1776

Hazlitt, William, *The Spirit of the Age*, 1825

Herrmann, Albert, *An Historical Atlas of China*, 1966

Holmes, R., *Coleridge: Early Visions*, 1989
— *Coleridge: Darker Reflections*, 1998

Impey, Lawrence, *Shang-tu, Summer Capital of Khubilai Khan*, 1925

Ji, Cheng, *The Craft of Gardens*, 1988

Jing, Anning, 'Portraits of Khubilai Khan', *Artibus Asiae* 54 1/2 1994

Jones, Sir William, *The Works of Sir William Jones*, 1976

Journal of Economic and Social History of the Orient, 1801

Keswick, Maggie, *The Chinese Garden*, 2003

Kircher, Athanasius, *China Illustratated*, 1667

Langlois, John D., *China under Mongol Rule*, 1981

Lattimore, Owen, *Inner Asian Frontiers of China*, 1988

Lawrence, Berta, *Coleridge and Wordsworth in Somerset*, 1970

Lewalski, Barbara K., *The Life of John Milton*, 2000

Magaillans Gabriel, *A New History of China*, 1688

Maiuri, Amedeo, *The Phlegraean Fields*, 1989

Map of the County of Somerset, from actual survey 1822

Miller, Lady Anna, *Poetical Amusements*, 1776

Murck, Alfreda, *Poetry and Painting in Song China*, 2000

Needham, Joseph, *Science and Civilization in China*, vol. 12, 2004

Olschki, Leonardo, *Marco Polo's Precursors*, 1943
— *Marco Polo's Asia*, 1960

Onon, Urgungge, *The History and the Life of Chinggis Khan*, 1990

Ortelius, Abraham, *Theatrum Orbis Terrarum*, 1570

Polo, Marco (ed.) Yule, *The Book of Ser Marco Polo, the Venetian*, 1903

Polwhele, R., *Poems by Gentlemen of Devon and Cornwall*, 1787

Porter, Roy, *Drugs and Narcotics in History*, 1995

Pritchard, R. E., *Odd Tom Coryat*, 2004

Purchas, Samuel, *Purchas his Pilgrimage*, 1613, 1614

Rack, Edmund, *Essays, Letters and Poems*, 1781

— Field notes and letters, 1782–87, manuscript, Somerset County Records Office and Bristol Records Office

Radtke, Kurt Werner, *Poetry of the Yuan Dynasty*, 1984

Rashīd al-Dīn Tabīb, *Rashīd al-Dīn's History of India*, 1965

— *The Successors of Genghis Khan*, 1971

Ratchnevsky, Paul, *Genghis Khan*, 1991

Rie, M. and R. Thurman, *The Sacred Art of Tibet*, 1991

Rossabi, Morris, *Khubilai Khan, His Life and Times*, 1988

Schafer, E. H., *The Golden Peaches of Samarcand*, 1963

— *The Vermilion bird. T'ang images of the South*, 1967

Schneider, E., *Coleridge, Opium and Kubla Khan*, 1953

Schwab, Raymond, *The Oriental Renaissance*, 1984

Sharp, Cecil J., *Folk Songs from Somerset*, 2nd edition 1911

Snellgrove, D. L., *The Hevajra tantra. A critical study*, 1959

Snodgrass, Adrian, *The Symbolism of the Stupa*, 1985

Somerset County Records Office. Parish Register for Porlock, 1750ff.

Taylor, J., *Odcombs Complaint or Coriats Funeral Epicedium*, 1613

The Bhagavat-Geeta or Dialogues of Krishna and Arjoon, 1846

The Gentleman's Magazine, lxiii.i.148, 1793

The Secret History of the Mongols, 1982

Turnbull, Stephen R., *Genghis Khan & the Mongol Conquests*, 2003

Uglow, Jenny, *The Lunar Men*, 2002

Wilkins, Sir Charles, *Grammar of the Sanskrita Language*, 1808

Wood, Frances, *The Silk Road*, 2002

Woolman, John, *Journals and Letters*, 1774

Yetkin, Serare, *Early Caucasian Carpets in Turkey*, 1978

Yule, Henry, *Cathay and the Way Thither*, 1866

— *The Book of Ser Marco Polo, the Venetian*, 1903

Zhong, Huanan, *The Art of Chinese Gardens*, 1982

Notes

Quotations in the text are mainly from Shakespeare, Virgil and Milton and these are given either in italics or quotation marks. Beyond the author's brief exploration of literary sources (p. 68), there are no quotations from Coleridge, although I have borrowed the verb 'aver' from *The Ancient Mariner*.

Epigraphs Xaindu was Samuel Purchas's spelling from which Coleridge derived Xanadu. *Purchas, His Pilgrimage*, 1613. Coleridge says he carried this volume, perhaps from Thomas Poole's library in Neither Stowey. It weighs about 8lbs.

First Parents or Grand parents: Adam and Eve, after Milton.

1 Culbone Wood stands between sea cliffs and the meadows leading up to an isolated farm house. *Serinde* (here pronounced with a long *i*) is western China and Central Asia. The *Yuan* dynasty was established in 1271 by the Mongolian, Kubilai Khan (this is a variant of one among many spellings). *Cathay*: Europeanised from Khitan (Manchuria), a term used by Marco Polo for northwestern China.

1 big with rich increese: Shakespeare, Sonnet 97.

2 Shepherd's smock: fiction.

3 abysm: borrowed from *The Tempest* I.ii.

prophetic fury: *Othello* III.4. 'From the hag', *Tom O'Bedlam*, 16th century ballad.

5 *pars densa* ...: Virgil, *Aeneid* VI: 7 'some pillage the woods, the thick coverts of game ...'. The verb is not relevant to context, which is a declivity resembling the terrain below the sanctuary at Cumae where Aeneas met the Sybil prior to his underworld voyage.

7 numbers: 18th century term for verses and/or the feet within them.

The dragonfly is *Anax imperator*, a large species which survives into late autumn.

Hier steh ich: Here I stand, a poor fool and know as little as before. Goethe, *Faust* Part I.

Vanessa atalanta: the Red Admiral.

8 This house ...: first of several references to, deformations of, or quotations from *The Tempest*. Here, Caliban's 'The isle is full of noises', *The Tempest* II.2.

9 quo lati: 'The huge side of the Euboean rock is hewn into a cavern, whither lead a hundred wide mouths, a hundred gateways, whence rush as many voices, the answers of the Sibyl.' *Aeneid* VI: 42–3.

Each line, except one of my own, is taken from a different song in Cecil Sharp's *Folk Song from Somerset*, vols 1 and 4.

11 hic labor: 'there that house of toil, a maze inextricable', *Aeneid* VI: 26.

12 Paukenwirbel: drum; and title given to Haydn's Symphony 103.

13 adspirate: 'breathe on what I've undertaken and bring down, from the world's beginning to the present, my unbroken song', Ovid, *Metamorphoses* I: 3–4.

ensevelate: coinage, from French *ensevelir*, to bury or shroud.

14 portrait: controversially attributed to Anige.

15 unseen in this portrait: Details are from an article on material life in the Yuan but I have lost the reference. Also Schafer: 1963.

stupa: Indian, then Tibetan and Chinese domed Buddhist reliquary.

Coleridge may not have had access to Marco Polo except in a very short translation by John Frampton from French 1579. All references to Marco are therefore probably anachronistic.

22 *Atlas* of Ortelius: see pp. 212–13. Marlowe used this for the composition of *Tambulaine*.

26 hymenoptera: the order of bees, wasps and ants.

27 Coryat described his manner as 'in the *Odcombian* vein'.

30 My thanks to Elizabeth Teller for help with Latin; some of it remains Odcombian.

33 the general: 'everyone' – as in *Hamlet* and elsewhere in Shakespeare.

38 *Sortes Virgilianae*: a medieval system of divination using randomly chosen passages from Virgil.

42 Ursprung: source; katabasis: descent to underworld.

45 ipse: Latin, 'itself or himself'. This repeated verbal tic is part of the writer's often quite irritating persona.

48 Phlegethon: one of the four infernal rivers described by Virgil.

49 Goethe, *Wandrers Nachtlied II*. Über allen Gipfeln Ist Ruh. In allen Wipfeln Spürest du Kaum einen Hauch. Die Vögelein schweigen in Walde. Warte nur, balde Ruhest du auch. Over all the hilltops is calm. In all the treetops you feel hardly a breath of air. The little birds fall silent in the woods. Only wait ... soon you'll also be at rest.

53 Friar Johannes Carpini, associate of St Francis, was papal emissary to the Mongols; he reached Karacoram 1245–46.

54 This song is made up. But 'There was an old man' is traditional, from Sharp's *Somerset Folk Songs*, 1911.

61 whirligig of time: deformed from *Twelfth Night* v.i.

62 Andrew Marvell, *The Garden*.

68 *Thalaba* VII: 6; *Gebir* III: 19; Bruce, *Travels to Discover the Source of the Nile*.

69 Sir William Jones: leading European Sanskritist of the period.

70 Campi Phlegraei: in the Vesuvian Avernus/Cumae region where the earth erupts underfoot with effluvia of Virgil's Hades. The passage *sub rupe sinistra*: 'under a cliff on the left, he sees a broad castle, circled by a three-fold wall, round which rushes a flood of torrential flames – Tartarean Phlegethon, which rolls thundering rocks in its path', *Aeneid* VI: 448ff.

71 Coleridge read some early translations from Sanskrit. The Baptist missionary William Carey (d.1834) translated some parts of the *Ramayana*, but it's unlikely that C. had access to these.

73 G. L. Giesecke, geologist and part author/originator of the libretto to Mozart's *Magic Flute*, arrived in Dublin from Greenland wearing skins covered in bird amulets – hence the character of Papageno.

73 passer ... puellae: 'Sparrow, my girl's pet object', Catullus II.

75 Nemi: the priest at Diana's temple where Those trees in whose dim shadow / The ghastly priest doth reign / The priest who slew the slayer / And shall himself be slain. Macaulay.

76 Buddhist religious teachers: these were Tibetan adepts who worked in around the Yuan court. See below Marco's account of Bacsis.

77 *Sympetrium niger*: medium sized 'darting' dragonfly species which also hovers.

78 Based on a carpet in the Ethnographic Museum, Istambul.

79 Jog on, jog on, the foot-path way / And merrily hent the stile-a: / A merry heart goes all the day, / Your sad tires in a mile-a, *The Winter's Tale* IV:3.

Words from the first line of this song return on the final page.

80 While most of the pseudo-Coleridge material is fictional, the *Essay* derives from 20th and 21st century scholarship.

81 There were four Khans within the Mongol imperium (*khaganate*). The supreme Khan was the *khagan*.

Nestorians: Christians who proclaimed Christ's human nature.

86 So shaken as we are: *Henry IV* I.i.

87 bodhisattva: mythological 'enlightenment being' of wisdom and compassion.

90 Anige's authorship of Kubilai's

portrait is doubtful. Morris Rossabi, personal communication.

The dialogue with Anige is based on sources. The conversation in no. 11 is fiction, as is the narrative of the journey in 10.

102 sovereigne eye: Shakespeare Sonnet 30.

105 Shi tsu: Kubilai's posthumous title which he could not have known.

110 unswept stone: the quotations are from Sonnets 55 and 71.

112 nautch girls were properly Indian not Chinese dancers.

116 knot and gender: *Othello* IV.2.

117 *deva-nagari*: Indian script used for both sacred and secular texts.

118 tiring: attiring.

The story of the Ismaili assassins is presumably apocryphal.

120 *The Mind Landscape*: see Cahill 1996.

125 Adapted from text in Yule 1903.

126 Adapted from text in Radtke 1984.

I dreamed of Xanadu. In compliment to Henry Vaughan: 'I saw Eternity the other night'.

127 krauncha birds: see p. 71.

138 Cellini's bronze is in the Renaissance gallery of the V&A.

139 Ovid, *Metamorphoses* II: 760ff. Dante, *Purgatorio* XIII: 70.

148 *clup*: a coinage.

150 *Erlkönig*: Schubert's setting of Goethe's ballad is implied.

The verses are quoted from Sharp 1911.

157 argle = ergo, therefore. Gravedigger, *Hamlet* V.1.

174 O, who can hold a fire in his hand: *Richard II* I.2.

bites shrewdly: *Hamlet* I.1.

175 'Ich weiss nicht was es soll bedeuten': Heine, *Die Lorelei*, 1822; may be an historical though perhaps not a cultural anachronism.

177 'It was the nightingale and not the lark ...': *Romeo and Juliet* III.v.2.

185 'Doppelgänger': from Heine's *Buch der Lieder*, 1827.

195 Conturbat me deforms Villon's *Timor mortis conturbat me.*

202 'Heaven the judicious sharp spectator sits': Walter Raleigh, 'What is our life'.

Tartarly and savage: Who killed John Keats? / 'I,' says the Quarterly, / So savage and Tartarly / ''Twas one of my feats.' Byron.

204 Tremblingly alive: Pope, *Essay on Man.*

205 So shaken as we are: as quoted p. 86.

206 Rev. Richard Polwhele, author of *History of Devon* and a seven volume *History of Cornwall*, wrote a eulogy on Rack's death.

How often with delight I trace / Thy varied life – and active scene; / Or mark the friend of human race / In sickness and in death serene! / To spread each saluary art, / By liberal plans with skill design'd, / And in historic strain impart / Some fresh instruction to the mind.

Polwhele's poem also contains the following line: 'Thrill'd with fine ardors *Collinsonias* glow.' A reference to a flower imported earlier in the century by Peter Collinson, who, like Rack, had been a cloth merchant and dyer.

207 Also the map folded into Billingsley's *General View of Somerset* indicates just one road from Taunton and then Dunster into Porlock. This terminates at Porlock to leave the far west of the county 'Mountainous Lands interspersed with fertile Vales'. No means of transport towards Porlock Weir or Culbone and Linton are indicated.

211 Two gates: *Aeneid* VI: 893ff, Dryden's translation.

voyages of fancy: I have avoided trespassing on the topic of fancy vs. the imagination and have used both terms loosely.

Illustrations

Cover image: Detail from Day and Masters, *Map of Somerset*, 1782, courtesy of Somerset Archives and Local Studies Service, reference number DD/SH/C1165/8

Frontispiece: Portrait of Kubilai Khan, National Palace Museum, Tapei

Page 108: Map from Emile Bretschneider, *Archaeological and Historical Researches on Peking and Its Environs*, Shanghai and London 1875, courtesy of Council for World Mission Archives and Manuscripts, SOAS

Page 206: Notes written at Culbone by Edmund Rack, *c.*1787, with markings by John Collinson, Smyth of Ashton Court Papers, courtesy of Bristol Record Office

Pages 212–13: North China and southwest England from Abraham Ortelius, *Theatrum Orbis Terrarum*, 1570, courtesy of the Wellcome Institute Library

Page 216: Thomas Coryat on elephant from *Thomas Coriate Traveller for the English Wits: Greeting from the Court of the Great Mogul*, 1616

First published in the United Kingdom in 2013 by
Shearsman Books, 50 Westons Hill Drive, Emersons
Green, Bristol, BS16 7DF

www.shearsman.com

ISBN 978 1 84861 229 7

Set in OurType Arnhem and Monotype Futura Bold by
Ewan Smith, London

Shearsman Books Ltd registered office
30–31 St James Place, Mangotsfield, Bristol BS16 9JB
(this address not for correspondence)

Printed in December 2022
by Rotomail Italia S.p.A., Vignate (MI) - Italy